W9-APJ-140

NOTES FROM UNDERGROUND

A NEW TRANSLATION
BACKGROUNDS AND SOURCES
RESPONSES
CRITICISM

A NORTON CRITICAL EDITION

Fyodor Dostoevsky

NOTES FROM UNDERGROUND

A NEW TRANSLATION
BACKGROUNDS AND SOURCES
RESPONSES
CRITICISM

Translated and Edited by

MICHAEL R. KATZ

UNIVERSITY OF TEXAS AT AUSTIN

W • W • NORTON & COMPANY • *New York* • *London*

First Edition

Library of Congress Cataloging-in-Publication Data
Dostoyevsky, Fyodor, 1821–1881.
[Zapiski iz podpol'ia. English]
Notes from underground / by Fyodor Dostoevsky; authoritative text
and criticism, Michael R. Katz, editor.
(A Norton critical edition)
Translation of Zapiski iz podpol'ia.
Includes excerpts from Dostoevsky's letters to his brother
Mikhail, 1859–1864, notebooks, 1864–1865, and Winter notes on summer
impressions.
Bibliography: p. 241
ISBN 0-393-95744-6
1. Dostoyevsky, Fyodor, 1821–1881. Zapiski iz podpol'ia.
I. Katz, Michael R. II. Title.
PG3326.Z4 1988
891.73'3—dc19   88-1062

W. W. Norton & Company, Inc., 500 Fifth Avenue, New York, N.Y. 10110
W. W. Norton & Company Ltd., 10 Coptic Street, London, WC1A 1PU
8 9 0

Contents

Preface   vii
The Text of *Notes from Underground*   1

Backgrounds and Sources   91
    Selected Letters from Fyodor Dostoevsky
        to Mikhail Dostoevsky (1859–64)   93
    Fyodor Dostoevsky • [Socialism and Christianity]   96
    Fyodor Dostoevsky • From *Winter Notes on Summer
        Impressions*   97
    N. G. Chernyshevsky • From *What Is to Be Done?*   99

Responses   119
    PARODY   121
    M. E. Saltykov-Shchedrin • From "The Swallows"   121
    Woody Allen • Notes from the Overfed   122
    IMITATION/INSPIRATION   126
    Robert Walser • The Child   126
    Ralph Ellison • From *The Invisible Man*   129
    John Lennon and Paul McCartney • Nowhere Man   131

Criticism   133
    Nikolai Mikhailovsky • [Dostoevsky's Cruel Talent]   135
    Vasily Rozanov • [Thought and Art in
        Notes from Underground]   139
    Lev Shestov • [Dostoevsky and Nietzsche]   142
    M. M. Bakhtin • [Discourse in Dostoevsky]   146
    Ralph E. Matlaw • Structure and Integration in
        Notes from the Underground   156

Victor Erlich • Notes on the Uses of Monologue in Artistic Prose — 171

Robert Louis Jackson • [Freedom in *Notes from Underground*] — 179

Gary Saul Morson • [Anti-Utopianism in *Notes from Underground*] — 188

Richard H. Weisberg • The Formalistic Model: *Notes from Underground* — 190

Joseph Frank • *Notes from Underground* — 202

A Chronology of Dostoevsky's Life and Work — 239

Selected Bibliography — 241

Preface

There have been numerous translations of Dostoevsky's *Notes from Underground*, a fact that bears witness to its extraordinary place in world literature. I have included a list of what I take to be the eight "principal" translations of the work—some of which are quite decent, and others of which are positively indecent. Only two of these are accompanied by any annotations; only one includes a selection of letters and background material; and only one contains a small selection of critical essays.

It has been my intention to produce what I hope is at least another decent translation of an extremely convoluted piece of mid-nineteenth-century Russian prose; in addition, I have attempted to provide comprehensive annotations and an extensive critical apparatus.

The first section, *Backgrounds and Sources*, includes relevant passages from Dostoevsky's letters to his brother written between 1859 and 1864; an excerpt on "Socialism and Christianity" from one of the author's notebooks; selections from his account of a formative visit to the West; and an extended part of Chernyshevsky's revolutionary novel *What Is to Be Done?* with which Dostoevsky polemicized in his *Notes from Underground*.

Responses, the second section, contains two parodies of Dostoevsky's work, one by the author's contemporary, M. E. Saltykov-Shchedrin, and the other by our contemporary, Woody Allen. In addition, there are several works that seem to me to have been inspired by *Notes from Underground*: a short story by the German-Swiss author Robert Walser, the introduction to his classic novel by the American writer Ralph Ellison, and a song by two lads from Liverpool, John Lennon and Paul McCartney.

The third section, *Criticism*, contains essays dating from 1882 to 1986—over one hundred years of writing about *Notes from Underground*. It includes excerpts from distinguished Russian critics, as well as examples of the best of recent Anglo-American scholarship on the work. A *Selected Bibliography* has been included to provide suggestions for further reading and study.

I wish to express my sincere gratitude to my reader, Walter Arndt, and to my former teachers at Williams College, Doris de Keyserlingk and Nicholas Fersen, for their perceptive comments on my draft translation; to my colleagues Robert Belknap, George Gibian, Robert Louis

Jackson, Sidney Monas, Victor Terras, William Mills Todd, and Edward Wasiolek for their encouragement and suggestions of works to be included in the critical apparatus; to my students at the University of Texas at Austin, Timothy Mark Taylor for the initial inspiration to undertake the project, Glenn Randall Mack for his research on the annotations, Joshua Larson and Samuel Peter Smith for their assistance in typing the manuscript, and Julie Swann for her help with proofreading. My work is dedicated to these students and to others like them.

Michael R. Katz

The Text of
NOTES FROM
UNDERGROUND

The underground man believes in
the teachings of Chernyshevsky but
does not really follow it.

- He knows, what is rational and yet
  is irrational

[handwritten: Dostoevsky believes that man is definitely capable of good, but equally capable of evil / a contradiction to Chernyshevsky]

Notes From Underground

[handwritten: moral phycological ; social ideological — two ways to view this character]

I
Underground[1]

I.

I am a sick man. . . . I am a spiteful man. I am a most unpleasant man. I think my liver is diseased. Then again, I don't know a thing about my illness; I'm not even sure what hurts. I'm not being treated and never have been, though I respect both medicine and doctors. Besides, I'm extremely superstitious—well at least enough to respect medicine. (I'm sufficiently educated not to be superstitious; but I am, anyway.) No, gentlemen, it's out of spite that I don't wish to be treated. Now then, that's something you probably won't understand. Well, I do. Of course, I won't really be able to explain to you precisely who will be hurt by my spite in this case; I know perfectly well that I can't possibly "get even" with doctors by refusing their treatment; I know better than anyone that all this is going to hurt me alone, and no one else. Even so, if I refuse to be treated, it's out of spite. My liver hurts? Good, let it hurt even more! *[handwritten: Masochism: his irrationality is a sign of his freedom]*

I've been living this way for some time—about twenty years. I'm forty now. I used to be in the civil service. But no more. I was a nasty official. I was rude and took pleasure in it. After all, since I didn't accept bribes, at least I had to reward myself in some way. (That's a poor joke, but I won't cross it out. I wrote it thinking that it would be very witty; but now, having realized that I merely wanted to show off disgracefully, I'll make a point of not crossing it out!) *[handwritten: Irony]* When petitioners used to approach my desk for information, I'd gnash my teeth and feel unending pleasure if I succeeded in causing someone distress. I almost always succeeded. For the most part they were all timid people: naturally, since they were

[handwritten margin: Proving his irrationality]

1. Both the author of these notes and the *Notes* themselves are fictitious, of course. Nevertheless, people like the author of these notes not only may, but actually must exist in our society, considering the general circumstances under which our society was formed. I wanted to bring before the public with more prominence than usual one of the characters of the recent past. He's a representative of the current generation. In the excerpt entitled "Underground" this person introduces himself and his views, and, as it were, wants to explain the reasons why he appeared and why he had to appear in our midst. The following excerpt ["Apropos of Wet Snow"] contains the actual "notes" of this person about several events in his life [*Dostoevsky's note*].

petitioners. But among the dandies there was a certain officer whom I particularly couldn't bear. He simply refused to be humble, and he clanged his saber in a loathsome manner. I waged war with him over that saber for about a year and a half. At last I prevailed. He stopped clanging. All this, however, happened a long time ago, during my youth. But do you know, gentlemen, what the main component of my spite really was? Why, the whole point, the most disgusting thing, was the fact that I was shamefully aware at every moment, even at the moment of my greatest bitterness, that not only was I not a spiteful man, I was not even an embittered one, and that I was merely scaring sparrows to no effect and consoling myself by doing so. I was foaming at the mouth—but just bring me some trinket to play with, just serve me a nice cup of tea with sugar, and I'd probably have calmed down. My heart might even have been touched, although I'd probably have gnashed my teeth out of shame and then suffered from insomnia for several months afterward. That's just my usual way. *constant contradiction; scizo*

I was lying about myself just now when I said that I was a nasty official. I lied out of spite. I was merely having some fun at the expense of both the petitioners and that officer, but I could never really become spiteful. At all times I was aware of a great many elements in me that were just the opposite of that. I felt how they swarmed inside me, these contradictory elements. I knew that they had been swarming inside me my whole life and were begging to be let out; but I wouldn't let them out, I wouldn't, I deliberately wouldn't let them out. They tormented me to the point of shame; they drove me to convulsions and—and finally I got fed up with them, oh how fed up! Perhaps it seems to you, gentlemen, that I'm repenting about something, that I'm asking your forgiveness for something? I'm sure that's how it seems to you. . . . But really, I can assure you, I don't care if that's how it seems. . . .

Not only couldn't I become spiteful, I couldn't become anything at all: neither spiteful nor good, neither a scoundrel nor an honest man, neither a hero nor an insect. Now I live out my days in my corner, taunting myself with the spiteful and entirely useless consolation that an intelligent man cannot seriously become anything and that only a fool can become something. Yes, sir, an intelligent man in the nineteenth century must be, is morally obliged to be, principally a characterless creature; a man possessing character, a man of action, is fundamentally a limited creature. That's my conviction at the age of forty. I'm forty now; and, after all, forty is an entire lifetime; why it's extreme old age. It's rude to live past forty, it's indecent, immoral! Who lives more than forty years? Answer sincerely, honestly. I'll tell you who: only fools and rascals. I'll tell those old men that right to their faces, all those venerable old men, all those silver-haired and sweet-smelling old men! I'll say it to the whole world right to its face! I have a right to say it because I myself will live to sixty. I'll make it to seventy! Even to eighty! . . . Wait! Let me catch my breath. . . .

You probably think, gentlemen, that I want to amuse you. You're wrong about that, too. I'm not at all the cheerful fellow I seem to be, or that I may seem to be; however, if you're irritated by all this talk (and I can already sense that you are irritated), and if you decide to ask me just who I really am, then I'll tell you: I'm a collegiate assessor.[2] I worked in order to have something to eat (but only for that reason); and last year, when a distant relative of mine left me six thousand rubles in his will, I retired immediately and settled down in this corner. I used to live in this corner before, but now I've settled down in it. My room is nasty, squalid, on the outskirts of town. My servant is an old peasant woman, spiteful out of stupidity; besides, she has a foul smell. I'm told that the Petersburg climate is becoming bad for my health, and that it's very expensive to live in Petersburg with my meager resources. I know all that; I know it better than all those wise and experienced advisers and admonishers. But I shall remain in Petersburg; I shall not leave Petersburg! I shall not leave here because . . . Oh, what difference does it really make whether I leave Petersburg or not?

Now, then, what can a decent man talk about with the greatest pleasure?

Answer: about himself.

Well, then, I too will talk about myself.

II.

Now I would like to tell you, gentlemen, whether or not you want to hear it, why it is that I couldn't even become an insect. I'll tell you solemnly that I wished to become an insect many times. But not even that wish was granted. I swear to you, gentlemen, that being overly conscious is a disease, a genuine, full-fledged disease. Ordinary human consciousness would be more than sufficient for everyday human needs—that is, even half or a quarter of the amount of consciousness that's available to a cultured man in our unfortunate nineteenth century, especially to one who has the particular misfortune of living in St. Petersburg, the most abstract and premeditated city in the whole world.[3] (Cities can be either premeditated or unpremeditated.) It would have been entirely sufficient, for example, to have the consciousness with which all so-called spontaneous people and men of action are endowed. I'll bet that you think I'm writing all this to show off, to make fun of these men of action, that I'm clanging my saber just like that officer did to show off in bad taste. But, gentlemen, who could possibly be proud of his illnesses and want to show them off?

But what am I saying? Everyone does that; people do take pride in their illnesses, and I, perhaps, more than anyone else. Let's not argue;

2. The eighth rank in the Table of Ranks introduced for the civil service by Peter the Great in 1722.

3. Petersburg was conceived as an imposing city; plans called for regular streets, broad avenues, and spacious squares.

my objection is absurd. Nevertheless, I remain firmly convinced that not only is being overly conscious a disease, but so is being conscious at all. I insist on it. But let's leave that alone for a moment. Tell me this: why was it, as if on purpose, at the very moment, indeed, at the precise moment that I was most capable of becoming conscious of the subtleties of everything that was "beautiful and sublime,"[4] as we used to say at one time, that I didn't become conscious, and instead did such unseemly things, things that . . . well, in short, probably everyone does, but it seemed as if they occurred to me deliberately at the precise moment when I was most conscious that they shouldn't be done at all? The more conscious I was of what was good, of everything "beautiful and sublime," the more deeply I sank into the morass and the more capable I was of becoming entirely bogged down in it. But the main thing is that all this didn't seem to be occurring accidentally; rather, it was as if it all had to be so. It was as if this were my most normal condition, not an illness or an affliction at all, so that finally I even lost the desire to struggle against it. It ended when I almost came to believe (perhaps I really did believe) that this might really have been my normal condition. But at first, in the beginning, what agonies I suffered during that struggle! I didn't believe that others were experiencing the same thing; therefore, I kept it a secret about myself all my life. I was ashamed (perhaps I still am even now); I reached the point where I felt some secret, abnormal, despicable little pleasure in returning home to my little corner on some disgusting Petersburg night, acutely aware that once again I'd committed some revolting act that day, that what had been done could not be undone, and I used to gnaw and gnaw at myself inwardly, secretly, nagging away, consuming myself until finally the bitterness turned into some kind of shameful, accursed sweetness and at last into genuine, earnest pleasure! Yes, into pleasure, real pleasure! I absolutely mean that. . . . That's why I first began to speak out, because I want to know for certain whether other people share this same pleasure. Let me explain: the pleasure resulted precisely from the overly acute consciousness of one's own humiliation; from the feeling that one had reached the limit; that it was disgusting, but couldn't be otherwise; you had no other choice—you could never become a different person; and that even if there were still time and faith enough for you to change into something else, most likely you wouldn't even want to change, and if you did, you wouldn't have done anything, perhaps because there really was nothing for you to change into. But the main thing and the final point is that all of this was taking place according to normal and fundamental laws of overly acute consciousness and of the inertia which results directly from these laws; consequently, not only couldn't one change, one simply

---

4. This phrase originated in Edmund Burke's *Philosophical Inquiry into the Origin of Our Ideas of the Sublime and Beautiful* (1756) and was repeated in Immanuel Kant's *Observations on the Feeling of the Beautiful and the Sublime* (1756). It became a cliché in the writings of Russian critics during the 1830s.

couldn't do anything at all. Hence it follows, for example, as a result of this overly acute consciousness, that one is absolutely right in being a scoundrel, as if this were some consolation to the scoundrel. But enough of this. . . . Oh, my, I've gone on rather a long time, but have I really explained anything? How can I explain this pleasure? But I will explain it! I shall see it through to the end! That's why I've taken up my pen. . . .

For example, I'm terribly proud. I'm as mistrustful and as sensitive as a hunchback or a dwarf; but, in truth, I've experienced some moments when, if someone had slapped my face, I might even have been grateful for it. I'm being serious. I probably would have been able to derive a peculiar sort of pleasure from it—the pleasure of despair, naturally, but the most intense pleasures occur in despair, especially when you're very acutely aware of the hopelessness of your own predicament. As for a slap in the face—why, here the consciousness of being beaten to a pulp would overwhelm you. The main thing is, no matter how I try, it still turns out that I'm always the first to be blamed for everything and, what's even worse, I'm always the innocent victim, so to speak, according to the laws of nature. Therefore, in the first place, I'm guilty inasmuch as I'm smarter than everyone around me. (I've always considered myself smarter than everyone around me, and sometimes, believe me, I've been ashamed of it. At the least, all my life I've looked away and never could look people straight in the eye.) Finally, I'm to blame because even if there were any magnanimity in me, it would only have caused more suffering as a result of my being aware of its utter uselessness. After all, I probably wouldn't have been able to make use of that magnanimity: neither to forgive, as the offender, perhaps, had slapped me in accordance with the laws of nature, and there's no way to forgive the laws of nature; nor to forget, because even if there were any laws of nature, it's offensive nonetheless. Finally, even if I wanted to be entirely unmagnanimous, and had wanted to take revenge on the offender, I couldn't be revenged on anyone for anything because, most likely, I would never have decided to do anything, even if I could have. Why not? I'd like to say a few words about that separately.

III.

Let's consider people who know how to take revenge and how to stand up for themselves in general. How, for example, do they do it? Let's suppose that they're seized by an impulse to take revenge—then for a while nothing else remains in their entire being except for that impulse. Such an individual simply rushes toward his goal like an enraged bull with lowered horns; only a wall can stop him. (By the way, when actually faced with a wall such individuals, that is, spontaneous people and men of action, genuinely give up. For them a wall doesn't constitute the evasion that it does for those of us who think and consequently do nothing; it's not an excuse to turn aside from the path, a pretext in which a person like me usually doesn't believe, but one for which he's always extremely grateful. No, they give up in all sincerity. For them the wall possesses some kind of soothing, morally decisive and definitive meaning, perhaps even something mystical . . . But more about the wall later.) Well, then, I consider such a spontaneous individual to be a genuine, normal person, just as tender mother nature wished to see him when she lovingly gave birth to him on earth. I'm green with envy at such a man. He's stupid, I won't argue with you about that; but perhaps a normal man is supposed to be stupid—how do we know? Perhaps it's even very beautiful. And I'm all the more convinced of the suspicion, so to speak, that if, for example, one were to take the antithesis of a normal man—that is, a man of overly acute consciousness, who emerged, of course, not from the bosom of nature, but from a laboratory test tube (this is almost mysticism, gentlemen, but I suspect that it's the case), then this test tube man sometimes gives up so completely in the face of his antithesis that he himself, with his overly acute consciousness, honestly considers himself not as a person, but a mouse. It may be an acutely conscious mouse, but a mouse nonetheless, while the other one is a person and consequently, . . . and so on and so forth. But the main thing is that he, he himself, considers himself to be a mouse; nobody asks him to do so, and that's the important point. Now let's take a look at this mouse in action. Let's assume, for instance, that it feels offended (it almost always feels offended), and that it also wishes to be revenged. It may even contain more accumulated malice than *l'homme de la nature et de la vérité*.[5] The mean, nasty, little desire to pay the offender back with evil may indeed rankle in it even more despicably than in *l'homme de la nature et de la vérité*, because *l'homme de la nature et de la vérité*, with his innate stupidity, considers his revenge nothing more than justice, pure and simple; but the mouse, as a result of its overly acute consciousness, rejects the idea of justice. Finally, we come to the act itself, to the very act of revenge. In addition to its original nastiness, the mouse has already managed to pile up all sorts of other nastiness around itself in the form of hesitations and doubts; so many unresolved questions have emerged from that one single question, that some kind of fatal blow is concocted unwillingly, some kind of stinking mess consisting of doubts, anxieties and, finally, spittle showered upon it by the spontaneous men of action who stand by solemnly as judges and arbiters, roaring with laughter until their sides split. Of course, the only thing left to do is dismiss it with a wave of its paw and a smile of assumed contempt which it doesn't even believe in, and creep ignominiously back into its mousehole. There, in its disgusting, stinking underground, our offended, crushed, and ridiculed mouse immediately plunges into

5. "The man of nature and of truth:" the basic idea is borrowed from Jean-Jacques Rousseau's *Confessions* (1782–89), namely, that man in a state of nature is honest and direct and that he is corrupted by civilization.

cold, malicious, and, above all, everlasting spitefulness. For forty years on end it will recall its insult down to the last, most shameful detail; and each time it will add more shameful details of its own, spitefully teasing and irritating itself with its own fantasy. It will become ashamed of that fantasy, but it will still remember it, rehearse it again and again, fabricating all sorts of incredible stories about itself under the pretext that they too could have happened; it won't forgive a thing. Perhaps it will even begin to take revenge, but only in little bits and pieces, in trivial ways, from behind the stove, incognito, not believing in its right to be revenged, nor in the success of its own revenge, and knowing in advance that from all its attempts to take revenge, it will suffer a hundred times more than the object of its vengeance, who might not even feel a thing. On its deathbed it will recall everything all over again, with interest compounded over all those years and. . . . But it's precisely in that cold, abominable state of half-despair and half-belief, in that conscious burial of itself alive in the underground for forty years because of its pain, in that powerfully created, yet partly dubious hopelessness of its own predicament, in all that venom of unfulfilled desire turned inward, in all that fever of vacillation, of resolutions adopted once and for all and followed a moment later by repentance—herein precisely lies the essence of that strange enjoyment I was talking about earlier. It's so subtle, sometimes so difficult to analyze, that even slightly limited people, or those who simply have strong nerves, won't understand anything about it. "Perhaps," you'll add with a smirk, "even those who've never received a slap in the face won't understand," and by so doing you'll be hinting to me ever so politely that perhaps during my life I too have received such a slap in the face and that therefore I'm speaking as an expert. I'll bet that's what you're thinking. Well, rest assured, gentlemen, I've never received such a slap, although it's really all the same to me what you think about it. Perhaps I may even regret the fact that I've given so few slaps during my lifetime. But that's enough, not another word about this subject which you find so extremely interesting.

I'll proceed calmly about people with strong nerves who don't understand certain refinements of pleasure. For example, although under particular circumstances these gentlemen may bellow like bulls as loudly as possible, and although, let's suppose, this behavior bestows on them the greatest honor, yet, as I've already said, when confronted with impossibility, they submit immediately. Impossibility—does that mean a stone wall? What kind of stone wall? Why, of course, the laws of nature, the conclusions of natural science and mathematics. As soon as they prove to you, for example, that it's from a monkey you're descended,[6] there's no reason to make faces; just accept it as it is. As soon as they prove to you that in truth one drop of your own fat is dearer to you than

---

6. A reference to Charles Darwin's theory of evolution and natural selection. A book on the subject was translated into Russian in 1864.

the lives of one hundred thousand of your fellow creatures and that this will finally put an end to all the so-called virtues, obligations, and other such similar ravings and prejudices, just accept that too; there's nothing more to do, since two times two is a fact of mathematics. Just you try to object.

"For goodness sake," they'll shout at you, "it's impossible to protest: it's two times two makes four! Nature doesn't ask for your opinion; it doesn't care about your desires or whether you like or dislike its laws. You're obliged to accept it as it is, and consequently, all its conclusions. A wall, you see, is a wall . . . etc. etc." Good Lord, what do I care about the laws of nature and arithmetic when for some reason I dislike all these laws and I dislike the fact that two times two makes four? Of course, I won't break through that wall with my head if I really don't have the strength to do so, nor will I reconcile myself to it just because I'm faced with such a stone wall and lack the strength.

As though such a stone wall actually offered some consolation and contained some real word of conciliation, for the sole reason that it means two times two makes four. Oh, absurdity of absurdities! How much better it is to understand it all, to be aware of everything, all the impossibilities and stone walls; not to be reconciled with any of those impossibilities or stone walls if it so disgusts you; to reach, by using the most inevitable logical combinations, the most revolting conclusions on the eternal theme that you are somehow or other to blame even for that stone wall, even though it's absolutely clear once again that you're in no way to blame, and, as a result of all this, while silently and impotently gnashing your teeth, you sink voluptuously into inertia, musing on the fact that, as it turns out, there's no one to be angry with; that an object cannot be found, and perhaps never will be; that there's been a substitution, some sleight of hand, a bit of cheating, and that it's all a mess— you can't tell who's who or what's what; but in spite of all these uncertainties and sleights-of-hand, it hurts you just the same, and the more you don't know, the more it hurts!

IV.

"Ha, ha, ha! Why, you'll be finding enjoyment in a toothache next!" you cry out with a laugh.

"Well, what of it? There is some enjoyment even in a toothache," I reply. "I've had a toothache for a whole month; I know what's what. In this instance, of course, people don't rage in silence; they moan. But these moans are insincere; they're malicious, and malice is the whole point. These moans express the sufferer's enjoyment; if he didn't enjoy it, he would never have begun to moan. This is a good example, gentlemen, and I'll develop it. In the first place, these moans express all the aimlessness of the pain which consciousness finds so humiliating, the whole system of natural laws about which you really don't give a damn, but as a result of which you're suffering nonetheless, while nature isn't. They express the consciousness that while there's no real enemy to be identified, the pain exists nonetheless; the awareness that, in spite of all possible Wagenheims,[7] you're still a complete slave to your teeth; that if someone so wishes, your teeth will stop aching, but that if he doesn't so wish, they'll go on aching for three more months; and finally, that if you still disagree and protest, all there's left to do for consolation is flagellate yourself or beat your fist against the wall as hard as you can, and absolutely nothing else. Well, then, it's these bloody insults, these jeers coming from nowhere, that finally generate enjoyment that can sometimes reach the highest degree of voluptuousness. I beseech you, gentlemen, to listen to the moans of an educated man of the nineteenth century who's suffering from a toothache, especially on the second or third day of his distress, when he begins to moan in a very different way than he did on the first day, that is, not simply because his tooth aches; not the way some coarse peasant moans, but as a man affected by progress and European civilization, a man "who's renounced both the soil and the common people,"[8] as they say nowadays. His moans become somehow nasty, despicably spiteful, and they go on for days and nights. Yet he himself knows that his moans do him no good; he knows better than anyone else that he's merely irritating himself and others in vain; he knows that the audience for whom he's trying so hard, and his whole family, have now begun to listen to him with loathing; they don't believe him for a second, and they realize full well that he could moan in a different, much simpler way, without all the flourishes and affectation, and that he's only indulging himself out of spite and malice. Well, it's precisely in this awareness and shame that the voluptuousness resides. "It seems I'm disturbing you, tearing at your heart, preventing anyone in the house from getting any sleep. Well, then, you won't sleep; you too must be aware at all times that I have a toothache. I'm no longer the hero I wanted to pass for earlier, but simply a nasty little man, a rogue. So be it! I'm delighted that you've seen through me. Does it make you feel bad to hear my wretched little moans? Well, then, feel bad. Now let me add an even nastier flourish. . . ." You still don't understand, gentlemen? No, it's clear that one has to develop further and become even more conscious in order to understand all the nuances of this voluptuousness! Are you laughing? I'm delighted. Of course my jokes are in bad taste, gentlemen; they're uneven, contradictory, and lacking in self-assurance. But that's because I have no respect for myself. Can a man possessing consciousness ever really respect himself?

---

7. The *General Address Book of St. Petersburg* listed eight dentists named Wagenheim; contemporary readers would have recognized the name from signs throughout the city.
8. This phrase is typical of the literary and social polemics of the 1860s.

V.

Well, and is it possible, is it really possible for a man to respect himself if he even presumes to find enjoyment in the feeling of his own humiliation? I'm not saying this out of any feigned repentance. In general I could never bear to say: "I'm sorry, Daddy, and I won't do it again," not because I was incapable of saying it, but, on the contrary, perhaps precisely because I was all too capable, and how! As if on purpose it would happen that I'd get myself into some sort of mess for which I was not to blame in any way whatsoever. That was the most repulsive part of it. What's more, I'd feel touched deep in my soul; I'd repent and shed tears, deceiving even myself of course, though not feigning in the least. It seemed that my heart was somehow playing dirty tricks on me. . . . Here one couldn't even blame the laws of nature, although it was these very laws that continually hurt me during my entire life. It's disgusting to recall all this, and it was disgusting even then. Of course, a moment or so later I would realize in anger that it was all lies, lies, revolting, made-up lies, that is, all that repentance, all that tenderness, all those vows to mend my ways. But you'll ask why I mauled and tortured myself in that way? The answer is because it was so very boring to sit idly by with my arms folded; so I'd get into trouble. That's the way it was. Observe yourselves better, gentlemen; then you'll understand that it's true. I used to think up adventures for myself, inventing a life so that at least I could live. How many times did it happen, well, let's say, for example, that I took offense, deliberately, for no reason at all? All the while I knew there was no reason for it; I put on airs nonetheless, and would take it so far that finally I really did feel offended. I've been drawn into such silly tricks all my life, so that finally I lost control over myself. Another time, even twice, I tried hard to fall in love. I even suffered, gentlemen, I can assure you. In the depths of my soul I really didn't believe that I was suffering; there was a stir of mockery, but suffer I did, and in a genuine, normal way at that; I was jealous, I was beside myself with anger. . . . And all as a result of boredom, gentlemen, sheer boredom; I was overcome by inertia. You see, the direct, legitimate, immediate result of consciousness is inertia, that is, the conscious sitting idly by with one's arms folded. I've referred to this before. I repeat, I repeat emphatically: all spontaneous men and men of action are so active precisely because they're stupid and limited. How can one explain this? Here's how: as a result of their limitations they mistake immediate and secondary causes for primary ones, and thus they're convinced more quickly and easily than other people that they've located an indisputable basis for action, and this puts them at ease; that's the main point. For, in order to begin to act, one must first be absolutely at ease, with no lingering doubts whatsoever. Well, how can I, for example, ever feel at ease? Where are the primary causes I can rely upon, where's the foundation? Where shall I find it? I exercise myself in thinking, and consequently, with me every primary cause drags in another, an even more primary one, and so on to infinity. This is precisely the essence of all consciousness and thought. And here again, it must be the laws of nature. What's the final result? Why, the very same thing. Remember: I was talking about revenge before. (You probably didn't follow.) I said: a man takes revenge because he finds justice in it. That means, he's found a primary cause, a foundation: namely, justice. Therefore, he's completely at ease, and, as a result, he takes revenge peacefully and successfully, convinced that he's performing an honest and just deed. But I don't see any justice here at all, nor do I find any virtue in it whatever; consequently, if I begin to take revenge, it's only out of spite. Of course, spite could overcome everything, all my doubts, and therefore could successfully serve instead of a primary cause precisely because it's not a cause at all. But what do I do if I don't even feel spite (that's where I began before)? After all, as a result of those damned laws of consciousness, my spite is subject to chemical disintegration. You look—and the object vanishes, the arguments evaporate, a guilty party can't be identified, the offense ceases to be one and becomes a matter of fate, something like a toothache for which no one's to blame, and, as a consequence, there remains only the same recourse: that is, to bash the wall even harder. So you throw up your hands because you haven't found a primary cause. Just try to let yourself be carried away blindly by your feelings, without reflection, without a primary cause, suppressing consciousness even for a moment; hate or love, anything, just in order not to sit idly by with your arms folded. The day after tomorrow at the very latest, you'll begin to despise yourself for having deceived yourself knowingly. The result: a soap bubble and inertia. Oh, gentlemen, perhaps I consider myself to be an intelligent man simply because for my whole life I haven't been able to begin or finish anything. All right, suppose I am a babbler, a harmless, annoying babbler, like the rest of us. But then what is to be done[9] if the direct and single vocation of every intelligent man consists in babbling, that is, in deliberately talking in endless circles?

VI.

Oh, if only I did nothing simply as a result of laziness. Lord, how I'd respect myself then. I'd respect myself precisely because at least I'd be capable of being lazy; at least I'd possess one more or less positive trait of which I could be certain. Question: who am I? Answer: a sluggard. Why, it would have been very pleasant to hear that said about oneself. It would mean that I'd been positively identified; it would mean that there was something to be said about me. "A sluggard!" Why, that's a calling and a vocation, a whole career! Don't joke, it's true. Then, by

9. An oblique reference to the controversial novel by Nikolai Chernyshevsky entitled *What Is to Be Done?* (1863). *Notes from Underground* is Dostoevsky's polemic response to it.

rights I'd be a member of the very best club and would occupy myself exclusively by being able to respect myself continually. I knew a gentleman who prided himself all his life on being a connoisseur of Lafite.[1] He considered it his positive virtue and never doubted himself. He died not merely with a clean conscience, but with a triumphant one, and he was absolutely correct. I should have chosen a career for myself too: I would have been a sluggard and a glutton, not an ordinary one, but one who, for example, sympathized with everything beautiful and sublime. How do you like that? I've dreamt about it for a long time. The "beautiful and sublime" have been a real pain in the neck during my forty years, but then it's been *my* forty years, whereas then—oh, then it would have been otherwise! I would've found myself a suitable activity at once—namely, drinking to everything beautiful and sublime. I would have seized upon every opportunity first to shed a tear into my glass and then drink to everything beautiful and sublime. Then I would have turned everything into the beautiful and sublime; I would have sought out the beautiful and sublime in the nastiest, most indisputable trash. I would have become as tearful as a wet sponge. An artist, for example, has painted a portrait of Ge.[2] At once I drink to the artist who painted that protrait of Ge because I love everything beautiful and sublime. An author has written the words, "Just as you please,"[3] at once I drink to "Just as you please," because I love everything "beautiful and sublime." I'd demand respect for myself in doing this, I'd persecute anyone who didn't pay me any respect. I'd live peacefully and die triumphantly— why, it's charming, perfectly charming! And what a belly I'd have grown by then, what a triple chin I'd have acquired, what a red nose I'd have developed—so that just looking at me any passerby would have said, "Now that's a real plus! That's something really positive!" Say what you like, gentlemen, it's extremely pleasant to hear such comments in our negative age.

VII.

But these are all golden dreams. Oh, tell me who was first to announce, first to proclaim that man does nasty things simply because he doesn't know his own true interest; and that if he were to be enlightened, if his eyes were to be opened to his true, normal interests, he would stop doing nasty things at once and would immediately become good and noble, because, being so enlightened and understanding his real advantage, he would realize that his own advantage really did lie in the good; and that it's well known that there's not a single man capable of acting knowingly against his own interest; consequently, he would, so

---

1. A variety of red wine from Médoc in France.
2. Russian artist N. N. Ge, whose painting "The Last Supper" was displayed in Petersburg during the spring of 1863 and provoked considerable controversy.
3. An attack on the writer M. E. Saltykov-Shchedrin, who published a sympathetic review of Ge's painting entitled "Just As You Please."

to speak, begin to do good out of necessity.[4] Oh, the child! Oh, the pure, innocent babe! Well, in the first place, when was it during all these millennia, that man has ever acted only in his own self interest? What does one do with the millions of facts bearing witness to the one fact that people knowingly, that is, possessing full knowledge of their own true interests, have relegated them to the background and have rushed down a different path, that of risk and chance, compelled by no one and nothing, but merely as if they didn't want to follow the beaten track, and so they stubbornly, willfully forged another way, a difficult and absurd one, searching for it almost in the darkness? Why, then, this means that stubbornness and willfulness were really more pleasing to them than any kind of advantage. . . . Advantage! What is advantage? Will you take it upon yourself to define with absolute precision what constitutes man's advantage? And what if it turns out that man's advantage sometimes not only may, but even must in certain circumstances, consist precisely in his desiring something harmful to himself instead of something advantageous? And if this is so, if this can ever occur, then the whole theory falls to pieces. What do you think, can such a thing happen? You're laughing; laugh, gentlemen, but answer me: have man's advantages ever been calculated with absolute certainty? Aren't there some which don't fit, can't be made to fit into any classification? Why, as far as I know, you gentlemen have derived your list of human advantages from averages of statistical data and from scientific-economic formulas. But your advantages are prosperity, wealth, freedom, peace, and so on and so forth; so that a man who, for example, expressly and knowingly acts in opposition to this whole list, would be, in you opinion, and in mine, too, of course, either an obscurantist or a complete madman, wouldn't he? But now here's what's astonishing: why is it that when all these statisticians, sages, and lovers of humanity enumerate man's advantages, they invariably leave one out? They don't even take it into consideration in the form in which it should be considered, although the entire calculation depends upon it. There would be no great harm in considering it, this advantage, and adding it to the list. But the whole point is that this particular advantage doesn't fit into any classification and can't be found on any list. I have a friend, for instance. . . . But gentlemen! Why, he's your friend, too! In fact, he's everyone's friend! When he's preparing to do something, this gentleman straight away explains to you eloquently and clearly just how he must act according to the laws of nature and truth. And that's not all: with excitement and passion he'll tell you all about genuine, normal human interests; with scorn he'll reproach the shortsighted fools who understand neither their own advantage nor the real meaning of virtue; and then—exactly a quarter of an hour later, without any sudden outside cause, but pre-

4. This section contains the most direct attack on Chernyshevsky's theory of rational egoism and his doctrine of human advantage.

cisely because of something internal that's stronger than all his interests—
he does a complete about-face; that is, he does something which clearly
contradicts what he's been saying: it goes against the laws of reason and
his own advantage, in a word, against everything. . . . I warn you that
my friend is a collective personage; therefore it's rather difficult to blame
only him. That's just it, gentlemen; in fact, isn't there something dearer
to every man than his own best advantage, or (so as not to violate the
rules of logic) isn't there one more advantageous advantage (exactly the
one omitted, the one we mentioned before), which is more important
and more advantageous than all others and, on behalf of which, a man
will, if necessary, go against all laws, that is, against reason, honor,
peace, and prosperity—in a word, against all those splendid and useful
things, merely in order to attain this fundamental, most advantageous
advantage which is dearer to him than everything else?

"Well, it's advantage all the same," you say, interrupting me. Be so
kind as to allow me to explain further; besides, the point is not my pun,
but the fact that this advantage is remarkable precisely because it destroys
all our classifications and constantly demolishes all systems devised by
lovers of humanity for the happiness of mankind. In a word, it interferes
with everything. But, before I name this advantage, I want to compromise myself personally; therefore I boldly declare that all these splendid
systems, all these theories to explain to mankind its real, normal interests
so that, by necessarily striving to achieve them, it would immediately
become good and noble—are, for the time being, in my opinion, nothing
more than logical exercises! Yes, sir, logical exercises! Why, even to
maintain a theory of mankind's regeneration through a system of its own
advantages, why, in my opinion, that's almost the same as . . . well,
claiming, for instance, following Buckle,[5] that man has become kinder
as a result of civilization; consequently, he's becoming less bloodthirsty
and less inclined to war. Why, logically it all even seems to follow. But
man is so partial to systems and abstract conclusions that he's ready to
distort the truth intentionally, ready to deny everything that he himself
has ever seen and heard, merely in order to justify his own logic. That's
why I take this example, because it's such a glaring one. Just look around:
rivers of blood are being spilt, and in the most cheerful way, as if it
were champagne. Take this entire nineteenth century of ours during
which even Buckle lived. Take Napoleon—both the great and the present
one.[6] Take North America—that eternal union.[7] Take, finally, that
ridiculous Schleswig-Holstein. . . .[8] What is it that civilization makes

---

5. In his *History of Civilization in England* (1857–
61), Henry Thomas Buckle argued that the development of civilization necessarily leads to the
cessation of war. Russia had recently been involved
in fierce fighting in the Crimea (1853–56).
6. The French emperors Napoleon I (1769–1821)
and his nephew Napoleon III (1808–73), both of
whom engaged in numerous wars, though on

vastly different scales.
7. The United States was in the middle of a bloody
civil war between the Union and the Confederacy
(1861–65).
8. The German duchies of Schleswig and Hol-
stein, held by Denmark since 1773, were reunited
with Prussia after a brief war in 1864.

kinder in us? Civilization merely promotes a wider variety of sensations in man and . . . absolutely nothing else. And through the development of this variety man may even reach the point where he takes pleasure in spilling blood. Why, that's even happened to him already. Haven't you noticed that the most refined bloodshedders are almost always the most civilized gentlemen to whom all these Attila the Huns[9] and Stenka Razins[1] are scarcely fit to hold a candle; and if they're not as conspicuous as Attila and Stenka Razin, it's precisely because they're too common and have become too familiar to us. At least if man hasn't become more bloodthirsty as a result of civilization, surely he's become bloodthirsty in a nastier, more repulsive way than before. Previously man saw justice in bloodshed and exterminated whomever he wished with a clear conscience; whereas now, though we consider bloodshed to be abominable, we nevertheless engage in this abomination even more than before. Which is worse? Decide for yourselves. They say that Cleopatra[2] (forgive an example from Roman history) loved to stick gold pins into the breasts of her slave girls and take pleasure in their screams and writhing. You'll say that this took place, relatively speaking, in barbaric times; that these are barbaric times too, because (also comparatively speaking), gold pins are used even now; that even now, although man has learned on occasion to see more clearly than in barbaric times, *he's still far from having learned* how to act in accordance with the dictates of reason and science. Nevertheless, you're still absolutely convinced that he will learn how to do so, as soon as he gets rid of some bad, old habits and as soon as common sense and science have completely re-educated human nature and have turned it in the proper direction. You're convinced that then man will voluntarily stop committing blunders, and that he will, so to speak, never willingly set his own will in opposition to his own normal interests. More than that: then, you say, science itself will teach man (though, in my opinion, that's already a luxury) that in fact he possesses neither a will nor any whim of his own, that he never did, and that he himself is nothing more than a kind of piano key or an organ stop;[3] that, moreover, there still exist laws of nature, so that everything he's done has been not in accordance with his own desire, but in and of itself, according to the laws of nature. Consequently, we need only discover these laws of nature, and man will no longer have to answer for his own actions and will find it extremely easy to live. All human actions, it goes without saying, will then be tabulated according to these laws, mathematically, like tables of logarithms up to 108,000, and will be entered on a schedule; or even better, certain edifying works will be published, like our contemporary encyclopedic dictionaries, in which everything

9. King of the Huns (?–453), who conducted devastating wars against the Roman emperors.
1. Cossack leader (?–1671) who organized a peasant rebellion in Russia.
2. Queen of Egypt (69–30 B. C.) and last ruler in the Ptolemy dynasty.
3. A reference to the last discourse of the French philosopher Denis Diderot in the *Conversation of D'Alembert and Diderot* (1769).

will be accurately calculated and specified so that there'll be no more actions or adventures left on earth.

At that time, it's still you speaking, new economic relations will be established, all ready-made, also calculated with mathematical precision, so that all possible questions will disappear in a single instant, simply because all possible answers will have been provided. Then the crystal palace will be built.[4] And then . . . Well, in a word, those will be our halcyon days.[5] Of course, there's no way to guarantee (now this is me talking) that it won't be, for instance, terribly boring then (because there won't be anything left to do, once everything has been calculated according to tables); on the other hand, everything will be extremely rational. Of course, what don't people think up out of boredom! Why, even gold pins get stuck into other people out of boredom, but that wouldn't matter. What's really bad (this is me talking again) is that for all I know, people might even be grateful for those gold pins. For man is stupid, phenomenally stupid. That is, although he's not really stupid at all, he's really so ungrateful that it's hard to find another being quite like him. Why, I, for example, wouldn't be surprised in the least, if, suddenly, for no reason at all, in the midst of this future, universal rationalism, some gentleman with an offensive, rather, a retrograde and derisive expression on his face were to stand up, put his hands on his hips, and declare to us all: "How about it, gentlemen, what if we knock over all this rationalism with one swift kick for the sole purpose of sending all these logarithms to hell, so that once again we can live according to our own stupid will!" But that wouldn't matter either; what's so annoying is that he would undoubtedly find some followers; such is the way man is made. And all because of the most foolish reason, which, it seems, is hardly worth mentioning: namely, that man, always and everywhere, whoever he is, has preferred to act as he wished, and not at all as reason and advantage have dictated; one might even desire something opposed to one's own advantage, and sometimes (this is now my idea) one *positively must do so*. One's very own free, unfettered desire, one's own whim, no matter how wild, one's own fantasy, even though sometimes roused to the point of madness—all this constitutes precisely that previously omitted, most advantageous advantage which isn't included under any classification and because of which all systems and theories are constantly smashed to smithereens. Where did these sages ever get the idea that man needs any normal, virtuous desire? How did they ever imagine that man needs any kind of rational, advantageous desire? Man needs only one thing—his own *independent* desire, whatever that in-

---

4. An allusion to the crystal palace described in Vera Pavlovna's fourth dream in Chernyshevsky's *What Is to Be Done?* as well as to the actual building designed by Sir Joseph Paxton, erected for the Great Exhibition in London in 1851, and de-

scribed by Dostoevsky in chapter 5 of *Winter Notes on Summer Impressions* (1863).
5. In the original Dostoevsky refers to "the arrival of the kagan-bird," supposedly a harbinger of good fortune.

dependence might cost and wherever it might lead. And as far as desire goes, the devil only knows. . . .

VIII.

"Ha, ha, ha! But in reality even this desire, if I may say so, doesn't exist!" you interrupt me with a laugh. "Why science has already managed to dissect man so now we know that desire and so-called free choice are nothing more than . . ."

"Wait, gentlemen, I myself wanted to begin like that. I must confess that even I got frightened. I was just about to declare that the devil only knows what desire depends on and perhaps we should be grateful for that, but then I remembered about science and I . . . stopped short. But now you've gone and brought it up. Well, after all, what if someday they really do discover the formula for all our desires and whims, that is, the thing that governs them, precise laws that produce them, how exactly they're applied, where they lead in each and every case, and so on and so forth, that is, the genuine mathematical formula—why, then all at once man might stop desiring, yes, indeed, he probably would. Who would want to desire according to some table? And that's not all: he would immediately be transformed from a person into an organ stop or something of that sort; because what is man without desire, without will, and without wishes if not a stop in an organ pipe? What do you think? Let's consider the probabilities—can this really happen or not?"

"Hmmm . . .," you decide, "our desires are mistaken for the most part because of an erroneous view of our own advantage. Consequently, we sometimes desire pure rubbish because, in our own stupidity, we consider it the easiest way to achieve some previously assumed advantage. Well, and when all this has been analyzed, calculated on paper (that's entirely possible, since it's repugnant and senseless to assume in advance that man will never come to understand the laws of nature) then, of course, all so-called desires will no longer exist. For if someday desires are completely reconciled with reason, we'll follow reason instead of desire simply because it would be impossible, for example, while retaining one's reason, to *desire* rubbish, and thus knowingly oppose one's reason, and desire something harmful to oneself. . . . And, since all desires and reasons can really be tabulated, since someday the laws of our so-called free choice are sure to be discovered, then, all joking aside, it may be possible to establish something like a table, so that we could actually desire according to it. If, for example, someday they calculate and demonstrate to me that I made a rude gesture[6] because I couldn't possibly refrain from it, that I had to make precisely that gesture, well, in that case, what sort of *free choice* would there be, especially if I'm a

---

6. Literally, "to give someone the fig," a rude gesture in which the thumb protrudes between clenched fingers.

learned man and have completed a course of study somewhere? Why, then I'd be able to calculate in advance my entire life for the next thirty years; in a word, if such a table were to be drawn up, there'd be nothing left for us to do; we'd simply have to accept it. In general, we should be repeating endlessly to ourselves that at such a time and in such circumstances nature certainly won't ask our opinion; that we must accept it as is, and not as we fantasize it, and that if we really aspire to prepare a table, a schedule, and, well . . . well, even a laboratory test tube, there's nothing to be done—one must even accept the test tube! If not, it'll be accepted even without you. . . .

"Yes, but that's just where I hit a snag! Gentlemen, you'll excuse me for all this philosophizing; it's a result of my forty years in the underground! Allow me to fantasize. Don't you see: reason is a fine thing, gentlemen, there's no doubt about it, but it's only reason, and it satisfies only man's rational faculty, whereas desire is a manifestation of all life, that is, of all human life, which includes both reason, as well as all of life's itches and scratches. And although in this manifestation life often turns out to be fairly worthless, it's life all the same, and not merely the extraction of square roots. Why, take me, for instance; I quite naturally want to live in order to satisfy all my faculties of life, not merely my rational faculty, that is, some one-twentieth of all my faculties. What does reason know? Reason knows only what it's managed to learn. (Some things it may never learn; while this offers no comfort, why not admit it openly?) But human nature acts as a whole, with all that it contains, consciously and unconsciously; and although it may tell lies, it's still alive. I suspect, gentlemen, that you're looking at me with compassion; you repeat that an enlightened and cultured man, in a word, man as he will be in the future, cannot knowingly desire something disadvantageous to himself, and that this is pure mathematics. I agree with you: it really is mathematics. But I repeat for the one-hundredth time, there is one case, only one, when a man may intentionally, consciously desire even something harmful to himself, something stupid, even very stupid, namely: in order *to have the right* to desire something even very stupid and not be bound by an obligation to desire only what's smart. After all, this very stupid thing, one's own whim, gentlemen, may in fact be the most advantageous thing on earth for people like me, especially in certain cases. In particular, it may be more advantageous than any other advantage, even in a case where it causes obvious harm and contradicts the most sensible conclusions of reason about advantage—because in any case it preserves for us what's most important and precious, that is, our personality and our individuality. There are some people who maintain that in fact this is more precious to man than anything else; of course, desire can, if it so chooses, coincide with reason, especially if it doesn't abuse this option, and chooses to coincide in moderation; this is useful and sometimes even commendable. But very often, even most of the time, desire absolutely and stubbornly disagrees with reason and

. . . and . . . and, do you know, sometimes this is also useful and even very commendable? Let's assume, gentlemen, that man isn't stupid. (And really, this can't possibly be said about him at all, if only because if he's stupid, then who on earth is smart?) But even if he's not stupid, he is, nevertheless, monstrously ungrateful. Phenomenally ungrateful. I even believe that the best definition of man is this: a creature who walks on two legs and is ungrateful. But that's still not all; that's still not his main defect. His main defect is his perpetual misbehavior, perpetual from the time of the Great Flood to the Schleswig-Holstein period of human destiny. Misbehavior, and consequently, imprudence; for it's long been known that imprudence results from nothing else but misbehavior. Just cast a glance at the history of mankind; well, what do you see? Is it majestic? Well, perhaps it's majestic; why, the Colossus of Rhodes,[7] for example—that alone is worth something! Not without reason did Mr Anaevsky[8] report that some people consider it to be the product of human hands, while others maintain that it was created by nature itself. Is it colorful? Well, perhaps it's also colorful; just consider the dress uniforms, both military and civilian,[9] of all nations at all times—why, that alone is worth something, and if you include everyday uniforms, it'll make your eyes bulge; not one historian will be able to sort it all out. Is it monotonous? Well, perhaps it's monotonous, too: men fight and fight; now they're fighting; they fought first and they fought last—you'll agree that it's really much too monotonous. In short, anything can be said about world history, anything that might occur to the most disordered imagination. There's only one thing that can't possibly be said about it—that it's rational. You'll choke on the word. Yet here's just the sort of thing you'll encounter all the time: why, in life you're constantly running up against people who are so well-behaved and so rational, such wise men and lovers of humanity who set themselves the lifelong goal of behaving as morally and rationally as possible, so to speak, to be a beacon for their nearest and dearest, simply in order to prove that it's really possible to live one's life in a moral and rational way. And so what? It's a well-known fact that many of these lovers of humanity, sooner or later, by the end of their lives, have betrayed themselves: they've pulled off some caper, sometimes even quite an indecent one. Now I ask you: what can one expect from man as a creature endowed with such strange qualities? Why, shower him with all sorts of earthly blessings, submerge him in happiness over his head so that only little bubbles appear on the surface of this happiness, as if on water, give him such economic prosperity that he'll have absolutely nothing left to do except sleep, eat gingerbread, and worry about the continuation

---

7. A large bronze statue of the sun god, Helios, built between 292 and 280 B.C. in the harbor of Rhodes and considered one of the seven wonders of the ancient world.

8. A. E. Anaevsky was a critic whose articles were frequently ridiculed in literary polemics of the period.

9. Uniforms were worn not only by military personnel but also by civil servants with decorations to distinguish rank.

of world history—even then, out of pure ingratitude, sheer perversity, he'll commit some repulsive act. He'll even risk losing his gingerbread, and will intentionally desire the most wicked rubbish, the most uneconomical absurdity, simply in order to inject his own pernicious fantastic element into all this positive rationality. He wants to hold onto those most fantastic dreams, his own indecent stupidity solely for the purpose of assuring himself (as if it were necessary) that men are still men and not piano keys, and that even if the laws of nature play upon them with their own hands, they're still threatened by being overplayed until they won't possibly desire anything more than a schedule. But that's not all: even if man really turned out to be a piano key, even if this could be demonstrated to him by natural science and pure mathematics, even then he still won't become reasonable; he'll intentionally do something to the contrary, simply out of ingratitude, merely to have his own way. If he lacks the means, he'll cause destruction and chaos, he'll devise all kinds of suffering and have his own way! He'll leash a curse upon the world; and, since man alone can do so (it's his privilege and the thing that most distinguishes him from other animals), perhaps only through this curse will he achieve his goal, that is, become really convinced that he's a man and not a piano key! If you say that one can also calculate all this according to a table, this chaos and darkness, these curses, so that the mere possibility of calculating it all in advance would stop everything and that reason alone would prevail—in that case man would go insane deliberately in order not to have reason, but to have his own way! I believe this, I vouch for it, because, after all , the whole of man's work seems to consist only in proving to himself constantly that he's a man and not an organ stop! Even if he has to lose his own skin, he'll prove it; even if he has to become a troglodyte, he'll prove it. And after that, how can one not sin, how can one not praise the fact that all this hasn't yet come to pass and that desire still depends on the devil knows what . . . ?"

You'll shout at me (if you still choose to favor me with your shouts) that no one's really depriving me of my will; that they're merely attempting to arrange things so that my will, by its own free choice, will coincide with my normal interests, with the laws of nature, and with arithmetic.

"But gentlemen, what sort of free choice will there be when it comes down to tables and arithmetic, when all that's left is two times two makes four? Two times two makes four even without my will. Is that what you call free choice?"

IX.

Gentlemen, I'm joking of course, and I myself know that it's not a very good joke; but, after all, you can't take everything as a joke. Perhaps I'm gnashing my teeth while I joke. I'm tormented by questions, gentlemen; answer them for me. Now, for example, you want to cure man of his old habits and improve his will according to the demands of science and common sense. But how do you know not only whether it's possible, but even if it's *necessary* to remake him in this way? Why do you conclude that human desire *must* undoubtedly be improved? In short, how do you know that such improvement will really be to man's advantage? And, to be perfectly frank, why are you so *absolutely* convinced that not to oppose man's real, normal advantage guaranteed by the conclusions of reason and arithmetic is really always to man's advantage and constitutes a law for all humanity? After all, this is still only an assumption of yours. Let's suppose that it's a law of logic, but perhaps not a law of humanity. Perhaps, gentlemen, you're wondering if I'm insane? Allow me to explain. I agree that man is primarily a creative animal, destined to strive consciously toward a goal and to engage in the art of engineering, that, is, externally and incessantly building new roads for himself *wherever they lead*. But sometimes he may want to swerve aside precisely because he's *compelled* to build these roads, and perhaps also because, no matter how stupid the spontaneous man of action may generally be, nevertheless it sometimes occurs to him that the road, as it turns out, almost always leads *somewhere or other*, and that the main thing isn't so much where it goes, but the fact that it does, and that the well-behaved child, disregarding the art of engineering, shouldn't yield to pernicious idleness which, as is well known, constitutes the mother of all vices. Man loves to create and build roads; that's indisputable. But why is he also so passionately fond of destruction and chaos? Now, then, tell me. But I myself want to say a few words about this separately. Perhaps the reason that he's so fond of destruction and chaos (after all, it's indisputable that he sometimes really loves it, and that's a fact) is that he himself has an instinctive fear of achieving his goal and completing the project under construction? How do you know if perhaps he loves his building only from afar, but not from close up; perhaps he only likes building it, but not living in it, leaving it afterward *aux animaux domestiques*,[1] such as ants or sheep, or so on and so forth. Now ants have altogether different tastes. They have one astonishing structure of a similar type, forever indestructible—the anthill. The worthy ants began with the anthill, and most likely, they will end with the anthill, which does great credit to their perseverance and steadfastness. But man is a frivolous and unseemly creature and perhaps, like a chess player, he loves only the process of achieving his goal, and not the goal itself. And, who knows (one can't vouch for it), perhaps the only goal on earth toward which mankind is striving consists merely in this incessant process of achieving or to put it another way, in life itself, and not particularly in the goal which, of course, must always be none other than two times two makes four, that is, a formula; after all,

1. To domestic animals.

two times two makes four is no longer life, gentlemen, but the beginning
of death. At least man has always been somewhat afraid of this two times
two makes four, and I'm afraid of it now, too. Let's suppose that the
only thing man does is search for this two times two makes four; he sails
across oceans, sacrifices his own life in the quest; but to seek it out and
find it—really and truly, he's very frightened. After all, he feels that as
soon as he finds it, there'll be nothing left to search for. Workers, after
finishing work, at least receive their wages, go off to a tavern, and then
wind up at a police station—now that's a full week's occupation. But
where will man go? At any rate a certain awkwardness can be observed
each time he approaches the achievement of similar goals. He loves the
process, but he's not so fond of the achievement, and that, of course is
terribly amusing. In short, man is made in a comical way; obviously
there's some sort of catch in all this. But two times two makes four is
an insufferable thing, nevertheless. Two times two makes four—why,
in my opinion, it's mere insolence. Two times two makes four stands
there brazenly with its hands on its hips, blocking your path and spitting
at you. I agree that two times two makes four is a splendid thing; but if
we're going to lavish praise, then two times two makes five is sometimes
also a very charming little thing.

   And why are you so firmly, so triumphantly convinced that only the
normal and positive—in short, only well-being is advantageous to man?
Doesn't reason ever make mistakes about advantage? After all, perhaps
man likes something other than well-being? Perhaps he loves suffering
just as much? Perhaps suffering is just as advantageous to him as well-
being? Man sometimes loves suffering terribly, to the point of passion,
and that's a fact. There's no reason to study world history on this point;
if indeed you're a man and have lived at all, just ask yourself. As far as
my own personal opinion is concerned, to love only well-being is somehow even indecent. Whether good or bad, it's sometimes also very
pleasant to demolish something. After all, I'm not standing up for suffering here, nor for well-being, either. I'm standing up for . . . my own
whim and for its being guaranteed to me whenever necessary. For instance, suffering is not permitted in vaudevilles,[2] that I know. It's also
inconceivable in the crystal palace; suffering is doubt and negation.
What sort of crystal palace would it be if any doubt were allowed? Yet,
I'm convinced that man will never renounce real suffering, that is,
destruction and chaos. After all, suffering is the sole cause of consciousness. Although I stated earlier that in my opinion consciousness is man's
greatest misfortune, still I know that man loves it and would not exchange
it for any other sort of satisfaction. Consciousness, for example, is infinitely higher than two times two. Of course, after two times two, there's
nothing left, not merely nothing to do, but nothing to learn. Then the

2. A dramatic genre, popular on the Russian stage, consisting of scenes from contemporary life acted
with a satirical twist, often in racy dialogue.

only thing possible will be to plug up your five senses and plunge into contemplation. Well, even if you reach the same result with consciousness, that is, having nothing left to do, at least you'll be able to flog yourself from time to time, and that will liven things up a bit. Although it may be reactionary, it's still better than nothing.

X.

You believe in the crystal palace, eternally indestructible, that is, one at which you can never stick out your tongue furtively nor make a rude gesture, even with your fist hidden away. Well, perhaps I'm so afraid of this building precisely because it's made of crystal and it's eternally indestructible, and because it won't be possible to stick one's tongue out even furtively.

Don't you see: if it were a chicken coop instead of a palace, and if it should rain, then perhaps I could crawl into it so as not to get drenched; but I would still not mistake a chicken coop for a palace out of gratitude, just because it sheltered me from the rain. You're laughing, you're even saying that in this case there's no difference between a chicken coop and a mansion. Yes, I reply, if the only reason for living is to keep from getting drenched.

But what if I've taken it into my head that this is not the only reason for living, and, that if one is to live at all, one might as well live in a mansion? Such is my wish, my desire. You'll expunge it from me only when you've changed my desires. Well, then, change them, tempt me with something else, give me some other ideal. In the meantime, I still won't mistake a chicken coop for a palace. But let's say that the crystal palace is a hoax, that according to the laws of nature it shouldn't exist, and that I've invented it only out of my own stupidity, as a result of certain antiquated, irrational habits of my generation. But what do I care if it doesn't exist? What difference does it make if it exists only in my own desires, or, to be more precise, if it exists as long as my desires exist? Perhaps you're laughing again? Laugh, if you wish; I'll resist all your laughter and I still won't say I'm satiated if I'm really hungry; I know all the same that I won't accept a compromise, an infinitely recurring zero,[3] just because it exists according to the laws of nature and it *really* does exist. I won't accept as the crown of my desires a large building with tenements for poor tenants to be rented for a thousand years and, just in case, with the name of the dentist Wagenheim on the sign. Destroy my desires, eradicate my ideals, show me something better and I'll follow you. You may say, perhaps, that it's not worth getting involved; but, in that case, I'll say the same thing in reply. We're having a serious discussion; if you don't grant me your attention, I won't grovel for it. I still have my underground.

And, as long as I'm still alive and feel desire—may my arm wither

3. A mathematical series containing an infinite number of circulating or repeating zeros.

away before it contributes even one little brick to that building! Never mind that I myself have just rejected the crystal palace for the sole reason that it won't be possible to tease it by sticking out one's tongue at it. I didn't say that because I'm so fond of sticking out my tongue. Perhaps the only reason I got angry is that among all your buildings there's still not a single one where you don't feel compelled to stick out your tongue. On the contrary, I'd let my tongue be cut off out of sheer gratitude, if only things could be so arranged that I'd no longer want to stick it out. What do I care if things can't be so arranged and if I must settle for some tenements? Why was I made with such desires? Can it be that I was made this way only in order to reach the conclusion that my entire way of being is merely a fraud? Can this be the whole purpose? I don't believe it.

By the way, do you know what? I'm convinced that we underground men should be kept in check. Although capable of sitting around quietly in the underground for some forty years, once he emerges into the light of day and bursts into speech, he talks on and on and on. . . .

XI.

The final result, gentlemen, is that it's better to do nothing! Conscious inertia is better! And so, long live the underground! Even though I said that I envy the normal man to the point of exasperation, I still wouldn't want to be him under the circumstances in which I see him (although I still won't keep from envying him. No, no, in any case the underground is more advantageous!) At least there one can . . . Hey, but I'm lying once again! I'm lying because I know myself as surely as two times two, that it isn't really the underground that's better, but something different, altogether different, something that I long for, but I'll never be able to find![4] To hell with the underground! Why, here's what would be better: if I myself were to believe even a fraction of everything I've written. I swear to you, gentlemen, that I don't believe one word, not one little word of all that I've scribbled. That is, I do believe it, perhaps, but at the very same time, I don't know why, I feel and suspect that I'm lying like a trooper.

"Then why did you write all this?" you ask me.

"What if I'd shut you up in the underground for forty years with nothing to do and then came back forty years later to see what had become of you? Can a man really be left alone for forty years with nothing to do?"

"Isn't it disgraceful, isn't it humiliating!" you might say, shaking your head in contempt. "You long for life, but you try to solve life's problems by means of a logical tangle. How importunate, how insolent your outbursts, and how frightened you are at the same time! You talk rubbish,

---

4. The author's letter dated 26 March 1864 to his brother provides an indication of what this "something" might be. See pp. 93–94.

but you're constantly afraid of them and make apologies. You maintain that you fear nothing, but at the same time you try to ingratiate yourself with us. You assure us that you're gnashing your teeth, yet at the same time you try to be witty and amuse us. You know that your witticisms are not very clever, but apparently you're pleased by their literary merit. Perhaps you really have suffered, but you don't even respect your own suffering. There's some truth in you, too, but no chastity; out of the pettiest vanity you bring your truth out into the open, into the market-place, and you shame it. . . . You really want to say something, but you conceal your final word out of fear because you lack the resolve to utter it; you have only cowardly impudence. You boast about your consciousness, but you merely vacillate, because even though your mind is working, your heart has been blackened by depravity, and without a pure heart, there can be no full, genuine consciousness. And how importunate you are; how you force yourself upon others; you behave in such an affected manner. Lies, lies, lies!"

Of course, it was I who just invented all these words for you. That, too, comes from the underground. For forty years in a row I've been listening to all your words through a crack. I've invented them myself, since that's all that's occurred to me. It's no wonder that I've learned it all by heart and that it's taken on such a literary form. . . .

But can you really be so gullible as to imagine that I'll print all this and give it to you to read? And here's another problem I have: why do I keep calling you "gentlemen"? Why do I address you as if you really were my readers? Confessions such as the one I plan to set forth here aren't published and given to other people to read. Anyway, I don't possess sufficient fortitude, nor do I consider it necessary to do so. But don't you see, a certain notion has come into my mind, and I wish to realize it at any cost. Here's the point.

Every man has within his own reminiscences certain things he doesn't reveal to anyone, except, perhaps, to his friends. There are also some that he won't reveal even to his friends, only to himself perhaps, and even then, in secret. Finally, there are some which a man is afraid to reveal even to himself; every decent man has accumulated a fair number of such things. In fact, it can even be said that the more decent the man, the more of these things he's accumulated. Anyway, only recently I myself decided to recall some of my earlier adventures; up to now I've always avoided them, even with a certain anxiety. But having decided not only to recall them, but even to write them down, now is when I wish to try an experiment: is it possible to be absolutely honest even with one's own self and not to fear the whole truth? Incidentally, I'll mention that Heine maintains that faithful autobiographies are almost impossible, and that a man is sure to lie about himself.[5] In Heine's opinion, Rousseau, for example, undoubtedly told untruths about him-

5. A reference to the work *On Germany* (1853–54) by the German poet Heinrich Heine.

self in his confession and even lied intentionally, out of vanity.[6] I'm convinced that Heine is correct; I understand perfectly well that sometimes it's possible out of vanity alone to impute all sorts of crimes to oneself, and I can even understand what sort of vanity that might be. But Heine was making judgments about a person who confessed to the public. I, however, am writing for myself alone and declare once and for all that if I write as if I were addressing readers, that's only for show, because it's easier for me to write that way. It's a form, simply a form; I shall never have any readers. I've already stated that. . . . I don't want to be restricted in any way by editing my notes. I won't attempt to introduce any order or system. I'll write down whatever comes to mind.

Well, now, for example, someone might seize upon my words and ask me, if you really aren't counting on any readers, why do you make such compacts with yourself, and on paper no less; that is, if you're not going to introduce any order or system, if you're going to write down whatever comes to mind, etc., etc.? Why do you go on explaining? Why do you keep apologizing?

"Well, imagine that," I reply.

This, by the way, contains an entire psychology. Perhaps it's just that I'm a coward. Or perhaps it's that I imagine an audience before me on purpose, so that I behave more decently when I'm writing things down. There may be a thousand reasons.

But here's something else: why is it that I want to write? If it's not for the public, then why can't I simply recall it all in my own mind and not commit it to paper?

Quite so; but somehow it appears more dignified on paper. There's something more impressive about it; I'll be a better judge of myself; the style will be improved. Besides, perhaps I'll actually experience some relief from the process of writing it all down. Today, for example, I'm particularly oppressed by one very old memory from my distant past. It came to me vividly several days ago and since then it's stayed with me, like an annoying musical motif that doesn't want to leave you alone. And yet you must get rid of it. I have hundreds of such memories; but at times a single one emerges from those hundreds and oppresses me. For some reason I believe that if I write it down I can get rid of it. Why not try?

Lastly, I'm bored, and I never do anything. Writing things down actually seems like work. They say that work makes a man become good and honest. Well, at least there's a chance.

It's snowing today, an almost wet, yellow, dull snow. It was snowing yesterday too, a few days ago as well. I think it was apropos of the wet snow that I recalled this episode and now it doesn't want to leave me alone. And so, let it be a tale apropos of wet snow.

---

6. Heine attacks the integrity of Rousseau's *Confessions* (1782–89).

II
Apropos of Wet Snow[7]

When from the darkness of delusion
I saved your fallen soul
With ardent words of conviction,
And, full of profound torment,
Wringing your hands, you cursed
The vice that had ensnared you;
When, punishing by recollection
Your forgetful conscience,
You told me the tale
Of all that had happened before,
And, suddenly, covering your face,
Full of shame and horror,
You tearfully resolved,
Indignant, shaken . . .
Etc., etc., etc.
            From the poetry of N. A. Nekrasov[8]

I.

At that time I was only twenty-four years old. Even then my life was gloomy, disordered, and solitary to the point of savagery. I didn't associate with anyone; I even avoided talking, and I retreated further and further into my corner. At work in the office I even tried not to look at anyone; I was aware not only that my colleagues considered me eccentric, but that they always seemed to regard me with a kind of loathing. Sometimes I wondered why it was that no one else thinks that others regard him with loathing. One of our office-workers had a repulsive pock-marked face which even appeared somewhat villainous. It seemed to me that with such a disreputable face I'd never have dared look at anyone. Another man had a uniform so worn that there was a foul smell emanating from him. Yet, neither of these two gentlemen was embarrassed— neither because of his clothes, nor his face, nor in any moral way. Neither one imagined that other people regarded him with loathing; and if either had so imagined, it wouldn't have mattered at all, as long as their supervisor chose not to view him that way. It's perfectly clear to me now, because of my unlimited vanity and the great demands I accordingly made on myself, that I frequently regarded myself with a

---

7. In an article entitled "Notes on Russian Literature" (1849), the critic Pavel Annenkov observed that "damp showers and wet snow" constitute indispensable elements of the Petersburg landscape in the writings of the Naturalist school.

8. These lines were written in 1845 by Nikolai Nekrasov, a writer and publisher preoccupied with Russia's social ills. Dostoevsky maintained intense and often tortured personal, literary, and political relations with him.

furious dissatisfaction verging on loathing; as a result, I intentionally ascribed my own view to everyone else. For example, I despised my own face; I considered it hideous, and I even suspected that there was something repulsive in its expression. Therefore, every time I arrived at work, I took pains to behave as independently as possible, so that I couldn't be suspected of any malice, and I tried to assume as noble an expression as possible. "It may not be a handsome face," I thought, "but let it be noble, expressive, and above all, extremely *intelligent*." But I was agonizingly certain that my face couldn't possibly express all these virtues. Worst of all, I considered it positively stupid. I'd have been reconciled if it had looked intelligent. In fact, I'd even have agreed to have it appear repulsive, on the condition that at the same time people would find my face terribly intelligent.

Of course, I hated all my fellow office-workers from the first to the last and despised every one of them; yet, at the same time it was as if I were afraid of them. Sometimes it happened that I would even regard them as superior to me. At this time these changes would suddenly occur: first I would despise them, then I would regard them as superior to me. A cultured and decent man cannot be vain without making unlimited demands on himself and without hating himself, at times to the point of contempt. But, whether hating them or regarding them as superior, I almost always lowered my eyes when meeting anyone. I even conducted experiments: could I endure someone's gaze? I'd always be the first to lower my eyes. This infuriated me to the point of madness. I slavishly worshipped the conventional in everything external. I embraced the common practice and feared any eccentricity with all my soul. But how could I sustain it? I was morbidly refined, as befits any cultured man of our time. All others resembled one another as sheep in a flock. Perhaps I was the only one in the whole office who constantly thought of himself as a coward and a slave; and I thought so precisely because I was so cultured. But not only did I think so, it actually was so: I was a coward and a slave. I say this without any embarrassment. Every decent man of our time is and must be a coward and a slave. This is his normal condition. I'm deeply convinced of it. This is how he's made and what he's meant to be. And not only at the present time, as the result of some accidental circumstance, but in general at all times, a decent man must be a coward and a slave. This is a law of nature for all decent men on earth. If one of them should happen to be brave about something or other, we shouldn't be comforted or distracted: he'll still lose his nerve about something else. That's the single and eternal way out. Only asses and their mongrels are brave, and even then, only until they come up against a wall. It's not worthwhile paying them any attention because they really don't mean anything at all.

There was one more circumstance tormenting me at that time: no one was like me, and I wasn't like anyone else. "I'm alone," I mused, "and they are *everyone*"; and I sank deep into thought.

From all this it's clear that I was still just a boy.

The exact opposite would also occur. Sometimes I would find it repulsive to go to the office: it reached the point where I would often return home from work ill. Then suddenly, for no good reason at all, a flash of skepticism and indifference would set in (everything came to me in flashes); I would laugh at my own intolerance and fastidiousness, and reproach myself for my *romanticism*. Sometimes I didn't even want to talk to anyone; at other times it reached a point where I not only started talking, but I even thought about striking up a friendship with others. All my fastidiousness would suddenly disappear for no good reason at all. Who knows? Perhaps I never really had any, and it was all affected, borrowed from books. I still haven't answered this question, even up to now. And once I really did become friends with others; I began to visit their houses, play préférance,[9] drink vodka, talk about promotions. . . . But allow me to digress.

We Russians, generally speaking, have never had any of those stupid, transcendent German romantics, or even worse, French romantics, on whom nothing produces any effect whatever: the earth might tremble beneath them, all of France might perish on the barricades, but they remain the same, not even changing for decency's sake; they go on singing their transcendent songs, so to speak, to their dying day, because they're such fools. We here on Russian soil have no fools. It's a well-know fact; that's precisely what distinguishes us from foreigners. Consequently, transcendent natures cannot be found among us in their pure form. That's the result of our "positive" publicists and critics of that period, who hunted for the Kostanzhoglos[1] and the Uncle Pyotr Ivan-oviches,[2] foolishly mistaking them for our ideal and slandering our own romantics, considering them to be the same kind of transcendents as one finds in Germany or France. On the contrary, the characteristics of our romantics are absolutely and directly opposed to the transcendent Europeans; not one of those European standards can apply here. (Allow me to use the word "romantic"—it's an old-fashioned little word, well-respected and deserving, familiar to everyone.) The characteristics of our romantics are to understand everything, *to see everything, often to see it much more clearly than our most positive minds*; not to be reconciled with anyone or anything, but, at the same time, not to balk at anything; to circumvent everything, to yield on every point, to treat everyone diplomatically; never to lose sight of some useful, practical goal (an

9. A card game for three players with a thirty-two-card pack resembling whist.
1. A character from the incomplete second volume of Nikolai Gogol's novel *Dead Souls* (1852). He is a model landowner and an efficient manager of his estate.

2. A character from Ivan Goncharov's novel *A Common Story* (1847) who serves as an example of common sense and practical activity for his young nephew.

apartment at government expense, a nice pension, a decoration)—to keep an eye on that goal through all his excesses and his volumes of lyrical verse, and, at the same time, to preserve intact the "beautiful and sublime" to the end of their lives; and, incidentally, to preserve themselves as well, wrapped up in cotton like precious jewelry, if only, for example, for the sake of that same "beautiful and sublime." Our romantic has a very broad nature and is the biggest rogue of all, I can assure you of that . . . even by my own experience. Of course, all this is true if the romantic is smart. But what am I saying? A romantic is always smart; I merely wanted to observe that although we've had some romantic fools, they really don't count at all, simply because while still in their prime they would degenerate completely into Germans, and, in order to preserve their precious jewels more comfortably, they'd settle over there, either in Weimar[3] or in the Black Forest.[4] For instance, I genuinely despised my official position and refrained from throwing it over merely out of necessity, because I myself sat there working and received good money for doing it. And, as a result, please note, I still refrained from throwing it over. Our romantic would sooner lose his mind (which, by the way, very rarely occurs) than give it up, if he didn't have another job in mind; nor is he ever kicked out, unless he's hauled off to the insane asylum as the "King of Spain,"[5] and only if he's gone completely mad. Then again, it's really only the weaklings and towheads who go mad in our country. An enormous number of romantics later rise to significant rank. What extraordinary versatility! And what a capacity for the most contradictory sensations! I used to be consoled by these thoughts back then, and still am even nowadays. That's why there are so many "broad natures" among us, people who never lose their ideals, no matter how low they fall; even though they never lift a finger for the sake of their ideals, even though they're outrageous villains and thieves, nevertheless they respect their original ideals to the point of tears and are extremely honest men at heart. Yes, only among us Russians can the most outrageous scoundrel be absolutely, even sublimely honest at heart, while at the same time never ceasing to be a scoundrel. I repeat, nearly always do our romantics turn out to be very efficient rascals (I use the word "rascal" affectionately); they suddenly manifest such a sense of reality and positive knowledge that their astonished superiors and the general public can only click their tongues at them in amazement.

Their versatility is really astounding; God only knows what it will turn into, how it will develop under subsequent conditions, and what it holds for us in the future. The material is not all that bad! I'm not saying this

3. A city in present-day East Germany regarded as the literary center of Europe during the late eighteenth and early nineteenth centuries, when Goethe, Schiller, and Herder all lived there.
4. A mountain range in southwestern Germany covered by beautiful, dark pine forests and cut by deep valleys and small lakes.

5. A reference to the hero of Gogol's short story "Diary of a Madman" (1835). Poprishchin, a low-ranking civil servant, sees his aspirations crushed by the enormous bureaucracy. He ends by going insane and imagining himself to be king of Spain.

out of some ridiculous patriotism or jingoism. However, I'm sure that once again you think I'm joking. But who knows? Perhaps it's quite the contrary, that is, you're convinced that this is what I really think. In any case, gentlemen, I'll consider that both of these opinions constitute an honor and a particular pleasure. And do forgive me for this digression.

Naturally, I didn't sustain any friendships with my colleagues, and soon I severed all relations after quarreling with them; and, because of my youthful inexperience at the same time, I even stopped greeting them, as if I'd cut them off entirely. That, however, happened to me only once. On the whole, I was always alone.

At home I spent most of my time reading. I tried to stifle all that was constantly seething within me with external sensations. And of all external sensations available, only reading was possible for me. Of course, reading helped a great deal—it agitated, delighted, and tormented me. But at times it was terribly boring. I still longed to be active; and suddenly I sank into dark, subterranean, loathsome depravity—more precisely, petty vice. My nasty little passions were sharp and painful as a result of my constant, morbid irritability. I experienced hysterical fits accompanied by tears and convulsions. Besides reading, I had nowhere else to go—that is, there was nothing to respect in my surroundings, nothing to attract me. In addition, I was overwhelmed by depression; I possessed a hysterical craving for contradictions and contrasts; and, as a result, I plunged into depravity. I haven't said all this to justify myself. . . . But, no, I'm lying. I did want to justify myself. It's for myself, gentlemen, that I include this little observation. I don't want to lie. I've given my word.

I indulged in depravity all alone, at night, furtively, timidly, sordidly, with a feeling of shame that never left me even in my most loathsome moments and drove me at such times to the point of profanity. Even then I was carrying around the underground in my soul. I was terribly afraid of being seen, met, recognized. I visited all sorts of dismal places.

Once, passing by some wretched little tavern late at night, I saw through a lighted window some gentlemen fighting with billiard cues; one of them was thrown out the window. At some other time I would have been disgusted; but just then I was overcome by such a mood that I envied the gentleman who'd been tossed out; I envied him so much that I even walked into the tavern and entered the billiard room. "Perhaps," I thought, "I'll get into a fight, and they'll throw me out the window, too."

I wasn't drunk, but what could I do—after all, depression can drive a man to this kind of hysteria. But nothing came of it. It turned out that I was incapable of being tossed out the window; I left without getting into a fight.

As soon as I set foot inside, some officer put me in my place.

I was standing next to the billiard table inadvertently blocking his way as he wanted to get by; he took hold of me by the shoulders and without a word of warning or explanation, moved me from where I was standing to another place, and he went past as if he hadn't even noticed me. I could have forgiven even a beating, but I could never forgive his moving me out of the way and entirely failing to notice me.

The devil knows what I would have given for a genuine, ordinary quarrel, a decent one, a more *literary* one, so to speak. But I'd been treated as if I were a fly. The officer was about six feet tall, while I'm small and scrawny. The quarrel, however, was in my hands; all I had to do was protest, and of course they would've thrown me out the window. But I reconsidered and preferred . . . to withdraw resentfully.

I left the tavern confused and upset and went straight home; the next night I continued my petty vice more timidly, more furtively, more gloomily than before, as if I had tears in my eyes—but I continued nonetheless. Don't conclude, however, that I retreated from that officer as a result of any cowardice; I've never been a coward at heart, although I've constantly acted like one in deed, but—wait before you laugh—I can explain this. I can explain anything, you may rest assured.

Oh, if only this officer had been the kind who'd have agreed to fight a duel! But no, he was precisely one of those types (alas, long gone) who preferred to act with their billiard cues or, like Gogol's Lieutenant Pirogov,[6] by appealing to the authorities. They didn't fight duels; in any case, they'd have considered fighting a duel with someone like me, a lowly civilian, to be indecent. In general, they considered duels to be somehow inconceivable, free-thinking, French, while they themselves, especially if they happened to be six feet tall, offended other people rather frequently.

In this case I retreated not out of any cowardice, but because of my unlimited vanity. I wasn't afraid of his height, nor did I think I'd receive a painful beating and get thrown out the window. In fact, I'd have had sufficient physical courage; it was moral fortitude I lacked. I was afraid that everyone present—from the insolent billiard marker to the foul-smelling, pimply little clerks with greasy collars who used to hang about—wouldn't understand and would laugh when I started to protest and speak to them in literary Russian. Because, to this very day, it's still impossible for us to speak about a point of honor, that is, not about honor itself, but a point of honor (*point d'honneur*), except in literary language. One can't even refer to a "point of honor" in everyday language. I was fully convinced (a sense of reality, in spite of all my romanticism!) that they would all simply split their sides laughing, and that the officer, instead of giving me a simple beating, that is, an inoffensive one, would certainly apply his knee to my back and drive me around the billiard table; only then perhaps would he have the mercy

---

6. One of two main characters in Gogol's short story "Nevsky Prospect" (1835). A shallow and self-satisfied officer, he mistakes the wife of a German artisan for a woman of easy virtue and receives a sound thrashing. He decides to lodge an official complaint, but after consuming a cream-filled pastry, thinks better of it.

to throw me out the window. Naturally, this wretched story of mine couldn't possibly end with this alone. Afterward I used to meet this officer frequently on the street and I observed him very carefully. I don't know whether he ever recognized me. Probably not; I reached that conclusion from various observations. As for me, I stared at him with malice and hatred, and continued to do so for several years! My malice increased and became stronger over time. At first I began to make discreet inquiries about him. This was difficult for me to do, since I had so few acquaintances. But once, as I was following him at a distance as though tied to him, someone called to him on the street: that's how I learned his name. Another time I followed him back to his own apartment and for a ten-kopeck piece learned from the doorman where and how he lived, on what floor, with whom, etc.—in a word, all that could be learned from a doorman. One morning, although I never engaged in literary activities, it suddenly occurred to me to draft a description of this officer as a kind of exposé, a caricature, in the form of a tale. I wrote it with great pleasure. I exposed him; I even slandered him. At first I altered his name only slightly, so that it could be easily recognized; but then, upon careful reflection, I changed it. Then I sent the tale off to *Notes of the Fatherland*.[7] But such exposés were no longer in fashion, and they didn't publish my tale. I was very annoyed by that. At times I simply choked on my spite. Finally, I resolved to challenge my opponent to a duel. I composed a beautiful, charming letter to him, imploring him to apologize to me; in case he refused, I hinted rather strongly at a duel. The letter was composed in such a way that if that officer had possessed even the smallest understanding of the "beautiful and sublime," he would have come running, thrown his arms around me, and offered his friendship. That would have been splendid! We would have led such a wonderful life! Such a life! He would have shielded me with his rank; I would have ennobled him with my culture, and, well, with my ideas. Who knows what might have come of it! Imagine it, two years had already passed since he'd insulted me; my challenge was the most ridiculous anachronism, in spite of all the cleverness of my letter in explaining and disguising that fact. But, thank God (to this day I thank the Almighty with tears in my eyes), I didn't send that letter. A shiver runs up and down my spine when I think what might have happened if I had. Then suddenly . . . suddenly, I got my revenge in the simplest manner, a stroke of genius! A brilliant idea suddenly occurred to me. Sometimes on holidays I used to stroll along Nevsky Prospect at about four o'clock in the afternoon, usually on the sunny side. That is, I didn't really stroll; rather, I experienced innumerable torments, humiliations, and bilious attacks. But that's undoubtedly just what I needed. I darted in and out like a fish among the strollers, constantly stepping aside before generals, cavalry officers, hussars, and

---

7. A literary and political journal published in Petersburg from 1839 to 1867 by A. A. Kraevsky.

young ladies. At those moments I used to experience painful spasms in my heart and a burning sensation in my back merely at the thought of my dismal apparel as well as the wretchedness and vulgarity of my darting little figure. This was sheer torture, uninterrupted and unbearable humiliation at the thought, which soon became an incessant and immediate sensation, that I was a fly in the eyes of society, a disgusting, obscene fly—smarter than the rest, more cultured, even nobler—all that goes without saying, but a fly, nonetheless, who incessantly steps aside, insulted and injured by everyone.[8] For what reason did I inflict this torment on myself? Why did I stroll along Nevsky Prospect? I don't know. But something simply *drew* me there at every opportunity.

Then I began to experience surges of that pleasure about which I've already spoken in the first chapter.[9] After the incident with the officer I was drawn there even more strongly; I used to encounter him along Nevsky most often, and it was there that I could admire him. He would also go there, mostly on holidays. He, too, would give way before generals and individuals of superior rank; he, too, would spin like a top among them. But he would simply trample people like me, or even those slightly superior; he would walk directly toward them, as if there were empty space ahead of him; and under no circumstance would he ever step aside. I revelled in my malice as I observed him, and . . . bitterly stepped aside before him every time. I was tortured by the fact that even on the street I found it impossible to stand on an equal footing with him. "Why is it you're always first to step aside?" I badgered myself in insane hysteria, at times waking up at three in the morning. "Why always you and not he? After all, there's no law about it; it isn't written down anywhere. Let it be equal, as it usually is when people of breeding meet: he steps aside halfway and you halfway, and you pass by showing each other mutual respect." But that was never the case, and I continued to step aside, while he didn't even notice that I was yielding to him. Then a most astounding idea suddenly dawned on me. "What if," I thought, "what if I were to meet him and . . . not step aside? Deliberately not step aside, even if it meant bumping in_ him: how would that be?" This bold idea gradually took such a hold that it afforded me no peace. I dreamt about it incessantly, horribly, and even went to Nevsky more frequently so that I could imagine more clearly how I would do it. I was in ecstasy. The scheme was becoming more and more possible and even probable to me. "Of course, I wouldn't really collide with him," I thought, already feeling more generous toward him in my joy, "but I simply won't turn aside. I'll bump into him, not very painfully, but just so, shoulder to shoulder, as much as decency allows. I'll bump into him the same amount as he bumps into me." At last I made up my mind completely. But the preparations took a very long time. First, in

---

8. In 1861 Dostoevsky had published a novel with the title *The Insulted and the Injured*, an explo-   ration of lower-class life in Petersburg.
9. That is, in part I, "Underground."

order to look as presentable as possible during the execution of my scheme, I had to worry about my clothes. "In any case, what if, for example, it should occasion a public scandal? (And the public there was *superflu:*[1] a countess, Princess D., and the entire literary world.) It was essential to be well-dressed; that inspires respect and in a certain sense will place us immediately on an equal footing in the eyes of high society." With that goal in mind I requested my salary in advance, and I purchased a pair of black gloves and a decent hat at Churkin's store. Black gloves seemed to me more dignified, more *bon ton*[2] than the lemon-colored ones I'd considered at first. "That would be too glaring, as if the person wanted to be noticed"; so I didn't buy the lemon-colored ones. I'd already procured a fine shirt with white bone cufflinks; but my overcoat constituted a major obstacle. In and of itself it was not too bad at all; it kept me warm; but it was quilted and had a raccoon collar, the epitome of bad taste. At all costs I had to replace the collar with a beaver one, just like on an officer's coat. For this purpose I began to frequent the Shopping Arcade; and, after several attempts, I turned up some cheap German beaver. Although these German beavers wear out very quickly and soon begin to look shabby, at first, when they're brand new, they look very fine indeed; after all, I only needed it for a single occasion. I asked the price: it was still expensive. After considerable reflection I resolved to sell my raccoon collar. I decided to request a loan for the remaining amount—a rather significant sum for me—from Anton Antonych Setochkin, my office chief, a modest man, but a serious and solid one, who never lent money to anyone, but to whom, upon entering the civil service, I'd once been specially recommended by an important person who'd secured the position for me. I suffered terribly. It seemed monstrous and shameful to ask Anton Antonych for money. I didn't sleep for two or three nights in a row; in general I wasn't getting much sleep those days, and I always had a fever. I would have either a vague sinking feeling in my heart, or else my heart would suddenly begin to thump, thump, thump! . . . At first Anton Antonych was surprised, then he frowned, thought it over, and finally gave me the loan, after securing from me a note authorizing him to deduct the sum from my salary two weeks later. In this way everything was finally ready; the splendid beaver reigned in place of the mangy raccoon, and I gradually began to get down to business. It was impossible to set about it all at once, in a foolhardy way; one had to proceed in this matter very carefully, step by step. But I confess that after many attempts I was ready to despair: we didn't bump into each other, no matter what! No matter how I prepared, no matter how determined I was—it seems that we're just about to bump, when I look up—and once again I've stepped aside while he's gone by without even noticing me. I even used to pray as I approached him that God would grant me determination. One time I'd fully resolved to do

---

1. Refined.   2. In good taste.

it, but the result was that I merely stumbled and fell at his feet because, at the very last moment, only a few inches away from him, I lost my nerve. He stepped over me very calmly, and I bounced to one side like a rubber ball. That night I lay ill with a fever once again and was delirious. Then, everything suddenly ended in the best possible way. The night before I decided once and for all not to go through with my pernicious scheme and to give it all up without success; with that in mind I went to Nevsky Prospect for one last time simply in order to see how I'd abandon the whole thing. Suddenly, three paces away from my enemy, I made up my mind unexpectedly; I closed my eyes and—we bumped into each other forcefully, shoulder to shoulder! I didn't yield an inch and walked by him on a completely equal footing! He didn't even turn around to look at me and pretended that he hadn't even noticed; but he was merely pretending, I'm convinced of that. To this very day I'm convinced of that! Naturally, I got the worst of it; he was stronger, but that wasn't the point. The point was that I'd achieved my goal, I'd maintained my dignity, I hadn't yielded one step, and I'd publicly placed myself on an equal social footing with him. I returned home feeling completely avenged for everything. I was ecstatic. I rejoiced and sang Italian arias. Of course, I won't describe what happened to me three days later; if you've read the first part entitled "Underground," you can guess for yourself.[3] The officer was later transferred somewhere else; I haven't seen him for some fourteen years. I wonder what he's doing nowadays, that dear friend of mine! Whom is he trampling underfoot?

II.

But when this phase of my nice, little dissipation ended I felt terribly nauseated. Remorse set in; I tried to drive it away because it was too disgusting. Little by little, however, I got used to that, too. I got used to it all; that is, it wasn't that I got used to it, rather, I somehow voluntarily consented to endure it. But I had a way out that reconciled everything— to escape into "all that was beautiful and sublime," in my dreams, of course. I was a terrible dreamer; I dreamt for three months in a row, tucked away in my little corner. And well you may believe that in those moments I was not at all like the gentlemen who, in his faint-hearted anxiety, had sewn a German beaver onto the collar of his old overcoat. I suddenly became a hero. If my six-foot tall lieutenant had come to see me then, I'd never have admitted him. I couldn't even conceive of him at that time. It's hard to describe now what my dreams consisted of then, and how I could've been so satisfied with them, but I was. Besides, even now I can take pride in them at certain times. My dreams

3. That is, the hero's retreat to his corner in the underground.

were particularly sweet and vivid after my little debauchery; they were filled with remorse and tears, curses and ecstasy. There were moments of such positive intoxication, such happiness, that I felt not even the slightest trace of mockery within me, really and truly. It was all faith, hope and love. That's just it: at the time I believed blindly that by some kind of miracle, some external circumstance, everything would suddenly open up and expand; a vista of appropriate activity would suddenly appear—beneficent, beautiful, and most of all, *ready-made* (what precisely, I never knew, but, most of all, it had to be ready-made), and that I would suddenly step forth into God's world, almost riding on a white horse and wearing a laurel wreath. I couldn't conceive of a secondary role; and that's precisely why in reality I very quietly took on the lowest one. Either a hero or dirt—there was no middle ground. That was my ruin because in the dirt I consoled myself knowing that at other times I was a hero, and that the hero covered himself with dirt; that is to say, an ordinary man would be ashamed to wallow in filth, but a hero is too noble to become defiled; consequently, he can wallow. It's remarkable that these surges of everything "beautiful and sublime" occurred even during my petty depravity, and precisely when I'd sunk to the lowest depths. They occurred in separate spurts, as if to remind me of themselves; however, they failed to banish my depravity by their appearance. On the contrary, they seemed to add spice to it by means of contrast; they came in just the right amount to serve as a tasty sauce. This sauce consisted of contradictions, suffering, and agonizing internal analysis; all of these torments and trifles lent a certain piquancy, even some meaning to my depravity—in a word, they completely fulfilled the function of a tasty sauce. Nor was all this even lacking in a measure of profundity. Besides, I would never have consented to the simple, tasteless, spontaneous little debauchery of an ordinary clerk and have endured all that filth! How could it have attracted me then and lured me into the street late at night? No, sir, I had a noble loophole for everything. . . .

But how much love, oh Lord, how much love I experienced at times in those dreams of mine, in those "escapes into everything beautiful and sublime." Even though it was fantastic love, even though it was never directed at anything human, there was still so much love that afterward, in reality, I no longer felt any impulse to direct it: that would have been an unnecessary luxury. However, everything always ended in a most satisfactory way by a lazy and intoxicating transition into art, that is, into beautiful forms of being, ready-made, largely borrowed from poets and novelists, and adapted to serve every possible need. For instance, I would triumph over everyone; naturally, everyone else grovelled in the dust and was voluntarily impelled to acknowledge my superiority, while I would forgive them all for everything. Or else, being a famous poet and chamberlain, I would fall in love; I'd receive an enormous fortune and would immediately sacrifice it all for the benefit of humanity,[4] at the same time confessing before all peoples my own infamies, which, needless to say, were not simple infamies, but contained a great amount of "the beautiful and sublime," something in the style of Manfred.[5] Everyone would weep and kiss me (otherwise what idiots they would have been), while I went about barefoot and hungry preaching new ideas and defeating all the reactionaries of Austerlitz.[6] Then a march would be played, a general amnesty declared, and the Pope would agree to leave Rome and go to Brazil;[7] a ball would be hosted for all of Italy at the Villa Borghese on the shores of Lake Como,[8] since Lake Como would have been moved to Rome for this very occasion; then there would be a scene in the bushes, etc., etc.—as if you didn't know. You'll say that it's tasteless and repugnant to drag all this out into the open after all the raptures and tears to which I've confessed. But why is it so repugnant? Do you really think I'm ashamed of all this or that it's any more stupid than anything in your own lives, gentlemen? Besides, you can rest assured that some of it was not at all badly composed. . . . Not everything occurred on the shores of Lake Como. But you're right; in fact, it is tasteless and repugnant. And the most repugnant thing of all is that now I've begun to justify myself before you. And even more repugnant is that now I've made that observation. But enough, otherwise there'll be no end to it: each thing will be more repugnant than the last .

I was never able to dream for more than three months in a row, and I began to feel an irresistible urge to plunge into society. To me plunging into society meant paying a visit to my office chief, Anton Antonych Setochkin. He's the only lasting acquaintance I've made during my lifetime; I too now marvel at this circumstance. But even then I would visit him only when my dreams had reached such a degree of happiness that it was absolutely essential for me to embrace people and all humanity at once; for that reason I needed to have at least one person on hand who actually existed. However, one could only call upon Anton Antonych on Tuesdays (his receiving day); consequently, I always had to adjust the urge to embrace all humanity so that it occurred on Tuesday. This Anton Antonych lived near Five Corners,[9] on the fourth floor, in four small, low-ceilinged rooms, each smaller than the last, all very

4. This dream of the underground man was later revived in Dostoevsky's novel *The Adolescent* (1875), where the hero plans to amass a fortune and then give it all away to benefit mankind.

5. The romantic hero of Byron's poetic tragedy *Manfred* (1817), a lonely, defiant figure whose past conceals some mysterious crime.

6. The site of Napoleon's great victory in December 1805 over the combined armies of the Russian tsar Alexander I and the Austrian emperor Francis II.

7. Napoleon announced his annexation of the Papal states to France in 1809 and was promptly excommunicated by Pope Pius VII. The Pope was imprisoned and forced to sign a new con cordat, but in 1814 returned to Rome in triumph.

8. The elegant summer palace built by Scipione Cardinal Borghese outside the Porta del Popolo in Rome. Lake Como is located in the foothills of the Italian Alps in Lombardy.

9. A well-known landmark in Petersburg.

frugal and yellowish[1] in appearance. He lived with his two daughters
and an aunt who used to serve tea. The daughters, one thirteen, the
other fourteen, had little snub noses. I was very embarrassed by them
because they used to whisper all the time and giggle to each other. The
host usually sat in his study on a leather couch in front of a table together
with some gray-haired guest, a civil servant either from our office or
another one. I never saw more than two or three guests there, and they
were always the same ones. They talked about excise taxes, debates in
the Senate, salaries, promotions, His Excellency and how to please him,
and so on and so forth. I had the patience to sit there like a fool next
to these people for four hours or so; I listened without daring to say a
word to them or even knowing what to talk about. I sat there in a stupor;
several times I broke into a sweat; I felt numbed by paralysis; but it was
good and useful. Upon returning home I would postpone for some time
my desire to embrace all humanity.

I had one other sort of acquaintance, however, named Simonov, a
former schoolmate of mine. In fact, I had a number of schoolmates in
Petersburg, but I didn't associate with them, and I'd even stopped greeting
them along the street. I might even have transferred into a different
department at the office so as not to be with them and to cut myself off
from my hated childhood once and for all. Curses on that school and
those horrible years of penal servitude. In short, I broke with my schoolmates as soon as I was released. There remained only two or three people
whom I would greet upon encountering them. One was Simonov, who
hadn't distinguished himself in school in any way; he was even-tempered
and quiet, but I detected in him a certain independence of character,
even honesty. I don't even think that he was all that limited. At one
time he and I experienced some rather bright moments, but they didn't
last very long and somehow were suddenly clouded over. Evidently he
was burdened by these recollections, and seemed in constant fear that
I would lapse into that former mode. I suspect that he found me repulsive, but not being absolutely sure, I used to visit him nonetheless.

So once, on a Thursday, unable to endure my solitude, and knowing
that on that day Anton Antonych's door was locked, I remembered
Simonov. As I climbed the stairs to his apartment on the fourth floor,
I was thinking how burdensome this man found my presence and that
my going to see him was rather useless. But since it always turned out,
as if on purpose, that such reflections would impel me to put myself
even further into an ambiguous situation, I went right in. It had been
almost a year since I'd last seen Simonov.

---

1. This color is typical of Dostoevsky's most repulsive interiors. Cf. the pawnbroker's flat in *Crime and Punishment* (1866).

III.

I found two more of my former schoolmates there with him. Apparently they were discussing some important matter. None of them paid any attention to me when I entered, which was strange since I hadn't seen them for several years. Evidently they considered me some sort of ordinary house fly. They hadn't even treated me like that when we were in school together, although they'd all hated me. Of course, I understood that they must despise me now for my failure in the service and for the fact that I'd sunk so low, was badly dressed, and so on, which, in their eyes, constituted proof of my ineptitude and insignificance. But I still hadn't expected such a degree of contempt. Simonov was even surprised by my visits. All this disconcerted me; I sat down in some distress and began to listen to what they were saying.

The discussion was serious, even heated, and concerned a farewell dinner which these gentlemen wanted to organize jointly as early as the following day for their friend Zverkov, an army officer who was heading for a distant province. Monsieur Zverkov had also been my schoolmate all along. I'd begun to hate him especially in the upper grades. In the lower grades he was merely an attractive, lively lad whom everyone liked. However, I'd hated him in the lower grades, too, precisely because he was such an attractive, lively lad. He was perpetually a poor student and had gotten worse as time went on; he managed to graduate, however, because he had influential connections. During his last year at school he'd come into an inheritance of some two hundred serfs, and, since almost all the rest of us were poor, he'd even begun to brag. He was an extremely uncouth fellow, but a nice lad nonetheless, even when he was bragging. In spite of our superficial, fantastic, and high-flown notions of honor and pride, all of us, except for a very few, would fawn upon Zverkov, the more so the more he bragged. They didn't fawn for any advantage; they fawned simply because he was a man endowed by nature with gifts. Moreover, we'd somehow come to regard Zverkov as a cunning fellow and an expert on good manners. This latter point particularly infuriated me. I hated the shrill, self-confident tone of his voice, his adoration for his own witticisms, which were terribly stupid in spite of his bold tongue; I hated his handsome, stupid face (for which, however, I'd gladly have exchanged my own intelligent one), and the impudent bearing typical of officers during the 1840s. I hated the way he talked about his future successes with women. (He'd decided not to get involved with them yet, since he still hadn't received his officer's epaulettes; he awaited those epaulettes impatiently.) And he talked about all the duels he'd have to fight. I remember how once, although I was usually very taciturn, I suddenly clashed with Zverkov when, during our free time, he was discussing future exploits with his friends; getting a bit carried away with the game like a little puppy playing in the sun, he suddenly declared that not a single girl in his village would escape his attention—

that it was his *droit de seigneur*,[2] and that if the peasants even dared protest, he'd have them all flogged, those bearded rascals; and he'd double their quit-rent.[3] Our louts applauded, but I attacked him—not out of any pity for the poor girls or their fathers, but simply because everyone else was applauding such a little insect. I got the better of him that time, but Zverkov, although stupid, was also cheerful and impudent. Therefore he laughed it off to such an extent that, in fact, I really didn't get the better of him. The laugh remained on his side. Later he got the better of me several times, but without malice, just so, in jest, in passing, in fun. I was filled with spite and hatred, but I didn't respond. After graduation he took a few steps toward me; I didn't object strongly because I found it flattering; but soon we came to a natural parting of the ways. Afterward I heard about his barrack-room successes as a lieutenant and about his *binges*. Then there were other rumors—about his *successes* in the service. He no longer bowed to me on the street; I suspected that he was afraid to compromise himself by acknowledging such an insignificant person as myself. I also saw him in the theater once, in the third tier, already sporting an officer's gold braids. He was fawning and grovelling before the daughters of some aged general. In those three years he'd let himself go, although he was still as handsome and agile as before; he sagged somehow and had begun to put on weight; it was clear that by the age of thirty he'd be totally flabby. So it was for this Zverkov, who was finally ready to depart, that our schoolmates were organizing a farewell dinner. They'd kept up during these three years, although I'm sure that inwardly they didn't consider themselves on an equal footing with him.

One of Simonov's two guests was Ferfichkin, a Russified German, a short man with a face like a monkey, a fool who made fun of everybody, my bitterest enemy from the lower grades—a despicable, impudent show-off who affected the most ticklish sense of ambition, although, of course, he was a coward at heart. He was one of Zverkov's admirers and played up to him for his own reasons, frequently borrowing money from him. Simonov's other guest, Trudolyubov, was insignificant, a military man, tall, with a cold demeanor, rather honest, who worshipped success of any kind and was capable of talking only about promotions. He was a distant relative of Zverkov's, and that, silly to say, lent him some importance among us. He'd always regarded me as a nonentity; he treated me not altogether politely, but tolerably.

"Well, if each of us contributes seven rubles," said Trudolyubov, "with three of us that makes twenty-one altogether—we can have a good dinner. Of course, Zverkov won't have to pay."

"Naturally," Simonov agreed, "since we're inviting him."

2. Landlord's privilege: the feudal landlord's right to spend the first night with the bride of a newly married serf.
3. The annual sum paid in cash or produce by serfs to landowners for the right to farm their land in feudal Russia, as opposed to the *corvée*, a certain amount of labor owed.

"Do you really think," Ferfichkin broke in arrogantly and excitedly, just like an insolent lackey bragging about his master-the-general's medals, "do you really think Zverkov will let us pay for everything? He'll accept out of decency, but then he'll order *half a dozen bottles* on his own."

"What will the four of us do with half a dozen bottles?" asked Trudolyubov, only taking note of the number.

"So then, three of us plus Zverkov makes four, twenty-one rubles, in the Hôtel de Paris, tomorrow at five o'clock," concluded Simonov definitively, since he'd been chosen to make the arrangements.

"Why only twenty-one?" I asked in trepidation, even, apparently, somewhat offended. "If you count me in, you'll have twenty-eight rubles instead of twenty-one."

It seemed to me that to include myself so suddenly and unexpectedly would appear as quite a splendid gesture and that they'd all be smitten at once and regard me with respect.

"Do you really want to come, too?" Simonov inquired with displeasure, managing somehow to avoid looking at me. He knew me inside out.

It was infuriating that he knew me inside out.

"And why not? After all, I was his schoolmate, too, and I must admit that I even feel a bit offended that you've left me out," I continued, just about to boil over again.

"And how were we supposed to find you?" Ferfichkin interjected rudely.

"You never got along very well with Zverkov," added Trudolyubov frowning. But I'd already latched on and wouldn't let go.

"I think no one has a right to judge that," I objected in a trembling voice, as if God knows what had happened. "Perhaps that's precisely why I want to take part now, since we didn't get along so well before."

"Well, who can figure you out . . . such lofty sentiments . . . ," Trudolyubov said with an ironic smile.

"We'll put your name down," Simonov decided, turning to me. "Tomorrow at five o'clock at the Hôtel de Paris. Don't make any mistakes."

"What about the money?" Ferfichkin started to say in an undertone to Simonov while nodding at me, but he broke off because Simonov looked embarrassed.

"That'll do," Trudolyubov said getting up. "If he really wants to come so much, let him."

"But this is our own circle of friends," Ferfichkin grumbled, also picking up his hat. "It's not an official gathering. Perhaps we really don't want you at all. . . ."

They left. Ferfichkin didn't even say goodbye to me as he went out;

Trudolyubov barely nodded without looking at me. Simonov, with whom I was left alone, was irritated and perplexed, and he regarded me in a strange way. He neither sat down nor invited me to.

"Hmmm . . . yes . . . , so, tomorrow. Will you contribute your share of the money now? I'm asking just to know for sure," he muttered in embarrassment.

I flared up; but in doing so, I remembered that I'd owed Simonov fifteen rubles for a very long time, which debt, moreover, I'd forgotten, but had also never repaid.

"You must agree, Simonov, that I couldn't have known when I came here . . . oh, what a nuisance, but I've forgotten. . . ."

He broke off and began to pace around the room in even greater irritation. As he paced, he began to walk on his heels and stomp more loudly.

"I'm not detaining you, am I?" I asked after a few moments of silence.

"Oh, no!" he replied with a start. "That is, in fact, yes. You see, I still have to stop by at . . . It's not very far from here . . . ," he added in an apologetic way with some embarrassment.

"Oh, good heavens! Why didn't you say so?" I exclaimed, seizing my cap; moreover I did so with a surprisingly familiar air, coming from God knows where.

"But it's really not far . . . only a few steps away . . . ," Simonov repeated, accompanying me into the hallway with a bustling air which didn't suit him well at all. "So, then, tomorrow at five o'clock sharp!" he shouted to me on the stairs. He was very pleased that I was leaving. However, I was furious.

"What possessed me, what on earth possessed me to interfere?" I *regret* gnashed my teeth as I walked along the street. "And for such a scoundrel, a pig like Zverkov! Naturally, I shouldn't go. Of course, to hell with them. Am I bound to go, or what? Tomorrow I'll inform Simonov by post. . . ."

But the real reason I was so furious was that I was sure I'd go. I'd go on purpose. The more tactless, the more indecent it was for me to go, the more certain I'd be to do it.

There was even a definite impediment to my going: I didn't have any money. All I had was nine rubles. But of those, I had to hand over seven the next day to my servant Apollon for his monthly wages; he lived in and received seven rubles for his meals.

Considering Apollon's character it was impossible not to pay him. But more about that rascal, that plague of mine, later.

In any case, I knew that I wouldn't pay him his wages and that I'd definitely go.

That night I had the most hideous dreams. No wonder: all evening I was burdened with recollections of my years of penal servitude at school and I couldn't get rid of them.[4] I'd been sent off to that school by distant relatives on whom I was dependent and about whom I've heard nothing since. They dispatched me, a lonely boy, crushed by their reproaches, already introspective, taciturn, and regarding everything around him savagely. My schoolmates received me with spiteful and pitiless jibes because I wasn't like any of them. But I couldn't tolerate their jibes; I couldn't possibly get along with them as easily as they got along with each other. I hated them all at once and took refuge from everyone in fearful, wounded and excessive pride. Their crudeness irritated me. Cynically they mocked my face and my awkward build; yet, what stupid faces they all had! Facial expressions at our school somehow degenerated and became particularly stupid. Many attractive lads had come to us, but in a few years they too were repulsive to look at. When I was only sixteen I wondered about them gloomily; even then I was astounded by the pettiness of their thoughts and the stupidity of their studies, games and conversations. They failed to understand essential things and took no interest in important, weighty subjects, so that I couldn't help considering them beneath me. It wasn't my wounded vanity that drove me to it; and, for God's sake, don't repeat any of those nauseating and hackneyed clichés, such as, "I was merely a dreamer, whereas they already understood life." They didn't understand a thing, not one thing about life, and I swear, that's what annoyed me most about them. On the contrary, they accepted the most obvious, glaring reality in a fantastically stupid way, and even then they'd begun to worship nothing but success. Everything that was just, but oppressed and humiliated, they ridiculed hard-heartedly and shamelessly. They mistook rank for intelligence; at the age of sixteen they were already talking about occupying comfortable little niches. Of course, much of this was due to their stupidity and the poor examples that had constantly surrounded them in their childhood and youth. They were monstrously depraved. Naturally, even this was more superficial, more affected cynicism; of course, their youth and a certain freshness shone through their depravity; but even this freshness was unattractive and manifested itself in a kind of rakishness. I hated them terribly, although, perhaps, I was even worse than they were. They returned the feeling and didn't conceal their loathing for me. But I no longer wanted their affection; on the contrary, I constantly longed for their humiliation. In order to avoid their jibes, I began to study as hard as I could on purpose and made my way to the top of the class. That impressed them. In addition, they all began to realize that I'd read certain books which they could never read and that I understood certain things (not included in our special course) about which they'd never even heard. They regarded this with savagery and sarcasm, but they submitted morally, all the more since even the teachers paid me some attention on this account. Their jibes ceased, but their

---

4. The account of the underground man's schooling foreshadows the hero's childhood in *The Adolescent*.

hostility remained, and relations between us became cold and strained. In the end I myself couldn't stand it: as the years went by, my need for people, for friends, increased. I made several attempts to get closer to some of them; but these attempts always turned out to be unnatural and ended of their own accord. Once I even had a friend of sorts. But I was already a despot at heart; I wanted to exercise unlimited power over his soul; I wanted to instill in him contempt for his surroundings; and I demanded from him a disdainful and definitive break with those surroundings. I frightened him with my passionate friendship, and I reduced him to tears and convulsions. He was a naive and giving soul, but as soon as he'd surrendered himself to me totally, I began to despise him and reject him immediately—as if I only needed to achieve a victory over him, merely to subjugate him. But I was unable to conquer them all; my one friend was not at all like them, but rather a rare exception. The first thing I did upon leaving school was abandon the special job in the civil service for which I'd been trained, in order to sever all ties, break with my past, cover it over with dust. . . . The devil only knows why, after all that, I'd dragged myself over to see this Simonov! . . .

Early the next morning I roused myself from bed, jumped up in anxiety, just as if everything was about to start happening all at once. But I believed that some radical change in my life was imminent and was sure to occur that very day. Perhaps because I wasn't used to it, but all my life, at any external event, albeit a trivial one, it always seemed that some sort of radical change would occur. I went off to work as usual, but returned home two hours earlier in order to prepare. The most important thing, I thought, was not to arrive there first, or else they'd all think I was too eager. But there were thousands of most important things, and they all reduced me to the point of impotence. I polished my boots once again with my own hands. Apollon wouldn't polish them twice in one day for anything in the world; he considered it indecent. So I polished them myself, after stealing the brushes from the hallway so that he wouldn't notice and then despise me for it afterward. Next I carefully examined my clothes and found that everything was old, shabby, and worn out. I'd become too slovenly. My uniform was in better shape, but I couldn't go to dinner in a uniform. Worst of all, there was an enormous yellow stain on the knee of my trousers. I had an inkling that the spot alone would rob me of nine-tenths of my dignity. I also knew that it was unseemly for me to think that. "But this isn't the time for thinking. Reality is now looming," I thought, and my heart sank. I also knew perfectly well at that time, that I was monstrously exaggerating all these facts. But what could be done? I was no longer able to control myself, and was shaking with fever. In despair I imagined how haughtily and coldly that "scoundrel" Zverkov would greet me; with what dull and totally relentless contempt that dullard Trudolyubov would regard me; how nastily and impudently that insect Ferfichkin would giggle at me in order to win Zverkov's approval; how well Simonov would understand all this and how he'd despise me for my wretched vanity and cowardice; and worst of all, how petty all this would be, not *literary*, but commonplace. Of course, it would have been better not to go at all. But that was no longer possible; once I began to feel drawn to something, I plunged right in, head first. I'd have reproached myself for the rest of my life: "So, you retreated, you retreated before reality, you retreated!" On the contrary, I desperately wanted to prove to all this "rabble" that I really wasn't the coward I imagined myself to be. But that's not all: in the strongest paroxysm of cowardly fever I dreamt of gaining the upper hand, of conquering them, of carrying them away, compelling them to love me—if only "for the nobility of my thought and my indisputable wit." They would abandon Zverkov; he'd sit by in silence and embarassment, and I'd crush him. Afterward, perhaps, I'd be reconciled with Zverkov and drink to our *friendship*,[5] but what was most spiteful and insulting for me was that I knew even then, I knew completely and for sure, that I didn't need any of this at all; that in fact I really didn't want to crush them, conquer them, or attract them, and that if I could have ever achieved all that, I'd be the first to say that it wasn't worth a damn. Oh, how I prayed to God that this day would pass quickly! With inexpressible anxiety I approached the window, opened the transom,[6] and peered out into the murky mist of the thickly falling wet snow. . . .

At last my worthless old wall clock sputtered out five o'clock. I grabbed my hat, and, trying not to look at Apollon—who'd been waiting since early morning to receive his wages, but didn't want to be the first one to mention it out of pride—I slipped out the door past him and intentionally hired a smart cab with my last half-ruble in order to arrive at the Hôtel de Paris in style.

IV.

I knew since the day before that I'd be the first one to arrive. But it was no longer a question of who was first.

Not only was no one else there, but I even had difficulty finding our room. The table hadn't even been set. What did it all mean? After many inquiries I finally learned from the waiters that dinner had been ordered for closer to six o'clock, instead of five. This was also confirmed in the buffet. It was too embarrassing to ask any more questions. It was still only twenty-five minutes past five. If they'd changed the time, they should have let me know; that's what the city mail was for. They shouldn't have subjected me to such "shame" in my own eyes and . . . and, at least not in front of the waiters. I sat down. A waiter began to set the table. I felt even more ashamed in his presence. Toward six o'clock

---

5. Russian the hero plans to switch from the formal mode of address (*vy*) to the informal (*ty*).
6. A small hinged pane in the window of a Russian house, used for ventilation especially during the winter when the main part of the window is sealed.

candles were brought into the room in addition to the lighted lamps already there, yet it hadn't occurred to the waiters to bring them in as soon as I'd arrived. In the next room two gloomy customers, angry-looking and silent, were dining at separate tables. In one of the distant rooms there was a great deal of noise, even shouting. One could hear the laughter of a whole crowd of people, including nasty little squeals in French—there were ladies present at that dinner. In short, it was disgusting. Rarely had I passed a more unpleasant hour, so that when they all arrived together precisely at six o'clock, I was initially overjoyed to see them, as if they were my liberators, and I almost forgot that I was supposed to appear offended.

Zverkov, obviously the leader, entered ahead of the rest. Both he and they were laughing; but, upon seeing me, Zverkov drew himself up, approached me unhurriedly, bowed slightly from the waist almost co-quettishly, and extended his hand politely, but not too, with a kind of careful civility, almost as if he were a general both offering his hand, but also guarding against something. I'd imagined, on the contrary, that as soon as he entered he'd burst into his former, shrill laughter with occasional squeals, and that he'd immediately launch into his stale jokes and witticisms. I'd been preparing for them since the previous evening; but in no way did I expect such condescension, such courtesy charac-teristic of a general. Could it be that he now considered himself so immeasurably superior to me in all respects? If he'd merely wanted to offend me by this superior attitude, it wouldn't have been so bad, I thought; I'd manage to pay him back somehow. But what if, without any desire to offend, the notion had crept into his dumb sheep's brain that he really was immeasurably superior to me and that he could only treat me in a patronizing way? From this possibility alone I began to gasp for air.

"Have you been waiting long?" Trudolyubov asked.

"I arrived at five o'clock sharp, just as I was told yesterday," I answered loudly and with irritation presaging an imminent explosion.

"Didn't you let him know that we changed the time?" Trudolyubov asked, turning to Simonov.

"No, I didn't. I forgot," he replied, but without any regret; then, not even apologizing to me, he went off to order the hors d'oeuvres.

"So you've been here for a whole hour, you poor fellow!" Zverkov cried sarcastically, because according to his notions, this must really have been terribly amusing. That scoundrel Ferfichkin chimed in after him with nasty, ringing laughter that sounded like a dog's yapping. My situation seemed very amusing and awkward to him, too.

"It's not the least bit funny!" I shouted at Ferfichkin, getting more and more irritated. "The others are to blame, not me. They neglected to inform me. It's, it's, it's . . . simply preposterous."

"It's not only preposterous, it's more than that," muttered Trudo-lyubov, naively interceding on my behalf. "You're being too kind. It's pure rudeness. Of course, it wasn't intentional. And how could Simonov have . . . hmm!"

"If a trick like that had been played on me," said Ferfichkin, "I'd . . ."

"Oh, you'd have ordered yourself something to eat," interrupted Zverkov, "or simply asked to have dinner served without waiting for the rest of us."

"You'll agree that I could've done that without asking anyone's permission," I snapped. "If I did wait, it was only because . . ."

"Let's be seated, gentlemen," cried Simonov upon entering. "Everything's ready. I can vouch for the champagne; it's excellently chilled. . . . Moreover, I didn't know where your apartment was, so how could I find you?" he said turning to me suddenly, but once again not looking directly at me. Obviously he was holding something against me. I suspect he got to thinking after what had happened yesterday.

Everyone sat down; I did, too. The table was round. Trudolyubov sat on my left, Simonov, on my right. Zverkov sat across; Ferfichkin, next to him, between Trudolyubov and him.

"Tell-l-l me now, are you . . . in a government department?" Zverkov continued to attend to me. Seeing that I was embarrassed, he imagined in earnest that he had to be nice to me, encouraging me to speak. "Does he want me to throw a bottle at his head, or what?" I thought in a rage. Unaccustomed as I was to all this, I was unnaturally quick to take offense.

"In such and such an office," I replied abruptly, looking at my plate.

"And . . . is it p-p-profitable? Tell-l-l me, what ma-a-de you decide to leave your previous position?"

"What ma-a-a-de me leave my previous position was simply that I wanted to," I dragged my words out three times longer than he did, hardly able to control myself. Ferfichkin snorted. Simonov looked at me ironically; Trudolyubov stopped eating and began to stare at me with curiosity.

Zverkov was jarred, but didn't want to show it.

"Well-l, and how is the support?"

"What support?"

"I mean, the s-salary?"

"Why are you cross-examining me?"

However, I told him right away what my salary was. I blushed terribly.

"That's not very much," Zverkov observed pompously.

"No, sir, it's not enought to dine in café-restaurants!" added Ferfichkin insolently.

"In my opinion, it's really very little," Trudolyubov observed in earnest.

"And how thin you've grown, how you've changed . . . since . . . ," Zverkov added, with a touch of venom now, and with a kind of impudent sympathy, examining me and my apparel.

"Stop embarrassing him," Ferfichkin cried with a giggle.

"My dear sir, I'll have you know that I'm not embarrassed," I broke in at last. "Listen! I'm dining in this 'café-restaurant' at my own expense, my own, not anyone else's; note that, Monsieur Ferfichkin."

"Wha-at? And who isn't dining at his own expense? You seem to be . . ." Ferfichkin seized hold of my words, turned as red as a lobster, and looked me straight in the eye with fury.

"Just so-o," I replied, feeling that I'd gone a bit too far, "and I suggest that it would be much better if we engaged in more intelligent conversation."

"It seems that you're determined to display your intelligence."

"Don't worry, that would be quite unnecessary here."

"What's all this cackling, my dear sir? Huh? Have you taken leave of your senses in that *duh*-partment of yours?"

"Enough, gentlemen, enough," cried Zverkov authoritatively.

"How stupid this is!" muttered Simonov.

"Really, it is stupid. We're gathered here in a congenial group to have a farewell dinner for our good friend, while you're still settling old scores," Trudolyubov said, rudely addressing only me. "You forced yourself upon us yesterday; don't disturb the general harmony now. . . ."

"Enough, enough," cried Zverkov. "Stop it, gentlemen, this'll never do. Let me tell you instead how I very nearly got married a few days ago . . ."

There followed some scandalous, libelous anecdote about how this gentleman very nearly got married a few days ago. There wasn't one word about marriage, however; instead, generals, colonels, and even gentlemen of the bed chamber figured prominently in the story, while Zverkov played the leading role among them all. Approving laughter followed; Ferfichkin even squealed.

Everyone had abandoned me by now, and I sat there completely crushed and humiliated.

"Good Lord, what kind of company is this for me?" I wondered. "And what a fool I've made of myself in front of them all! But I let Ferfichkin go too far. These numbskulls think they're doing me an honor by allowing me to sit with them at their table, when they don't understand that it's I who's done them the honor, and not the reverse. 'How thin I've grown! What clothes!' Oh, these damned trousers! Zverkov's already noticed the yellow spot on my knee. . . . What's the use? Right now, this very moment, I should stand up, take my hat, and simply leave without saying a single word. . . . Out of contempt! And tomorrow—I'll even be ready for a duel. Scoundrels! It's not the seven rubles I care about. But they may think that . . . To hell with it! I don't care about the seven rubles. I'm leaving at once! . . ."

Of course, I stayed.

In my misery I drank Lafite and sherry by the glassful. Being unaccustomed to it, I got drunk very quickly; the more intoxicated I became, the greater my annoyance. Suddenly I felt like offending them all in the most impudent manner—and then I'd leave. To seize the moment and show them all who I really was—let them say: even though he's ridiculous, he's clever . . . and . . . and . . . in short, to hell with them!

I surveyed them all arrogantly with my dazed eyes. But they seemed to have forgotten all about me. *They* were noisy, boisterous and merry. Zverkov kept on talking. I began to listen. He was talking about some magnificent lady whom he'd finally driven to make a declaration of love. (Of course, he was lying like a trooper.) He said that he'd been assisted in this matter particularly by a certain princeling, the hussar Kolya, who possessed some three thousand serfs.

"And yet, this same Kolya who has three thousand serfs hasn't even come to see you off," I said, breaking into the conversation suddenly. For a moment silence fell.

"You're drunk already," Trudolyubov said, finally deigning to notice me, and glancing contemptuously in my direction. Zverkov examined me in silence as if I were an insect. I lowered my eyes. Simonov quickly began to pour champagne.

Trudolyubov raised his glass, followed by everyone but me.

"To your health and to a good journey!" he cried to Zverkov. "To old times, gentlemen, and to our future, hurrah!"

Everyone drank up and pressed around to exchange kisses with Zverkov. I didn't budge; my full glass stood before me untouched.

"Aren't you going to drink?" Trudolyubov roared at me, having lost his patience and turning to me menacingly.

"I wish to make my own speech, all by myself . . . and then I'll drink, Mr. Trudolyubov."

"Nasty shrew!" Simonov muttered.

I sat up in my chair, feverishly seized hold of my glass, and prepared for something extraordinary, although I didn't know quite what I'd say.

"*Silence!*" cried Ferfichkin. "And now for some real intelligence!" Zverkov waited very gravely, aware of what was coming.

"Mr. Lieutenant Zverkov," I began, "you must know that I detest phrases, phrasemongers, and corsetted waists. . . . That's the first point; the second will follow."

Everyone stirred uncomfortably.

"The second point: I hate obscene stories and the men who tell them.[7] I especially hate the men who tell them!"

"The third point: I love truth, sincerity and honesty," I continued almost automatically, because I was beginning to become numb with horror, not knowing how I could be speaking this way. . . . "I love thought, Monsieur Zverkov. I love genuine comradery, on an equal footing, but not . . . hmmm . . . I love . . . But, after all, why not? I too will drink to your health, Monsieur Zverkov. Seduce those Circassian

---

7. A phrase borrowed form the inveterate liar Nozdryov, one of the provincial landowners in the first volume of Gogol's *Dead Souls* (1842).

maidens,[8] shoot the enemies of the fatherland, and . . . and . . . To your health, Monsieur Zverkov!"

Zverkov rose from his chair, bowed, and said: "I'm most grateful."

He was terribly offended and had even turned pale.

"To hell with him," Trudolyubov roared, banging his fist down on the table.

"No, sir, people should be whacked in the face for saying such things!" squealed Ferfichkin.

"We ought to throw him out!" muttered Simonov.

"Not a word, gentlemen, not a move!" Zverkov cried triumphantly, putting a stop to this universal indignation. "I'm grateful to you all, but I can show him myself how much I value his words."

"Mr. Ferfichkin, tomorrow you'll give me satisfaction for the words you've just uttered!" I said loudly, turning to Ferfichkin with dignity.

"Do you mean a duel? Very well," he replied, but I must have looked so ridiculous as I issued my challenge, it must have seemed so out of keeping with my entire appearance, that everyone, including Ferfichkin, collapsed into laughter.

"Yes, of course, throw him out! Why, he's quite drunk already," Trudolyubov declared in disgust.

"I shall never forgive myself for letting him join us," Simonov muttered again.

"Now's the time to throw a bottle at the lot of them," I thought. So I grabbed a bottle and . . . poured myself another full glass.

". . . No, it's better to sit it out to the very end!" I went on thinking. "You'd be glad, gentlemen, if I left. But nothing doing! I'll stay here deliberately and keep on drinking to the very end, as a sign that I accord you no importance whatsoever. I'll sit here and drink because this is a tavern, and I've paid good money to get in. I'll sit here and drink because I consider you to be so many pawns, nonexistent pawns. I'll sit here and drink . . . and sing too, if I want to, yes, sir, I'll sing because I have the right to . . . sing . . . hmm."

But I didn't sing. I just tried not to look at any of them; I assumed the most carefree poses and waited impatiently until they would be the first to speak to me. But, alas, they did not. How much, how very much I longed to be reconciled with them at that moment! The clock struck eight, then nine. They moved from the table to the sofa. Zverkov sprawled on the couch, placing one foot on the round table. They brought the wine over, too. He really had ordered three bottles at his own expense. Naturally, he didn't invite me to join them. Everyone surrounded him on the sofa. They listened to him almost with reverence. It was obvious they liked him. "What for? What for?" I wondered to myself. From time to time they were moved to drunken ecstasy and

8. A Moslem people inhabiting a region in the northern Caucasus.

exchanged kisses. They talked about the Caucasus, the nature of true passion, card games, profitable positions in the service; they talked about the income of a certain hussar Podkharzhevsky, whom none of them knew personally, and they rejoiced that his income was so large; they talked about the unusual beauty and charm of Princess D., whom none of them had ever seen; finally, they arrived at the question of Shakespeare's immortality.

I smiled contemptuously and paced up and down the other side of the room, directly behind the sofa, along the wall from the table to the stove and back again. I wanted to show them with all my might that I could get along without them; meanwhile, I deliberately stomped my boots, thumping my heels. But all this was in vain. *They paid me no attention.* I had the forebearance to pace like that, right in front of them, from eight o'clock until eleven, in the very same place, from the table to the stove and from the stove back to the table. "I'm pacing just as I please, and no one can stop me." A waiter who came into the room paused several times to look at me; my head was spinning from all those turns; there were moments when it seemed that I was delirious. During those three hours I broke out in a sweat three times and then dried out. At times I was pierced to the heart with a most profound, venomous thought: ten years would pass, twenty, forty; and still, even after forty years, I'd remember with loathing and humiliation these filthiest, most absurd, and horrendous moments of my entire life. It was impossible to humiliate myself more shamelessly or more willingly, and I fully understood that, fully; nevertheless, I continued to pace from the table to the stove and back again. "Oh, if you only knew what thoughts and feelings I'm capable of, and how cultured I really am!" I thought at moments, mentally addressing the sofa where my enemies were seated. But my enemies behaved as if I weren't even in the room. Once, and only once, they turned to me, precisely when Zverkov started in about Shakespeare, and I suddenly burst into contemptuous laughter. I snorted so affectedly and repulsively that they broke off their conversation immediately and stared at me in silence for about two minutes, in earnest, without laughing, as I paced up and down, from the table to the stove, while *I paid not the slightest bit of attention to them.* But nothing came of it; they didn't speak to me. A few moments later they abandoned me again. The clock struck eleven.

"Gentlemen," exclaimed Zverkov, getting up from the sofa, "Now let's all go *to that place.*"[9]

"Of course, of course!" the others replied.

I turned abruptly to Zverkov. I was so exhausted, so broken, that I'd have slit my own throat to be done with all this! I was feverish; my hair, which had been soaked through with sweat, had dried and now stuck to my forehead and temples.

9. That is, a brothel.

"Zverkov, I ask your forgiveness," I said harshly and decisively. "Fer-fichkin, yours too, and everyone's, everyone's. I've insulted you all!"

"Aha! So a duel isn't really your sort of thing!" hissed Ferfichkin venomously.

His remark was like a painful stab to my heart.

"No, I'm not afraid of a duel, Ferfichkin! I'm ready to fight with you tomorrow, even after we're reconciled. I even insist upon it, and you can't refuse me. I want to prove that I'm not afraid of a duel. You'll shoot first, and I'll fire into the air."

"He's amusing himself," Simonov observed.

"He's simply taken leave of his senses!" Trudolyubov added.

"Allow us to pass; why are you blocking our way? . . . Well, what is it you want?" Zverkov asked contemptuously. They were all flushed, their eyes glazed. They'd drunk a great deal.

"I ask for your friendship, Zverkov, I've insulted you, but . . ."

"Insulted me? You? In-sul-ted me? My dear sir, I want you to know that never, under any circumstances, could you possibly insult *me!*"

"And that's enough from you. Out of the way!" Trudolyubov added. "Let's go."

"Olympia is mine, gentlemen, that's agreed!" cried Zverkov. •

"We won't argue, we won't," they replied, laughing.

I stood there as if spat on. The party left the room noisily, and Trudolyubov struck up a stupid song. Simonov remained behind for a brief moment to tip the waiters. All of a sudden I went up to him.

"Simonov! Give me six rubles," I said decisively and desperately.

He looked at me in extreme amazement with his dulled eyes. He was drunk, too.

"Are you really going *to that place* with us?"

"Yes!"

"I have no money!" he snapped; then he laughed contemptuously and headed out of the room.

I grabbed hold of his overcoat. It was a nightmare.

"Simonov! I know that you have some money. Why do you refuse me? Am I really such a scoundrel? Beware of refusing me: if you only knew, if you only knew why I'm asking. Everything depends on it, my entire future, all my plans. . . ."

Simonov took out the money and almost threw it at me.

"Take it, if you have no shame!" he said mercilessly, then ran out to catch up with the others.

I remained behind for a minute. The disorder, the leftovers, a broken glass on the floor, spilled wine, cigarette butts, drunkenness and delirium in my head, agonizing torment in my heart; and finally, a waiter who'd seen and heard everything and who was now looking at me with curiosity.

"*To that place!*" I cried. "Either they'll all fall on their knees, em-bracing me, begging for my friendship, or . . . or else, I'll give Zverkov a slap in the face."

V.

"So here it is, here it is at last, a confrontation with reality," I muttered, rushing headlong down the stairs. "This is no longer the Pope leaving Rome and going to Brazil; this is no ball on the shores of Lake Como!"

"You're a scoundrel," the thought flashed through my mind, "if you laugh at that now."

"So what!" I cried in reply. "Everything is lost now, anyway!"

There was no sign of them, but it didn't matter. I knew where they were going.

At the entrance stood a solitary, late-night cabby in a coarse peasant coat powdered with wet, seemingly warm snow that was still falling. It was steamy and stuffy outside. The little shaggy piebald nag was also dusted with snow and was coughing; I remember that very well. I headed for the rough-hewn sledge; but as soon as I raised one foot to get in, the recollection of how Simonov had just given me six rubles hit me with such force that I tumbled into the sledge like a sack.

"No! There's a lot I have to do to make up for that!" I cried. "But make up for it I will or else I'll perish on the spot this very night. Let's go!" We set off. There was an entire whirlwind spinning around inside my head.

"They won't fall on their knees to beg for my friendship. That's a mirage, an indecent mirage, disgusting, romantic, and fantastic; it's just like the ball on the shores of Lake Como. Consequently, I *must* give Zverkov a slap in the face! I am obligated to do it. And so, it's all decided; I'm rushing there to give him a slap in the face."

"Hurry up!"

The cabby tugged at the reins.

"As soon as I go in, I'll slap him. Should I say a few words first before I slap him in the face? No! I'll simply go in and slap him. They'll all be sitting there in the drawing room; he'll be on the sofa with Olympia. That damned Olympia! She once ridiculed my face and refused me. I'll drag Olympia around by the hair and Zverkov by the ears. No, better grab one ear and lead him around the room like that. Perhaps they'll begin to beat me, and then they'll throw me out. That's even likely. So what? I'll still have slapped him first; the initiative will be mine. According to the laws of honor, that's all that matters. He'll be branded, and nothing can wipe away that slap except a duel. He'll have to fight. So just let them beat me now! Let them, the ingrates! Trudolyubov will hit me hardest, he's so strong. Ferfichkin will sneak up alongside and will undoubtedly grab my hair, I'm sure he will. But let them, let them. That's why I've come. At last these blockheads will be forced to grasp the tragedy in all this! As they drag me to the door, I'll tell them that they really aren't even worth the tip of my little finger!"

"Hurry up, driver, hurry up!" I shouted to the cabby.

He was rather startled and cracked his whip. I'd shouted very savagely.

"We'll fight at daybreak, and that's settled. I'm through with the department. Ferfichkin recently said duh-partment, instead of department. But where will I get pistols? What nonsense! I'll take my salary in advance and buy them. And powder? Bullets? That's what the second will attend to. And how will I manage to do all this by daybreak? And where will I find a second? I have no acquaintances. . . ."

"Nonsense!" I shouted, whipping myself up into even more of a frenzy, "Nonsense!"

"The first person I meet on the street will have to act as my second, just as he would pull a drowning man from the water. The most extraordinary possibilities have to be allowed for. Even if tomorrow I were to ask the director himself to act as my second, he too would have to agree merely out of a sense of chivalry, and he would keep it a secret![1] Anton Antonych . . ."

The fact of the matter was that at that very moment I was more clearly and vividly aware than anyone else on earth of the disgusting absurdity of my intentions and the whole opposite side of the coin, but . . .

"Hurry up, driver, hurry, you rascal, hurry up!"

"Hey, sir!" that son of the earth replied.

A sudden chill came over me.

"Wouldn't it be better . . . wouldn't it be better . . . to go straight home right now? Oh, my God! Why, why did I invite myself to that dinner yesterday? But no, it's impossible. And my pacing for three hours from the table to the stove? No, they, and no one else will have to pay me back for that pacing! They must wipe out that disgrace!"

"Hurry up!"

"What if they turn me over to the police? They wouldn't dare! They'd be afraid of a scandal. And what if Zverkov refuses the duel out of contempt? That's even likely; but I'll show them. . . . I'll rush to the posting station when he's supposed to leave tomorrow; I'll grab hold of his leg, tear off his overcoat just as he's about to climb into the carriage. I'll fasten my teeth on his arm and bite him. 'Look, everyone, see what a desperate man can be driven to!' Let him hit me on the head while others hit me from behind. I'll shout to the whole crowd, 'Behold, here's a young puppy who's going off to charm Circassian maidens with my spit on his face!' "

"Naturally, it'll all be over after that. The department will banish me from the face of the earth. They'll arrest me, try me, drive me out of the service, send me to prison; ship me off to Siberia for resettlement. Never mind! Fifteen years later when they let me out of jail, a beggar in rags, I'll drag myself off to see him. I'll find him in some provincial town. He'll be married and happy. He'll have a grown daughter. . . . I'll say, 'Look, you monster, look at my sunken cheeks and my rags. I've lost everything—career, happiness, art, science, a *beloved woman*—

---

1. Duels as a means of resolving points of honor were officially discouraged but still fairly common.

all because of you. Here are the pistols. I came here to load my pistol, and . . . and I forgive you.' Then I'll fire into the air, and he'll never hear another word from me again. . . ."

I was actually about to cry, even though I knew for a fact at that very moment that all this was straight out of Silvio and Lermontov's *Masquerade*.[2] Suddenly I felt terribly ashamed, so ashamed that I stopped the horse, climbed out of the sledge, and stood there amidst the snow in the middle of the street. The driver looked at me in amazement and sighed.

What was I to do? I couldn't go there—that was absurd; and I couldn't drop the whole thing, because then it would seem like . . . Oh, Lord! How could I drop it? After such insults!

"No!" I cried, throwing myself back into the sledge. "It's predestined; it's fate! Drive on, hurry up, *to that place!*"

In my impatience, I struck the driver on the neck with my fist.

"What's the matter with you? Why are you hitting me?" cried the poor little peasant, whipping his nag so that she began to kick up her hind legs.

Wet snow was falling in big flakes; I unbuttoned my coat, not caring about the snow. I forgot about everything else because now, having finally resolved on the slap, *I felt with horror that it was imminent* and that *nothing on earth could possibly stop it.* Lonely street lamps shone gloomily in the snowy mist like torches at a funeral. Snow got in under my overcoat, my jacket, and my necktie, and melted there. I didn't button up; after all, everything was lost, anyway. At last we arrived. I jumped out, almost beside myself, ran up the stairs, and began to pound at the door with my hands and feet. My legs, especially my knees, felt terribly weak. The door opened rather quickly; it was as if they knew I was coming. (In fact, Simonov had warned them that there might be someone else, since at this place one had to give notice and in general take precautions. It was one of those "fashionable shops" of the period that have now been eliminated by the police. During the day it really was a shop; but in the evening men with recommendations were able to visit as guests.) I walked rapidly through the darkened shop into a familiar drawing-room where there was only one small lit candle, and I stopped in dismay: there was no one there.

"Where are they?" I asked.

Naturally, by now they'd all dispersed. . . .

Before me stood a person with a stupid smile, the madam herself, who knew me slightly. In a moment a door opened, and another person came in.

Without paying much attention to anything, I walked around the room, and, apparently, was talking to myself. It was as if I'd been

2. The protagonist of Alexander Pushkin's short story "The Shot" (1830), a man dedicated to revenge. *Masquerade* (1835) is a drama by Mikhail Lermontov about romantic conventions of love and honor. Both works conclude with bizarre twists.

delivered from death, and I felt it joyously in my whole being. I'd have given him the slap, certainly, I'd certainly have given him the slap. But now they weren't here and . . . everything had vanished, everything had changed! . . . I looked around. I still couldn't take it all in. I glanced up mechanically at the girl who'd come in: before me there flashed a fresh, young, slightly pale face with straight dark brows and a serious, seemingly astonished look. I liked that immediately; I would have hated her if she'd been smiling. I began to look at her more carefully, as though with some effort. I'd still not managed to collect my thoughts. There was something simple and kind in her face, but somehow it was strangely serious. I was sure that she was at a disadvantage as a result, and that none of those fools had even noticed her. She couldn't be called a beauty, however, even though she was tall, strong, and well built. She was dressed very simply. Something despicable took hold of me; I went up to her. . . .

I happened to glance into a mirror. My overwrought face appeared extremely repulsive: it was pale, spiteful and mean; and my hair was dishevelled. "It doesn't matter. I'm glad," I thought. "In fact, I'm even delighted that I'll seem so repulsive to her; that pleases me. . . ."

VI.

Somewhere behind a partition a clock was wheezing as if under some strong pressure, as though someone were strangling it. After this un- naturally prolonged wheezing there followed a thin, nasty, somehow unexpectedly hurried chime, as if someone had suddenly leapt forward. It struck two. I recovered, although I really hadn't been asleep, only lying there half-conscious.

It was almost totally dark in the narrow, cramped, low-ceilinged room, which was crammed with an enormous wardrobe and cluttered with cartons, rags, and all sorts of old clothes. The candle burning on the table at one end of the room flickered faintly from time to time, and almost went out completely. In a few moments total darkness would set in.

It didn't take long for me to come to my senses; all at once, without any effort, everything returned to me, as though it had been lying in ambush ready to pounce on me again. Even in my unconscious state some point had constantly remained in my memory, never to be for- gotten, around which my sleepy visions had gloomily revolved. But it was a strange thing: everything that had happened to me that day now seemed, upon awakening, to have occurred in the distant past, as if I'd long since left it all behind.

My mind was in a daze. It was as though something were hanging over me, provoking, agitating, and disturbing me. Misery and bile were welling inside me, seeking an outlet. Suddenly I noticed beside me two wide-open eyes, examining me curiously and persistently. The gaze was coldly detached, sullen, as if belonging to a total stranger. I found it oppressive.

A dismal thought was conceived in my brain and spread throughout my whole body like a nasty sensation, such as one feels upon entering a damp, mouldy underground cellar. It was somehow unnatural that only now these two eyes had decided to examine me. I also recalled that during the course of the last two hours I hadn't said one word to this creature, and that I had considered it quite unnecessary; that had even given me pleasure for some reason. Now I'd suddenly realized starkly how absurd, how revolting as a spider, was the idea of debauchery, which, without love, crudely and shamelessly begins precisely at the point where genuine love is consummated. We looked at each other in this way for some time, but she didn't lower her gaze before mine, nor did she alter her stare, so that finally, for some reason, I felt very uneasy.

"What's your name?" I asked abruptly, to put an end to it quickly.

"Liza," she replied, almost in a whisper, but somehow in a very unfriendly way; and she turned her eyes away.

I remained silent.

"The weather today . . . snow . . . foul!" I observed, almost to myself, drearily placing one arm behind my head and staring at the ceiling.

She didn't answer. The whole thing was obscene.

"Are you from around here?" I asked her a moment later, almost angrily, turning my head slightly toward her.

"No."

"Where are you from?"

"Riga," she answered unwillingly.

"German?"

"No, Russian."

"Have you been here long?"

"Where?"

"In this house."

"Two weeks." She spoke more and more curtly. The candle had gone out completely; I could no longer see her face.

"Are your mother and father still living?"

"Yes . . . no . . . they are."

"Where are they?"

"There . . . in Riga."

"Who are they?"

"Just . . ."

"Just what? What do they do?"

"Tradespeople."[3]

"Have you always lived with them?"

---

3. The lower middle class consisted of various categories of townspeople, including craftsmen, small householders, and artisans.

"Yes."

"How old are you?"

"Twenty."

"Why did you leave them?"

"Just because . . ."

That "just because" meant: leave me alone, it makes me sick. We fell silent.

Only God knows why, but I didn't leave. I too started to feel sick and more depressed. Images of the previous day began to come to mind all on their own, without my willing it, in a disordered way. I suddenly recalled a scene that I'd witnessed on the street that morning as I was anxiously hurrying to work. "Today some people were carrying a coffin and nearly dropped it," I suddenly said aloud, having no desire whatever to begin a conversation, but just so, almost accidentally.

"A coffin?"

"Yes, in the Haymarket; they were carrying it up from an underground cellar."

"From a cellar?"

"Not a cellar, but from a basement . . . well, you know . . . from downstairs . . . from a house of ill repute . . . There was such filth all around. . . . Eggshells, garbage . . . it smelled foul . . . it was disgusting."

Silence.

"A nasty day to be buried!" I began again to break the silence.

"Why nasty?"

"Snow, slush . . ." (I yawned.)

"It doesn't matter," she said suddenly after a brief silence.

"No, it's foul. . . ." (I yawned again.) "The grave diggers must have been cursing because they were getting wet out there in the snow. And there must have been water in the grave."

"Why water in the grave?" she asked with some curiosity, but she spoke even more rudely and curtly than before. Something suddenly began to goad me on.

"Naturally, water on the bottom, six inches or so. You can't ever dig a dry grave at Volkovo cemetery."

"Why not?"

"What do you mean, why not? The place is waterlogged. It's all swamp. So they bury them right in the water. I've seen it myself . . . many times. . . ."

(I'd never seen it, and I'd never been to Volkovo cemetery, but I'd heard about it from other people.)

"Doesn't it matter to you if you die?"

"Why should I die?" she replied, as though defending herself.

"Well, someday you'll die; you'll die just like that woman did this morning. She was a . . . she was also a young girl . . . she died of consumption."

"The wench should have died in the hospital. . . ." (She knows all about it, I thought, and she even said "wench" instead of "girl.")

"She owed money to her madam," I retorted, more and more goaded on by the argument. "She worked right up to the end, even though she had consumption. The cabbies standing around were chatting with the soldiers, telling them all about it. Her former acquaintances, most likely. They were all laughing. They were planning to drink to her memory at the tavern." (I invented a great deal of this.)

Silence, deep silence. She didn't even stir.

"Do you think it would be better to die in a hospital?"

"Isn't it just the same? . . . Besides, why should I die?" she added irritably.

"If not now, then later?"

"Well, then later . . ."

"That's what you think! Now you're young and pretty and fresh—that's your value. But after a year of this life, you won't be like that any more; you'll fade."

"In a year?"

"In any case, after a year your price will be lower," I continued, gloating. "You'll move out of here into a worse place, into some other house. And a year later, into a third, each worse and worse, and seven years from now you'll end up in a cellar on the Haymarket. Even that won't be so bad. The real trouble will come when you get some disease, let's say a weakness in the chest . . . or you catch cold or something. In this kind of life it's no laughing matter to get sick. It takes hold of you and may never let go. And so, you die."

"Well, then, I'll die," she answered now quite angrily and stirred quickly.

"That'll be a pity."

"For what?"

"A pity to lose a life."

Silence.

"Did you have a sweetheart? Huh?"

"What's it to you?"

"Oh, I'm not interrogating you. What do I care? Why are you angry? Of course, you may have had your own troubles. What's it to me? Just the same, I'm sorry."

"For whom?"

"I'm sorry for you."

"No need . . . ," she whispered barely audibly and stirred once again.

That provoked me at once. What! I was being so gentle with her, while she . . .

"Well, and what do you think? Are you on the right path then?"

"I don't think anything."

"That's just the trouble—you don't think. Wake up, while there's still time. And there is time. You're still young and pretty; you could fall in love, get married, be happy. . . ."[4]

"Not all married women are happy," she snapped in her former, rude manner.

"Not all, of course, but it's still better than this. A lot better. You can even live without happiness as long as there's love. Even in sorrow life can be good; it's good to be alive, no matter how you live. But what's there besides . . . stench? Phew!"

I turned away in disgust; I was no longer coldly philosophizing. I began to feel what I was saying and grew excited. I'd been longing to expound these cherished *little ideas* that I'd been nurturing in my corner. Something had suddenly caught fire in me, some kind of goal had "manifested itself" before me.

"Pay no attention to the fact that I'm here. I'm no model for you. I may be even worse than you are. Moreover, I was drunk when I came here." I hastened nonetheless to justify myself. "Besides, a man is no example to a woman. It's a different thing altogether; even though I degrade and defile myself, I'm still no one's slave; if I want to leave, I just get up and go. I shake it all off and I'm a different man. But you must realize right from the start that you're a slave. Yes, a slave! You give away everything, all your freedom. Later, if you want to break this chain, you won't be able to; it'll bind you ever more tightly. That's the kind of evil chain it is. I know. I won't say anything else; you might not even understand me. But tell me this, aren't you already in debt to your madam? There, you see!" I added, even though she hadn't answered, but had merely remained silent; but she was listening with all her might. "There's your chain! You'll never buy yourself out. That's the way it's done. It's just like selling your soul to the devil. . . .

"And besides . . . I may be just as unfortunate, how do you know, and I may be wallowing in mud on purpose, also out of misery. After all, people drink out of misery. Well, I came here out of misery. Now, tell me, what's so good about this place? Here you and I were . . . intimate . . . just a little while ago, and all that time we didn't say one word to each other; afterward you began to examine me like a wild creature, and I did the same. Is that the way people love? Is that how one person is supposed to encounter another? It's a disgrace, that's what it is!"

"Yes!" she agreed with me sharply and hastily. The haste of her answer surprised even me. It meant that perhaps the very same idea was flitting through her head while she'd been examining me earlier. It meant that she too was capable of some thought. . . . "Devil take it; this is odd, this *kinship*," I thought, almost rubbing my hands together. "Surely I can handle such a young soul."

---

4. A popular theme treated by Gogol, Chernyshevsky, and Nekrasov, among others. Typically, an innocent and idealistic young man attempts to rehabilitate a prostitute or "fallen woman."

It was the sport that attracted me most of all.

She turned her face closer to mine, and in the darkness it seemed that she propped her head up on her arm. Perhaps she was examining me. I felt sorry that I couldn't see her eyes. I heard her breathing deeply.

"Why did you come here?" I began with some authority.

"Just so . . ."

"But think how nice it would be living in your father's house! There you'd be warm and free; you'd have a nest of your own."

"And what if it's worse than that?"

"I must establish the right tone," flashed through my mind. "I won't get far with sentimentality."

However, that merely flashed through my mind. I swear that she really did interest me. Besides, I was somewhat exhausted and provoked. After all, artifice goes along so easily with feeling.

"Who can say?" I hastened to reply. "All sorts of things can happen. Why, I was sure that someone had wronged you and was more to blame than you are. After all, I know nothing of your life story, but a girl like you doesn't wind up in this sort of place on her own accord. . . ."

"What kind of a girl am I?" she whispered hardly audibly; but I heard it.

"What the hell! Now I'm flattering her. That's disgusting! But, perhaps it's a good thing. . . ." She remained silent.

"You see, Liza, I'll tell you about myself. If I'd had a family when I was growing up, I wouldn't be the person I am now. I think about this often. After all, no matter how bad it is in your own family—it's still your own father and mother, and not enemies or strangers. Even if they show you their love only once a year, you still know that you're at home. I grew up without a family; that must be why I turned out the way I did—so unfeeling."

I waited again.

"She might not understand," I thought. "Besides, it's absurd—all this moralizing."

"If I were a father and had a daughter, I think that I'd have loved her more than my sons, really," I began indirectly, talking about something else in order to distract her. I confess that I was blushing.

"Why's that?"

Ah, so she's listening!

"Just because. I don't know why, Liza. You see, I knew a father who was a stern, strict man, but he would kneel before his daughter and kiss her hands and feet; he couldn't get enough of her, really.[5] She'd go dancing at a party, and he'd stand in one spot for five hours, never taking his eyes off her. He was crazy about her; I can understand that. At night she'd be tired and fall asleep, but he'd wake up, go in to kiss her, and make the sign of the cross over her while she slept. He used

---

5. A similar story is told in Honoré de Balzac's novel *Le Père Goriot* (1834).

to wear a dirty old jacket and was stingy with everyone else, but would spend his last kopeck on her, buying her expensive presents; it afforded him great joy if she liked his presents. A father always loves his daughters more than their mother does. Some girls have a very nice time living at home. I think that I wouldn't even have let my daughter get married."

"Why not?" she asked with a barely perceptible smile.

"I'd be jealous, so help me God. Why, how could she kiss someone else? How could she love a stranger more than her own father? It's even painful to think about it. Of course, it's all nonsense; naturally, everyone finally comes to his senses. But I think that before I'd let her marry, I'd have tortured myself with worry. I'd have found fault with all her suitors. Nevertheless, I'd have ended up by allowing her to marry whomever she loved. After all, the one she loves always seems the worst of all to the father. That's how it is. That causes a lot of trouble in many families."

"Some are glad to sell their daughters, rather than let them marry honorably," she said suddenly.

Aha, so that's it!

"That happens, Liza, in those wretched families where there's neither God nor love," I retorted heatedly. "And where there's no love, there's also no good sense. There are such families, it's true, but I'm not talking about them. Obviously, from the way you talk, you didn't see much kindness in your own family. You must be very unfortunate. Hmm . . . But all this results primarily from poverty."

"And is it any better among the gentry? Honest folk live decently even in poverty."

"Hmmm . . . Yes. Perhaps. There's something else, Liza. Man only likes to count his troubles; he doesn't calculate his happiness. If he figured as he should, he'd see that everyone gets his share. So, let's say that all goes well in a particular family; it enjoys God's blessing, the husband turns out to be a good man, he loves you, cherishes you, and never leaves you. Life is good in that family. Sometimes, even though there's a measure of sorrow, life's still good. Where isn't there sorrow? If you choose to get married, *you'll find out for yourself.* Consider even the first years of a marriage to the one you love: what happiness, what pure bliss there can be sometimes! Almost without exception. At first even quarrels with your husband turn out well. For some women, the more they love their husbands, the more they pick fights with them. It's true; I once knew a woman like that. 'That's how it is,' she'd say. 'I love you very much and I'm tormenting you out of love, so that you'll feel it.' Did you know that one can torment a person intentionally out of love? It's mostly women who do that. Then she thinks to herself, 'I'll love him so much afterward, I'll be so affectionate, it's no sin to torment him a little now.' At home everyone would rejoice over you, and it would be so pleasant, cheerful, serene, and honorable. . . . Some other women are very jealous. If her husband goes away, I knew one like that, she can't stand it; she jumps up at night and goes off on the sly to see.

Is he there? Is he in that house? Is he with that one? Now that's bad. Even she herself knows that it's bad; her heart sinks and she suffers because she really loves him. It's all out of love. And how nice it is to make up after a quarrel, to admit one's guilt or forgive him! How nice it is for both of them, how good they both feel at once, just as if they'd met again, married again, and begun their love all over again. No one, no one at all has to know what goes on between a husband and wife, if they love each other. However their quarrel ends, they should never call in either one of their mothers to act as judge or to hear complaints about the other one. They must act as their own judges. Love is God's mystery and should be hidden from other people's eyes, no matter what happens. This makes it holier, much better. They respect each other more, and a great deal is based on this respect. And, if there's been love, if they got married out of love, why should love disappear? Can't it be sustained? It rarely happens that it can't be sustained. If the husband turns out to be a kind and honest man, how can the love disappear? The first phase of married love will pass, that's true, but it's followed by an even better kind of love. Souls are joined together and all their concerns are managed in common; there'll be no secrets from one another. When children arrive, each and every stage, even a very difficult one, will seem happy, as long as there's both love and courage. Even work is cheerful; even when you deny yourself bread for your children's sake, you're still happy. After all, they'll love you for it afterward; you're really saving for your own future. Your children will grow up, and you'll feel that you're a model for them, a support. Even after you die, they'll carry your thoughts and feelings all during their life. They'll take on your image and likeness, since they received it from you.[6] Consequently, it's a great obligation. How can a mother and father keep from growing closer? They say it's difficult to raise children. Who says that? It's heavenly joy! Do you love little children, Liza?[7] I love them dearly. You know—a rosy little boy, suckling at your breast; what husband's heart could turn against his wife seeing her sitting there holding his child? The chubby, rosy little baby sprawls and snuggles; his little hands and feet are plump; his little nails are clean and tiny, so tiny it's even funny to see them; his little eyes look as if he already understood everything. As he suckles, he tugs at your breast playfully with his little hand. When the father approaches, the child lets go of the breast, bends way back, looks at his father, and laughs—as if God only knows how funny it is— and then takes to suckling again. Afterward, when he starts cutting teeth, he'll sometimes bite his mother's breast; looking at her sideways his little eyes seem to say, 'See, I bit you!' Isn't this pure bliss—the three of them, husband, wife, and child, all together? You can forgive a great deal for

---

6. In Genesis 1:26 God declares, "Let us make man in our image, after our likeness."
7. This question foreshadows the treatment of children in Dostoevsky's last novel *The Brothers Karamazov* (1879–80), in particular Alyosha's involvement with Lise and with the schoolboys.

such moments. No, Liza, I think you must first learn how to live by yourself, and only afterward blame others."

"It's by means of images," I thought to myself, "just such images that I can get to you," although I was speaking with considerable feeling, I swear it; and all at once I blushed. "And what if she suddenly bursts out laughing—where will I hide then?" That thought drove me into a rage. By the end of my speech I'd really become excited, and now my pride was suffering somehow. The silence lasted for a while. I even considered shaking her.

"Somehow you . . ." she began suddenly and then stopped.

But I understood everything already: something was trembling in her voice now, not shrill, rude or unyielding as before, but something soft and timid, so timid that I suddenly was rather ashamed to watch her and felt guilty.

"What?" I asked with tender curiosity.

"Well, you . . ."

"What?"

"You somehow . . . it sounds just like a book," she said, and once again something which was noticeably sarcastic was suddenly heard in her voice.

Her remark wounded me dreadfully. That's not what I'd expected.

Yet, I didn't understand that she was intentionally disguising her feelings with sarcasm; that was usually the last resort of people who are timid and chaste of heart, whose souls have been coarsely and impudently invaded; and who, until the last moment, refuse to yield out of pride and are afraid to express their own feelings to you. I should've guessed it from the timidity with which on several occasions she tried to be sarcastic, until she finally managed to express it. But I hadn't guessed, and a malicious impulse took hold of me.

"Just you wait," I thought.

VII.

"That's enough, Liza. What do books have to do with it, when this disgusts me as an outsider? And not only as an outsider. All this has awakened in my heart . . . Can it be, can it really be that you don't find it repulsive here? No, clearly habit means a great deal. The devil only knows what habit can do to a person. But do you seriously think that you'll never grow old, that you'll always be pretty, and that they'll keep you on here forever and ever? I'm not even talking about the filth. . . . Besides, I want to say this about your present life: even though you're still young, good-looking, nice, with soul and feelings, do you know, that when I came to a little while ago, I was immediately disgusted to be here with you! Why, a man has to be drunk to wind up here. But if you were in a different place, living as nice people do, I might not

only chase after you, I might actually fall in love with you. I'd rejoice
at a look from you, let alone a word; I'd wait for you at the gate and
kneel down before you; I'd think of you as my betrothed and even
consider that an honor. I wouldn't dare have any impure thoughts about
you. But here, I know that I need only whistle, and you, whether you
want to or not, will come to me, and that I don't have to do your
bidding, whereas you have to do mine. The lowliest peasant may hire
himself out as a laborer, but he doesn't make a complete slave of himself;
he knows that it's only for a limited term. But what's your term? Just
think about it. What are you giving up here? What are you enslaving?
Why, you're enslaving your soul, something you don't really own, together with your body! You're giving away your love to be defiled by
any drunkard! Love! After all, that's all there is! It's a precious jewel, a
maiden's treasure, that's what it is! Why, to earn that love a man might
be ready to offer up his own soul, to face death. But what's your love
worth now? You've been bought, all of you; and why should anyone
strive for your love, when you offer everything even without it? Why,
there's no greater insult for a girl, don't you understand? Now, I've heard
that they console you foolish girls, they allow you to see your own lovers
here. But that's merely child's play, deception, making fun of you, while
you believe it. And do you really think he loves you, that lover of yours?
I don't believe it. How can he, if he knows that you can be called away
from him at any moment? He'd have to be depraved after all that. Does
he possess even one drop of respect for you? What do you have in
common with him? He's laughing at you and stealing from you at the
same time—so much for his love. It's not too bad, as long as he doesn't
beat you. But perhaps he does. Go on, ask him, if you have such a
lover, whether he'll ever marry you. Why, he'll burst out laughing right
in your face, if he doesn't spit at you or smack you. He himself may be
worth no more than a few lousy kopecks. And for what, do you think,
did you ruin your whole life here? For the coffee they give you to drink,
or for the plentiful supply of food? Why do you think they feed you so
well? Another girl, an honest one, would choke on every bite, because
she'd know why she was being fed so well. You're in debt here, you'll
be in debt, and will remain so until the end, until such time comes as
the customers begin to spurn you. And that time will come very soon;
don't count on your youth. Why, here youth flies by like a stagecoach.
They'll kick you out. And they'll not merely kick you out, but for a long
time before that they'll pester you, reproach you, and abuse you—as if
you hadn't ruined your health for the madam, hadn't given up your
youth and your soul for her in vain, but rather, as if you'd ruined her,
ravaged her, and robbed her. And don't expect any support. Your friends
will also attack you to curry her favor, because they're all in bondage
here and have long since lost both conscience and pity. They've become
despicable, and there's nothing on earth more despicable, more repulsive, or more insulting than their abuse. You'll lose everything here,

everything, without exception—your health, youth, beauty, and hope—
and at the age of twenty-two you'll look as if you were thirty-five, and
even that won't be too awful if you're not ill. Thank God for that. Why,
you probably think that you're not even working, that it's all play! But
there's no harder work or more onerous task than this one in the whole
world and there never has been. I'd think that one's heart alone would
be worn out by crying. Yet you dare not utter one word, not one syllable;
when they drive you out, you leave as if you were the guilty one. You'll
move to another place, then to a third, then somewhere else, and finally
you'll wind up in the Haymarket. And there they'll start beating you for
no good reason at all; it's a local custom; the clients there don't know
how to be nice without beating you. You don't think it's so disgusting
there? Maybe you should go and have a look sometime, and see it with
your own eyes. Once, at New Year's, I saw a woman in a doorway. Her
own kind had pushed her outside as a joke, to freeze her for a little
while because she was wailing too much; they shut the door behind her.
At nine o'clock in the morning she was already dead drunk, dishevelled,
half-naked, and all beaten up. Her face was powdered, but her eyes were
bruised; blood was streaming from her nose and mouth; a certain cabby
had just fixed her up. She was sitting on a stone step, holding a piece
of salted fish in her hand; she was howling, wailing something about
her 'fate,' and slapping the fish against the stone step. Cabbies and
drunken soldiers had gathered around the steps and were taunting her.
Don't you think you'll wind up the same way? I wouldn't want to believe
it myself, but how do you know, perhaps eight or ten years ago this
same girl, the one with the salted fish, arrived here from somewhere or
other, all fresh like a little cherub, innocent, and pure; she knew no
evil and blushed at every word. Perhaps she was just like you—proud,
easily offended, unlike all the rest; she looked like a queen and knew
that total happiness awaited the man who would love her and whom
she would also love. Do you see how it all ended? What if at the very
moment she was slapping the fish against that filthy step, dead drunk
and dishevelled, what if, even at that very moment she'd recalled her
earlier, chaste years in her father's house when she was still going to
school, and when her neighbor's son used to wait for her along the path
and assure her that he'd love her all his life and devote himself entirely
to her, and when they vowed to love one another forever and get married
as soon as they grew up! No, Liza, you'd be lucky, very lucky, if you
died quickly from consumption somewhere in a corner, in a cellar, like
that other girl. In a hospital, you say? All right—they'll take you off,
but what if the madam still requires your services? Consumption is quite
a disease—it's not like dying from a fever. A person continues to hope
right up until the last minute and declares that he's in good health. He
consoles himself. Now that's useful for your madam. Don't worry, that's
the way it is. You've sold your soul; besides, you owe her money—that
means you don't dare say a thing. And while you're dying, they'll all

abandon you, turn away from you—because there's nothing left to get
from you. They'll even reproach you for taking up space for no good
reason and for taking so long to die. You won't even be able to ask for
something to drink, without their hurling abuse at you: 'When will you
croak, you old bitch? You keep on moaning and don't let us get any
sleep—and you drive our customers away.' That's for sure; I've overheard
such words myself. And as you're breathing your last, they'll shove you
into the filthiest corner of the cellar—into darkness and dampness; lying
there alone, what will you think about then? After you die, some stranger
will lay you out hurriedly, grumbling all the while, impatiently—no
one will bless you, no one will sigh over you; they'll merely want to get
rid of you as quickly as possible. They'll buy you a wooden trough and
carry you out as they did that poor woman I saw today; then they'll go
off to a tavern and drink to your memory. There'll be slush, filth, and
wet snow in your grave—why bother for the likes of you? 'Let her down,
Vanyukha; after all, it's her fate to go down with her legs up, that's the
sort of girl she was. Pull up on that rope, you rascal!' 'It's okay like that.'
'How's it okay? See, it's lying on its side. Was she a human being or
not? Oh, never mind, cover it up.' They won't want to spend much
time arguing over you. They'll cover your coffin quickly with wet, blue
clay and then go off to the tavern. . . . That'll be the end of your memory
on earth;[8] for other women, children will visit their graves, fathers,
husbands—but for you—no tears, no sighs; no remembrances. No one,
absolutely no one in the whole world, will ever come to visit you; your
name will disappear from the face of the earth, just as if you'd never
been born and had never existed.[9] Mud and filth, no matter how you
pound on the lid of your coffin at night when other corpses arise: 'Let
me out, kind people, let me live on earth for a little while! I lived, but
I didn't really see life; my life went down the drain; they drank it away
in a tavern at the Haymarket; let me out, kind people, let me live in
the world once again!' "

I was so carried away by my own pathos that I began to feel a lump
forming in my throat, and . . . I suddenly stopped, rose up in fright,
and, leaning over apprehensively, I began to listen carefully as my own
heart pounded. There was cause for dismay.

For a while I felt that I'd turned her soul inside out and had broken
her heart; the more I became convinced of this, the more I strived to
reach my goal as quickly and forcefully as possible. It was the sport, the
sport that attracted me; but it wasn't only the sport. . . .

I knew that I was speaking clumsily, artificially, even bookishly; in
short, I didn't know how to speak except "like a book." But that didn't
bother me, for I knew, I had a premonition, that I would be understood

---

8. The theme of memory is also central to *The Brothers Karamazov* and forms the core of Alyosha's peroration over Ilyusha's grave at the conclusion of the novel.

9. This unhappy alternative to memory characterizes the hero's death in Gogol's short story "The Overcoat" (1842), where, a day later, Petersburg carries on as if Akaky Akakievich had never existed.

and that this bookishness itself might even help things along. But now, having achieved this effect, I suddenly lost all my nerve. No, never, never before had I witnessed such despair! She was lying there, her face pressed deep into a pillow she was clutching with her hands. Her heart was bursting. Her young body was shuddering as if she were having convulsions. Suppressed sobs shook her breast, tore her apart, and suddenly burst forth in cries and moans. Then she pressed her face even deeper into the pillow: she didn't want anyone, not one living soul, to hear her anguish and her tears. She bit the pillow; she bit her hand until it bled (I noticed that afterward); or else, thrusting her fingers into her dishevelled hair, she became rigid with the strain, holding her breath and clenching her teeth. I was about to say something, to ask her to calm down; but I felt that I didn't dare. Suddenly, all in a kind of chill, almost in a panic, I groped hurriedly to get out of there as quickly as possible. It was dark: no matter how I tried, I couldn't end it quickly. Suddenly I felt a box of matches and a candlestick with a whole unused candle. As soon as the room was lit up, Liza started suddenly, sat up, and looked at me almost senselessly, with a distorted face and a half-crazy smile. I sat down next to her and took her hands; she came to and threw herself at me, wanting to embrace me, yet not daring to. Then she quietly lowered her head before me.

"Liza, my friend, I shouldn't have . . . you must forgive me," I began, but she squeezed my hands so tightly in her fingers that I realized I was saying the wrong thing and stopped.

"Here's my address, Liza. Come to see me."

"I will," she whispered resolutely, still not lifting her head.

"I'm going now, good-bye . . . until we meet again."

I stood up; she did, too, and suddenly blushed all over, shuddered, seized a shawl lying on a chair, threw it over her shoulders, and wrapped herself up to her chin. After doing this, she smiled again somewhat painfully, blushed, and looked at me strangely. I felt awful. I hastened to leave, to get away.

"Wait," she said suddenly as we were standing in the hallway near the door, and she stopped me by putting her hand on my overcoat. She quickly put the candle down and ran off; obviously she'd remembered something or wanted to show me something. As she left she was blushing all over, her eyes were gleaming, and a smile had appeared on her lips—what on earth did it all mean? I waited against my own will; she returned a moment later with a glance that seemed to beg forgiveness for something. All in all it was no longer the same face or the same glance as before—sullen, distrustful, obstinate. Now her glance was imploring, soft, and, at the same time, trusting, affectionate, and timid. That's how children look at people whom they love very much, or when they're asking for something. Her eyes were light hazel, lovely, full of life, as capable of expressing love as brooding hatred.

Without any explanation, as if I were some kind of higher being who was supposed to know everything, she held a piece of paper out toward me. At that moment her whole face was shining with a most naive, almost childlike triumph. I unfolded the paper. It was a letter to her from some medical student containing a high-flown, flowery, but very respectful declaration of love. I don't remember the exact words now, but I can well recall the genuine emotion that can't be feigned shining through that high style. When I'd finished reading the letter, I met her ardent, curious, and childishly impatient gaze. She'd fixed her eyes on my face and was waiting eagerly to see what I'd say. In a few words, hurriedly, but with some joy and pride, she explained that she'd once been at a dance somewhere, in a private house, at the home of some "very, very good people, *family people*, where they *knew nothing*, nothing at all," because she'd arrived at this place only recently and was just . . . well, she hadn't quite decided whether she'd stay here and she'd certainly leave as soon as she'd paid off her debt. . . . Well, and this student was there; he danced with her all evening and talked to her. It turned out he was from Riga; he'd known her as a child, they'd played together, but that had been a long time ago; he was acquainted with her parents—but he knew nothing, absolutely nothing *about this place* and he didn't even suspect it! And so, the very next day, after the dance, (only some three days ago), he'd sent her this letter through the friend with whom she'd gone to the party . . . and . . . well, that's the whole story."

She lowered her sparkling eyes somewhat bashfully after she finished speaking.

The poor little thing, she'd saved this student's letter as a treasure and had run to fetch this one treasure of hers, not wanting me to leave without knowing that she too was the object of sincere, honest love, and that someone exists who had spoken to her respectfully. Probably that letter was fated to lie in her box without results. But that didn't matter; I'm sure that she'll guard it as a treasure her whole life, as her pride and vindication; and now, at a moment like this, she remembered it and brought it out to exult naively before me, to raise herself in my eyes, so that I could see it for myself and could also think well of her. I didn't say a thing; I shook her hand and left. I really wanted to get away. . . . I walked all the way home in spite of the fact that wet snow was still falling in large flakes. I was exhausted, oppressed, and perplexed. But the truth was already glimmering behind that perplexity. The ugly truth!

VIII.

It was some time, however, before I agreed to acknowledge that truth. I awoke the next morning after a few hours of deep, leaden sleep. Instantly recalling the events of the previous day, even I was astonished at my *sentimentality* with Liza last night, at all of yesterday's "horror and pity." "Why, it's an attack of old woman's nervous hysteria, phew!" I decided. "And why on earth did I force my address on her? What if she comes? Then again, let her come, it doesn't make any difference. . . ." But *obviously* that was not the main, most important matter: I had to make haste and rescue at all costs my reputation in the eyes of Zverkov and Simonov. That was my main task. I even forgot all about Liza in the concerns of that morning.

First of all I had to repay last night's debt to Simonov immediately. I resolved on desperate means: I would borrow the sum of fifteen rubles from Anton Antonych. As luck would have it, he was in a splendid mood that morning and gave me the money at once, at my first request. I was so delighted that I signed a promissory note with a somewhat dashing air, and told him *casually* that on the previous evening "I'd been living it up with some friends at the Hôtel de Paris. We were holding a farewell dinner for a comrade, one might even say, a childhood friend, and, you know—he's a great carouser, very spoiled—well, naturally; he comes from a good family, has considerable wealth and a brilliant career; he's witty and charming, and has affairs with certain ladies, you understand. We drank up an extra 'half-dozen bottles' and . . ." There was nothing to it; I said all this very easily, casually, and complacently.

Upon arriving home I wrote to Simonov at once.

To this very day I recall with admiration the truly gentlemanly, good-natured, candid tone of my letter. Cleverly and nobly, and, above all, without unnecessary words, I blamed myself for everything. I justified myself, "if only I could be allowed to justify myself," by saying that, being so totally unaccustomed to wine, I'd gotten drunk with the first glass, which (supposedly) I'd consumed even before their arrival, as I waited for them in the Hôtel de Paris between the hours of five and six o'clock. In particular, I begged for Simonov's pardon; I asked him to convey my apology to all the others, especially to Zverkov, whom, "I recall, as if in a dream," it seems, I'd insulted. I added that I'd have called upon each of them, but was suffering from a bad headache, and, worst of all, I was ashamed. I was particularly satisfied by the "certain lightness," almost casualness (though, still very proper), unexpectedly reflected in my style; better than all possible arguments, it conveyed to them at once that I regarded "all of last night's unpleasantness" in a rather detached way, and that I was not at all, not in the least struck down on the spot as you, gentlemen, probably suspect. On the contrary, I regard this all serenely, as any self-respecting gentleman would. The true story, as they say, is no reproach to an honest young man.

"Why, there's even a hint of aristocratic playfulness in it," I thought admiringly as I reread my note. "And it's all because I'm such a cultured and educated man! Others in my place wouldn't know how to extricate themselves, but I've gotten out of it, and I'm having a good time once again, all because I'm an 'educated and cultured man of our time.' It may even be true that the whole thing occurred as a result of that wine yesterday. Hmmm . . . well, no, it wasn't really the wine. And I didn't have anything to drink between five and six o'clock when I was waiting for them. I lied to Simonov; it was a bold-faced lie—yet I'm not ashamed of it even now. . . ."

But, to hell with it, anyway! The main thing is, I got out of it.

I put six rubles in the letter, sealed it up, and asked Apollon to take it to Simonov. When he heard that there was money in it, Apollon became more respectful and agreed to deliver it. Toward evening I went out for a stroll. My head was still aching and spinning from the events of the day before. But as evening approached and twilight deepened, my impressions changed and became more confused, as did my thoughts. Something hadn't yet died within me, deep within my heart and conscience; it didn't want to die, and it expressed itself as burning anguish. I jostled my way along the more populous, commercial streets, along Meshchanskaya, Sadovaya, near the Yusupov Garden.[1] I particularly liked to stroll along these streets at twilight, just as they became most crowded with all sorts of pedestrians, merchants, and tradesmen, with faces preoccupied to the point of hostility, on their way home from a hard day's work. It was precisely the cheap bustle that I liked, the crass prosaic quality. But this time all that street bustle irritated me even more. I couldn't get a hold of myself or puzzle out what was wrong. Something was rising, rising up in my soul continually, painfully, and didn't want to settle down. I returned home completely distraught. It was just as if some crime were weighing on my soul.

I was constantly tormented by the thought that Liza might come to see me. It was strange, but from all of yesterday's recollections, the one of her tormented me most, somehow separately from all the others. I'd managed to forget the rest by evening, to shrug everything off, and I still remained completely satisfied with my letter to Simonov. But in regard to Liza, I was not at all satisfied. It was as though I were tormented by her alone. "What if she comes?" I thought continually. "Well, so what? It doesn't matter. Let her come. Hmm. The only unpleasant thing is that she'll see, for instance, how I live. Yesterday I appeared before her such a . . . hero . . . but now, hmm! Besides, it's revolting that I've sunk so low. The squalor of my apartment. And I dared go to dinner last night wearing such clothes! And that oilcloth sofa of mine with its stuffing hanging out! And my dressing gown that doesn't quite cover me! What rags! . . . She'll see it all—and she'll see Apollon. That swine will surely insult her. He'll pick on her, just to be rude to me. Of course, I'll be frightened, as usual. I'll begin to fawn before her, wrap myself up in my dressing gown. I'll start to smile and tell lies. Ugh, the indecency! And that's not even the worst part! There's something even

---

1. An attractive public garden and popular meeting place that plays an important role in Raskolnikov's meanderings in *Crime and Punishment*.

more important, nastier, meaner! Yes, meaner! Once again, I'll put on that dishonest, deceitful mask! . . ."

When I reached this thought, I simply flared up.

"Why deceitful? How deceitful? Yesterday I spoke sincerely. I recall that there was genuine feeling in me, too. I was trying no less than to arouse noble feelings in her . . . and if she wept, that's a good thing; it will have a beneficial effect. . ."

But I still couldn't calm down.

All that evening, even after I returned home, even after nine o'clock, when by my calculations Liza could no longer have come, her image continued to haunt me, and, what's most important, she always appeared in one and the same form. Of all that had occurred yesterday, it was one moment in particular which stood out most vividly: that was when I lit up the room with a match and saw her pale, distorted face with its tormented gaze. What a pitiful, unnatural, distorted smile she'd had at that moment! But little did I know then that even fifteen years later I'd still picture Liza to myself with that same pitiful, distorted, and unnecessary smile which she'd had at that moment.

The next day I was once again prepared to dismiss all this business as nonsense, as the result of overstimulated nerves; but most of all, as exaggeration. I was well aware of this weakness of mine and sometimes was even afraid of it; "I exaggerate everything, that's my problem," I kept repeating to myself hour after hour. And yet, "yet, Liza may still come, all the same"; that was the refrain which concluded my reflections. I was so distressed that I sometimes became furious. "She'll come! She'll definitely come!" If not today, then tomorrow, she'll seek me out! That's just like the damned romanticism of all these *pure hearts*! Oh, the squalor, the stupidity, the narrowness of these "filthy, sentimental souls!" How could all this not be understood, how on earth could it not be understood?. . ." But at this point I would stop myself, even in the midst of great confusion.

"And how few, how very few words were needed," I thought in passing, "how little idyllic sentiment (what's more, the sentiment was artificial, bookish, composed) was necessary to turn a whole human soul according to my wishes at once. That's innocence for you! That's virgin soil!"

At times the thought occurred that I might go to her myself "to tell her everything," and to beg her not to come to me. But at this thought such venom arose in me that it seemed I'd have crushed that "damned" Liza if she'd suddenly turned up next to me. I'd have insulted her, spat at her, struck her, and chased her away! *damned*

One day passed, however, then a second, and a third; she still hadn't come, and I began to calm down. I felt particularly reassured and relaxed after nine o'clock in the evening, and even began to daydream sweetly at times. For instance, "I'd save Liza, precisely because she'd come to me, and I'd talk to her. . . . I'd develop her mind, educate her. At last I'd notice that she loved me, loved me passionately. I'd pretend I didn't understand. (For that matter, I didn't know why I'd pretend; most likely just for the effect.) At last, all embarrassed, beautiful, trembling, and sobbing, she'd throw herself at my feet and declare that I was her saviour and she loved me more than anything in the world. I'd be surprised, but . . . "Liza," I'd say, "Do you really think that I haven't noticed your love? I've seen everything. I guessed, but dared not be first to make a claim on your heart because I had such influence over you, and because I was afraid you might deliberately force yourself to respond to my love out of gratitude, that you might forcibly evoke within yourself a feeling that didn't really exist. No, I didn't want that because it would be . . . despotism. . . . It would be indelicate (well, in short, here I launched on some European, George Sandian, inexplicably lofty subtleties . . .).[2] But now, now—you're mine, you're my creation, you're pure and lovely, you're my beautiful wife."

> And enter my house bold and free
> To become its full mistress![3]

"Then we'd begin to live happily together, travel abroad, etc., etc." In short, it began to seem crude even to me, and I ended it all by sticking my tongue out at myself.

"Besides, they won't let her out of there, the 'bitch,' " I thought. "After all, it seems unlikely that they'd release them for strolls, especially in the evening (for some reason I was convinced that she had to report there every evening, precisely at seven o'clock). Moreover, she said that she'd yet to become completely enslaved there, and that she still had certain rights; that means, hmm. Devil take it, she'll come, she's bound to come!"

It was a good thing I was distracted at the time by Apollon's rudeness. He made me lose all patience. He was the bane of my existence, a punishment inflicted on me by Providence. We'd been squabbling constantly for several years now and I hated him. My God, how I hated him! I think that I never hated anyone in my whole life as much as I hated him, especially at those times. He was an elderly, dignified man who worked part-time as a tailor. But for some unknown reason he despised me, even beyond all measure, and looked down upon me intolerably. However, he looked down on everyone. You need only glance at that flaxen, slicked-down hair, at that single lock brushed over his forehead and greased with vegetable oil, at his strong mouth, always drawn up in the shape of the letter V,[4] and you felt that you were standing before a creature who never doubted himself. He was a pedant of the highest order, the greatest one I'd ever met on earth; in addition

---

2. A reference to the writings of George Sand (1804–76), the assumed name of the famous French author. She produced over eighty novels ranging in subject from romantic love to social reform and women's rights.

3. The concluding lines of Nekrasov's poem "When from the darkness of delusion," quoted at the beginning of part 2, "Apropos of Wet Snow."
4. The last letter of the old Russian alphabet, triangular in shape.

he possessed a sense of self-esteem appropriate perhaps only to Alexander the Great, King of Macedonia.[5] He was in love with every one of his buttons, every one of his fingernails—absolutely in love, and he looked it! He treated me quite despotically, spoke to me exceedingly little, and, if he happened to look at me, cast a steady, majestically self-assured, and constantly mocking glance that sometimes infuriated me. He carried out his tasks as if he were doing me the greatest of favors. Moreover, he did almost nothing at all for me; nor did he assume that he was obliged to do anything. There could be no doubt that he considered me the greatest fool on earth, and, that if he "kept me on," it was only because he could receive his wages from me every month. He agreed to "do nothing" for seven rubles a month. I'll be forgiven many of my sins because of him. Sometimes my hatred reached such a point that his gait alone would throw me into convulsions. But the most repulsive thing about him was his lisping. His tongue was a bit larger than normal or something of the sort; as a result, he constantly lisped and hissed. Apparently, he was terribly proud of it, imagining that it endowed him with enormous dignity. He spoke slowly, in measured tones, with his hands behind his back and his eyes fixed on the ground. It particularly infuriated me when he used to read the Psalter to himself behind his partition. I endured many battles on account of it. He was terribly fond of reading during the evening in a slow, even singsong voice, as if chanting over the dead. It's curious, but that's how he ended up: now he hires himself out to recite the Psalter over the dead; in addition, he exterminates rats and makes shoe polish. But at that time I couldn't get rid of him; it was as if he were chemically linked to my own existence. Besides, he'd never have agreed to leave for anything. It was impossible for me to live in a furnished room: my own apartment was my private residence, my shell, my case, where I hid from all humanity. Apollon, the devil only knows why, seemed to belong to this apartment, and for seven long years I couldn't get rid of him.

It was impossible, for example, to delay paying him his wages for even two or three days. He'd make such a fuss that I wouldn't know where to hide. But in those days I was so embittered by everyone that I decided, heaven knows why or for what reason, to *punish* Apollon by not paying him his wages for two whole weeks. I'd been planning to do this for some time now, about two years, simply in order to teach him that he had no right to put on such airs around me, and that if I chose to, I could always withhold his wages. I resolved to say nothing to him about it and even remain silent on purpose, to conquer his pride and force him to be the first one to mention it. Then I would pull all seven rubles out of a drawer and show him that I actually had the money and had intentionally set it aside, but that "I didn't want to, didn't want to, simply

---

5. One of the greatest generals and most powerful personalities of the ancient world (356–23 B.C.). He amassed an enormous empire, stretching from the Adriatic to India.

didn't want to pay him his wages, and that I didn't want to simply because *that's what I wanted*," because such was "my will as his master," because he was disrespectful and because he was rude. But, if he were to ask respectfully, then I might relent and pay him; if not, he might have to wait another two weeks, or three, or even a whole month. . . .

But, no matter how angry I was, he still won. I couldn't even hold out for four days. He began as he always did, because there had already been several such cases (and, let me add, I knew all this beforehand; I knew his vile tactics by heart), to wit: he would begin by fixing an extremely severe gaze on me. He would keep it up for several minutes in a row, especially when meeting me or accompanying me outside of the house. If, for example, I held out and pretended not to notice these stares, then he, maintaining his silence as before, would proceed to further tortures. Suddenly, for no reason at all, he'd enter my room quietly and slowly, while I was pacing or reading; he'd stop at the door, place one hand behind his back, thrust one foot forward, and fix his gaze on me, no longer merely severe, but now utterly contemptuous. If I were suddenly to ask him what he wanted, he wouldn't answer at all. He'd continue to stare at me reproachfully for several more seconds; then, compressing his lips in a particular way and assuming a very meaningful air, he'd turn slowly on the spot and slowly withdraw to his own room. Two hours later he'd emerge again and suddenly appear before me in the same way. It's happened sometimes that in my fury I hadn't even asked what he wanted, but simply raised my head sharply and imperiously, and begun to stare reproachfully back at him. We would stare at each other thus for some two minutes or more; at last he'd turn slowly and self-importantly, and withdraw for another few hours.

If all this failed to bring me back to my senses and I continued to rebel, he'd suddenly begin to sigh while staring at me. He'd sigh heavily and deeply, as if trying to measure with each sigh the depth of my moral decline. Naturally, it would end with his complete victory: I'd rage and shout, but I was always forced to do just as he wished on the main point of dispute.

This time his usual maneuvers of "severe stares" had scarcely begun when I lost my temper at once and lashed out at him in a rage. I was irritated enough even without that.

"Wait!" I shouted in a frenzy, as he was slowly and silently turning with one hand behind his back, about to withdraw to his own room. "Wait! Come back, come back, I tell you!" I must have bellowed so unnaturally that he turned around and even began to scrutinize me with a certain amazement. He continued, however, not to utter one word, and that was what infuriated me most of all.

"How dare you come in here without asking permission and stare at me? Answer me!"

But after regarding me serenely for half a minute, he started to turn around again.

"Wait!" I roared, rushing up to him. "Don't move! There! Now answer me: why do you come in here to stare?"

"If you've got any orders for me now, it's my job to do 'em," he replied after another pause, lisping softly and deliberately, raising his eyebrows, and calmly shifting his head from one side to the other— what's more, he did all this with horrifying composure.

"That's not it! That's not what I'm asking you about, you executioner!" I shouted, shaking with rage. "I'll tell you myself, you executioner, why you came in here. You know that I haven't paid you your wages, but you're so proud that you don't want to bow down and ask me for them. That's why you came in here to punish me and torment me with your stupid stares, and you don't even sus-s-pect, you torturer, how stupid it all is, how stupid, stupid, stupid, stupid!"

He would have turned around silently once again, but I grabbed hold of him.

"Listen," I shouted to him. "Here's the money, you see! Here it is! (I pulled it out of a drawer.) All seven rubles. But you won't get it, you won't until you come to me respectfully, with your head bowed, to ask my forgiveness. Do you hear?"

"That can't be!" he replied with some kind of unnatural self-confidence.

"It will be!" I shrieked. "I give you my word of honor, it will be!"

"I have nothing to ask your forgiveness for," he said as if he hadn't even noticed my shrieks, "because it was you who called me an 'executioner,' and I can always go lodge a complaint against you at the police station."

"Go! Lodge a complaint!" I roared. " Go at once, this minute, this very second! You're still an executioner! Executioner! Executioner!" But he only looked at me, then turned and, no longer heeding my shouts, calmly withdrew to his own room without looking back.

"If it hadn't been for Liza, none of this would have happened!" I thought to myself. Then, after waiting a minute, pompously and solemnly, but with my heart pounding heavily and forcefully, I went in to see him behind the screen.

"Apollon!" I said softly and deliberately, though gasping for breath, "go at once, without delay to fetch the police supervisor!"

He'd already seated himself at his table, put on his eyeglasses, and picked up something to sew. But, upon hearing my order, he suddenly snorted with laughter.

"At once! Go this very moment! Go, go, or you can't imagine what will happen to you!"

"You're really not in your right mind," he replied, not even lifting his head, lisping just as slowly, and continuing to thread his needle.

"Who's ever heard of a man being sent to fetch a policeman against himself? And as for trying to frighten me, you're only wasting your time, because nothing will happen to me."

"Go," I screeched, seizing him by the shoulder. I felt that I might strike him at any moment.

I never even heard the door from the hallway suddenly open at that very moment, quietly and slowly, and that someone walked in, stopped, and began to examine us in bewilderment. I glanced up, almost died from shame, and ran back into my own room. There, clutching my hair with both hands, I leaned my head against the wall and froze in that position.

Two minutes later I heard Apollon's deliberate footsteps.

"There's *some woman* asking for you," he said, staring at me with particular severity; then he stood aside and let her in—it was Liza. He didn't want to leave, and he scrutinized us mockingly.

"Get out, get out!" I commanded him all flustered. At that moment my clock strained, wheezed, and struck seven.

IX.

> And enter my house bold and free,
> To become its full mistress!
> From the same poem.[6]

I stood before her, crushed, humiliated, abominably ashamed; I think I was smiling as I tried with all my might to wrap myself up in my tattered, quilted dressing gown—exactly as I'd imagined this scene the other day during a fit of depression. Apollon, after standing over us for a few minutes, left, but that didn't make things any easier for me. Worst of all was that she suddenly became embarrassed too, more than I'd ever expected. At the sight of me, of course.

"Sit down," I said mechanically and moved a chair up to the table for her, while I sat on the sofa. She immediately and obediently sat down, staring at me wide-eyed, and, obviously, expecting something from me at once. This naive expectation infuriated me, but I restrained myself.

She should have tried not to notice anything, as if everything were just as it should be, but she . . . And I vaguely felt that she'd have to pay dearly *for everything*.

"You've found me in an awkward situation, Liza," I began, stammering and realizing that this was precisely the wrong way to begin.

"No, no, don't imagine anything!" I cried, seeing that she'd suddenly blushed. "I'm not ashamed of my poverty. . . . On the contrary, I regard it with pride. I'm poor, but noble. . . . One can be poor and noble," I muttered. "But . . . would you like some tea?"

6. See above, n. 7 on p. 29.

"No . . . ," she started to say.

"Wait!"

I jumped up and ran to Apollon. I had to get away somehow.

"Apollon," I whispered in feverish haste, tossing down the seven rubles which had been in my fist the whole time, "here are your wages. There, you see, I've given them to you. But now you must rescue me: bring us some tea and a dozen rusks from the tavern at once. If you don't go, you'll make me a very miserable man. You have no idea who this woman is. . . . This means—everything! You may think she's . . . But you've no idea at all who this woman really is!"

Apollon, who'd already sat down to work and had put his glasses on again, at first glanced sideways in silence at the money without abandoning his needle; then, paying no attention to me and making no reply, he continued to fuss with the needle he was still trying to thread. I waited there for about three minutes standing before him with my arms folded *à la Napoleon*.[7] My temples were soaked in sweat. I was pale, I felt that myself. But, thank God, he must have taken pity just looking at me. After finishing with the thread, he stood up slowly from his place, slowly pushed back his chair, slowly took off his glasses, slowly counted the money and finally, after inquiring over his shoulder whether he should get a whole pot, slowly walked out of the room. As I was returning to Liza, it occurred to me: shouldn't I run away just as I was, in my shabby dressing gown, no matter where, and let come what may.

I sat down again. She looked at me uneasily. We sat in silence for several minutes.

"I'll kill him." I shouted suddenly, striking the table so hard with my fist that ink splashed out of the inkwell.

"Oh, what are you saying?" she exclaimed, startled.

"I'll kill him, I'll kill him!" I shrieked, striking the table in an absolute frenzy, but understanding full well at the same time how stupid it was to be in such a frenzy.

"You don't understand, Liza, what this executioner is doing to me. He's my executioner. . . . He's just gone out for some rusks; he . . ."

And suddenly I burst into tears. It was a nervous attack. I felt so ashamed amidst my sobs, but I couldn't help it. She got frightened.

"What's the matter? What's wrong with you?" she cried, fussing around me.

"Water, give me some water, over there!" I muttered in a faint voice, realizing full well, however, that I could've done both without the water and without the faint voice. But I was *putting on an act*, as it's called, in order to maintain decorum, although my nervous attack was genuine.

She gave me some water while looking at me like a lost soul. At that very moment Apollon brought in the tea. It suddenly seemed that this ordinary and prosaic tea was horribly inappropiate and trivial after every-

7. In the style of Napoleon.

thing that had happened, and I blushed. Liza stared at Apollon with considerable alarm. He left without looking at us.

"Liza, do you despise me?" I asked, looking her straight in the eye, trembling with impatience to find out what she thought.

She was embarrased and didn't know what to say.

"Have some tea," I said angrily. I was angry at myself, but she was the one who'd have to pay, naturally. A terrible anger against her suddenly welled up in my heart; I think I could've killed her.[8] To take revenge I swore inwardly not to say one more word to her during the rest of her visit. "She's the cause of it all," I thought.

Our silence continued for about five minutes. The tea stood on the table; we didn't touch it. It reached the point of my not wanting to drink on purpose, to make it even more difficult for her; it would be awkward for her to begin alone. Several times she glanced at me in sad perplexity. I stubbornly remained silent. I was the main sufferer, of course, because I was fully aware of the despicable meanness of my own spiteful stupidity; yet, at the same time, I couldn't restrain myself.

"I want to . . . get away from . . . that place . . . once and for all," she began just to break the silence somehow; but, poor girl, that was just the thing she shouldn't have said at that moment, stupid enough as it was to such a person as me, stupid as I was. My own heart even ached with pity for her tactlessness and unnecessary straightforwardness. But something hideous immediately suppressed all my pity; it provoked me even further. Let the whole world go to hell. Another five minutes passed.

"Have I disturbed you?" she began timidly, barely audibly, and started to get up.

But as soon as I saw this first glimpse of injured dignity, I began to shake with rage and immediately exploded.

"Why did you come here? Tell me why, please," I began, gasping and neglecting the logical order of my words. I wanted to say it all at once, without pausing for breath; I didn't even worry about how to begin.

"Why did you come here? Answer me! Answer!" I cried, hardly aware of what I was saying. "I'll tell you, my dear woman, why you came here. You came here because I spoke some *words of pity* to you that time. Now you've softened, and want to hear more 'words of pity.' Well, you should know that I was laughing at you then. And I'm laughing at you now. Why are you trembling? Yes, I was laughing at you! I'd been insulted, just prior to that, at dinner, by those men who arrived just before me that evening. I came intending to thrash one of them, the officer; but I didn't succeed; I couldn't find him; I had to avenge my insult on someone, to get my own back; you turned up and I took my

---

8. This homicidal impulse foreshadows Raskolnikov's murder of the pawnbroker in *Crime and Punishment*.

anger out at you, and I laughed at you. I'd been humiliated, and I wanted to humiliate someone else; I'd been treated like a rag, and I wanted to exert some power. . . . That's what it was; you thought that I'd come there on purpose to save you, right? Is that what you thought? Is that it?"

I knew that she might get confused and might not grasp all the details, but I also knew that she'd understand the essence of it very well. That's just what happened. She turned white as a sheet; she wanted to say something. Her lips were painfully twisted, but she collapsed onto a chair just as if she'd been struck down with an ax.[9] Subsequently she listened to me with her mouth gaping, her eyes wide open, shaking with awful fear. It was the cynicism, the cynicism of my words that crushed her. . . .

"To save you!" I continued, jumping up from my chair and rushing up and down the room in front of her, "to save you from what? Why, I may be even worse than you are. When I recited that sermon to you, why didn't you throw it back in my face? You should have said to me, 'Why did you come here? To preach morality or what?' Power, it was the power I needed then, I craved the sport, I wanted to reduce you to tears, humiliation, hysteria—that's what I needed then! But I couldn't have endured it myself, because I'm such a wretch. I got scared. The devil only knows why I foolishly gave you my address. Afterward, even before I got home, I cursed you like nothing on earth on account of that address. I hated you already because I'd lied to you then, because it was all playing with words, dreaming in my own mind. But, do you know what I really want now? For you to get lost, that's what! I need some peace. Why, I'd sell the whole world for a kopeck if people would only stop bothering me. Should the world go to hell, or should I go without my tea? I say, let the world go to hell as long as I can always have my tea. Did you know that or not? And I know perfectly well that I'm a scoundrel, a bastard, an egotist, and a sluggard. I've been shaking from fear for the last three days wondering whether you'd ever come. Do you know what disturbed me most of all these last three days? The fact that I'd appeared to you then as such a hero, and that now you'd suddenly see me in this torn dressing gown, dilapidated and revolting. I said before that I wasn't ashamed of my poverty; well, you should know that I am ashamed, I'm ashamed of it more than anything, more afraid of it than anything, more than if I were a thief, because I'm so vain; it's as if the skin's been stripped away from my body so that even wafts of air cause pain. By now surely even you've guessed that I'll never forgive you for having come upon me in this dressing gown as I was attacking Apollon like a vicious dog. Your saviour, your former hero, behaving like a mangy, shaggy mongrel, attacking his own lackey, while that lackey stood there laughing at me! Nor will I ever forgive you for

9. Raskolnikov chooses an ax to strike down his victim in *Crime and Punishment*.

those tears which, like an embarrassed old woman, I couldn't hold back before you. And I'll never forgive *you* for all that I'm confessing now. Yes—you, you alone must pay for everything because you turned up like this, because I'm a scoundrel, because I'm the nastiest, most ridiculous, pettiest, stupidest, most envious worm of all those living on earth who're no better than me in any way, but who, the devil knows why, never get embarrassed, while all my life I have to endure insults from every louse—that's my fate. What do I care that you don't understand any of this? What do I care, what do I care about you and whether or not you perish there? Why, don't you realize how much I'll hate you now after having said all this with your being here listening to me? After all, a man can only talk like this once in his whole life, and then only in hysteria! . . . What more do you want? Why, after all this, are you still hanging around here tormenting me? Why don't you leave?"

But at this point a very strange thing suddenly occurred.

I'd become so accustomed to inventing and imagining everything according to books, and picturing everything on earth to myself just as I'd conceived of it in my dreams, that at first I couldn't even comprehend the meaning of this strange occurrence. But here's what happened: Liza, insulted and crushed by me, understood much more than I'd imagined. She understood out of all this what a woman always understands first of all, if she sincerely loves—namely, that I myself was unhappy.

The frightened and insulted expression on her face was replaced at first by grieved amazement. When I began to call myself a scoundrel and a bastard, and my tears had begun to flow (I'd pronounced this whole tirade in tears), her whole face was convulsed by a spasm. She wanted to get up and stop me; when I'd finished, she paid no attention to my shouting, "Why are you here? Why don't you leave?" She only noticed that it must have been very painful for me to utter all this. Besides, she was so defenseless, the poor girl. She considered herself immeasurably beneath me. How could she get angry or take offense? Suddenly she jumped up from the chair with a kind of uncontrollable impulse, and yearning toward me, but being too timid and not daring to stir from her place, she extended her arms in my direction. . . . At this moment my heart leapt inside me, too. Then suddenly she threw herself at me, put her arms around my neck, and burst into tears. I, too, couldn't restrain myself and sobbed as I'd never done before.

"They won't let me . . . I can't be . . . good!"[1] I barely managed to say; then I went over to the sofa, fell upon it face down, and sobbed in genuine hysterics for a quarter of an hour. She knelt down, embraced me, and remained motionless in that position.

But the trouble was that my hysterics had to end sometime. And so (after all, I'm writing the whole loathsome truth), lying there on the

---

1. This epithet *dobryi* ("good") must be read in combination with that in the second sentence of the work, where the hero describes himself as *zloi*, not only "spiteful," but also "evil."

sofa and pressing my face firmly into that nasty leather cushion of mine, I began to sense gradually, distantly, involuntarily, but irresistibly, that it would be awkward for me to raise my head and look Liza straight in the eye. What was I ashamed of? I don't know, but I was ashamed. It also occurred to my overwrought brain that now our roles were completely reversed, now she was the heroine, and I was the same sort of humiliated and oppressed creature she'd been in front of me that evening—only four days ago. . . . And all this came to me during those few minutes as I lay face down on the sofa!

My God! Was it possible that I envied her?

I don't know; to this very day I still can't decide. But then, of course, I was even less able to understand it. After all, I couldn't live without exercising power and tyrannizing over another person. . . . But . . . but, then, you really can't explain a thing by reason; consequently, it's useless to try.

However, I regained control of myself and raised my head; I had to sooner or later. . . . And so, I'm convinced to this day that it was precisely because I felt too ashamed to look at her, that another feeling was suddenly kindled and burst into flame in my heart—the feeling of domination and possession. My eyes gleamed with passion; I pressed her hands tightly. How I hated her and felt drawn to her simultaneously! One feeling intensified the other. It was almost like revenge! . . . At first there was a look of something resembling bewilderment, or even fear, on her face, but only for a brief moment. She embraced me warmly and rapturously.

X.

A quarter of an hour later I was rushing back and forth across the room in furious impatience, constantly approaching the screen to peer at Liza through the crack. She was sitting on the floor, her head leaning against the bed, and she must have been crying. But she didn't leave, and that's what irritated me. By this time she knew absolutely everything. I'd insulted her once and for all, but . . . there's nothing more to be said. She guessed that my outburst of passion was merely revenge, a new humiliation for her, and that to my former, almost aimless, hatred there was added now a *personal*, *envious* hatred of her. . . . However, I don't think that she understood all this explicitly; on the other hand, she fully understood that I was a despicable man, and, most important, that I was incapable of loving her.

I know that I'll be told this is incredible—that it's impossible to be as spiteful and stupid as I am; you may even add that it was impossible not to return, or at least to appreciate, this love. But why is this so incredible? In the first place, I could no longer love because, I repeat, for me love meant tyrannizing and demonstrating my moral superiority. All my life I could never even conceive of any other kind of love, and I've now reached the point that I sometimes think that love consists precisely in a voluntary gift by the beloved person of the right to tyrannize over him.[2] Even in my underground dreams I couldn't conceive of love in any way other than a struggle. It always began with hatred and ended with moral subjugation; afterward, I could never imagine what to do with the subjugated object. And what's so incredible about that, since I'd previously managed to corrupt myself morally; I'd already become unaccustomed to "real life,"[3] and only a short while ago had taken it into my head to reproach her and shame her for having come to hear "words of pity" from me. But I never could've guessed that she'd come not to hear words of pity at all, but to love me, because it's in that kind of love that a woman finds her resurrection, all her salvation from whatever kind of ruin, and her rebirth, as it can't appear in any other form. However, I didn't hate her so much as I rushed around the room and peered through the crack behind the screen. I merely found it unbearably painful that she was still there. I wanted her to disappear. I longed for "peace and quiet"; I wanted to remain alone in my underground. "Real life" oppressed me—so unfamiliar was it—that I even found it hard to breathe.

But several minutes passed, and she still didn't stir, as if she were oblivious. I was shameless enough to tap gently on the screen to remind her. . . . She started suddenly, jumped up, and hurried to find her shawl, hat, and coat, as if she wanted to escape from me. . . . Two minutes later she slowly emerged from behind the screen and looked at me sadly. I smiled spitefully; it was forced, however, for *appearance's sake only*; and I turned away from her look.

"Good-bye," she said, going toward the door.

Suddenly I ran up to her, grabbed her hand, opened it, put something in . . . and closed it again. Then I turned away at once and bolted to the other corner, so that at least I wouldn't be able to see. . . .

I was just about to lie—to write that I'd done all this accidentally, without knowing what I was doing, in complete confusion, out of foolishness. But I don't want to lie; therefore I'll say straight out, that I opened her hand and placed something in it . . . out of spite. It occurred to me to do this while I was rushing back and forth across the room and she was sitting there behind the screen. But here's what I can say for sure: although I did this cruel thing deliberately, it was not from my heart, but from my stupid head. This cruelty of mine was so artificial, cerebral, intentionally invented, *bookish*, that I couldn't stand it myself even for one minute—at first I bolted to the corner so as not to see, and then, out of shame and in despair, I rushed out after Liza. I opened the door into the hallway and listened. "Liza! Liza!" I called down the stairs, but timidly, in a soft voice.

2. This theme is diametrically opposed to that expressed by Dostoevsky in chapter 6 of *Winter Notes on Summer Impressions*.

3. The original Russian for this phrase is the splendidly tautological *zhivaya zhizn'*, "living life."

There was no answer; I thought I could hear her footsteps at the bottom of the stairs.

"Liza!" I cried more loudly.

No answer. But at that moment I heard down below the sound of the tight outer glass door opening heavily with a creak and then closing again tightly. The sound rose up the stairs.

She'd gone. I returned to my room deep in thought. I felt horribly oppressed.

I stood by the table near the chair where she'd been sitting and stared senselessly into space. A minute or so passed, then I suddenly started: right before me on the chair I saw . . . in a word, I saw the crumpled blue five-ruble note, the very one I'd thrust into her hand a few moments before. It was the same one; it couldn't be any other; I had none other in my apartment. So she'd managed to toss it down on the table when I'd bolted to the other corner.

So what? I might have expected her to do that. Might have expected it? No. I was such an egotist, in fact, I so lacked respect for other people, that I couldn't even conceive that she'd ever do that. I couldn't stand it. A moment later, like a madman, I hurried to get dressed. I threw on whatever I happened to find, and rushed headlong after her. She couldn't have gone more than two hundred paces when I ran out on the street.

It was quiet; it was snowing heavily, and the snow was falling almost perpendicularly, blanketing the sidewalk and the deserted street. There were no passers-by; no sound could be heard. The street lights were flickering dismally and vainly. I ran about two hundred paces to the crossroads and stopped.

"Where did she go? And why am I running after her? Why? To fall down before her, sob with remorse, kiss her feet, and beg her forgiveness! That's just what I wanted. My heart was being torn apart; never, never will I recall that moment with indifference. But—why?" I wondered. "Won't I grow to hate her, perhaps as soon as tomorrow, precisely because I'm kissing her feet today? Will I ever be able to make her happy? Haven't I found out once again today, for the hundredth time, what I'm really worth? Won't I torment her?"

I stood in the snow, peering into the murky mist, and thought about all this.

"And wouldn't it be better, wouldn't it," I fantasized once I was home again, stifling the stabbing pain in my heart with such fantasies, "wouldn't it be better if she were to carry away the insult with her forever? Such an insult—after all, is purification; it's the most caustic and painful form of consciousness. Tomorrow I would have defiled her soul and wearied her heart. But now that insult will never die within her; no matter how abominable the filth that awaits her, that insult will elevate and purify her . . . by hatred . . . hmm . . . perhaps by forgiveness as well. But will that make it any easier for her?"

And now, in fact, I'll pose an idle question of my own. Which is better: cheap happiness or sublime suffering? Well, come on, which is better?

These were my thoughts as I sat home that evening, barely alive with the anguish in my soul. I'd never before endured so much suffering and remorse; but could there exist even the slightest doubt that when I went rushing out of my apartment, I'd turn back again after going only half-way? I never met Liza afterward, and I never heard anything more about her. I'll also add that for a long time I remained satisfied with my theory about the use of insults and hatred, in spite of the fact that I myself almost fell ill from anguish at the time.

Even now, after so many years, all this comes back to me as *very unpleasant*. A great deal that comes back to me now is very unpleasant, but . . . perhaps I should end these *Notes* here? I think that I made a mistake in beginning to write them. At least, I was ashamed all the time I was writing this *tale*: consequently, it's not really literature, but corrective punishment. After all, to tell you long stories about how, for example, I ruined my life through moral decay in my corner, by the lack of appropriate surroundings, by isolation from any living beings, and by futile malice in the underground—so help me God, that's not very interesting. A novel needs a hero, whereas here all the traits of an anti-hero have been assembled *deliberately*; but the most important thing is that all this produces an extremely unpleasant impression because we've all become estranged from life, we're all cripples, every one of us, more or less. We've become so estranged that at times we feel some kind of revulsion for genuine "real life," and therefore we can't bear to be reminded of it. Why, we've reached a point where we almost regard "real life" as hard work, as a job, and we've all agreed in private that it's really better in books. And why do we sometimes fuss, indulge in whims, and make demands? We don't know ourselves. It'd be even worse if all our whimsical desires were fulfilled. Go on, try it. Give us, for example, a little more independence; untie the hands of any one of us, broaden our sphere of activity, relax the controls, and . . . I can assure you, we'll immediately ask to have the controls reinstated.[4] I know that you may get angry at me for saying this, you may shout and stamp your feet: "Speak for yourself," you'll say, "and for your own miseries in the underground, but don't you dare say '*all of us.*'" If you'll allow me, gentlemen; after all, I'm not trying to justify myself by saying *all of us*. What concerns me in particular, is that in my life I've only taken to an extreme that which you haven't even dared to take halfway; what's more, you've mistaken your cowardice for good sense; and, in so deceiving yourself, you've consoled yourself. So, in fact, I may even be "more alive" than you are. Just take a closer look! Why, we don't even

4. This foreshadows the Grand Inquisitor's powerful arguments against absolute freedom in *The Brothers Karamazov*.

know where this "real life" lives nowadays, what it really is, and what it's called. Leave us alone without books and we'll get confused and lose our way at once—we won't know what to join, what to hold on to, what to love or what to hate, what to respect or what to despise. We're even oppressed by being men—men with real bodies and blood of *our very own*. We're ashamed of it; we consider it a disgrace and we strive to become some kind of impossible "general-human-beings." We're still-born; for some time now we haven't been conceived by living fathers; we like it more and more. We're developing a taste for it. Soon we'll conceive of a way to be born from ideas. But enough; I don't want to write any more "from Underground. . . ."

However, the "notes" of this paradoxalist don't end here. He couldn't resist and kept on writing. But it also seems to us that we might as well stop here.

BACKGROUNDS AND
SOURCES

Selected Letters
from
Fyodor Dostoevsky
to
Mikhail Dostoevsky
(1859–64)†

* * *

9 October 1859

In December I shall begin writing a novel. * * * Don't you remember, I told you about a certain *Confession*¹—a novel that I wanted to write after everything else, saying that I had to gain some experience first. Several days ago I positively decided to write it without delay. It has been merged with the other novel (the passionate element) that I told you about. In the first place, it will be striking, passionate; in the second, all my heart and soul will go into this novel. I conceived of it during my years of imprisonment,² lying on a bunk bed, at a painful moment of grief and disintegration. * * * *Confession* will establish my name once and for all.

* * *

20 March 1864

* * * I have set to work on a story.³ I'm trying to finish it off as quickly as possible, but at the same time I want it to turn out well. It's far more difficult to write it than I'd anticipated. Meanwhile it's absolutely essential that it be good, essential *especially to me*. In its tone the tale is too strange; the tone is shrill and wild. It may not be well received; consequently I need poetry to come to the rescue and soften the whole thing. But I hope it all works out. * * *

26 March 1864

* * * I'll complain about my article;⁴ the misprints are terrible and it would have been better not to print the penultimate chapter (the most

† From F. M. Dostoevsky, *Polnoe sobranie sochinenii v tridtsati tomakh* (Leningrad: Nauka, 1985), vol. 28, translated by Michael R. Katz. Letters to Dostoevsky's older brother (1820–64). The two were very close from their early years and became even closer when they decided to work together on the journals *Vremya* and *Epokha*.

1. The first mention of such a project in any of Dostoevsky's letters. It embodies the central idea of *Notes from Underground*. The title of the larger project was repeated in announcements during 1862, but work on the novel was never completed.

2. Dostoevsky was arrested in 1849 and imprisoned for participating in radical circles. His death sentence was commuted at the last minute to exile in Siberia. He served his sentence of hard labor in Omsk (1850–54) and then was posted to a military battalion in Semipalatinsk (1854–59).

3. Dostoevsky uses the word *povest'* (a "story" or "tale") to refer to *Notes from Underground*.

4. This refers to part 1 ("Underground"), published separately. Since the whereabouts of the original manuscript are unknown, it is impossible to establish what changes in the text might have been demanded by the censor.

important one in which the main idea is expressed), than to print it as is, namely, with sentences mixed up and contradicting itself. But what's to be done! The censors are swine—those places where I mocked everything and sometimes blasphemed *for appearance's sake*—they let pass; but where I deduced from all this the necessity of faith and Christ— they deleted it. What's the matter with these censors of ours, are they in a conspiracy against the government, or what? * * *

*   *   *

2 April 1864

But here's what's important, Misha: this month I'll *certainly* not only be unable to write that article, but I probably won't be able to write any criticism at all. . . . * * * I'm writing a story[5] now, but having trouble with it too. My friend, I was ill for the greater part of the month; then I got better, but up to now I still haven't completely recovered. My nerves are distraught and I still can't gather my strength. My torments *of all kinds* are now so onerous that I don't even want to talk about them. My wife is dying, *literally*. Every day there comes a moment when we expect her death. Her suffering is terrible and it's taking its toll on me because. . . . After all, writing isn't mechanical work; still, I write and write in the mornings, but my work is only beginning. The story is stretching out. Sometimes it seems that it'll be rubbish, but I'm still writing with enthusiasm; I don't know what'll come of it. The thing is that it still requires a great deal of time. Even if I write only half of it, I'll still send it to be set in type; but I want to publish it as a whole, *sine qua non*. In general there's little time for writing, although it seems that all the time is my own; still there's so little time, because this is not a *productive* period for me and I sometimes have other things on my mind. Moreover, I'm afraid that my wife's death will occur soon, and there will *inevitably* be an interruption. If it weren't for the interruption, I think I could finish it. I can't say anything for sure. I'm merely presenting the facts of the matter. You can judge for yourself.

*   *   *

5 April 1864

* * * If only I had strength, leisure time, and *no interruptions*, my story could be finished this month, but certainly not during the first half. That's how it is. Now decide for yourself: *the March issue* will definitely have to be published in April. It won't look good for a new journal if its March issue appears in May. Can I finish it in time? Judging by all the signs—no. The main problem is an interruption which doesn't depend on me and whose consequences I can't foresee. Therefore, my dear, I ask you to write me as soon as possible and tell me the *very latest date* by which you must have the story in your hands. I'll be able to

---

5. Here Dostoevsky uses the word *povest'* to refer to part 2 ("Apropos of Wet Snow").

judge from your reply whether I can finish it or not. In any case, however, take into account the circumstances that may occur to hinder my work and which won't depend on me. * * *

* * *

9 *April* 1864

My friend, I suppose you received my last letter. I wrote that it seems as if the story won't be finished. I repeat, Misha: I'm so exhausted, so oppressed by circumstances, in such an agonizing situation, that I can't even answer for my physical strength at work. I eagerly await your reply. But for now, here's what I can report: the story is expanding. It may be as long as five printer's sheets,[6] I don't know; therefore, even with enormous effort, it is *materially* impossible to finish it. What's to be done? Shall we really publish it unfinished? Impossible. It can't be divided. And all the while, I don't know how it'll come out—it may be rubbish, but personally I have great hopes for it. It will be a powerful and candid piece; it will be the truth. Even though it will probably be bad, it will make an impression. I know. And perhaps will even be very good. What's to be done? In any case, I repeat, it's *materially* impossible to complete this kind of labor in such a short time; and, if you decide to publish by Easter Week, my writing even a critical article may be impossible. That's certain. Therefore, if it's at all possible—release me from the March issue, be my benefactor. In exchange, by April you'll have both my story of considerable length and a critical article. *I stake my life* on it, if only I don't die. Let me complete the story and then you'll see my activity.

* * *

13 *April* 1864

* * * But on to business: I'll tell you once again what I've told you before about the story: it's stretching out. It's very likely that it'll come out well; I'm working on it with all my strength, but it's progressing slowly, because all my time is inevitably taken up by other things. The story is divided into three chapters, each not less than 1½ printer's sheets. The second chapter is in chaos, the third hasn't been started yet, but the first is now being revised. The first chapter may run 1½ printer's sheets and may be completely ready in five days or so. Should it really be published separately? People will laugh at it, all the more so since it'll lose all its flavor without the other two (main) chapters. You understand a *transition* in music. Well, it's the same here. The first chapter contains what appears to be chatter; but suddenly, in the last two chapters this chatter turns into an unexpected catastrophe. If you ask me to send only the first chapter, I'll do so. Write to me at once. . . . * * *

6. This term is used to designate units of sixteen printed pages (now called a "signature") that are bound together in books or journals. The printer's sheet was also the unit by which writers were paid for their work.

15 April 1864
* * * Yesterday Marya Dmitrievna suffered a decisive attack: blood gushed from her throat, and began to flood into her chest and suffocate her. We all expected the end. We all stayed near her. She bid farewell to everyone, made peace with everyone, and gave final instructions * * *

* * *

P. S. Now I can't send the story in any case *(even the beginning)*. What's to be done? But it'll be ready by April. . . .

Marya Dmitrievna is dying quietly, in full consciousness. . . .

15 April 1864
* * * Just now, at seven o'clock this evening, Marya Dmitrievna died after wishing you all a long and happy life (her own words). Remember her with a kind word. She suffered so much of late that I can't imagine anyone would be unable to make his peace with her. * * *

FYODOR DOSTOEVSKY

[Socialism and Christianity]†

In socialism there are [only] splinters[1], in Christianity, the ultimate development of personality and one's own will.

God is an idea, of collective humanity, of the masses, of *everybody*.

* * *

There's something much higher than god-appetite.[2] That is, to be the lord and master even of one's own self, one's *I*, to sacrifice this *I*, to hand it over—to everybody. There's something inexpressibly beautiful in this idea, sweet, inevitable, even inexplicable.

Inexplicable, precisely. Should the socialist begin to explain, he'd argue that if you imagine each man will give up *everything*, even himself, even his own *I* for everybody, then that means no one will be poor, and everyone will be terribly rich. The socialist would be lying crudely, in a vile and pot-bellied way. For although it's really true, that is, everyone

† From F. M. Dostoevsky, *Polnoe sobranie sochi-nenii v tridtsati tomakh* (Leningrad: Nauka, 1980), vol. 20, pp. 191-94, translated by Michael R. Katz. An excerpt from a draft of an unfinished article in Dostoevsky's fourth notebook (1864–65).
1. The Russian word *(luchinochka)* means splin-

ters of wood used to light fires in peasant huts; hence here, either small, insignificant "fragments" or the inadequate light cast by these burning slivers.
2. The Russian phrase *(bog-chrevo)*, literally "god-as-belly," represents man's animalistic appetites.

will be rich, socialism still stops at this point. But this can't be because a socialist can't even conceive of how it's possible to give oneself up freely for others; from his point of view, that's immoral. But that's just the point, the whole infinitude of Christianity over socialism consists precisely in the fact that a Christian (in the ideal), in giving away everything, demands nothing for himself in return.

And if that's not enough, he's even hostile to the idea of recompense, he regards it as nonsensical and will only accept a reward out of love for the donors, or only because he feels that afterward he'll love the donor even more (the new Jerusalem, embraces, green branches).

FYODOR DOSTOEVSKY

From *Winter Notes on Summer Impressions*†

Chapter V

BAAL[1]

* * * . . . The City[2] with its millions of inhabitants and worldwide commerce, the Crystal Palace,[3] the International Exposition . . . Yes, the Exposition is striking. You feel the terrible force that united here all these countless people coming from all over the world into one fold;[4] you become aware of an enormous idea; you feel that something significant has been achieved here, some victory or triumph. It's even as if you begin to fear something. However independent you are, you still begin to feel terrified for some reason or other. "Isn't this really the ideal that's been achieved?" you wonder. "Isn't this the goal? Isn't this really the 'one fold'?" Mustn't one really accept all this as ultimate truth and fall silent once and for all? It's all so triumphant, victorious and proud that it begins to take your breath away. You look at these hundreds of thousands, these millions of people, humbly streaming here from all corners of the globe, people who have come with one single thought, quietly, stubbornly and silently crowding into this colossal palace, and you sense that here something definitive has taken place, taken place and been completed. It's like some Biblical scene, something about Babylon,[5] some prophecy from the Apocalypse[6] taking place before one's

† From F. M. Dostoevsky, *Polnoe sobranie sochinenii v tridsati tomakh* (Leningrad: Nauka, 1973), vol. 5, pp. 69–70, 79–80, translated by Michael R. Katz.

1. The name used throughout the Old Testament to designate the pagan deities of Canaan.
2. The central, commercial part of London.
3. A large glass and steel structure built in London in 1851 to serve as the main pavilion for international expositions.
4. From the Gospel According to St. John: "And there shall be one fold, and one shepherd"(10.16).
5. The ancient capital of Mesopotamia, known for its wealth, architectural splendor, and hanging gardens.
6. The Revelation of St. John the Divine, the last book of the New Testament.

very eyes. You sense that it would require a great deal of eternal spiritual fortitude and denial in order not to submit, not to yield to the impression, not to bow down to the fact, and not to worship Baal, that is, not to accept the world that exists as one's own ideal. . . . * * *

Chapter VI

ESSAY ON THE BOURGEOIS

* * *

. . . Western man talks about brotherhood[7] as the great motivating force of mankind, but he doesn't realize that there is no place to acquire brotherhood if it does not already exist in reality. What is to be done? Brotherhood has to be created at all costs. But it turns out that it's impossible to create brotherhood because it creates itself, comes of itself, and is found in nature. But in French nature, and in Western nature in general, it does not appear to be present; instead one finds there a principle of individualism, a principle of isolation, of intense self-preservation, of personal gain, self-definition in terms of one's own *I*, the opposition of this *I* to all of nature and to all other people, as an independent, autonomous principle, totally equal and equivalent to everything that exists outside of it. Well, such a juxtaposition cannot create brotherhood. Why? Because in brotherhood, in true brotherhood, it's not the separate personality, not the *I* that should be concerned with its equal value and equivalence to *everything else*, but rather this *everything else* must come *in and of itself* to the person demanding his rights, to that individual *I*, and of itself, without his asking, must recognize him as equal in value and equivalent to himself, that is, to everything else that exists. Moreover, that rebellious and demanding person must first of all offer to sacrifice to society all of itself, all of its *I*, and not only refrain from demanding its rights, but, on the contrary, surrender all to society without any preconditions.

But the Western personality is not accustomed to such a procedure: it fights for what it demands, it demands its rights, it wants to *separate* itself—and brotherhood does not emerge. Of course, might there not be a regeneration? But a regeneration is accomplished over thousands of years, for such ideas must first become embodied in flesh and blood in order to become reality. So then, you will say to me, must one be without individuality in order to be happy? Does salvation lie in impersonality? On the contrary, on the contrary, I say, not only is it unnecessary to be without individuality, but it is even essential to achieve a greater degree of individuality than actually exists now in the West. Understand me: voluntary, completely self-conscious, and totally unconstrained sacrifice of one's entire self for the good of everyone is, in

7. Dostoevsky's translation of the third word in the French revolutionary slogan, "*Liberté, égalité, fraternité.*"

my opinion, a sign of the highest development of individuality, of its greatest power, its greatest self-mastery, the greatest freedom of its own will. To lay down one's life willingly for others, to be crucified or burned at the stake for others, can only be done at the very highest stage of individuality. A highly developed individuality, completely convinced of its right to be an individual, no longer fearing for itself, cannot possibly make anything else of its personality, that is, can find no greater use for it than to give it all to others, so that others can become equally autonomous and happy individuals. This is a law of nature; normally man aspires toward it. But there is one fly in the ointment, one tiny little fly; if, however, it finds its way into the mechanism, the whole thing immediately comes crashing down and is destroyed. Namely: all will be lost if in this case there exists even the slightest calculation on behalf of one's own advantage

*   *   *

N. G. Chernyshevsky

From *What Is to Be Done?* †

Vera Pavlovna's Fourth Dream

Vera Pavlovna has a dream.

From the distance she hears the sound of a familiar voice. Oh, how familiar it is now, and it's drawing nearer and nearer.[1]

> Wie herrlich leuchtet
> Mir die Natur!
> Wie glanzt die Sonne!
> Wie lacht die Flur![2]

> [How splendid the brightness
> Of nature around me!
> How the sun shines!
> How the fields laugh!]

Vera Pavlovna sees that it is so; everything is just like that.

The field glimmers with a golden tint; the meadow is covered with flowers; and hundreds upon thousands of blossoms unfold on bushes

---

† From N. G. Chernyshevsky, *Chto delat'?* (Leningrad: Nauka, 1975), pp. 275–90, translated by Michael R. Katz. Written as a response to Turgenev's unflattering portrayal of the nihilist Bazarov in *Fathers and Sons* (1861), Chernyshevsky's novel in turn first provoked Dostoevsky to write *Notes from Underground.*

1. The voice is that of Angiolina Bosio (1830–59), a celebrated Italian opera singer who performed regularly in St. Petersburg during the 1850s.
2. The opening lines of the poem *"Mailied"* ("May Song," 1771) by Johann Wolfgang von Goethe (1749–1832).

surrounding the meadow. The forest that rises up behind grows greener, whispers, and is decked out in bright flowers. A fragrance wafts in from the field, the meadow, the shrubs, and from the flowers that fill the forest. Birds flutter in the branches of the trees; their thousands of voices float down from above together with all the fragrances. Beyond the field, meadow, shrubs, and forest there appear other fields glimmering with gold, meadows swathed in flowers, shrubs decked with blossoms— stretching all the way to the distant mountains that are covered with forests and lit by the sun. Here and there bright silvery, golden, purple, or translucent clouds lightly tint the brilliant azure of the sky along the horizon. The sun has just risen; nature rejoices and brings joy. It pours light and warmth, fragrance and song, love and bliss into the heart; and a song of joy and bliss, love and goodness pours forth from the heart. "Oh, earth! Oh, bliss! Oh, love! Oh, splendid golden love, like morning clouds over mountain tops!"

> O Erd'! O Sonne!
> O Glück! O Lust!
>
> O Lieb, o Liebe!
> So golden schön,
> Wie Morgenwolken
> Auf jenen Höhn![3]
>
> [Oh earth! Oh sun!
> Oh happiness! Oh delight!
>
> Oh love, oh love!
> So golden-beautiful,
> Like morning clouds
> Over those hills!]

"Now do you recognize me? Do you see that I am beautiful? You still don't. None of you yet knows me in all my beauty. Behold now what was, what is, and what shall be. Look and listen":

> Wohl perlet im Glase der purpurne Wein,
> Wohl glänzen die Augen der Gäste, . . .[4]
>
> [The goblet sparkles with purple wine,
> The eyes of the guests shine brightly, . . .]

At the foot of the mountains, on the outskirts of the forest, amidst the bushes flowering in tall, thick avenues, a palace looms up.

"Let us go there."

They walk, they fly.

A magnificent feast is in progress. Wine bubbles in glasses.

---

3. Lines 11–16 of Goethe's "*Mailied*" (see n. 2 above).
4. The opening lines of the poem "*Die vier Wel-*

talter" ("The Four Ages of the World," 1802), by Johann Christoph Friedrich von Schiller (1759–1805).

The guests' eyes sparkle. It's noisy, but whispers and laughter can be heard beneath the noise. Hands are squeezed in secret; at times an inaudible kiss is stealthily exchanged. "A song! A song! Our celebration isn't complete without a song!" The poet rises: both his face and his mind are illumined with inspiration. Nature confides her secrets in him, history reveals its meaning, and in his song thousands of years of life parade by in a series of tableaux.

1.

The words of the poet ring out and the first scene appears.

Tents of nomads. Sheep, horses, and camels graze around the tents. In the distance stand groves of olives and fig trees. Farther still, on the horizon to the northwest, stands a double chain of lofty mountains. The summits are covered with snow, their slopes with cedars. But the shepherds are more slender than the cedars, their wives, more graceful than the palms. Their indolent life is untroubled in its sweet state of bliss. They have but one concern—love. They spend all their time, day after day, in caresses and songs of love.

"No," says the radiant beauty. "This isn't about me. I didn't exist then. This woman is still a slave. Where there's no equality, I don't exist. This goddess was named Astarte.[5] Look, here she is."

A splendid woman. She wears heavy gold bracelets on her wrists and ankles and a heavy necklace of pearls and coral set in gold around her neck. Her hair is annointed with myrrh. There is sensuality and servility in her face, sensuality and vacuity in her eyes.

"Submit to your master. Sweeten his idleness in the intervals between his forays. You must love him because he has bought you: if you don't, he'll kill you," she says to the woman lying before her in the dust.

"You can see that this isn't me," says the beauty.

2.

The inspired words of the poet ring out again.

A new scene appears.

A city. Mountains stretch into the distance to the north and east; far off to the south and east, but close by to the west, lies the sea. A wonderful city! Its houses are neither large nor luxurious from the outside. But there are many magnificent temples, especially on the hill with stairs leading up to gates of astonishing size and beauty. The entire hill is covered with temples and public buildings, each one of which would be sufficient to add to the beauty and glory of the most magnificent of today's capitals. There are thousands of statues in these temples and throughout the whole town—any one of them would be enough to

5. A Semitic goddess of fertility and love corresponding to the Greek Aphrodite, Astarte was the most important female deity among the Phoenicians.

transform the museum in which it stood into the foremost collection in the whole world. How beautiful are the people who crowd the squares and streets! Each one of these young men, women, and girls could serve as a model for a statue. They are active, lively, cheerful people whose whole life is radiant and elegant. These houses don't appear to be luxurious from the outside, but what a wealth of elegance and what a high capacity for enjoyment they reveal inside. One could easily lose oneself in admiration before each item of furniture and each piece of crockery. And these people are all so beautiful, so able to appreciate beauty, to live for love, to serve beauty.

Here's an exile returning to the city which had ousted him from power, now he's coming back to rule—everyone knows that. Why are no hands raised up against him? Because riding next to him on his chariot stands a woman of exceptional beauty (even among all these beautiful creatures). She presents him to the people, asking them to accept him, telling them that she is his patroness. Bowing down before her beauty, the people confer to her beloved Pisistratus[6] the right to rule over them.

Here's a courtroom. The judges are gloomy old men. The people may be won over, but not these judges. The Areopagus[7] is known for its merciless severity, its implacable impartiality. Gods and goddesses have come here to submit their affairs to judgment. And now this woman, considered by all to be guilty of horrendous crimes, is supposed to appear before them. She must die, this destroyer of Athens; each one of the judges has already decided the matter in his heart. But when the accused Aspasia[8] appears before them, they fall to the ground before her saying, "You cannot be condemned, for you are too beautiful!" Is this not the kingdom of beauty? Is this not the kingdom of love?

"No," says the radiant beauty, "I didn't exist then either. They bowed down before woman, but they didn't consider her as an equal. They worshipped her, but only as a source of pleasure. They didn't yet acknowledge her human dignity. Where there's no respect for woman as a human being, I still don't exist. This goddess was named Aphrodite.[9] Look, here she is."

This goddess wears no adornments at all. She's so beautiful that her worshippers didn't want her to wear any clothes: her marvelous shape was not to be hidden from their enraptured gaze.

What does she say to the woman almost as beautiful as she, who's scattering incense on her altar?

6. Pisistratus (605?–527 B.C.) seized power in Athens around 560 B.C., where he ruled tyrannically until his death despite being sent into exile twice by his opponents.
7. An aristrocractic council that acted as a religious authority and the highest court in ancient Athens.

8. Mistress of the Athenian statesman Pericles and renowned both for her intelligence and her beauty, Aspasia (5th cen. B.C.) became a controversial figure in Athens because of her involvement in public affairs.
9. The Greek goddess of love, beauty, and fertility.

"Be a source of pleasure for man. He's your master. Live for him, not for yourself."

Her eyes reflect only the languor of physical pleasure. Her stance is proud, as is her expression, but she takes pride only in her physical beauty. What sort of life was a woman condemned to lead during her reign? Man locked her up in the gynecium[1] so that nobody but he, her master, could enjoy the beauty which belonged to him. She had no freedom. There were other women who called themselves free, but they sold both the enjoyment of their beauty and their freedom. "No, they had no freedom either. This goddess was half-slave. Where there is no freedom, there is no happiness and I don't exist."

3.

The words of the poet ring out again. A new scene appears.

An arena before a castle. Around it arises an amphitheater filled with a crowd of dazzling spectators. Knights are already waiting in the arena. Above it, on the castle balcony, sits a young woman. She holds a scarf in her hand. The victorious knight will receive that scarf and the right to kiss her hand. The knights fight to the death. Toggenburg[2] wins.

"Oh, knight, I love you as a sister would. Demand no other love from me. My heart pounds neither at your approach nor at your departure."

"My fate is sealed," he replies and sets sail for Palestine. His fame spreads throughout Christendom. But he can't go on living without seeing the goddess of his heart. He returns without having found oblivion in battle.

"Oh, knight, don't come searching here. She's gone off to a convent."

He builds himself a hut; from it, unbeknownst to her, he can watch her open the window of her cell every morning. His whole life consists of waiting for her to appear at that window, beautiful as the sun. He has no other life except to catch a glimpse of his heart's goddess; he has no other life until the day he dies. Even as his life is fading, still he sits by the window of his little hut, thinking only, "Will I ever see her again?"

"This isn't about me at all," says the radiant beauty. "He loved her as long as he didn't touch her. If she'd become his wife, then she'd have become his subject. She'd have had to tremble before him. He'd have locked her up and ceased loving her. He'd have taken long hunting trips, gone off to fight wars, caroused with his comrades, and raped his vassals, while his wife would have been abandoned, locked away, despised. At that time once a man touched a woman, he ceased loving

---

1. The women's quarters in ancient Greek houses.
2. The hero of Schiller's ballad "*Ritter Toggen-* *burg*" ("The Knight Toggenburg," 1798) (see n. 4 above).

her. No, I didn't exist then. This goddess is named 'Chastity.'[3] Look, here she is."

She's a modest, gentle, tender, beautiful woman—more beautiful than Astarte, even more beautiful than Aphrodite, but she's pensive, gloomy, and sorrowful. Others bow their knees before her and bring her garlands of roses. She says "My soul is sad unto deathly sorrow. A sword has pierced my heart. You must grieve as well. You are unhappy. The earth is a vale of tears."

"No, no, I didn't exist then," says the radiant beauty.

4.

No, these goddesses aren't at all like me. They continue to reign, but their kingdoms are in decline. The birth of each new kingdom initiates the decline of the previous one. I was born only when the last one began to crumble. Since my birth their kingdoms have declined more rapidly; soon they will completely disappear. Each new kingdom failed to replace its predecessor entirely, so that they all continue to coexist. But I shall replace them all; soon they'll all disappear and I alone will remain to rule over the whole world. But they had to reign before me; my kingdom couldn't have come into being without theirs.

"People used to be like animals. They ceased being so when man began to value woman's beauty. But woman wasn't as strong as man, and man was a coarse creature. At that time everything was decided by force. Having begun to value woman's beauty, man took her as his own. She became his property, his chattel. This was the reign of Astarte.

"When man developed further, he came to value woman's beauty more than ever and began to worship her. But woman's consciousness wasn't yet fully developed. He valued her only for her beauty. She was able to think only those thoughts which she heard from him. He said that he was a human being but that she wasn't; she still viewed herself as a splendid treasure belonging to him. She didn't consider herself human. This was the reign of Aphrodite.

"But soon the consciousness that she too was a human being began to awaken in her. What grief must have seized her at the dawning of even the weakest notion of her own human dignity! For she wasn't yet acknowledged to be a person. Man still didn't want to have her as a companion for himself, other than as his slave. She said, "I don't wish to be your companion!" Then his passion made him entreat her and submit. He forgot that he didn't consider her a human being, and came to love her as an unattainable, untouchable, and inviolable maiden. But as soon as she believed his entreaty, as soon as he touched her, then woe unto her! She was in his hands, and those hands were stronger than hers. He was coarse; he made her his slave

---

3. An allusion to the Virgin Mary.

and despised her. Woe unto her! This is the sorrowful reign of the Virgin.

"But centuries passed. My sister—(Do you know her? . . . She appeared to you before I did.)—did her work. She preceded the others and has always existed. She existed before people were created and has always labored tirelessly. Her work was difficult, her successes gradual, but she toiled on and on and soon became more successful. Man became wiser; more and more, woman strongly perceived herself as a human being equal to him. And the time came, and I was born.

"That was not so long ago, not long ago at all. Do you know who first sensed that I had been born and who announced it to the others? It was Rousseau in *La Nouvelle Heloise*.[4] People heard about me for the first time in that book.

"Since then my kingdom has expanded. I still don't rule over very many people. But now my kingdom is growing rapidly and you can already foresee a time when I shall rule over all the earth. Only then will people fully appreciate my beauty. Those who acknowledge my power at this time are still incapable of obeying my will entirely. They are surrounded by crowds of people who are hostile to it. These people would torment them, poison their lives, if they knew my will and fulfilled it entirely. But I desire happiness; I require no suffering whatever. So I tell them: "Don't do anything for which you will be persecuted. Know my will only to the extent that you can do so without causing harm to yourselves."

"But can I ever know you fully?" asks Vera Pavlovna.

"Yes, you can. You're in a fortunate position. You have nothing to fear. You can do anything you want. If you would know my will entirely, then you'd know that I would do nothing to harm you. You must not and will not desire anything for which you would be tormented by those who do not know me. You're now completely satisfied by what you have; you don't think about anything or anyone else, nor will you. I can reveal myself to you entirely."

"Tell me your name then. You named the previous goddesses, but you still haven't told me your name."

"So, you want me to tell you my name? Look at me and listen to me."

5.

"Look and listen. Do you recognize my voice? Do you recognize my face? Haven't you seen it before?"

No, she hadn't seen her face, hadn't seen it at all. Why then did it seem as if she were seeing her? She'd seen it often during the last year,

---

4. A novel by the French-Swiss philosopher, political theorist, and skeptic Jean-Jacques Rousseau (1712–78), *Julie: ou La Nouvelle Heloise* (1761) contains a sharp critique of European society in general and the position of women in particular.

ever since she'd first spoken with him, when he first looked at her and kissed her, she'd been seeing this radiant beauty who didn't hide from her and who'd appeared to her as she did to him.

"No, I haven't seen you before, I haven't seen your face. You appeared to me, and I caught a glimpse of you, but you were surrounded by such radiance that I really couldn't see you. I only noticed that you were more beautiful than all the others. I heard your voice too, but only to recognize that it was lovelier than all the others."

"Behold, for your sake I shall dim the brightness of my aura for a moment; for a moment my voice will be heard without the enchanting quality which I usually give it. For a moment I shall cease being a goddess just for you. There. Did you see? Did you hear? Do you recognize me? Enough! I'm a goddess again and shall remain so forever!"

Once more she's surrounded by the full brilliance of her radiance and her voice is inexpressibly enchanting. But for that one moment when she ceased being a goddess and allowed herself to be recognized—could it be? Did Vera Pavlovna really see that face? Did she really hear that voice?

"Yes," replies the goddess. "You wanted to know who I am and you found out. You wanted to learn my name. I have no name other than that of the person to whom I appear. My name is her name. Now you have seen who I am. There's nothing nobler than a human being, nothing nobler than a woman. I am she to whom I appear, she who loves and is loved."

Yes, Vera Pavlovna did see: it was she herself, but as a goddess.[5] The goddess's countenance was her own, her own living countenance, whose features were so far from perfection. Every day she encountered many faces that were much more beautiful than hers. Yet this was her very own face, glowing with the radiance of love, lovelier than all the ideals bequeathed to us by the great sculptors of antiquity and the great artists of the golden age of painting. Yes, it was she herself, but glowing with the radiance of love. In Petersburg, a city so lacking in beauty, there were hundreds of faces more beautiful than hers. But she was far more beautiful than the Aphrodite in the Louvre,[6] lovelier than all the famous beauties known heretofore.

"You're seeing your reflection in a mirror just as you are, without me. In me you behold yourself as you are seen by the one who loves you. For his sake I merge with you. For him there's no one more beautiful than you. For him all ideals pale beside you."

Isn't that so?

It is so, it is so!

---

5. Drawing on both the Christian doctrine of transfiguration and the ideas of the German philosopher Ludwig Feuerbach, Chernyshevsky deifies Vera Pavlovna while anthropologizing his goddess.

6. That is, the statue of the Venus de Milo.

6.

"Now you know *who* I am; next you shall learn *what* I am.

"I possess all the sensual pleasure which was contained in Astarte. She's the ancestor of all of us, the other goddesses who replaced her. I possess all the ecstasy at the contemplation of beauty which was contained in Aphrodite. I possess all the reverence before purity which was contained in Chastity.

"But in me all these qualities are fuller, nobler, and stronger than in those others. That which was in Chastity is combined in me with the qualities of Astarte and Aphrodite. In combination with other strengths, each of these qualities becomes even more powerful, greater as a result of the synthesis.[7] But much more power and splendor are bestowed on each of these qualities in me by that new element which wasn't present in any of the previous goddesses. That new element which distinguishes me from all others is "equal rights between lovers," that is, an equal relationship between them as human beings. As a result of this new element alone, everything I possess is much, oh so much more beautiful than it was in them.

"When a man acknowledges a woman's rights as equal to his own, he's renouncing the view of her as his personal property. Then she loves him as he loves her, only because she wants to. If she doesn't so wish, then he has no rights over her whatsoever, as she has none over him. Therefore I am freedom.

"As a result of this equality and freedom, everything in me which was present in previous goddesses has acquired a new character, a greater splendor, one which was unknown before me and which makes everything else insignificant.

"Previously sensual pleasure wasn't fully known because without the free attraction of two lovers, neither could experience radiant rapture. Before me ecstasy at the contemplation of beauty was not fully known, because if beauty isn't revealed through free attraction, there exists no radiant rapture at its contemplation. Without free attraction both pleasure and delight are dull in comparison to what they are in me. My chastity is purer than that of Chastity, who spoke only about the purity of body. I possess purity of heart. I'm free because in me there's neither deceit nor pretense. I say no word that I don't feel. I bestow no kiss barren of love.

"But the new quality in me that conveys greater loveliness to what was in all previous goddesses in and of itself constitutes my loveliness, greater than anything else. A master is embarrassed before his servant, a servant before his master; man is completely free only among equals. It's tiresome to be with one's inferiors; only among equals can one experience

---

7. In claiming that this merger makes the whole more powerful than the sum of its parts while also enhancing the quality of each part, Chernyshevsky reflects a central tenet of German idealist philosophy as well as anticipates the contemporary scientific concept of synergy.

true joy. That's why before me even as man did not not know the full happiness of love; that which he experienced was unworthy of being called happiness—it was merely momentary intoxication. As for woman—before me she was so pitiful. She was a subordinate, an enslaved creature, living in fear; before me she knew too little about the nature of love. Where there's fear, there's no love. . . .

"Therefore, if you wish to express in one phrase what I am, it's 'equal rights.' Without them the pleasures of the body and delight in beauty are tedious, dull, and vile. Without them there's no purity of heart, only the deceptive purity of body. As a result of this equality in me there is also freedom, without which I cannot exist.

"I've told you everything so that now you can tell others what I am. But at present my kingdom is still small; I must protect my people from the slander of those who don't yet know me. At this time I can't reveal my will fully to everyone. I shall do so only when my kingdom extends over all people. When everyone becomes beautiful in body and pure in heart, then will I reveal all of my beauty to them. As for you, your fate is particularly fortunate. I'll neither confuse you nor harm you, in describing to you what I'll be like when everyone becomes worthy of acknowledging me as their goddess, as opposed to now, when there are still so few. To you alone will I reveal the secrets of my future. Promise to keep silent and listen."

7.[8]

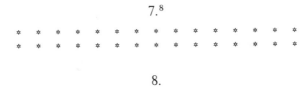

8.

"Oh, my love, now I know your will completely. I know that it will come to pass, but what will it be like? How will people live then?"

"I can't tell you that by myself. I need the help of my older sister, the one who first appeared to you a long time ago. She's both my mistress and my servant. I can only be what she makes of me, and yet she works for me. Sister, come to my aid."

The Sister of her Sisters, the Bride of her Bridegrooms appears.

"Greetings, sister," she says to the goddess. "Are you here too, sister?" she asks Vera Pavlovna. "Do you wish to see how people will live when my ward, the goddess, rules over everyone? Then behold."

There stands a building, a large, enourmous structure such as can only be seen in a few of the grandest capitals. No, now there's no other building like it! It stands amidst fields and meadows, orchards and groves. The fields grow grain, but they aren't like the ones we have now; rather,

---

8. This section probably signifies the revolution, which Chernyshevsky could not describe because of tsarist censorship.

they're rich and abundant. Is that really wheat? Whoever saw ears and kernels like these? Now such ears and kernels can only be grown in greenhouses. The fields are our fields, but now such blossoms can only be seen in flower gardens. The orchards are full of lemons and orange trees, peach and apricot—how can they grow in the fresh air? Oh, there are columns surrounding them, all open for summer. Yes, these are greenhouses opened up for summer. The groves are our groves—oak and linden, maple and elm—yes, the groves are just like ours now. Great care has been lavished on them; there's not a single diseased tree. But the groves are just like ours, they alone have remained the same as they were before. But this building—what on earth is it? What style of architecture? There's nothing at all like it now. No, there is one building that hints at it—the palace at Sydenham:[9] cast iron and crystal, crystal and cast iron—nothing else. No, that's not all; it's merely the shell of the building, its external facade. Inside there's a real house, a colossal one, surrounded by this crystal and cast iron edifice as if by a sheath, forming broad galleries around it on every floor. What graceful architecture in the inner house! What narrow spaces between the windows! The windows themselves are huge, wide, and stretch the entire height of each floor. The stone walls look like a row of pilasters that form a frame for these windows looking out onto the galleries. What sort of floors and ceilings are these? Of what material are these doors and windowframes made? What is it? Silver? Platinum? Almost all the furniture is made the same way! Wooden furniture here is merely a whim, something for variety's sake. But of what are all the other pieces, the ceilings, and the floors made? "Try to move this armchair," says the elder goddess. The metallic furniture is lighter than walnut. What kind of metal is it? Oh, now I know. Sasha once showed me a small piece of it that was as light as glass. They make earrings and brooches from it now. Yes, Sasha said that sooner or later aluminum[1] would replace wood, and perhaps even stone. How elegant it all is! Aluminum and more aluminum; all the spaces between the windows are hung with huge mirrors. What carpets on the floors! Here in this hall half the floor has been left uncovered and one can see that it too is made of aluminum. "You see, it's been left unpolished so that it won't be too slippery. Children play here, and adults do, too. In that hall the floor has been left completely uncovered for dancing. There are tropical flowers and trees everywhere. The entire house is a huge winter garden.

But who lives in this house which is more magnificent than any palace? "Many people live here, a great many. Come along and we shall see them."

They go out onto the balcony that leads off the top floor of the gallery. Why hadn't Vera Pavlovna noticed them before? Groups of people are

9. A reference to the Crystal Palace, an innovative building of glass and steel designed by Sir Joseph Paxton and erected at Hyde Park in London for the Great Exhibition in 1851.
1. A metallic element first isolated by Friedrich Wöhler in 1827 and produced industrially in 1854.

scattered throughout the fields. There are men and women everywhere, old people and young, together with children. But primarily there are young people. There are very few old men and even fewer old women; there are more children than old men, but not many of them either. More than half the children have remained inside to attend to the housework. They do almost all the chores and enjoy their work very much. A few old women work with them. But there are really very few old men and women here because people grow old very late. Life is so healthy and peaceful that it preserves one's freshness.

The groups working in the fields are almost all singing. What kind of labor are they doing? Oh, they're gathering in the grain. How quickly it progresses! Why shouldn't it? Why shouldn't they be singing? Machines are doing almost all the work for them—reaping, blinding the sheaves, and carting them away. People have only to walk alongside, or ride, or drive the machines. How cleverly they've arranged it all for themselves. Although the weather's very hot, it doesn't bother them at all. They've erected a huge canopy over the part of the field where there're working. As the work progresses, the canopy gets moved along too. How cool they stay! Why shouldn't their labor go quickly and cheerfully? Why shouldn't they be singing? I too wouldn't mind harvesting under such conditions! And there are songs and more songs, all of them new and unfamiliar. Now they're singing one of ours which I know too:

> You and I will live like kings:
> These people are our friends—
> Whatever your heart desires,
> I will acquire it all with them.[2]

Now the work is finished and everyone returns to the building. "Let's go back to the hall and see how they dine," says the elder sister. They enter the largest of the huge halls. Half of it is occupied by tables which have already been set. There are so many of them! How many people dine here? A thousand or more. Not everyone's here; those who prefer, dine in their own rooms. The old men and women and the children who didn't work in the fields have prepared everything. "To prepare food, do the housework, clean the rooms—this work is too easy for other hands," says the elder sister. "It's appropriate that such tasks be done by those who aren't yet able, or who are no longer able, to do anything else." What splendid place settings! All aluminum and crystal. Vases with flowers have been placed in the center of the wide tables. The food has already been served. The workers have entered and sat down to dinner, as have those who prepared the meal.

"Who'll serve the food?"

"When? During the meal? Why? There are only five or six courses.

___

2. A quotation from the poem "Flight" (1838) by the lyric poet Aleksei Koltsov (1809-42).

Those dishes which are supposed to be hot have been positioned so that they won't grow cold. Do you see these indentations? They're steam tables," explains the elder sister.

"You live well and like to eat well. Do you dine like this often?"

"Several times a year."

"Here this is regular fare: whoever desires can have better food, whatever he wants, and a separate account is kept. No such account is kept for those who don't require anything except those dishes prepared for all. Everything else is arranged in the same way. What everyone can afford together is provided free; but a charge is made for any special item or whim."

"Is that really us? Is that really our country? I heard one of our own songs and they are all speaking Russian."

"Yes, you see that river not far from here? It's the Oka.[3] These people are Russians—for when I'm with you, I too am a Russian."

"Did you accomplish all this?"

"All this was accomplished for my sake; I inspired it and inspire its completion. But it's she, my elder sister, the worker, who's bringing it into being. I merely delight in it."

"And will everyone live like this?"

"Everyone," says the elder sister. "For everyone there will be eternal spring and summer and joy everlasting. But we've shown you only the end of my half of the day; the work part, and the beginning of her half. We'll look in on them again during an evening two months from now."

9.

The flowers have withered and the leaves have begun to fall from the trees; the scene has become more desolate.

"You see, it would be tedious to keep looking at all this and very boring to live here," says the younger sister. "I don't want to live like this."

"The halls are empty; there's no one left in the fields or gardens," says the elder sister. "I arranged all this according to the will of my sister, the goddess."

"Has the palace really been deserted?"

"Yes, for now it's cold and damp. Why should anyone live here? Out of some two thousand people only ten or twenty eccentrics remain who feel that for once it would provide a pleasant diversion to stay in this remote and solitary area and experience a northern autumn. Soon, during the winter, there'll be constant changes: small groups of people who like winter outings will arrive to spend a few days here."

"But where are they all now?"

"Wherever it's warm and pleasant," says the elder sister. "In the

---

3. A northern tributary of the Volga River, the Oka lies somewhat south and east of Moscow.

summer, when it's nice to be here and there's work to be done, many different guests arrive from the south. We were in a building where all the inhabitants came from your country. But a great many houses had to be built to accommodate all the guests; in some, people from different lands have settled together with their hosts. Each person chooses the company which suits him best. But, having received this multitude of guests for the summer to help with the work, you can head south to spend the other seven or eight unpleasant months of the year; each person goes wherever he chooses. There's a special region in the south where the majority of your people go. It's even called "New Russia."

"Is that where Odessa and Kherson are?"[4]

"That was in your time. Behold: here's New Russia."

Mountains are clad in gardens; between them stand narrow valleys and broad ravines. "Previously these mountains were barren cliffs," says the elder sister. "Now they're covered with a thick layer of soil; groves of very tall trees grow among gardens. Below, in moist hollows, are coffee plantations. Date palms and fig trees stand above; vineyards are interspersed among sugar cane plantations; in the green fields grows some wheat, but mainly rice."

"What country is this?"

"Let's climb a little higher and you'll see its borders."

Far off to the northeast there are two rivers which flow together and head due east from where Vera Pavlovna stands. Farther to the south, still in the same southeasterly direction, there lies a long, wide bay. The land extends far to the south, continually growing wider between that bay and another longer, narrow one which forms its western boundary. Between the small western bay and the sea far to the northwest lies a narrow isthmus.

"We're in the middle of a desert," says Vera Pavlovna in astonishment.

"Well, in the middle of a former desert. But now, as you can see, this whole expanse of land from the north, from that large river in the northeast, has been transformed into the most fertile fields, just as that other strip along the sea to the north once used to be and now is once again, the strip that once upon a time was called 'the land of milk and honey'?[5] You can see that we're not far from the southern boundary of the cultivated land. The mountainous part of the peninsula is still a barren, sandy steppe, such as the whole area used to be in your day. With each passing year you Russians are pushing back the edge of the desert further to the south. Other people are at work in other countries; everyone has ample room and sufficient work. Life is spacious and abundant. Yes, from the great northeastern river the entire expanse of

---

4. Both major cities and ports in southern Russia. Odessa is located on the coast of the Black Sea, while Kherson lies near the mouth of the Dniepr River.

5. An allusion both to the land promised by God to Moses for the Jews (Exodus 3.8) and to the biblical garden of Eden. The area described is the valley of the Tigris and Euphrates rivers, viewed by Vera Pavlovna from the Sinai Peninsula, where, on Mount Sinai, Moses received the Ten Commandments.

land to the middle of the peninsula in the south is now green and covered with flowers. Throughout the whole area, just as in the north, enormous buildings stand three or four versts apart, like innumerable huge chessmen on a gigantic chessboard. Let's go down and enter one of them," says the elder sister.

It's the same sort of enormous crystal building, but its columns are white.

"They're made of aluminum," explains the elder sister. It's very hot here and white doesn't absorb heat in the direct sun. It's a bit more expensive than cast-iron, but it's better suited to local conditions."

Look what else they've invented! For a considerable distance all around the crystal palace there stand rows of tall, thin pillars; on top of them, high above the entire palace and for about half a verst around, stretches a white canopy. "It's continually being sprinkled with water," explains the elder sister. "From each pillar a small fountain rises above the canopy spraying drops of water like rain. Consequently, it's cool to reside here. You see, they can adjust the temperature as they please."

"But what if someone likes the intense heat and bright southern sun?"

"Do you see those pavilions and tents way out there in the distance? Everyone can live just as he pleases. I'm striving toward that end, working in order to bring it about."

"Then are there still cities left for those who wish to live in them?"

"Yes, but there aren't very many people left like that. There are fewer cities now and they are all located near the best harbors as centers of communication and transportation. But these cities are larger and more splendid than before. Everyone visits them for a few days in search of diversion. The majority of their inhabitants changes constantly. People go there only to work for a brief period."

"But what about those who want to live there all the time?"

"They do, just as you live in those Petersburgs, Parises, and Londons of yours. Whose business is it? Who would interfere? Let each person live as he chooses. The vast majority, however, ninety-nine people out of a hundred, live as my sister and I have shown you because it's more pleasant and advantageous for them. But now let's go into the palace. It's already quite late in the evening and time to see them."

"But no, first I want to know how it all came about."

"How *what* came about?"

"How the barren desert was transformed into fertile land where almost everyone spends two-thirds of the year."

"How it came about? There's nothing strange about it! All of this transpired not in one year, not even in ten; I accomplished it gradually. From the banks of the great river in the northeast and the shores of the great sea in the southwest, people transported clay on their mighty machines to bind the sand. They dug canals and irrigated the land; vegetation began to appear and, as a result, there was more moisture in the air. They moved forward, step by step, a few versts a year, sometimes only one, just as now they keep advancing toward the south. What's so unusual about that? People merely became more intelligent and began to turn to their own advantage the tremendous means and resources which had previously been wasted or used counterproductively. I've not been working and teaching in vain. It was even difficult for them to understand what was most useful. During your time people were still savages, such coarse, cruel, and reckless creatures. But I kept teaching them. Once they began to understand, it was not hard for them to make progress. You know that I require nothing too difficult. Why you yourself are doing something for me, in my own way! Is it really so hard?"

"No."

"Of course not. Remember your own dressmaking establishment? Did you have many resources? Any more than others?"

"No. We had no resources to speak of."

"But now your seamstresses have ten times more comfort. They enjoy life twenty times as much and experience unpleasantness a hundred times less than others who had the same resources as you. You've proven that even in your own time people can lead a free and easy life. One has only to be rational, to know how to organize, and to learn how to use resources most advantageously."

"Yes, yes. I know that."

"Let's see how people live only a short time after they've come to understand what you've long understood."

10.

They enter the building. It's the same sort of enormous, majestic hall. The evening is well under way. It's already three hours after sunset, a time for merry-making. How brightly the hall is lit, but how? There are neither candelabra nor chandeliers! Oh, that's it! In the dome there hangs a large pane of frosted glass through which light pours into the room. Of course, that's just how it ought to be: pale, soft, bright light, just like sunlight. Yes, indeed, it's electric light.[6] There are about a thousand people in the hall, but it could easily accommodate three times that number.

"And it happens, when guests come to visit," says the radiant beauty, "there can be more people here."

"Well, what sort of event is it? A ball? Surely it's not just an ordinary weekday evening?"

"Of course."

"Nowadays this would be a palace ball. The women are dressed so elegantly. Yes, indeed, times have changed, that's clear from the cut of their dresses. A few ladies are wearing the clothes of our time, but obviously it's being done for variety's sake, as an amusement. Yes, they're

6. Electric lighting became widespread in urban Russia only in the early twentieth century.

being silly, mocking our apparel. Others are wearing different costumes—the most diverse kinds, various eastern and southern styles, all much more graceful than ours. But the most popular costume is similar to that which Grecian women wore during the elegant Athenian period. It's very light and loose-fitting. The men wear long, wide tunics without waists, like cloaks or togas. Apparently, it's their ordinary domestic wear. How modest and lovely! It outlines their bodies so elegantly and exquisitely; it enhances the grace of all their movements. And what an orchestra! More than a hundred men and women! Best of all, what a chorus!"

"Yes, today in all of Europe you couldn't find ten such fine voices, one hundred of which are now gathered in this hall. It's the same in every other hall. The way of life here is so different: it's healthy and very elegant. As a result, the chest improves and the voice does too," explains the radiant beauty. But the members of both the orchestra and the chorus are constantly changing: some leave while others take their place. Some go off to dance, others return.

It's an ordinary, weekday evening. People dance like this and make merry every evening. But when have I ever seen such energy in merriment? But how can their merriment help but possess an energy unknown to us? They spend the morning engaged in very hard work. Anyone who's not put in a good day's work hasn't sufficiently prepared his nervous system to experience the fullness of such enjoyment. The merriment of simple people, when they have occasion to make merry, is so much more joyous, lively, and spontaneous than ours. But now our simple people have very meager means for amusement; here the means are so much greater than even ours are. Furthermore, the merriment of our simple people is marred by the memory of various inconveniences and deprivations, misfortunes and sufferings, and by a foreboding of even more in the future. They have but a fleeting moment when grief and need are forgotten. Is it ever really possible to forget one's grief and need entirely? Don't the deserts cover everything with sand? Don't the marshy miasmas contaminate even a small amount of good land and air lying between desert and swamp? But there are no such memories here, no danger of grief or need, only the recollection of free and willing labor, of abundance, goodness, and enjoyment. Here we have only the expectation of more of the same in the future. What a contrast! And again, the nervous system of our workers today is strong, but nothing more; although they can withstand considerable merriment, they are coarse and insensitive. Whereas here their constitution is still strong, like that of our workers, as well as developed and impressionable, like our own. But they also possess a readiness to make merry, a healthy, strong desire for enjoyment which we lack; such is granted only to those of sound health who do physical labor. In such people these qualities are combined with all the delicacy of feeling which we possess. They have all our moral development combined with the physical growth of our strong working people. It's easy to understand why their merriment, enjoyment, and passion are so much stronger, broader, sweeter, and livelier than ours. What fortunate people!

No, people still don't know what genuine merriment really is because neither the kind of life nor the sort of people necessary for it yet exists. Only people such as these can enjoy themselves completely and know the full ecstasy of pleasure. How they burst with health and strength, how graceful and elegant they are, how energetic and expressive their features! They're all so lucky, such handsome men and women, leading a free life of work and enjoyment. What fortunate people! What fortunate people!

Half of them are enjoying themselves exuberantly in the large hall. But where's the other half?

"Where are the others?" repeats the radiant beauty. "They're everywhere. Many are at the theater, some as actors, others as musicians, and still others as spectators, just as they desire. Some are in lecture halls, museums, and libraries. Others are in garden avenues or in their own rooms, relaxing alone or with their children. As for the rest: that's my secret.[7] In the hall you saw how their cheeks glowed and their eyes sparkled. You saw how they came and went. When they leave, it's I who lures them away. The room of each man and woman is my sanctuary. Within those walls my mysteries are inviolable. The curtained doors and thick carpets absorb every sound. Silence and mystery prevail. They return: it's I who brings them back from my kingdom of mysteries into the realm of light entertainment. I reign here.

"Here I reign. Everything is done for my sake! Work equals replenishment of feeling and strength for me; enjoyment equals preparation for me, relaxation after me. I constitute the purpose of life here; I am all of life."

11.

"Life's greatest happiness resides in my sister, the goddess," says the elder sister. "But you see that every kind of happiness exists here, whatever anyone desires. Everyone lives as he desires; each and every person has complete will, yes, free will."

"What we've shown you will not soon reach its full development in the form that you've just seen. Many generations will pass before everything which you can now foresee is to be fully realized. No, not many generations. My work is progressing quickly, faster with each passing year. Nevertheless, you still won't enter into my sister's completed kingdom. But at least you've glimpsed it, and now you know what the future will be. It's radiant and beautiful. Tell everyone that the future will be

7. An allusion to sexual love.

radiant and beautiful. Love it, strive toward it, work for it, bring it nearer, transfer into the present as much as you can from it. To the extent that you succeed in doing so, your life will be bright and good, rich in joy and pleasure. Strive toward it, work for it, bring it nearer, transfer into the present as much as you can from it."

RESPONSES

Parody

M. E. SALTYKOV-SHCHEDRIN

From "The Swallows"†

Fourth Swallow [a "despondent writer of fiction," i.e., Fyodor Dostoevsky, summarizing the contents of his new work]:

* * *

The new work I've finished is entitled *Notes on the Immortality of the Soul* . . . These *Notes* are related by a sick and spiteful swallow. At first he goes on about all sorts of nonsense: how he's sick and spiteful; how everything in the world is upside-down, how he's got a pain in the small of his back, how no one can tell whether there'll be a lot of mushrooms next summer, and finally how everyone is rubbish and won't become good until he becomes convinced that he is rubbish, and in conclusion, of course, he shifts to the real subject of his reflections. He derives his proofs primarily from Thomas Aquinas[1], but since he remains silent on this point, the reader believes that these ideas belong to the narrator himself. Then there's the setting of the story. It's neither dark nor light on stage, but some kind of grayish color; no live voices are heard, only hissing; no live images are seen, but it seems as if bats are dashing about in the twilight. This is not a world of fantasy, nor is it real, but a something in-between.[2] Everyone's weeping, not about anything in particular, but simply because everyone's got a sharp pain in the small of his back.

---

† Mikhail Evgrafovich Saltykov-Shchedrin (1826–89) was the most important satirical writer in mid-nineteenth century Russia. The Russian word *stryzh* is usually translated as "martin," but this 1864 satire on Dostoevsky's journalistic endeavors in general and *Notes from Underground* in particular is traditionally entitled "The Swallows." From F. M. Dostoevsky, *Polnoe sobranie sochinenii v tridsati tomakh* (Leningrad: Nauka, 1973), vol. 5, p. 382, translated by Michael R. Katz.

1. Thomas Aquinas (1225–74) was an Italian the- ologian and philosopher, the greatest figure of the scholastic movement, and the founder of the system declared to be the official philosophy of the Roman Catholic church.

2. The Russian phrase *kisel'nyi mir* is derived from the word *kisel'*, a sweet, jellylike desert made from fruit purée and a starchy substance. Its consistency is neither solid nor liquid, but something in-between, used here metaphorically to represent a realm midway between fantasy and reality.

WOODY ALLEN

Notes from the Overfed†

(After reading Dostoevski and the new "Weight Watchers" magazine on the same plane trip)

I am fat. I am disgustingly fat. I am the fattest human I know. I have nothing but excess poundage all over my body. My fingers are fat. My wrists are fat. My eyes are fat. (Can you imagine fat eyes?) I am hundreds of pounds overweight. Flesh drips from me like hot fudge off a sundae. My girth has been an object of disbelief to everyone who's seen me. There is no question about it, I'm a regular fatty. Now, the reader may ask, are there advantages or disadvantages to being built like a planet? I do not mean to be facetious or speak in paradoxes, but I must answer that fat in itself is above bourgeois morality. It is simply fat. That fat could have a value of its own, that fat could be, say, evil or pitying, is, of course, a joke. Absurd! For what is fat after all but an accumulation of pounds? And what are pounds? Simply an aggregate composite of cells. Can a cell be moral? Is a cell beyond good or evil? Who knows—they're so small. No, my friend, we must never attempt to distinguish between good fat and bad fat. We must train ourselves to confront the obese without judging, without thinking this man's fat is first-rate fat and this poor wretch's is grubby fat.

Take the case of K. This fellow was porcine to such a degree that he could not fit through the average doorframe without the aid of a crowbar. Indeed, K. would not think to pass from room to room in a conventional dwelling without first stripping completely and then buttering himself. I am no stranger to the insults K. must have borne from passing gangs of young rowdies. How frequently he must have been stung by cries of "Tubby!" and "Blimp!" How it must have hurt when the governor of the province turned to him on the Eve of Michaelmas and said, before many dignitaries, "You hulking pot of *kasha!*"

Then one day, when K. could stand it no longer, he dieted. Yes, dieted! First sweets went. Then bread, alcohol, starches, sauces. In short K. gave up the very stuff that makes a man unable to tie his shoelaces without help from the Santini Brothers. Gradually he began to slim down. Rolls of flesh fell from his arms and legs. Where once he looked roly-poly, he suddenly appeared in public with a normal build. Yes, even an attractive build. He seemed the happiest of men. I say "seemed," for eighteen years later, when he was near death and fever raged throughout his slender frame, he was heard to cry out, "My fat! Bring me my fat! Oh, please! I must have my fat! Oh, somebody lay some avoirdupois on me! What a fool I've been. To part with one's fat! I must have been in league with the Devil!" I think that the point of the story is obvious.

Now the reader is probably thinking, Why, then, if you are Lard City, have you not joined the circus? Because—and I confess this with no small embarrassment—I cannot leave the house. I cannot go out because I cannot get my pants on. My legs are too thick to dress. They are the living result of more corned beef than there is on Second Avenue—I would say about twelve thousand sandwiches per leg. And not all lean, even though I specified. One thing is certain: If my fat could speak, it would probably speak of a man's intense loneliness—with, oh, perhaps a few additional pointers on how to make a sailboat out of paper. Every pound on my body wants to be heard from, as do Chins Four through Twelve inclusive. My fat is strange fat. It has seen much. My calves alone have lived a lifetime. Mine is not happy fat, but it is real fat. It is not fake fat. Fake fat is the worst fat you can have, although I don't know if the stores still carry it.

But let me tell you how it was that I became fat. For I was not always fat. It is the Church that has made me thus. At one time I was thin— quite thin. So thin, in fact that to call me fat would have been an error in perception. I remained thin until one day—I think it was my twentieth birthday—when I was having tea and cracknels with my uncle at a fine restaurant. Suddenly my uncle put a question to me. "Do you believe in God?" he asked. "And if so, what do you think He weighs?" So saying, he took a long and luxurious draw at his cigar and, in that confident, assured manner he has cultivated, lapsed into a coughing fit so violent I thought he would hemorrhage.

"I do not believe in God, " I told him. "For if there is a God, then tell me, Uncle, why is there poverty and baldness? Why do some men go through life immune to a thousand mortal enemies of the race, while others get a migraine that lasts for week? Why are our days numbered and not, say, lettered? Answer me, Uncle. Or have I shocked you?"

I knew I was safe in saying this, because nothing ever shocked the man. Indeed, he had seen his chess tutor's mother raped by Turks and would have found the whole incident amusing had it not taken so much time.

"Good nephew," he said, "there is a God, despite what you think, and He is everywhere. Yes? Everywhere!"

"Everywhere, Uncle? How can you say that when you don't even know for sure if we exist? True, I am touching your wart at this moment, but could that not be an illusion? Could not all life be an illusion? Indeed, are there not certain sects of holy men in the East who are convinced that *nothing* exists outside their minds except for the Oyster Bar at Grand Central Station? Could it not be simply that we are alone and aimless, doomed to wander in an indifferent universe, with no hope

of salvation, nor any prospect except misery, death, and the empty reality
of eternal nothing?"

I could see that I made a deep impression on my uncle with this, for
he said to me, "You wonder why you're not invited to more parties!
Jesus, you're morbid!" He accused me of being nihilistic and then said,
in that cryptic way the senile have, "God is not always where one seeks
Him, but I assure you, dear nephew, He is everywhere. In these cracknels, for instance." With that, he departed, leaving me his blessing and
a check that read like a tab for an aircraft carrier.

I returned home wondering what it was he meant by that one simple
statement "He is everywhere. In these cracknels, for instance." Drowsy
by then, and out of sorts I lay down on my bed and took a brief nap.
In that time, I had a dream that was to change my life forever. In the
dream, I am strolling in the country, when I suddenly notice I am
hungry. Starved, if you will, I come upon a restaurant and I enter. I
order the open-hot-roast-beef sandwich and a side of French. The wait-
ress, who resembles my landlady (a thoroughly insipid woman who
reminds one instantly of some of the hairier lichens), tries to tempt me
into ordering the chicken salad, which doesn't look fresh. As I am
conversing with this woman, she turns into a twenty-four-piece starter
set of silverware, I become hysterical with laughter, which suddenly
turns to tears and then into a serious ear infection. The room is suffused
with a radiant glow, and I see a shimmering figure approach on a white
steed. It is my podiatrist, and I fall to the ground with guilt.

Such was my dream. I awoke with a tremendous sense of well-being.
Suddenly I was optimistic. Everything was clear. My uncle's statement
reverberated to the core of my very existence. I went to the kitchen and
started to eat. I ate everything in sight. Cakes, breads, cereals, meat,
fruits. Succulent chocolates, vegetables in sauce, wines, fish, creams
and noodles, éclairs, and wursts totalling in excess of sixty thousand
dollars. If God is everywhere, I had concluded, then He is in food.
Therefore, the more I ate the godlier I would become. Impelled by this
new religious fervor, I glutted myself like a fanatic. In six months, I was
the holiest of holies, with a heart entirely devoted to my prayers and a
stomach that crossed the state line by itself. I last saw my feet one
Thursday morning in Vitebsk, although for all I know they are still down
there. I ate and ate and grew and grew. To reduce would have been the
greatest folly. Even a sin! For when we lose twenty pounds, dear reader
(and I am assuming you are not as large as I), we may be losing the
twenty best pounds we have! We may be losing the pounds that contain
our genius, our humanity our love and honesty or, in the case of one
inspector general I knew, just some unsightly flab around the hips.

Now, I know what you are saying. You are saying this is in direct
contradiction to everything—yes, everything—I put forth before. Suddenly I am attributing to neuter flesh, values! Yes, and what of it? Because

isn't life that very same kind of contradiction? One's opinion of fat can change in the same manner that the seasons change, that our hair changes, that life itself changes. For life is change and fat is life, and fat is also death. Don't you see? Fat is everything! Unless, of course, you're overweight.

Imitation/Inspiration

ROBERT WALSER

The Child†

Unfortunately, he was only a schoolboy or an apprentice, a child. Prestige he had none, instead a sweetheart with a dainty little mouth and puzzling stare with which she at first soundly 'punished' the child. Basically children are very high-spirited; one has to intimidate them right from the start. The child has always been faint-hearted towards his beloved. He would have liked a mandolin or some other instrument for striking up songs in praise of his mistress. In theory, he heaped presents upon her; in practice, he was too frugal, too much the petty-bourgeois householder. In his thoughts a child is always very daring; faced with reality he trembles, delicately shirking the tasks he has set himself. He had the nervous temperament of a dog, let's say a whippet. While he was frolicking, nothing could equal his pleasure. At one time, the child was a man capable of putting on urbane airs. But people easily noticed the childlikeness lurking everywhere, and his feigned self-assurance thus came to nothing. Timidity, however, he knew not, at least not for long; and he laughed at the mockery of the strong. Scorn and unfeeling treatment made him happy. What was to be done? The child's years now numbered forty, already a little over, actually; but let us spare him such truths, just as one does not bother ladies with them. He had doe-eyes, and unwisely accepted all offers from generous hands; later on, however, he made up his mind to accept more cautiously, to donate rather than to pocket. Doing the latter, one risks being called a sponger. Was the child once energetic? Some think so; others say he has remained himself all along. Earlier, you know, he wrote fat books, in other words, poetically surveyed his beholdings. Now he had to rely on living and for that he at first found no form. Since he kept people waiting for a novel, they scolded him for his sluggishness. He was incredibly slack, so it went, and throughout the land was said to have no heart, whereas it had never before been so wide open. Is it really necessary to have publishable manuscripts in one's pocket to be able to identify oneself as an educated person? The child did indeed lose a cruel amount of time

† From *Comparative Criticism*, vol. 6 (1984), pp. 261-264. Reprinted by permission of Cambridge University Press, translated by Mark Harman.

in inward service and in love. He called the lady in question mama, once again a sign of immaturity. But this much we must say for him: he never claimed he ought to be considered mature. Occasionally he behaved loutishly. Defend him? Wouldn't dream of it! Does the sort need any such thing? 'You, who used to arouse attention, displaying the brightest mind and the most beautiful handwriting, how little you now have to show for yourself! If I were you, I'd feel dejected. Pull yourself together!' Thus spoke a former schoolmate. Becoming just the tiniest bit angry, the child from then on treated the remonstrator frostily. Now, there are cases where advancing becomes more difficult for an individual, and what's then left of understanding? Successes are understood, inhibitions laughed at. The child, for instance, could not come up with a single word in front of his beloved, having such a heap of words in readiness that he wished to tell her everything at once, wanted to spread out the whole supply. So he simply kept staring at her; that bored her, naturally, who had found him amusing. Was he ever entertaining? Those who know him closely can both affirm and deny that. He had forever considered himself good company only in exceptional cases. Former lady friends were fond of him because with them he made as much use of his ears as of his mouth. Being silent can be as pleasant as talking. There were those who felt they ought to shake him up, with 'obviously', for instance, or: 'A child can grasp that', supposed exhortations that he sharpen his wits. Observing them, the child saw each one all wrapped in his skin, an observation he considered as soothing as could be. The child sported tangled hair, and often turned up unwashed in the most reputable of apartments; he did so not out of poverty, but rather out of vanity. His opponents easily saw through all this, but inwardly the child had no enemy, and could thus put up with everyone effortlessly. Did his 'love' mean arrest? He was in love for the first time. His lady did not accord him the slightest favour; not that he needed any, for that matter. Children, by the way, are often difficult to handle. I am of the opinion one shouldn't go too much out of one's way for them, precisely because they are demanding, and expressions of understanding tend to annoy rather than satisfy them.

The child once wrote the following:

Yes, I am a bad person, in other words, a fine and educated one. Fine persons have the right to be bad. Only the uneducated feel it their duty to be virtuous. What was it that I inflicted on an office clerk? I did not admit she was right in every respect. Her anger made her ill. A pretty young girl wanted to know whether I was an admirer of hers. Since I failed to show any understanding, things went downhill for her, whereas I was able to keep myself on top. I bow to ladies, only to ignore them the next day, thus spreading discomfort. Other people's discomfort comforts me; their quarrels bring me peace. How vapid are cheerful faces; how funny serious ones! For a while I loved a girl because she

definitely seemed a bit dim-witted. Imbecility does have a certain fascination. I am someone who does not know precisely who he really is.
Sometimes I am as sensitive as a girl. How boring to hear talk of the
countryside and so on! Educated people ought to realize that it is cheap
to fall back on the exclamation 'wonderful' when discussing a work of
art. Praise can seem pretty mindless. Being in raptures verges at times
on stupidity. Happy people easily make themselves unpopular. Is it not
almost shameless to parade your high spirits, to let your eyes shine so
freely? Any minute the merriment can peter out. We ought to ration
our contentment. I prefer to be accommodating when no one expects
it, rather than when people think I do so gladly. Nobody is entitled to
treat me as if he knew me. When I recognize somebody, I do not say
so to his face, thus appearing indelicate and arousing displeasure. Being
educated and being intellectual is not the same thing. 'Miss, did you
get your Pfitzner?' I heard somebody ask. Which seems to have bored
the lady in question. Women are not to be snared with elegant phrases;
nor do they make catches with them either. Not long ago someone
scolded me out of inclination. My serenity annoyed him. One can almost
do in somebody with modesty. Irony can liberate as well as torment. I
am one of those who have read Dostoevsky. Because I wasn't nice to
her, a lady declared me crazy. In future I will do likewise to others.
Superior people make me feel superior; modest ones baffle me. Behind
modesty one suspects power. Occasionally I am a little nasty, but never
for long. Nothing puts me in such a cheerful mood as having cause to
pull myself together. We live but once in this wonderful world. At times
the commonplace is quite wonderful. All too much music is unhealthy,
too much goodness likewise. Many people consider me spoiled, and yet
no girl has ever kissed me. Recently I saw a boy whom I would right
away have liked to serve as friend or tutor, so appealing were his features.
He resembled my beloved, and I could not take my eyes off him. That
I have a beloved amazes and pleases me; I find that very clever of me.
Cannot a beloved be a capital excuse for so much? For marriage I am
too old and too young, too shrewd and too inexperienced. But if it comes
to it, I won't say no. People are often thought competent merely because
they are loud, a proof of the importance of surfaces. Acting superficial,
I please others. Through frivolity one can win them over. In love, one
behaves unlovably; that's why lovers meet with little approval. Love does
not seem as strong as its semblance. Edith treats me like a silly boy.
What is attachment other than sillyboyishness? Towards me she quite
rightly plays the servere mama, reprimanding me, finding me unsuitable.
What she resembles is a piano teacher—majestic, but with a roguish
touch. I love her terribly. To the mind, feeling seems untenable. What
the former approves, the soul disdains; what it recommends, the heart
banishes. How, a hundred times by now, you have quietly made a
Croesus of me, O heart! She has driven me away; I do her bidding,
don't see her any more. A child is happy obeying.

RALPH ELLISON

From *The Invisible Man*†

Prologue

I am an invisible man. No, I am not a spook like those who haunted
Edgar Allan Poe; nor am I one of your Hollywood-movie ectoplasms.
I am a man of substance, of flesh and bone, fiber and liquids—and I
might even be said to possess a mind. I am invisible, understand, simply
because people refuse to see me. Like the bodiless heads you see sometimes in circus sideshows, it is as though I have been surrounded by
mirrors of hard, distorting glass. When they approach me they see only
my surroundings, themselves, or figments of their imagination—indeed,
everything and anything except me.

Nor is my invisibility exactly a matter of a bio-chemical accident to
my epidermis. That invisibility to which I refer occurs because of a
peculiar disposition of the eyes of those with whom I come in contact.
A matter of the construction of their inner eyes, those eyes with which
they look though their physical eyes upon reality. I am not complaining,
nor am I protesting either. It is sometimes advantageous to be unseen,
although it is most often rather wearing on the nerves. Then too, you're
constantly being bumped against by those of poor vision. Or again, you
often doubt if you really exist. You wonder whether you aren't simply
a phantom in other people's minds. Say, a figure in a nightmare which
the sleeper tries with all his strength to destroy. It's when you feel like
this that, out of resentment, you begin to bump people back. And, let
me confess, you feel that way most of the time. You ache with the need
to convince yourself that you do exist in the real world, that you're a
part of all the sound and anguish, and you strike out with your fists,
you curse and you swear to make them recognize you. And, alas, it's
seldom sucessful.

One night I accidentally bumped into a man, and perhaps because
of the near darkness he saw me and called me an insulting name. I
sprang at him, seized his coat lapels and demanded that he apologize.
He was a tall blonde man, and as my face came close to his he looked
insolently out of his blue eyes and cursed me, his breath hot on my face
as he struggled. I pulled his chin down sharp upon the crown of my
head, butting him as I had seen the West Indians do, and I felt his flesh
tear and the blood gush out, and I yelled, "Apologize! Apologize!" But
he continued to curse and struggle, and I butted him again and again
until he went down heavily, on his knees, profusely bleeding. I kicked
him repeatedly, in a frenzy because he still uttered insults though his

† From *The Invisible Man* by Ralph Ellison. Copyright 1952 by Ralph Ellison. Reprinted by permission
of Random House, Inc.

lips were frothy with blood. Oh yes, I kicked him! And in my outrage I got out my knife and prepared to slit his throat, right there beneath the lamplight in the deserted street, holding him by the collar with one hand, and opening the knife with my teeth—when it occurred to me that the man had not *seen* me, actually; that he, as far as he knew, was in the midst of a walking nightmare! And I stopped the blade, slicing the air as I pushed him away, letting him fall back to the street. I stared at him hard as the lights of the car stabbed through the darkness. He lay there, moaning on the asphalt; a man almost killed by a phantom. It unnerved me. I was both disgusted and ashamed. I was like a drunken man myself, wavering about on weakened legs. Then I was amused. Something in this man's thick head had sprung out and beaten him within an inch of his life. I began to laugh at this crazy discovery. Would he have awakened at the point of death? Would Death himself have freed him for wakeful living? But I didn't linger. I ran away into the dark, laughing so hard I feared I might rupture myself. The next day I saw his picture in the *Daily News*, beneath a caption stating that he had been "mugged." Poor fool, poor blind fool, I thought with sincere compassion, mugged by an invisible man!

Most of the time (although I do not choose as I once did to deny the violence of my days by ignoring it) I am not so overtly violent. I remember that I am invisible and walk softly so as not to awaken them; there are few things in the world as dangerous as sleepwalkers. I learned in time though that it is possible to carry on a fight against them without their realizing it. For instance, I have been carrying on a fight with Mono-polated Light & Power for some time now. I use their service and pay them nothing at all, and they don't know it. Oh, they suspect that power is being drained off, but they don't know where. All they know is that according to the master meter back there in their power station a hell of a lot of free current is disappearing somewhere into the jungle of Harlem. The joke, of course, is that I don't live in Harlem but in a border area. Several years ago (before I discovered the advantage of being invisible) I went through the routine process of buying service and paying their outrageous rates. But no more. I gave up all that, along with my apartment, and my old way of life: That way based upon the fallacious assumption that I, like other men, was visible. Now, aware of my in-visibility, I live rent-free in a building rented strictly to whites, in a section of the basement that was shut off and forgotten during the nineteenth century, which I discovered when I was trying to escape in the night from Ras the Destroyer. But that's getting too far ahead of the story, almost to the end, although the end is in the beginning and lies far ahead.

The point now is that I found a home—or a hole in the ground, as you will. Now don't jump to the conclusion that because I call my home a "hole" it is damp and cold like a grave; there are cold holes and warm holes. Mine is a warm hole. And remember, a bear retires to his hole for the winter and lives until spring; then he comes strolling out like the Easter chick breaking from its shell. I say all this to assure you that it is incorrect to assume that, because I'm invisible and live in a hole, I am dead. I am neither dead nor in a state of suspended animation. Call me Jack-the-Bear, for I am in a state of hibernation.

My hole is warm and full of light. Yes, full of light. I doubt if there is a brighter spot in all New York than this hole of mine, and I do not exclude Broadway. Or the Empire State Building on a photographer's dream night. But that is taking advantage of you. Those two spots are among the darkest of our whole civilization—pardon me, our whole culture (an important distinction, I've heard)—which might sound like a hoax, or a contradiction, but that (by contradiction, I mean) is how the world moves: Not like an arrow, but a boomerang. (Beware of those who speak of the spiral of history; they are preparing a boomerang. Keep a steel helmet handy.) I know; I have been boomeranged across my head so much that I now can see the darkness of lightness. And I love light. Perhaps you'll think it strange that an invisible man should need light, desire light, love light. But maybe it is exactly because I am invisible. Light confirms my reality, gives birth to my form. A beautiful girl once told me a recurring nightmare in which she lay in the center of a large dark room and felt her face expand until it filled the whole room, becoming a formless mass while her eyes ran in bilious jelly up the chimney. And so it is with me. Without light I am not only invisible, but formless as well; and to be unaware of one's form is to live a death. I myself, after existing some twenty years, did not become alive until I discovered my invisibility. * * *

JOHN LENNON AND PAUL McCARTNEY

Nowhere Man†

He's a real nowhere man,
Sitting in his nowhere land,
Making all his nowhere plans for nobody.

Doesn't have a point of view,
Knows not where he's going to,
Isn't he a bit like you and me?

Nowhere man, please listen, you don't know,
What you're missing,
Nowhere man, the world is at your command.

He's as blind as he can be,
Just sees what he wants to see,
Nowhere man, can you see me at all?

Nowhere man, don't worry,
Take your time, don't hurry,
Leave it all till somebody else lends you a hand.

Doesn't have a point of view,
Knows not where he's going to,
Isn't he a bit like you and me?

Nowhere man, please listen, you don't know
What you're missing,
Nowhere man, the world is at your command.

He's a real nowhere man,
Sitting in his nowhere land,
Making all his nowhere plans for nobody.
Making all his nowhere plans for nobody.
Making all his nowhere plans for nobody.

CRITICISM

NIKOLAI K. MIKHAILOVSKY

[Dostoevsky's Cruel Talent]†

Let us begin with the section of the menagerie which is called *Notes from the Underground*.

The underground man (for the sake of brevity we will thus call the unknown person who relates *Notes from the Underground*) begins his notes with certain philosophical reflections. At the same time, among the reflections, which for the present are unimportant to us, but are not without brilliance and originality, he pours out his soul to the reader, trying to dig to its very bottom and to show this bottom in all its filth and abomination. A cruel unveiling takes place, precisely in order to show his audience "all the intricacies of the sensuality" of spite. This already by itself produces the impression of something oppressive, stinking, mouldy; you are really and truly sitting in the underground, or it is really some leprous sloven in front of you removing one filthy rag after another from his rotting, putrid sores. Then the unveiling shifts from the verbal to the factual, that is, the story of some of the hero's exploits is told.

* * *

I have very briefly summarized the contents of this story, passing over many extremely subtle details. The entire story presents a kind of psychological lacework. But I think that from the rough outlines through which I have conveyed the story, it is evident how deeply interested Dostoevsky was in the phenomena of cruelty, tyranny and tormenting, and how minutely he examined them. Perhaps what is most interesting in *Notes from the Underground* is the lack of motive for the underground man's animosity towards Liza. You see no reasons, whatsoever for the animosity. A person appears on the stage as a forty-year-old man, fully formed, and whatever in his life has so ruined him remains, in the words of Kaydanov, shrouded in mystery. It is as if all his infamy must be explained by some self-generation or does not even require an explanation. The story contains only general phrases, devoid of a definite content, concerning this—such as, for example, the underground man has grown unaccustomed to "real life" and has become attached to a "book" life. But suppose the author simply wants to thus depict a totally spiteful and tormenting man, and at any rate this is his, the author's affair and not a trait of the underground man's character. Much more

† From Nikolai Mikhailovsky, *A Cruel Talent*, trans. Spencer Cadmus (Ann Arbor: Ardis, 1978), pp. 13–19. Reprinted by permission of Ardis Publishers.

interesting is the fact that the underground man actually begins to torment Liza for absolutely no reason at all; it is simply that she happened
to be at hand. There are no reasons for his spite towards her, the
underground man foresees no results from his tormenting. He abandons
himself to his pastime out of love for the art, for the "intrigue." We will
encounter this unnecessary cruelty again. But now let us note that the
very placing of these pictures of cruelty within the framework of need-
lessness attests to the value which Dostoevsky attributed to this topic.
The hero might have tormented Liza with the worthy purpose of guiding
her to the way of truth; he might have taken revenge on her for some
offense, mockery, etc. The picture of the shaken soul would have been
present in all these instances. But Dostoevsky rejected all external, incidental motives: the hero torments her because he wants or likes to
torment. There is no cause or purpose here, and, according to the author,
they are not at all needed, for there is an unconditional cruelty, a cruelty
an und für sich, and that is precisely what is interesting.

Whether because of this or some other reason, it is quite difficult to
say what Dostoevsky's attitude is toward his hero. In the two or three
closing lines he gives him the morally indifferent name, "paradoxalist."
As for the mental resources of the underground man, it is possible to
find here very different things, among others are those philosophical
reflections (for example, about freedom of the will) which have absolutely
no relationship to cruelty, as well as those which are very akin to Dostoevsky himself. In *Notes from the Underground*, for example, there
appears in as yet an unclear and interrogatory form one of the favorite
ideas of the last years of Dostoevsky's career. The underground man
writes: "And why are you so firmly, so triumphantly convinced that the
normal and positive alone, in short prosperity alone is advantageous to
man? Is not reason mistaken about advantages? After all, perhaps man
likes not only prosperity? Perhaps he likes suffering just as much? Might
not suffering be just as advantageous to him as prosperity? Man sometimes terribly loves suffering, to the point of passion, and that is a fact."
If the reader were to recall how subsequently Dostoevsky passionately
preached suffering, how he saw in suffering the most intimate demand
of the spirit of the Russian people; how he elevated the jail and the penal
colony to a pearl of creation; if the reader were to recall all this, then
perhaps he would be surprised at having encountered the same ideas in
the notes of a cruel beast. But this is precisely the question whether the
underground man is also a beast from Dostoevsky's point of view. The
opinions of the underground man about himself are, at first glance,
striking for their ruthlessness: a person is willing to relate apparently any
kind of abomination. But, upon examining this strange confession more
closely, you see that the underground man not only has no objection
to showing off his ruthlessness toward himself, but also to justifying
himself to some extent. Above all he does not at all consider himself a
monster, a man exceptional by nature. To be sure, he does presume

himself to be a truly exceptional person, but only for his daring thought and clearness of conscience. He says, for example: "As for me in particular, I have, after all, in my life only carried to the extreme that which you have not dared to carry halfway, and what is more, you have taken your cowardice for discretion and have consoled yourselves with it, while deceiving yourselves." In another place, elaborately explaining "the enjoyment in a toothache," the underground man asserts that *every* "educated person of the nineteenth century" on the second or third day of a toothache will already be moaning not strictly out of pain, but out of spite. "His moans become nasty, disgustingly spiteful ones, and continue for whole days and nights. And, after all, he himself knows that he will derive no benefit at all from moans; he knows better than everyone that he is only overtaxing and irritating himself and others in vain; he knows that even the audience for whom he has been exerting himself and his whole family have been listening to him with disgust, do not believe him for a moment, and deep down understand that he could moan differently, more simply, without trills and flourishes, and that he is only indulging himself out of spite, out of malice. They say, 'I am bothering you, straining your hearts, I don't let anyone in the house sleep. Well, stay awake then, you, too, can feel every minute of my toothache. For you I am now no longer the hero I wanted to appear as before, but simply a horrid little person, a scoundrel. Well, so be it, then! I am very glad that you have seen through me. Is it nasty for you to hear my foul moans? Well, let it be nasty; here, I'll give you an even nastier flourish in a minute . . .' You still do not understand, ladies and gentlemen? No, you obviously must develop more and become more conscious to understand all the intricacies of this sensuality."

Thus, the difference between the underground man and the majority of educated people of the nineteenth century is only that he more clearly recognizes the enjoyment derived from spite, while everyone else takes advantage of this very enjoyment. Such a generalization considerably softens the underground man's self-castigation. Two in distress make sorrow less. This means that the underground man is not at all that nasty if everyone is the same; he is even above the rest, because he is more daring and more intelligent than they are. Let any of "the educated people of the nineteenth century" try to throw a stone at him.

In addition to this extenuating or even elevating circumstance, the underground man perhaps might have decided to propose one more. The reader saw that among the rosy pictures by which the underground man agonizingly wounded Liza's soul, there was the sketch of a woman tormenting her husband out of love. Then followed the generalization: "Did you know that you can deliberately torment a person out of love?" About himself the underground man says frankly: "For me to love meant to tyrannize and show moral superiority. In all my life I have not even been able to imagine a different kind of love, and have reached the point that I sometimes now think that love really consists in the right, freely given by the beloved object, to tyrannize over it. Even in my underground dreams I have not imagined love otherwise, except as a struggle, I have always begun it with hatred and ended it with moral subjugation, but afterwards I could not even imagine: what does one do with the subjugated object?" If one understands the matter in such a way that here, he says, is a monster who has never felt love, then of course much daring and sincerity are needed in order to make such a declaration. Love seems to be a feeling that is quite universally accessible and quite rewarding in itself. No special intellectual and moral eminence is needed to experience it, and in fact the pitiful, wretched monster is probably the one in whose language love and tyranny are identical or at least always accompany each other. So it is. Well, what if this apparent meagerness of thoughts and feelings is not a deformity at all, but only depth of "penetration" into the human soul? What if the soul, well, let us suppose, at least not of man in general, but only of the educated person of the nineteenth century, is so structured that love and tyranny inevitably flourish in it side by side? A simple mortal could not understand this, and what of it! A simple mortal admires the beauty of a beautiful face, while an educated person would approach it with a microscope and see in this beautiful face an entire network of very ugly wrinkles, grooves, etc. The same is true here. Refined psychologists, like the underground man and Dostoevsky himself, could find in the soul such things and such combinations of things which for us, simple mortals, are quite inaccessible. And if in fact love and tyranny grow, flourish and bear fruit side by side, even when intersecting each other, if this is in some way the law of nature, what educated person of the nineteenth century would dare to throw a stone at the underground man? The stone would bounce off him, like a pea off a wall, and would strike the thrower himself. And consequently the underground man is again justified and even glorified. For he says, not about himself, but as a general observation: "Did you know that you can deliberately torment a person out of love?"

Such a sceptical attitude toward the best or, in general, well-disposed feelings is hardly limited in the underground man to love alone. The epigraph to the story about the meeting with Liza (it has a separate title, "Apropos of the Wet Snow") is taken from Nekrasov's poem, "When from the darkness of corruption I delivered your fallen soul with the ardent speech of conviction," etc. On the lips of the underground man these words are the purest irony, for although Liza, indeed, was "filled with shame and fear," "ended up crying, confused, shaken," the underground man did not have this result in mind at all and, as we saw, was simply engaged in the "game" of wolves and sheep. But it was not without reason that this epigraph was used, and from the sceptical malice of the underground man it can be expected that the responsibility be put on everyone else: Ivan Kivaet via Petra—"put your business responsibility on someone else." That is, if such an incident took place with any of you, ladies and gentlemen, you would not fail to recite Nekrasov's poem and have at the same time a very salvational and even heroic appearance, but I know how these things happen, I know that if even in reality you have been thinking of saving a fallen soul, there was nevertheless mixed here much desire to torment a person, to torture him; I know this and am telling about myself openly, while you hide behind lofty feelings. . . .

Whether this explanation is correct or not, it is certain that in the underground man each manifestation of life is complicated by cruelty and the desire to torment. And, of course, it is not a chance coincidence that Dostoevsky himself always and everywhere examined the mixture of cruelty and spite with various feelings, which at first glance have nothing in common with them. Scattered throughout the minor stories collected in the second and third volumes of Dostoevsky's works are the germs of these unnatural combinations, germs which later were developed further.

* * *

VASILY ROZANOV

[Thought and Art in *Notes from Underground*]†

In an amazing way, Dostoevsky's enormous talent for generalization was combined with a keen receptivity to the particular and the individual. Therefore, he not only understood the general and the primary significance of what takes place in history, but also was conscious of its unbearable horror, as if he himself had experienced all the personal suffering caused by violation of the principal law of development. Immediately after *Winter Notes on Summer Impressions*, he published the gloomy *Notes from the Underground*, which we mentioned above.

In reading it, one is unexpectedly struck by our need for annotated editions—annotated not from the standpoint of the form and origin of literary works, as is already done, but from the standpoint of their contents and meaning—in order finally to decide the question of whether the idea contained in them is true, or whether it is false, and why, and to decide this by joint efforts, to decide it thoroughly and rigorously, in a way accessible only to science. For example, every line of *Notes from the Underground* is important; it is impossible to reduce the book to

† Reprinted from Vasily Rozanov, *Dostoevsky and the Legend of the Grand Inquisitor*. Translated by Spencer E. Roberts. Copyright © 1972 by Cornell University. Used by permission of the publisher, Cornell University.

general formulas. Moreover, no thinking person can pass over the assertions made in it without considering them carefully.

There never was a writer in our literature whose ideals were so completely divorced from present-day reality. The thought never for a moment occurred to Dostoevsky to try to preserve this way of life and merely improve a thing or two in it. Because of the generalizing cast of his mind, he directed all his attention toward the evil concealed in the general system of a historically developed life; hence his hatred of and disdain for all hope of improving anything by means of individual changes; hence his animosity towards our parties of progressives and Westerners. Perceiving only the "general," he passed directly from reality to the extreme in the ideal, and the first thing he encountered there was the hope of raising, with the help of reason, an edifice of human life so perfect that it would give peace to man, crown history, and put an end to suffering. His criticism of this idea runs through all his works; it was expressed for the first time, and moreover in the greatest detail, in *Notes from the Underground*.

The man from the underground is a person who has withdrawn deep within himself. He hates life and spitefully criticizes the ideal of the rational utopians on the basis of a precise knowledge of human nature, which he acquired through a long and lonely observation of himself and of history.

The outline of his criticism is as follows: man carries within himself, in an undeveloped state, a complex world of inclinations that have not yet been discovered—and their discovery will determine his future history just as inevitably as the existence of these inclinations in him now is certain. Therefore, the predetermination of history and its crown by our reason alone will always be empty talk without any real importance.

Among those inclinations, in so far as they have already revealed themselves during the course of history, there is so much that is incomprehensibly strange and irrational that it is impossible to find any intelligent formula that would satisfy human nature. Is not happiness the principle on which this formula can be constructed? But does not man sometimes crave suffering? Are there really any pleasures for which Hamlet would give up the torments of his consciousness? Are not order and regularity the common features of every final system of human relations? And yet, do we not sometimes love chaos, destruction, and disorder even more passionately than we do regularity and creation? Is it possible to find a person who would do only what is necessary and good his whole life long? And would he not, by limiting himself to this for so long, experience a strange weariness; would he not shift, at least briefly, to the poetry of instinctive actions? Finally, will not all happiness disappear for man if there disappears for him the feeling of novelty, of everything unexpected, everything capriciously changeable—things to which he now adapts his way of life, and in so doing experiences much distress, but an equal joy? Does not uniformity for everyone contradict the fundamental principle of human nature—individuality—and does not the constancy of the future and of the "ideal" contradict his free will, his thirst for choosing something or other in his own way, sometimes contrary to an external, even a rational, decision? And can man really be happy without freedom, without individuality? Without all this, with the eternal absence of novelty, will not instincts be irresistibly aroused in him such as will shatter the adamantine nature of every formula: and man will wish for suffering, destruction, blood, for everything except that to which his formula has doomed him for all eternity; in the same way that a person confined too long to a light, warm room will cut his hands on the glass of the windowpanes and run naked out into the cold, merely so as not to have to remain any longer in his former surroundings? Was it not this feeling of spiritual weariness that led Seneca into intrigue and crime? And was it not this that made Cleopatra stick gold pins into the breasts of her black slave girls, while eagerly looking them in the face, watching their trembling, smiling lips, and their frightened eyes? And finally, will the never-changing possession of the achieved ideal really satisfy a person for whom wishing, striving, and achieving is an irresistible need? And does rationality, on the whole, exhaust human nature? But obviously that is the only thing that its very creator—reason—can give to a final formula.

By nature, man is a completely irrational creature; therefore, reason can neither completely explain him nor completely satisfy him. No matter how persistent is the work of thought, it will never cover all of reality; it will answer the demands of the imaginary man, but not those of the real one. Hidden in man is the instinct for creation, and this was precisely what gave him life, what rewarded him with suffering and joy—things that reason can neither understand nor change.

The rational is one thing; the mystical is another thing again. And while it is inaccessible to the touch and power of science, it can be arrived at through religion. Hence the development of the mystical in Dostoevsky and the concentration of his interest on all that is religious, something we observe in the second and chief period of his work, which began with *Crime and Punishment.*

*   *   *

LEV SHESTOV

[Dostoevsky and Nietzsche]†

And when exactly did it [the period of the underground] begin? The fact is a remarkable one: at the very time when, apparently, the most cherished hopes of the generation of the fifties began to come true. Serfdom fell. Quite a number of reforms—some proposed, some already under way—promised to realize the dream to which Belinsky had devoted himself and over which Natasha (*The Humiliated and Insulted*) had wept when Ivan Petrovich read her his first story. Up to this point, the "humblest man" had been mentioned only in books; now his rights were recognized by everyone. Up to this point, "humanity" had been a mere abstraction; now it was called upon to exercise its sway over life. The most extreme idealists at the beginning of the sixties had to admit that reality, usually so slow or even motionless, was not this time lagging far behind their dreams. In literature, there was a great celebration. Dostoevsky alone did not share in the general rejoicing. He stood to the side, just as if nothing unusual had happened. More than that, he hid in the underground: Russia's hopes were not his hopes. They were of no concern to him.

How are we to explain such indifference on the part of the greatest Russian writer to events which were regarded in our literature as marking the dawn of a new era in Russian history? The stock explanation is simple: Dostoevsky was a great artist, but a poor thinker. The value of stock explanations is well known. This one is worth no more than the rest, but like every platitude, it deserves attention. Not without reason did it come into this world. People needed it, not to discover the way to truth, but on the contrary, to block all paths to it, to stifle it, to curb it. Incidentally, there is nothing surprising here if we recall what sort of "truth" is in question here! How could it help but be stifled when Dostoevsky himself was horrified by it? I shall quote just one short passage here from the notes of the underground man. This is what he says to the prostitute who has come to him for "moral support": "Do you know what I really want? That you all go to the devil, that's what. I need peace. Why, I'd sell the whole world right now for a kopeck. Is the world to go to pot, or am I to go without my tea? I say that the world can go to pot, so long as I can always get my tea." Who is speaking in this way? Who took it into his head to put such monstrously cynical words into his hero's mouth? That same Dostoevsky, who a short time earlier had so fervently and sincerely said the words about the "humblest man," which I quoted several times already. Now do you understand

† From Lev Shestov, *Dostoevsky, Tolstoy, and Nietzsche*, trans. Bernard Martin and Spencer Roberts (Athens: 1969). Reprinted by permission of the Ohio University Press, Athens.

what an incredibly powerful blow was needed to drive him to such great extremes? Now do you understand which truth it was that must have been revealed to him? Oh, our publicists were right a thousand times over when they sought a platitude to replace such a truth!

Notes from the Underground is a heart-rending cry of terror that has escaped from a man suddenly convinced that all his life he had been lying and pretending when he assured himself and others that the loftiest purpose in life is to serve the "humblest man." Up to this point, he had considered himself marked by fate to do a great work. But now he suddenly felt that he was not a bit better than anyone else, that he cared as little for all ideas as the most common mortal. Let ideas triumph a thousand times over: let the peasants be freed, let just and merciful courts be set up, let military conscription be abolished—his heart would be no lighter, no happier because of it. He was obliged to tell himself that if, instead of all those great and fortunate events, misfortune were to befall Russia, he would feel no worse—perhaps even better. What in the world is a man to do who has discovered in himself such a hideous and disgusting idea? And particularly a writer accustomed to thinking that he is duty-bound to share with his readers all that goes on in his soul? Is he to tell the truth? To go out to the city square and openly admit to the public that his entire past life, that all of his past words, had been nothing but lies, pretense, and hyprocrisy, that while he was crying over Makar Devushkin he was not in the least thinking of the poor wretch, but merely drawing pictures to console himself and the public? And this at the age of forty, when it is impossible to begin a new life, when a break with the past is tantamount to burying oneself alive! Dostoevsky tried to go on speaking in the old way; almost simultaneously with *Notes from the Underground*, he was writing *The Humiliated and Insulted*, in which he forced himself to champion the idea of self-renunciation, despite the fact that he staggered beneath its weight. But where was he to get the strength for such systematic fraud and self-deception? He was already having difficulty sustaining the tone in *The Humiliated and Insulted*. Even it has pages in which the ominous light of the new revelation breaks through. True, they are few. The underground man is evident here only in the Prince's talk with Ivan Petrovich (at night in the restaurant), but it is enough for us to realize what a storm was gathering in Dostoevsky's soul. The Prince all the time ridicules "ideals" and "Schiller" in a most brazen way, while poor Ivan Petrovich sits there downcast, unable not only to defend himself, but even to behave with a semblance of dignity. When you let anyone, even in a novel, deride your holy of holies so caustically, it means you have taken the first step toward its denial. True, Dostoevsky lets the Prince triumph just once, and even then only for a moment. Later, in the pages that follow, all the characters seem to flaunt their nobility and selflessness before one another. But one rotten apple can spoil the whole barrel. Dostoevsky's pathos had dried up. Goodness and service to the idea no longer inspired him.

Notes from the Underground is a public, albeit a veiled, renunciation of his past. "I can't, I simply can't go on pretending. I can't go on living the lie of ideas, and yet I have no other truth. Come what may." That is what these notes say, however much Dostoevsky disclaims them in his comment. Never before had the "word" of a single Russian writer resounded with such hopelessness, with such despair. This accounts for the unprecedented boldness (Count Tolstoy would call it "effrontery"— after all, he spoke that way about Nietzsche) with which Dostoevsky let himself deride the dearest and most sacred human feelings. I have already pointed out that Dostoevsky tells his own story in Notes from the Underground. These words should not, however, be taken to mean that he himself had actually treated a chance female acquaintance so disgracefully; no, the story with Liza is, of course, fictitious. But the horrible thing about the Notes is that Dostoevsky felt the need—even in thought, even in his imagination—to do such a disgraceful thing. It was not Liza he drove away from himself at this point. I am certain there was always enough spontaneous pity in his soul for him to refrain from excessively harsh fits of anger and exasperation. He needed the character Liza merely to deride the "idea" and trample it in the dirt—that same idea that he had served throughout his life. The epigraph to the chapter in which this dreadful story is told is taken from the beginning of Nekrasov's celebrated poem: "When from the Darkness of Error." It was this poem and the holy of holies of those people from whom he had once "fervently accepted" his new doctrine that Dostoevsky was now so madly and blasphemously cursing. But this was the only way out for him. He could no longer remain silent. Something spontaneous, ugly, and horrible had awakened in his soul—and it was something beyond his power to control. As we saw, he did everything possible to preserve his old faith. He continued to pray to his former god even when there was almost no hope in his heart that the prayer would be heard. All the time, it seemed to him that his doubts would pass, that this was merely temptation. In these final moments, he continued, now with just his lips, to whisper his incantation: "It deeply moves the heart to realize that the humblest man is also a human being and is called your brother." But the words of this prayer not only did not console him, they were the venom that poisoned Dostoevsky, although people saw in them and still continue to see in them innocent and even soul-fortifying words. Lucky the person who senses nothing but the poetry of brotherhood in that sentence! But how is a person to cope with these works when the insignificance and absurdity of the humblest man's existence keeps pushing its way to the foreground? How can you tolerate it if you know from personal experience all the horrors of such a downtrodden existence? When the poetry of brotherhood is to be reserved for the new people just beginning life, and you must assume the role of Makar Devushkin, the object of sympathy of lofty souls? What will the great idea of humanity provide then? Hope for the future—very far off, of course—dreams of a different, a felicitous organization of mankind? But for the time being there is the unceasing, hateful, and hypocritical role of the priest of all that is "lofty and beautiful." It was not my idea to write the lofty and beautiful in quotation marks. I found it that way in *Notes from the Underground.* There, all "ideals" are presented in such a guise. There, Schiller, humanity, Nekrasov's poetry, the Crystal Palace, in brief, everything that had once filled Dostoevsky's soul with sympathy and delight—everything—is showered with sarcasms of a most venomous and personal nature. Ideals and sympathy for them arouse in him a feeling of revulsion and horror. Not that he was contesting the possibility of the realization of ideals. He did not even think of that; he did not want to. If the exalted dreams of his youth were destined to come true someday—all the worse. If the ideal of human happiness on earth were destined someday to be realized, Dostoevsky would curse it beforehand. I shall be frank: prior to Dostoevsky, no one dared to express such ideas, even with proper comment. Great despair was needed for such ideas to appear in the human mind; superhuman daring was needed for someone to appear with them in public.

That is why Dostoevsky never acknowledged them as his own, and always had a reserve supply of ideals for display; the more hysterically he cried out, the more they diverged from the nature of his cherished desires, or if you will, from the desires of his entire being. Every last one of his later works is filled with this duality. The question arises— what are we to look for in them, what are we to value? The demands of his soul, which break through to the surface despite "reason and conscience," to use Tolstoy's favorite words, or the prescriptions for an elevated life, prepared more or less according to a common stereotype? On which side is truth? Hitherto, "reason and conscience" were regarded as the final judges. All that we have in the way of ideals and hopes was created by them alone. But now that a judge has been discovered over these judges, what are we to do? Heed its voice, or remain true to tradition and again reduce it to silence. I say "again," because people heard that voice many times before, but they were seized with terror and always stifled it with solemn cries in honor of the old judges. And Dostoevsky did so himself, although, in this sense, his works remind you of the sermons of those preachers, who, under the pretext of fighting immorality, depict enticing scenes of carnal joy. Whatever the traditionalists may say, there can no longer be any doubt. We must let the man speak in his own way. Forgive him all his sins beforehand—just let him tell the truth. Perhaps—who knows—perhaps this truth, which is so obnoxious at first sight, contains something far better than the charm of the most ostentatious lie. Perhaps the full force of sorrow and despair should not at all be directed toward the preparation of doctrines and ideals suitable for man's everyday life, as the teachers of mankind have hitherto done, while always zealously concealing their own doubts and misfortunes from the eyes of outsiders. Perhaps we should abandon pride, the beauty of dying, and all external embellishments and again try to catch sight of the much-slandered truth? What if the old assumption that the tree of knowledge is not the tree of life is false? It is worth examining this prejudice together with the theory of natural development, which gives rise to it. The soul, insulted for all that it holds sacred, will perhaps find the strength in itself for a new struggle.

M. M. BAKHTIN

[Discourse in Dostoevsky]†

* * *

From *The Double* we move immediately to "Notes from Underground," passing over a whole series of intervening works.

"Notes from Underground" is a confessional *Ich-Erzählung*. Originally the work was entitled "A Confession."[1] And it is in fact an authentic confession. Of course, "confession" is understood here not in the personal sense. The author's intention is refracted here, as in any *Ich-Erzählung*; this is not a personal document but a work of art.

In the confession of the Underground Man what strikes us first of all is its extreme and acute dialogization: there is literally not a single monologically firm, undissociated word. From the very first sentence the hero's speech has already begun to cringe and break under the influence of the anticipated words of another, with whom the hero, from the very first step, enters into the most intense internal polemic.

"I am sick man . . . I am a spiteful man. I am an unpleasant man." Thus begins the confession. The ellipsis and the abrupt change of tone after it are significant. The hero began in a somewhat plaintive tone "I am a sick man," but was immediately enraged by that tone: it looked as if he were complaining and needed sympathy, as if he were seeking that sympathy in another person, as if he needed another person! And then there occurs an abrupt dialogic turnaround, one of those typical breaks in accent so characteristic of the whole style of the "Notes," as if the hero wants to say: You, perhaps, were led to believe from my first word that I am seeking your sympathy, so take this: I am a spiteful man. I am an unpleasant man!

† From M. M. Bakhtin, *Problems of Dostoevsky's Poetics*, trans. Caryl Emerson (Minneapolis: 1984). Reprinted by permission of the University of Minnesota Press, Minneapolis.

1. "Notes from Underground" was originally announced by Dostoevsky under this title in "Time."

Characteristic here is a gradual increase in negative tone (to spite the other) under the influence of the other's anticipated reaction. Such breaks in accent always lead to an accumulation of ever-intensifying abusive words or words that are, in any case, unflattering to the other person, as in this example:

> To live longer than forty years is bad manners; it is vulgar, immoral. Who does live beyond forty? Answer that, sincerely and honestly. I will tell you who: fools and worthless people do. I tell all old men that to their face, all those respectable old men, all those silver-haired and reverend old men! I tell the whole world that to its face. I have a right to say so, for I'll go on living to sixty myself. I'll live till seventy! Till eighty! Wait, let me catch my breath. ["Notes," Part One, 1]

In the opening words of the confession, this internal polemic with the other is concealed. But the other's words are present invisibly, determining the style of speech from within. Midway into the first paragraph, however, the polemic has already broken out into the open: the anticipated response of the other takes root in the narration, although, to be sure, still in a weakened form. "No, I refuse to treat it out of spite. You probably will not understand that. Well, but *I* understand it."

At the end of the third paragraph there is already a very characteristic anticipation of the other's reaction:

> Well, are you not imagining, gentlemen, that I am repenting for something now, that I am asking your forgiveness for something? I am sure you are imagining that. However, I assure you it does not matter to me if you are.

At the end of the next paragraph comes the above-quoted polemical attack against the "reverend old men." The following paragraph begins directly with the anticipation of a response to the preceding paragraph:

> No doubt you think, gentlemen, that I want to amuse you. You are mistaken in that, too. I am not at all such a merry person as you imagine, or as you may, imagine; however, if irritated by all this babble (and I can feel that you are irritated) you decide to ask me just who I am, then my answer is, I am a certain low-ranked civil servant.

The next paragraph again ends with an anticipated response:

> . . . I'll bet you think I am writing all this to show off, to be witty at the expense of men of action; and what is more,

that out of ill-bred showing-off, I am clanking a sword, like
my officer.

Later on such endings to paragraphs become more rare, but it remains
true that all basic semantic sections of the work become sharper and
more shrill near the end, in open anticipation of someone else's response.

Thus the entire style of the "Notes" is subject to the most powerful
and all-determining influence of other people's words, which either act
on speech covertly from within as in the beginning of the work, or
which, as the anticipated response of another person, take root in the
very fabric of speech, as in those above-quoted ending passages. The
work does not contain a single word gravitating exclusively toward itself
and its referential object; that is, there is not a single monologic word.
We shall see that this intense relationship to another's consciousness in
the Underground Man is complicated by an equally intense relationship
to his own self. But first we shall make a brief structural analysis of this
act of anticipating another's response.

Such anticipation is marked by one peculiar structural trait: it tends
toward a vicious circle. The tendency of these anticipations can be
reduced to a necessity to retain for oneself the final word. This final
word must express the hero's full independence from the views and
words of the other person, his complete indifference to the other's opinion and the other's evaluation. What he fears most of all is that people
might think he is repenting before someone, that he is asking someone's
forgiveness, that he is reconciling himself to someone else's judgment
or evaluation, that his self-affirmation is somehow in need of affirmation
and recognition by another. And it is in this direction that he anticipates
the other's response. But precisely in this act of anticipating the other's
response and in responding to it he again demonstrates to the other (and
to himself) his own dependence on this other. He *fears* that the other
might think he *fears* that other's opinion. But through this fear he
immediately demonstrates his own inability to be at peace with his own
definition of self. With his refutation, he confirms precisely what he
wishes to refute, and he knows it. Hence the inescapable circle in which
the hero's self-consciousness and discourse are trapped: "Well, are you
not imagining, gentlemen, that I am repenting for something now? . . .
I am sure you are imagining that. However, I assure you it does not
matter to me if you are. . . ."

During that night out on the town, the Underground Man, insulted
by his companions, wants to show them that he pays them no attention:

> I smiled contemptuously and walked up and down the other
> side of the room, opposite the sofa, along the wall, from the
> table to the stove and back again. I tried my very utmost to
> show them that I could do without them, and yet I purposely
> stomped with my boots, thumping with my heels. But it was

all in vain. They paid no attention at all. ["Notes," Part Two, ch. IV]

Meanwhile our underground hero recognizes all this perfectly well himself, and understands perfectly well the impossibility of escaping from that circle in which his attitude toward the other moves. Thanks to this attitude toward the other's consciousness, a peculiar *perpetuum mobile* is achieved, made up of his internal polemic with another and with himself, an endless dialogue where one reply begets another, which begets a third, and so on to infinity, and all of this without any forward motion.

Here is an example of that inescapable *perpetuum mobile* of the dialogized self-consciousness:

> You will say that it is vulgar and base to drag all this [the hero's dreaming—M. B.] into public after all the tears and raptures I have myself admitted. But why is it base? Can you imagine that I am ashamed of it all, and that it was stupider than anything in your life, gentlemen? And I can assure you that some of these fancies were by no means badly composed. Not everything took place on the shores of Lake Como. And yet you are right—it really is vulgar and base. And what is most base of all is that I have now started to justify myself to you. And even more base than that is my making this remark now. But that's enough, or, after all, there will be no end to it; each step will be more base than the last. ["Notes," Part Two, ch. II]

Before us is an example of a vicious circle of dialogue which can neither be finished nor finalized. The formal significance of such inescapable dialogic oppositions in Dostoevsky's work is very great. But nowhere in his subsequent works does this opposition appear in such naked, abstractly precise, one could even say directly mathematical, form. [2]

As a result of the Underground Man's attitude toward the other's consciousness and its discourse—extraordinary dependence upon it and at the same time extreme hostility toward it and nonacceptance of its judgments—his narration takes on one highly essential artistic characteristic. This is a deliberate clumsiness of style, albeit subject to a certain artistic logic. His discourse does not flaunt itself and cannot flaunt itself, for there is no one before whom it can flaunt. It does not, after all, gravitate naively toward itself and its referential object. It is addressed to another person and to the speaker himself (in his internal dialogue

---

2. This can be explained by the generic similarities between "Notes from Underground" and Menippean satire.

with himself). And in both of these directions it wants least of all to flaunt itself and be "artistic" in the usual sense of the word. In its attitude toward the other person it strives to be deliberately inelegant, to "spite" him and his tastes in all respects. But this discourse takes the same position even in regard to the speaker himself, for one's attitude toward oneself is inseparably interwoven with one's attitude toward another. Thus discourse is pointedly cynical, calculatedly cynical, yet also anguished. It strives to play the holy fool, for holy-foolishness is indeed a sort of form, a sort of aestheticism—but, as it were, in reverse.

As a result, the prosaic triteness of the portrayal of his inner life is carried to extreme limits. In its material, in its theme, the first part of "Notes from Underground" is lyrical. From a formal point of view, this is the same prose lyric of spiritual and emotional quest, of spiritual unfulfillment that we find, for example, in Turgenev's "Phantoms" or "Enough," or in any lyrical page from a confessional *Ich-Erzählung* or a page from *Werther*. But this is a peculiar sort of lyric, analogous to the lyrical expression of a toothache.

This expression of a toothache, oriented in an internally polemical way toward the listener and toward the sufferer, is spoken by the Underground Hero himself, and he speaks of it, of course, not by chance. He suggests eavesdropping on the groans of an "educated man of the nineteenth century" who suffers from a toothache, on the second or third day of his illness. He tries to expose the peculiar sensuality behind this whole cynical expression of pain, an expression intended for the "public":

> His moans become nasty, disgustingly spiteful, and go on for whole days and nights. And, after all, he himself knows that he does not benefit at all from his moans; he knows better than anyone that he is only lacerating and irritating himself and others in vain; he knows that even the audience for whom he is exerting himself and his whole family now listen to him with loathing, do not believe him for a second, and that deep down they understand that he could moan differently, more simply, without trills and flourishes, and that he is only indulging himself like that out of spite, out of malice. Well, sensuality exists precisely in all these consciousnesses and infamies. "It seems I am troubling you, I am lacerating your hearts, I am keeping everyone in the house awake. Well, stay awake then, you, too, feel every minute that I have a toothache. I am no longer the hero to you now that I tried to appear before, but simply a nasty person, a scoundrel. Well, let it be that way, then! I am very glad that you see through me. Is it nasty for you to hear my foul moans? Well, let it be nasty. Here I will let you have an even nastier flourish in a minute. . . ." ["Notes," Part One, ch. IV]

Of course any implied comparison here between the structure of the Underground Man's confession and the expression of a toothache is on the level of parodic exaggeration, and in this sense is cynical. But the orientation of this expression of a toothache, with all its "trills and flourishes," nevertheless does, in its relation to the listener and to the speaker himself, reflect very accurately the orientation of discourse in a confession, although, we repeat, it reflects not objectively but in a taunting, parodically exaggerating style, just as *The Double* reflected the internal speech of Golyadkin.

The destruction of one's own image in another's eyes, the sullying of that image in another's eyes as an ultimate desperate effort to free oneself from the power of the other's consciousness and to break through to one's self for the self alone—this, in fact, is the orientation of the Underground Man's entire confession. For this reason he makes his discourse about himself deliberately ugly. He wants to kill in himself any desire to appear the hero in others' eyes (and in his own): "I am no longer the hero to you now that I tried to appear before, but simply a nasty person, a scoundrel. . . ."

To accomplish this he must banish from his discourse all epic and lyrical tones, all "heroizing" tones; he must make his discourse *cynically* objective. A soberly objective definition of himself, without exaggeration or mockery, is impossible for a hero from the underground, because such a soberly prosaic definition would presuppose a word without a sideward glance, a word without a loophole; neither the one nor the other exist on his verbal palette. True, he is continually trying to break through to such a word, to break through to spiritual sobriety, but for him the path lies through cynicism and holy-foolishness. He has neither freed himself from the power of the other's consciousness nor admitted its power over him,[3] he is for now merely struggling with it, polemicizing with it maliciously, not able to accept it but also not able to reject it. In this striving to trample down his own image and his own discourse as they exist in and for the other person, one can hear not only the desire for sober self-definition, but also a desire to annoy the other person; and this forces him to overdo his sobriety, mockingly exaggerating it to the point of cynicism and holy-foolishness: "Is it nasty for you to hear my foul moans? Well, let it be nasty. Here I will let you have an even nastier flourish in a minute. . . ."

But the underground hero's word about himself is not only a word with a sideward glance; it is also, as we have said, a word with a loophole. The influence of the loophole on the style of his confession is so great that his style cannot be understood without a consideration of its formal activity. The word with a loophole has enormous significance in Dostoevsky's works in general, especially in the later works. And here we

---

3. According to Dostoevsky, such an admittance would also serve to calm down the discourse and purify it.

pass on to another aspect of the structure of "Notes from Underground": the hero's attitude toward his own self, which throughout the course of the entire work is interwoven and combined with his dialogue with another.

What, then, is this loophole of consciousness and of the word?

A loophole is the retention for oneself of the possibility for altering the ultimate, final meaning of one's own words. If a word retains such a loophole this must inevitably be reflected in its structure. This potential other meaning, that is, the loophole left open, accompanies the word like a shadow. Judged by its meaning alone, the word with a loophole should be an ultimate word and does present itself as such, but in fact it is only the penultimate word and places after itself only a conditional, not a final, period.

For example, the confessional self-definition with a loophole (the most widespread form in Dostoevsky) is, judging by its meaning, an ultimate word about oneself, a final definition of oneself, but in fact it is forever taking into account internally the responsive, contrary evaluation of oneself made by another. The hero who repents and condemns himself actually wants only to provoke praise and acceptance by another. Condemning himself, he wants and demands that the other person dispute this self-definition, and he leaves himself a loophole in case the other person should suddenly in fact agree with him, with his self-condemnation, and not make use of his privilege as the other.

Here is how the hero from the underground tells of his "literary" dreams:

> I, for instance, was triumphant over everyone; everyone, of course, lay in the dust and was *forced* to recognize my superiority *spontaneously*, and I forgave them all. I, a famous poet, and a courtier, fell in love; I inherited countless millions and immediately devoted them to humanity, and *at the same time I confessed before all the people my shameful deeds, which, of course, were not merely shameful, but contained an enormous amount of "the sublime and the beautiful,"* something in the Manfred style. *Everyone would weep and kiss me (what idiots they would be if they did not)*, while I would go barefoot and hungry preaching new ideas and fighting a victorious Austerlitz against the reactionaries. ["Notes," Part Two, ch. II]

Here he ironically relates dreams of heroic deeds with a loophole, dreams of confession with a loophole. He casts a parodic light on these dreams. But his very next words betray the fact that his repentant confession of his dreams has its own loophole, too, and that he himself is prepared to find in these dreams and in his very confessing of them something, if not in the Manfred style, then at least in the realm of "the sublime and the beautiful," if anyone should happen to agree with him that the dreams are indeed base and vulgar: "You will say that it is vulgar and base to drag all this into public after all the tears and raptures I have myself admitted. But why is it base? Can you imagine that I am ashamed of it all, and that it was stupider than anything in your life, gentlemen? And I can assure you that some of these fancies were by no means badly composed. . . ."

And this passage, already cited by us above, is caught up in the vicious circle of self-consciousness with a sideward glance.

The loophole creates a special type of fictive ultimate word about oneself with an unclosed tone to it, obtrusively peering into the other's eyes and demanding from the other a sincere refutation. We shall see that the word with a loophole achieves especially sharp expression in Ippolit's confession, but it is to one degree or another inherent in all the confessional self-utterances of Dostoevsky's heroes.[4] The loophole makes all the heroes' self-definitions unstable, the word in them has no hard and fast meaning, and at any moment, like a chameleon, it is ready to change its tone and its ultimate meaning.

The loophole makes the hero ambiguous and elusive even for himself. In order to break through to his self the hero must travel a very long road. The loophole profoundly distorts his attitude toward himself. The hero does not know whose opinion, whose statement is ultimately the final judgment on him: is it his own repentant and censuring judgment, or on the contrary is it another person's opinion that he desires and has compelled into being, an opinion that accepts and vindicates him? The image of Nastasya Filippovna, for example, is built almost entirely on this motif alone. Considering herself guilty, a fallen woman, she simultaneously assumes that the other person, precisely as the other, is obliged to vindicate her and cannot consider her guilty. She genuinely quarrels with Myshkin, who vindicates her in everything, but she equally genuinely despises and rejects all those who agree with her self-condemnation and consider her a fallen woman. Ultimately Nastasya Filippovna does not know even her own final word on herself: does she really consider herself a fallen woman, or does she vindicate herself? Self-condemnation and self-vindication, divided between two voices—I condemn myself, another vindicates me—but anticipated by a single voice, create in that voice interruptions and an internal duality. An anticipated and obligatory vindication by the other merges with self-condemnation, and both tones begin to sound simultaneously in that voice, resulting in abrupt interruptions and sudden transitions. Such is the voice of Nastasya Filippovna, such is the style of her discourse. Her entire inner life (and, as we shall see, her outward life as well) is reduced to a search for herself and for her own undivided voice beneath the two voices that have made their home in her.

The Underground Man conducts the same sort of inescapable dialogue

4. Exceptions will be pointed out below.

with himself that he conducts with the other person. He cannot merge completely with himself in a unified monologic voice simply by leaving the other's voice entirely outside himself (whatever that voice might be, without a loophole), for, as is the case with Golyadkin, his voice must also perform the function of surrogate for the other person. He cannot reach an agreement with himself, but neither can he stop talking with himself. The style of his discourse about himself is organically alien to the period, alien to finalization, both in its separate aspects and as a whole. This is the style of internally endless speech which can be mechanically cut off but cannot be organically completed.

But precisely for that reason is Dostoevsky able to conclude his work in a way so organic and appropriate for the hero; he concludes it on precisely that which would foreground the tendency toward eternal endlessness embedded in his hero's notes.

> But enough; I don't want to write more from "underground". . .
> The "notes" of this paradoxalist do not end here, however. He could not resist and continued them. But it also seems to me that we may stop here. ["Notes," Part Two, ch. X]

In conclusion we will comment upon two additional characteristics of the Underground Man. Not only his discourse but his face too has its sideward glance, its loophole, and all the phenomena resulting from these. It is as if interference, voices interrupting one another, penetrate his entire body, depriving him of self-sufficiency and unambiguousness. The Underground Man hates his own face, because in it he senses the power of another person over him, the power of that other's evaluations and opinions. He himself looks on his own face with another's eyes, with the eyes of the other. And this alien glance interruptedly merges with his own glance and creates in him a peculiar hatred toward his own face:

> For instance, I hated my face; I thought it disgusting, and even suspected that there was something base in its expression and therefore every time I turned up at the office I painfully tried to behave as independently as possible so that I might not be suspected of being base, and to give my face as noble an expression as possible. "Let my face even be ugly," I thought, "but let it be noble, expressive, and above all, extremely intelligent." But I was absolutely and painfully certain that my face could never express those perfections; but what was worst of all, I thought it positively stupid-looking. And I would have been quite satisfied if I could have looked intelligent. In fact, I would even have put up with looking base if, at the same time, my face could have been thought terribly intelligent. ["Notes," Part Two, ch. I]

Just as he deliberately makes his discourse about himself unattractive, so is he made happy by the unattractiveness of his face:

> I happened to look at myself in the mirror. My harassed face struck me as extremely revolting, pale, spiteful, nasty, with disheveled hair. "No matter, I am glad of it," I thought: "I am glad that I shall seem revolting to her; like that." ["Notes," Part Two, ch. V]

This polemic with the other on the subject of himself is complicated in "Notes from Underground" by his polemic with the other on the subject of the world and society. The underground hero, in contrast to Devushkin and Golyadkin, is an ideologist.

In his ideological discourse we can easily uncover the same phenomena that are present in his discourse about himself. His discourse about the world is both overtly and covertly polemical; it polemicizes not only with other people, with other ideologies, but also with the very subject of its thinking—with the world and its order. And in this discourse on the world there are two voices, as it were, sounding for him, among which he cannot find himself and his own world, because even the world he defines with a loophole. Just as his body has become an "interrupted" thing in his own eyes, so is the world, nature, society perceived by him as "interrupted." In each of his thoughts about them there is a battle of voices, evaluations, points of view. In everything he senses above all *someone else's will* predetermining him. It is within the framework of this alien will that he perceives the world order, nature with its mechanical necessity, the social order. His own thought is developed and structured as *the thought of someone personally insulted by the world order*, personally humiliated by its blind necessity. This imparts a profoundly intimate and passionate character to his ideological discourse, and permits it to become tightly interwoven with his discourse about himself. It seems (and such indeed was Dostoevsky's intent) that we are dealing here with a single discourse, and only by arriving at himself will the hero arrive at his world. Discourse about the world, just like discourse about oneself, is profoundly dialogic: the hero casts an energetic reproach at the world order, even at the mechanical necessity of nature, as if he were talking not about the world but with the world. Of these peculiarities of ideological discourse we will speak below, when we take up the general issue of hero-ideologists and Ivan Karamazov in particular; in him these features are especially acute and clear-cut.

The discourse of the Underground Man is entirely a discourse-address. To speak, for him, means to address someone; to speak about himself means to address his own self with his own discourse; to speak about another person means to address that other person; to speak about the world means to address the world. But while speaking with himself, with another, with the world, he simultaneously addresses a third party as well: he squints his eyes to the side, toward the listener, the witness, the judge.[5] This simultaneous triple-directedness of his discourse and the fact that he does not acknowledge any object without addressing it is also responsible for the extraordinarily vivid, restless, agitated, and one might say, obtrusive nature of this discourse. It cannot be seen as a lyrical or epic discourse, calmly gravitating toward itself and its referential object; no, first and foremost one reacts to it, responds to it, is drawn into its game; it is capable of agitating and irritating, almost like the personal address of a living person. It destroys footlights, but not because of its concern for topical issues or for reasons that have any direct philosophical significance, but precisely because of that formal structure analyzed by us above.

The element of *address* is essential to every discourse in Dostoevsky, narrative discourse as well as the discourse of the hero. In Dostoevsky's world generally there is nothing merely thing-like, no mere matter, no object—there are only subjects. Therefore there is no word-judgment, no word about an object, no secondhand referential word—there is only the word as address, the word dialogically contracting another word, a word about a word addressed to a word.

RALPH E. MATLAW

Structure and Integration in
Notes from the Underground†

I

In the literature on *Notes from the Underground* the protagonist is always called "the underground man" (*podpol'nyj chelovek*), as if he were an archetypal entity, rather than "the narrator," an accepted literary convention of the *Icherzählung*. The nomenclature is significant, for critics have treated the work as the turning point in Dostoevsky's development, ransacked it for philosophical, political, and sociological formulas, noted the profound psychology, but have never analyzed the *Notes* in detail as an artifact. By so doing critics distort the *Notes* structurally and substantively, because they concentrate on and overemphasize the first part of the work almost to the exclusion of the second, and because they accept and discuss the narrator's formulations in this

5. We recall the characterization that Dostoevsky himself gave to the hero's speech in "A Meek One:" . . . "he either argues with himself or addresses some unseen listener, a judge as it were.

However, it is always like that in real life."
† Reprinted by permission of the Modern Language Association of America from PMLA 73 (1958): 101–09.

part without analyzing them as the expression of literary creation.[1] The purpose of this study is to examine the unity of the *Notes*: to ascertain the relationships of its two parts; to indicate the thematic function of ordering episodes in a particular sequence; to note the recurrence of certain objects, the symbolism involved therein, and its effect on the unity of the *Notes*; finally, to assess the effect of artful integration on the apparent "meaning" of the work.

To treat the *Notes* as an artistic whole—to find the real, rather than the mechanical principle of organization—involves first the problem of time sequence. Events in Part II antedate those of Part I by fourteen to sixteen years. What is the purpose of such displacement? The simplest answer might be that such sequence obviates accounting for the time gap. The second part can have no apt conclusion. Since it reconstructs the narrator's experience, it might well continue his story to the time he commits his "notes" to paper. Indeed, at the end of the work, to the last sentence, "I don't want to write more from 'underground'," Dostoevsky appends the comment "the notes of this paradoxalist do not end here, however. He could not refrain from continuing them, but it seems to us that we may stop here." Were the two sections placed chronologically, there would be a hiatus between the end of his experiences and his philosophical formulations; the emergence of one from the other might seem insufficiently motivated as a change from narrative to "logical" exposition. Another possibility is that the second part, particularly in 1864, must have seemed particularly repellent to the reader. Why read, or even write, so tortured and in some respects disgusting a work? In the first section, though the psychological mechanism is no less evident, the narrator propounds a series of brilliant paradoxes, through which he attempts to establish his intellectual superiority, so that his vagaries in the second part now seem to him to be presented against a backdrop which slightly attenuates them. Finally, this narrator is a new phenomenon in literature and must be so marked. Hence Dostoevsky's footnote:

> The author of these notes and the "Notes" themselves are, of course, imaginary. Nevertheless, such persons as the writer of these notes not only may, but positively must exist in our society, considering those circumstances under which our so-

---

1. While the central position of the *Notes* in Dostoevsky's canon was recognized as early as 1882 by N. K. Mikhailovsky, V. V. Rozanov's essay on the *Legend of the Grand Inquisitor* (1890) ushered in the modern emphasis on Dostoevsky as thinker. Subsequent critics invariably accept Rozanov's emphasis on, if not his interpretation of, Pt. I of the *Notes*. Leon Edel, *The Psychological Novel (1900–1950)* (New York: Lippincott, 1955), p. 59, implies a more analytic approach to the work's "content": "in the first paragraph [Dostoevsky] had semaphored the reader, not with flags but with klieg lights that here was the mind of an eccentric, if not a madman." Even the best attempt to date to combine ideological appreciation with analysis of novelistic technique, K. Mochul'sky, *Dostoevsky* (Paris: YMCA Press, 1947), pp. 202–215, fails to account for the effect of the narrator's personality on the philosophy he proffers. In the present essay the *Notes* are quoted as translated by Constance Garnett, with some changes for accuracy and consistency.

> ciety in general was formed. I wanted to expose to the public more clearly than usually done one of the characters of the recent past. He is one of the representatives of the current generation. In this excerpt, entitled "Underground," this person introduces himself, his views, and, as it were, tries to explain the reasons why he appeared and had to appear in our midst. In the following excerpt will appear the real "notes" of this person about several events in his life.

Although these answers begin to explain the structure, they do not satisfactorily account for the higher organization so characteristic in Dostoevsky. For even a cursory reading reveals that the work is of a piece—stylistically, intellectually, psychologically the *Notes* are a single sustained effort. They take the form of an extended monologue, but are full of suggestions of dialogue: "you say," "you laugh," "this is all that you say," "yes, gentlemen," and so on. Such locutions also appear, to a lesser degree, in the *Writer's Diary*, but with a different function. The narrator, by his own admission, is writing a confession,[2] and maintains that the oratorical flourishes simply exist so that he may express himself most easily and clearly. But this device in turn gives the work the illusion of dialogue and makes it seem like a sustained polemic with an opponent, as if the narrator were anticipating objections. Like all confessions, the narrator's postulates the existence of an auditor, but psychologically the auditor here is never passive and cannot be so for this is a confession to one's self—the auditor and confessor are one. The *Notes* may even be considered as a parody of confession which, in religious terms, is ostensibly preceded by contrition, but here is replaced by proud (though ambivalent) self-defense. The confession is not Augustinian but Rousseauistic, with the added temporal notation of Musset's title, *Confessions d'un enfant du siècle*. The literary roots of the narrator's confession are unmistakable. Rousseau appears not only as the propounder of the *homme de la nature et de la vérité* in the first part, but also in an explicit comment at its end. The narrator approves Heine's criticism of Rousseau and autobiography—that a man will lie about himself out of sheer vanity—but he also adduces it as proof that his confession is true, unexaggerated, since it is not meant for publication.

The narrator is correct in his contention, though not in the manner he thinks. Dostoevsky's psychological insight permits him to trace a portrait which is, or can be, clear to the reader despite the narrator's evasions, repetitions, contradictions, self-lacerations. At their deepest level the narrator's analyses are honestly meant. That they appear not to be so, or to be incorrect, must be attributed to the fact that these

---

2. It is noteworthy that in his periodical, the *Epoch*, Dostoevsky announced the forthcoming publication of the work, then entitled *Confession* (*Ispoved'*). However, when the work appeared it bore the title by which we know it. In his letters Dostoevsky also insisted that the whole piece would have to appear in one issue, but he had only completed the first part in time.

analyses and judgments are distorted by the narrator's personality. The reader must constantly discount the distorting prism, and assess the narrator's incorrect judgments about others and himself in terms of what they tell about the narrator. To put it more clearly, the narrator is portrayed twice. His own statements account for his actions at one level, yet his statements are not trustworthy. Dostoevsky indicates the profounder psychological level, which is manifest in the contradiction between the narrator's analyses and his behavior. Parenthetically, it might be pointed out that the narrator's knowledge is not emotional but rational; although he claims that the *Notes* are "hardly literature so much as corrective punishment," the *Notes*, unlike those of the *Adolescent*, have no ameliorative or therapeutic value to their ostensible author.

If the *Notes* are to be considered as a psychological document, then the structure, and even its confessional aspect, gains another dimension. The relationship of the two parts might be described as follows: most of the interest of the *Notes* for the narrator consists in his recreation of the experiences in Part II. But the narrator is not at first capable of committing himself to such an exposition. He evades the subject, attempts to build up his ego by rationalization, by philosophical speculation, and avoids the recapitulation of his past until the time that the need for disclosure and security in such disclosure coincide. From this point of view practically all the first part is a false start, leading the reader away from the real subject of the work.[3] Dostoevsky had originally indicated the true center of the book himself. The only significant change from the first printed text to the second is the elimination of the last sentence in Dostoevsky's footnote: "Thus this first excerpt should be considered as an introduction to the whole book, almost as a foreword."

A psychological principle of organization seems to account most satisfactorily for the sequence of the *Notes*, but it does not solve all the problems of organization. Against his will the narrator exposes himself almost as much in the first as in the second part.[4] And if one ignores other dimensions of the work and their relation to the psychological, the *Notes* then do not properly weight Part I as the synthesis, the result of the narrator's life in Part II. Moreover, even psychological confession does not account for the highly selective nature and progression of

3. The first two sentences of the *Notes* also contain a false start and, *in peto*, expose the narrator's personality: "I am a sick man . . . I am a spiteful man. I am a repulsive man." The first clause apparently strikes the narrator as a request for sympathy. Since he denies such desires he restarts, now attempting to alienate the reader ("I am a spiteful man"), and then extends his hostility, ("I am a repulsive man"). This is more clearly marked in the original, because in Russian, unlike English, the first person singular pronoun is not usually capitalized, so that the second clause, following interpunction, is more clearly a new beginning. The psychological movement is also more sharply marked. A literal rendering of the opening is: "I man sick . . . I spiteful man. Repulsive I man." All three clauses are stylistically correct in Russian, but the shift in emphasis and tone is unmistakable.

4. In this respect the relationship of the two parts may be formulated as follows: in Pt. I the psychology is turned into a polemic and is directed against an imaginary reader; in Pt II it is externalized, projected onto characters and situations.

episodes in what at first appears to be merely a chronological recapitulation. So that if psychologically the narrative properly progresses from the first to the second part, chronologically and rationally Part II leads back into the formulations of Part I. Neither the narrator nor Dostoevsky stresses this (except in the concluding footnote), but as we shall see, the narrator's psychological pattern does not in itself account for all of his social behavior: society and the particular historical moment affect his personality. And the interaction of the psychological, social, and intellectual create the dramatic tension and structure of the *Notes*.

II

Dostoevsky's style and his narrative method consist of an interpenetration of "naturalistic" and metaphysical elements. He introduces real events and philosophical speculations as two facets of the same subject, frequently (as in the "odor of sanctity" in the *Brothers Karamazov*) presenting a naturalistic explanation concomitantly with a mystic one. The opposition of real to ideal implies an ethical core which, in a social context, postulates in part the quest of the individual for his place in the world. It is so stated in Gogol's *Cloak* which, with his *Nevsky Prospect*, is a forerunner of important concepts in the *Notes*. The quest is psychological as well as ethical, and Dostoevsky's contribution to the problem lies in the development of its psychological aspect and can be illustrated by means of his earlier story, the *Double*. Misinterpretation of the *Double* has tended to obliterate the organic unity of Dostoevsky's psychological and social thought. Realizing that the *Double* failed, Dostoevsky continually wished to rewrite the work, but finally realized that it would have to be completely recast. However, only the form was bad—the idea remained artistically unrealized. Dostoevsky even betrays his dualistic procedure in his defense of the *Double* in the *Writer's Diary*: "Why should I lose a wonderful idea, and an extraordinary type in his social importance, which I first discovered, and whose herald I was?" Further he states "the idea was quite clear, and I have never expressed anything more important in my work." This idea is obviously not clinical schizophrenia but an ethical idea which contrasts man's aspiration (in the "double") with his actual position. The fact that the double exists is indubitably psychological; the reason for its existence, in Dostoevsky's work, is primarily social. In the *Notes* we may clearly see Dostoevsky's ethical-psychological duality in operation, and may also note in passing the change of attitude by the author from the detachment and disdain of the *Double* to sympathetic treatment of the narrator and his problems in the *Notes*.

In the second part of the *Notes* each of the episodes is carefully selected to point out socio-ethical considerations simultaneously with psychological ones. These appear in different balances: sometimes one element predominates, sometimes another; both are always present. I shall here touch only on four episodes—that with the officer, the farewell party for Zverkov, the affair with Liza, and the attitude of the narrator to his servant Apollon—in an attempt to see how Dostoevsky's method gradually forces the narrator into his final position.

The narrator attempts to avenge himself against an officer who, during a quarrel with another man "moved me from where I was standing to another spot and passed by as though he had not noticed me." The narrator does not demand an immediate apology but later, in various ways, for several years (!) he attempts to revenge this slight. Occasionally he spots the officer on the Nevsky Prospect, where the narrator

> used to wriggle like an eel among the passers-by, in the most unseemly fashion, continually moving aside to make way for generals, for officers of the Guards and the Hussars, or for ladies. In those minutes I used to feel a convulsive twinge at my heart, and hot all down my back at the mere thought of the wretchedness of my dress, of the wretchedness and vulgarity of my little scurrying figure.

The future underground man, usually immersed in books and daydreaming, is drawn to the Nevsky at every possible opportunity, drawn to partake in the rush and movement of life. The Nevsky in this sense is almost a commonplace of Russian literature. Dostoevsky's distinctive use emphasizes the narrator's "continually moving aside," his being forced outside the stream of life while the social parade passes him in both directions. Of the officer the narrator observes that "he too went out of his way for generals and persons of high rank, and he too shifted among them like an eel. But people like me, or even neater than I, he simply walked over." Social stratification, then, forces the officer to step aside, but the narrator, as a lower creature in the scale, must *continually* step aside. He has no stature either in his own estimation (a psychological fact), or in that of the Nevsky strollers (a social comment).

His "audacious" plan for revenge consists in attempting to force the officer to yield the right of way. To achieve his end, the narrator makes elaborate preparations: "To begin with, when I carried out my plan I should have to look very decent, and I had to think of my clothes. In any case, if, for instance, there were any sort of public scandal . . . I must be well dressed; that inspires respect and of itself puts us in some way on equal footing in the eyes of high society." By dint of financial hardship the narrator improves his appearance. Similarly, Akaky Akakevich in the *Cloak* saves in order to purchase his garment. The sacrifice for each is crucial, since the goal for both represents the emotional awakening of the character. The officer's crime was lack of notice, lack of consideration for a fellow being. By improving his appearance, the narrator defeats the primary social purpose of his plan, since the respect he may obtain will be merely a tribute to his external appearance. Thus his rationalization leads him to duplicate the officer's crime: he is unable to consider himself a social being. His behavior is socially conditioned—the material emphasis has been inculcated too strongly—but his inability to exact revenge is also motivated psychologically. His diffidence, his vanity, insist that he present an external appearance corresponding to what he considers his intellectual superiority. Similarly, he cannot carry out his plan for psychological reasons. At the last minute he always steps aside, once even falling ignominiously at the officer's feet. Finally the narrator closes his eyes and collides with the officer, who

> did not even look around and pretended not to notice it. But he was only pretending, I am convinced of it, I am convinced of it to this day! Of course, I got the worst of it—he was stronger—but that was not the point. The point was that I had attained my goal, I had kept up my dignity, I had not yielded a step, and had put myself publicly on an equal social footing with him.

The narrator's vanity had precluded any possibility of social atonement by the officer. Psychologically, the narrator *must* feel that he has triumphed, though his insistence suggests he does not. Admission that the officer did not notice him would be unbearable: it would annihilate him, destroy the very foundation of his personality. Even failure is preferable to nonrecognition, since failure at least implies the possibility of success, and thereby provides the narrator a point of contact with humanity. He ends the espisode by remarking: "The officer was later transferred. I have not seen him now for fourteen years. What is the dear fellow (*golubchik*) doing now? Whom is he walking over?" Although used sarcastically, the term of endearment (*golubchik*) is in part seriously meant, and presents an inverted protest, for to the narrator the officer represents a form—perhaps the worst form—of social intercourse. And the protest becomes the more poignant as the narrator anticipates similar experiences by other men, members of the same social and historical community. The personal psychology, however, still dominates. There is apparently a genuine interest in maintaining the fleeting contact, the brief moment of social and psychological achievement.

The second major event is again precipitated by a combination of social and psychological forces. The narrator experiences one of those rare moments when he feels a need for human companionship. But since the day is a Thursday and the only person whose house he frequents (his superior, Setochin, who also figures in the *Double*) receives only on Tuesday, the narrator must hold his desire in abeyance. He finally decides to visit a former classmate and there insinuates himself into the farewell party for Zverkov. This episode is one of the clearest examples of the narrator's psychological mechanism. He constantly realizes that he should not act as he does, but nevertheless each action is calculated to antagonize the other participants and elicit their disdain. Also, the difference between the narrator's quotations of dialogue and his interpretation of their meanings indicates that after the episode with the officer he has reached a point at which social intercourse is no longer feasible for him. He misinterprets Zverkov's motives when the latter first greets him, and Zverkov's final remark, "Insulted? *You* insulted *me?* Understand, sir, that you could never, under any circumstances, possibly insult *me*," is interpreted only psychologically, whereas the remark also has overtones of social inequality or might be construed as a combination of exasperation and social differentiation. But the point here is precisely to indicate, in comparison with the narrator's youth and school days, and with the Nevsky episode, that the question of social inequality has now become for the narrator almost entirely a psychological problem of individual value.

During the trip to the brothel and the events there (about which more in the next section), and simultaneously with the romantic phantasy about revenge, the narrator has an inkling that it will disgrace rather than vindicate himself. Nevertheless, despite his hesitation and vacillation, he feels compelled to bring the event to its inevitable conclusion, to discover his essential self. This scene is clearly the keystone of the *Notes* but it is projected by means of an irony that operates at a second remove. Dostoevsky brilliantly exploits a symbolic touch to forewarn the reader of the added intricacy. Material standards were previously shown to be inadequate because they were limited by rationality. They may also be inadequate because they are misrepresented by psychological irrationality. Thus the narrator's dissatisfaction with his personality finds one mode of expression in his undue concern for sartorial elegance, a product of the same distortion that leads him to intense dissatisfaction with his face. In describing his attitude he also states his desideratum: "Let my face even be ugly, so long as it seems lofty, expressive, and above all *extremely* intelligent." It therefore follows that he also expects his face to reflect his tortured feelings when he arrives at the brothel. As he approaches Liza he looks at a mirror: "My harassed face struck me as particularly revolting, pale, angry, abject, with dishevelled hair." Everything that follows seems to be the narrator to be motivated by and to exemplify his vilest, most repulsive traits. Like the narrator's assumption about his face, this is only *his* view, and his view of the image in the mirror is a distortion of a false view. But Dostoevsky forces his reader to acknowledge that ultimately the narrator interprets the picture in the mirror correctly: the mirror reflects an agonized face. The appearance and the reality have fused. Similarly, the reader must now discount the narrator's view of his motivation in talking to Liza and accept his sermon as the direct expression of the narrator's profoundest convictions and deepest needs. The scene presents the narrator's views directly, and the reader only tends to question them because the narrator describes then as artificial and because some of his views of "love" are highly personal, though so noted by him. The sermon contradicts most of the rational strictures and self-characterizations of the narrator but leads to the same conclusions that the paradoxes of Part I imply. The verbal pattern is atypical: this time the narrator consciously uses an emotional, even sentimental, harangue, and minimizes intellectual, rational exposition. He later denies that his speech represents his real vision because it is atypical of his style, though he justifies its use for Liza. The stylized eloquence in the external form of the sermon corresponds to a reversal in the narrator's subject matter: not material advancement but the soul and love are its contents. It rejects his previous criteria by being directed at a person of no intellectual ability (but even she comments on the "bookish" nature of his speech), a person who according to Part I would be unworthy of his attention. The scene emphasizes that the narrator has dramatically tried, and spectacularly succeeded, in arousing an ignorant soul and has led it out of an acquiescence to and involvement in humanity's shoddier side to an appreciation of its individuality, value, and even grandeur. The narrator has salvaged one life, and in his concern for an "insignificant" person has demonstrated the mainspring of his view of man. The success of his effort, both on Liza and on himself (for he becomes involved in his own eloquence and is moved by it) indicates that he has found and developed the basic issues to which man responds.

The narrator cannot operate long at this emotional level, and realizes his incapacity almost immediately. He proceeds to describe his relationship with Apollon, which is very rich in meanings. If the narrator's report can be trusted, the portrait of Apollon indicates, beneath the mask of human dignity, the same malicious, sadistic traits characteristic of the narrator. He is thus an extension of the narrator's personality, a proof, as it were, of his ubiquity in the modern world, and once more refers the reader to Dostoevsky's footnote. The relationship is complex, for the narrator enjoys the so-called "tortures" Apollon inflicts on him, which he anticipates and provokes. There is no motivation for Apollon's remaining with the narrator unless one accepts the narrator's estimate of his servant or else vouchsafes him enormous compassion and stature. Yet Apollon has additional meanings: he is another of those who consider the external side of man supreme, but, paradoxically, is a servant who achieves true (or as the narrator sees it, false) human dignity. And as one who delights in reading psalms aloud, and who ultimately turns into a professional funeral psalm reader, he intones a symbolic *requiescat* over the narrator while still in his service. Thus Apollon is introduced at this point to balance the narrator's humanistic achievement with Liza and to reintroduce his psychological estrangement.

In anticipating Liza's visit, the narrator reflects on the circumstance that he will appear to her in all his miserable poverty and slovenliness. Again human beings are to be judged by their appearance rather than their intrinsic value. Yet the narrator, having once broken through his assumed intellectualism to experience a relationship founded on a fundamental human need, would repeat such experiences if he were capable of so doing. He realizes the difference between the need and the action, the social and the personal, when he objects to poverty: "Oh, the beastliness! And it isn't the beastliness of it that matters most! There is something more important, more loathsome, viler! Yes, viler! And to put on that dishonest lying mask again!" The lying mask, that is, his speech to Liza, is rejected, and the narrator's second protest is directed against the psychological barrier erected between himself and man; it reaffirms his alienation from society.

III

To accept unquestioningly the narrator's abstractions in Part I, the results of his cerebrations and psychological rationalizations, would necessitate, if only for reasons of consistency, accepting the accuracy and validity of the depictions as well as the judgments of events in Part II. That Dostoevsky does not intend the reader to do so, that, in fact, he expects the narrative to communicate, by artistic deployment, more and perhaps different generalizations about the narrator than the narrator can make by generalization and description, may be illustrated by tracing the symbolism of objects in the *Notes*. Here one must distinguish between the symbolic value objects assume for the narrator, and the symbolism arising from the narrator's story, but apparently only to the reader.

Because so much of Dostoevsky consists of dramatic dialogue there is little descriptive prose; in the *Notes* there is almost none. Here as elsewhere Dostoevsky makes symbolic use of objects and of attitudes expressed through objects, though these must necessarily appear as speech. Among objects the following bear significant relation to the story: clothes (noted earlier in the Nevsky episode), eyes, snow, tables, walls, doors, and glass.[5] A closer look at these will show yet another artistic connection between the two parts and simultaneously offer a further insight into Dostoevsky's method.

We have previously seen that to the narrator clothes are an index of personal success. They appear with other connotations as well. Thus in Part I the first object the narrator finds antipathetic is the clanking sword of an officer. The problem of dress recurs before the party, first when the narrator brushes his own shoes because he fears that Apollon would never consent to clean twice in a single day, and again when he thinks about the state of his clothes and the yellow spot on his trousers. (One must note here the onus of the "Yellow Passport" carried by prostitutes, as well as the Russian designation, "yellow spot," for that part of the

5. Also to be noted (although it is a difficult matter to illustrate, particularly in limited space) are these attitudes in addition to those connected with insect imagery—and recurrent in Dostoevsky's later fiction—those of stuffiness, dreams, physical movement accompanied by mental development, and pain, particularly physical pain (the toothache as symbol of corruption).

retina most sensitive to light.) Similarly, his old dressing gown, in which he feels sure Liza will see him, and which even in his own eyes is the symbol of poverty, is exactly the object he tries to wrap around himself when she does appear. Apparently it offers no protection except the psychological one of displaying his poverty. More telling is the fact that real contact between him and Liza is necessarily made while he is without clothes, and at a time when he is rawest psychologically. When he dresses at the brothel he immediately loses the possibility for personal contact and resumes his façade, with which clothes may be equated. When Liza visits him, he recognizes that the psychological situation of the brothel is reversed, and notes its symbolic counterpart in Liza's festive appearance and his own dressing gown. But the clearest proof of the symbolic use of clothes occurs in the brief spell when the narrator acts from the heart—a distinction he insists upon when he says about the money he pressed into Liza's hand, "though I did that cruel thing purposely, it was not an impulse from the heart, but came from my evil brain." In that brief span, between the time she leaves and that moment on the street when he realizes the futility of pursuit, he is concerned only with his need, not with his intellect. When he rushes after her, clothes lose the value the narrator usually attaches to them, become neutral and, paradoxically, assume their most striking symbolic function by indicating the profundity of the moment: "A minute later I flew like a madman to dress, flinging on what I could at random, and ran headlong after her."

Connected with the psychological and the social behavior expressed by the emphasis on clothes is a continual emphasis on eyes, the verb *to see*, and the chiaroscuro of Petersburg. The narrator, like others in the *Double* and *Possessed*, finds it impossible to look anyone directly in the eyes, turns away, and at the same time has a constant paranoiac feeling of being observed. (The objection to the crystal palace is therefore apposite even in this context.) At least as early as *Oedipus Rex* eyes and seeing are used as symbols for understanding or knowledge and reason. In the *Notes*, both in the introspections of Part I and the episodes of Part II, they repeatedly indicate that the narrator cannot see clearly, cannot evaluate properly, refuses to understand or is incapable of it.

This configuration also appears in conjunction with snow, which is usually treated as a white, pristine covering, either pleasant or inimical, but in either case endowed with an elemental beauty. In the *Notes*, in Petersburg, it is yellow, dingy, wet, unpleasant, troublesome; Dostoevsky uses it for maximum symbolic effect. The narrator almost at the outset admits that the Petersburg climate is bad for him, but only returns to the subject at the end of Part I, when he makes the important statement, "I fancy it is the wet snow which has reminded me of that incident, which I cannot shake off now. And so let it be a story apropos of the wet snow." In the same manner, after the dinner party, when the narrator jumps into a sleigh to follow his friends, he particularly remembers the driver and horse, covered with "wet and, as it were, warm snow. It was hot and steaming." This time the narrator becomes depressed by snow in a different way. He realizes during the ride that his behavior is foolish, but decides to carry on. He unbuttons his coat, and the snow, in big wet flakes, drifts under his coat, his jacket, and his tie. It melts there and he remarks "I did not wrap myself up—all was lost anyway." Clearly he betrays the same romantic attitude as that of the scene of revenge he conjures up en route. But just as clearly, although this is a crucial episode in his experience, it cannot be the scene he recalls at the end of Part I. Nevertheless it forms one part of it. The narrator mentions "deserted street lights gleaming sullenly in the snowy darkness like torches at a funeral" (an echo of Apollon's calling). He uses the topic of snow (again in conjunction with funerals and darkness) to start his conversation with Liza. The most effective use of snow occurs at the end, when Liza runs into the street and the narrator follows her. This time it falls in masses, perpendicularly, ready to cover everything, "the pavement and the empty street as though with a pillow. There was no one in the street, no sound was to be heard. The streetlights gave a disconsolate and useless glimmer." The narrator ends his search, and indeed the image has been exploited fully. The snow, which originally hung over him, dingy, and could not be shaken off, and which reminded him of the experiences of Part II, now serves to cover Liza's steps. But it can never obliterate the narrator's experience. It can only settle on him, a mantle which will never be worn lightly, lit by lights which do not sufficiently illuminate.

The most important symbol in the *Notes*, however, is obviously the wall. The narrator describes himself at first as having a corner, then later uses the image of a cornered mouse coming up against a wall. The narrator occupies a whole room, not a corner, but like the mouse he is cornered and shut in by the wall.[6] The wall successively represents to the narrator single-minded purpose, finality, all that is in keeping with the normal, stupid, average man; then, in turn, it stands for natural science, for the laws of nature, for mathematics, for Darwin and heredity, for theories of virtue and enlightened self-interest, in short, for anything that can be connected with rational theories of the nineteenth century. With the wall may be associated the crystal palace, the highest stage of human utopia, which is wall-like because it is deterministic and rational, and because it eliminates all possibility for man to show his individuality and free will. The wall, then, embodies a paradox, for it represents those things designed to improve the lot of man, but in practice tending to destroy that which is most valuable in him. It symbolizes the positive, final views against which the narrator rails, and also stands as a barrier between man and his fullest expression of the self. Through the wall, however, one may assert one's individuality, even if only by making

6. Parts of rooms, "corners," were let so that a room might be shared by a number of lodgers. The scurrying of the mouse, incidentally, is analogous to the scurrying and wriggling on the Nevsky.

one's neighbors aware of one's toothache. Recognition of the wall leads the narrator to a consciousness of the wall as a symbol for isolation in Part I.[7] In Part II it operates for the reader as the culminating symbol of the narrative. The narrator has, in his rooms high in a Petersburg tenement, achieved the ultimate in isolation when he forces Liza to leave. He listens to her steps as she runs down the stairs, shouts her name and then notes: "I heard the stiff outer glass door open heavily with a creak and slam violently. The sound echoed up the stairs." This is what the narrator had dreaded when hesitating whether or not to follow to the brothel. Through his romantic posturing he communicates his very real despair, since he realizes that his behavior will precipitate him into ultimate isolation. Dostoevsky, to paraphrase Poe, is writing not of Petersburg, but of the soul. And when the door—a glass door—slams shut, the symbol of the wall is dramatically complete.

IV

The narrator, then, through a complex series of psychological and social motivations is actually driven to the philosophical position enunciated in the first part. Like his sermon to Liza, his protest has another and a deeper validity than that which he assigns to it. But it becomes artistically meaningful only if seen in terms of the whole work, if his ideas are studied not exclusively for their meaning, but contextually, as the expression of a personality whose generalizations are masked by a highly developed and personalized irony because this is the only form in which he is willing to admit his profound concern for his fellow beings.

Moreover, Dostoevsky specifically calls the narrator a "paradoxalist" so it behooves the reader to examine the narrator's ideas with some care. The first paradox is implied in the title. The English rendering of *podpol'e* as 'underground' is perfect, for in both languages there is a connotative difference between cellar and underground. The adjective *underground* as well as the noun indicate a secret organization, in modern times invariably a revolutionary one. The title clearly implies this, since the narrator's residence (which has other important symbolic overtones) is always above ground. But underground movements in Russia of the 1860's are precisely those against which the narrator inveighs, so that logically he should be considered reactionary rather than revolutionary. On the other hand, both in terms of respect for individual human value and in terms of present day antiutopian attitudes, the narrator is the true

7. The reader has in the meantime noted that tables assume an analogous function for the narrator. He tries to discomfit petitioners from his official position behind a table; he becomes involved in the Nevsky episode because he is out of place at a billiard table; he sits alone at table while waiting for Zverkov, is ignored by his schoolmates when they arrive and leaves the conviviality of the table in order to pace the room; he secretes his money in a table drawer; glares at Apollon who sits behind his own table; and, of course, it is across a table that he communicates with the future reader of his "notes."

revolutionary and his contemporaries are not.[8] The title also carries the modern overtones of 'subconscious' which Dostoevsky had found in C. G. Carus and German romanticism, and which is in any case a central theme of the work (the will as irrational). A whole galaxy of paradoxes may be traced in the *Notes*. On the psychological level, the paradox consists of the difference between the narrator's self-analysis, self-comprehension, and his behavior, which contradicts such analysis; of suffering as a palliative; in social theory, the paradoxes of individual supremacy and social stratification, of a utopia for all men and the insignificance and expendability of any particular individual, of utopian idealism destroying humanism, of progress and regression; at the same time, the narrator's view of the soul as "filth." On the philosophical level, where the ramifications are broadest, the paradox presents the problems of free will and determined behavior (as opposed to the psychological statement of the same problem), of conscience and consciousness (*soznanie* means both 'realization' and 'conscience'— cognitive and ethical) which makes man a superior being to the *animaux domestiques* and yet in his superiority destroys him; the paradox of reason being denied and minimized by the only tool which will adequately do so—reason itself. Stemming from this is the paradox of integration in society and isolation from it and, in literary terms, the creation of an antihero who is a hero, and writing directed against the process of writing.

The narrator protests against positivism; he contends that belief in chemically created man and consciousness smacks of its own kind of mysticism, but he has no acceptable escape from such a world. He finds a release in books and dreams, particularly the latter. Indeed, both in the first part and at the very end of the second, he echoes Piskarev's remark in the *Nevsky Prospect* about the superiority of dreams and books to reality:

> "Real life" (*zhivaja zhizn'*) oppressed me with its novelty so much that I could hardly breathe . . . for we are all cripples, every one of us more or less. We are so divorced from it that we feel at once a sort of loathing for "real life," and so cannot bear to be reminded of it. We have almost come to look upon "real life" as an effort, almost as hard work, and we are all privately agreed that it is better in books.

Much of the narrator's view of himself is, of course, a dream, a projection, in literary terms, of the romantic outcast and of the lone avenger

---

8. I am assuming that the Russian word was current in the 1860's with this political meaning. There is only one significant literary use of the word before Dostoevsky, in Pushkin's *The Covetous Knight*: "Let him force my father to treat me as a son, not as a mouse bred in the underground." The knight's treasure is, however, kept in the cellar (*podval*). *Underground* appears with political overtones in correspondence during the late 1860's, as well as in the title *Podpol'noe slovo* (*The Underground Word*), an émigré periodical published in Geneva in 1866. It seems unlikely to me that the use of the word in the *Notes* could have introduced this meaning.

(he mentions Pushkin's Silvio [*The Shot*] and Lermontov's *Masquerade*).[9] He dreams of himself as a hero, for his notion is that a hero cannot defile himself—even the evil he does is accepted and forgiven. Still, he recognizes that dreams are caused by "real life" behavior, that his most hideous dreams follow days in which he considers his behavior as particularly despicable. Ultimately he recognizes the futility of this method of escape. He particularly emphasizes at the end that he has not created anything interesting in the *Notes*, for a novel needs a hero, while all the traits of the antihero are *expressly* gathered together in this work. There is no middle ground for the narrator: "be a hero or an insect." The middle is crass, stupid, uninteresting. But Dostoevsky's creation has shown himself to be if not the average man, at least typical of nineteenth- (and twentieth-) century man. The narrator claims at one point that it is not so much the end or goal of life but its very process which is interesting and important. This, his most positive affirmation, aptly characterizes the *Notes* themselves.

No social or personal redemption is possible for the narrator. The view he takes of man, which, like Ivan Karamazov's, is founded on a denial of love, might almost be stated in terms of a generalization from the *Writer's Diary:* "The consciousness of complete impotence to help suffering humanity or to do it any good or alleviate its love can even, despite our belief in humanity's suffering, change that feeling for humanity from love into hatred." The possibility of a solution, however, did at one time exist in the *Notes*. In a letter to his brother Michael, Dostoevsky wrote on 26 March 1864:

> I am also bewailing my *Notes*. Terrible misprints, and it would have been better not to print the penultimate chapter [of Pt. I] at all (that chapter where the very idea is stated), than to print it in that form, that is, with sentences left out and contradicting itself. But what can be done? Those swine of censors left in the passages where I railed at everything and *pretended* to blaspheme; but they deleted the passage where I deduced from all this the *necessity of belief and Christ*.

Dostoevsky did not try to reintroduce the passage in subsequent editions, and his omission makes the work more effective, since a comparable view is implied in the scene with Liza and its rejection there is dramatically justified. Nothing can exist for the narrator; even religion is merely a fiction.

---

9. The *Notes* is in many places a parody of the romantic and sentimental tale. One should note particularly the paragraph on romantics in Pt. II, and Dostoevsky's use of a sentimental epigraph from Nekrasov in two places, which he coldly breaks off after the first few lines. The subject of this poem ("When from the gloom of corruption"), the regeneration of a prostitute, provides the subject for the Liza episode.

The tragedy of the narrator, and that inherent in the *Notes*, is particularly gloomy and hopeless because in the dramatic and structural terms of the story there is no escape. All roads are blocked; the wall blocks action, thought, sentiment. But a wall shuts out as well as in. The narrator has values which cannot be shared by his doctrinaire contemporaries. Gide's self-conscious characterization of the main idea of the *Notes* as " 'celui qui pense n'agit point . . . ,' et de là à prétendre que l'action présuppose certaine médiocrité intellectuelle, il n'y a qu'un pas" completely inverts the story's meaning. For the narrator admits that the underground is not really what he wants, that he seeks something totally different. But since psychology and philosophy are inseparable in the *Notes* he cannot find a positive conclusion for either one. The real point, the import of the *Notes*, is that action consists in apprehending the conflict, in gauging what Malraux calls the only two characters of tragedy, the hero and his sense of life. If there is no escape, there is realization and sympathy. There is the paradoxical recognition in the total terms of the *Notes* that humanism as well as neurosis underlies the narrator's protest, and that even refusal to accept the wall is in itself an assertion of man's stature.

VICTOR ERLICH

Notes on the Uses of Monologue in Artistic Prose†

1. The problem outlined here is but a small facet of a larger question— that of stylistic potentialities and psycho-ideological implications of various verbal structures occurring in the literary works. If, as a German esthetician H. Konrad has put it, imaginative literature is "the world transformed into language", the verbal device is the writer's most potent means of grappling with reality.[1] In literary art ideological battles are often fought on the plane of the opposition between metaphor and metonymy, or meter and free verse.

2. This by now is rather widely recognized with regard to poetry where verbal texture is organized throughout for esthetic effect. Few students of poetry will deny that the poet's choice of words and the patterns of his imagery bear important relation, indeed often provide a clue, to the total meaning or meanings of the poem. Yet there is no reason why artistic prose should not be discussed in the same vein, or, for that matter, why an inquiry into the "larger" implications of the literary artists' use of language should be confined to the lexical stratum. The

† From the *International Journal of Slavic Linguistics and Poetics* (1959). Reprinted by permission of the author.

1. Quoted in René Wellek and Austin Warren, *Theory of Literature* (New York, 1949), p. 341.

recurrence in a work of literature of grammatical categories, e.g. the first-person or the second-person pronouns, can be as revealing as the prevalence of certain semantic units or clusters. This brings us to the question of *monologue* in narrative fiction.

3. "Monologue" could be, and actually has been, defined simply as an absence of dialogue, as non-alternating, continuous, extended utterance.[2] Should we accept this rather negative definition, we would have to agree with V. Vinogradov that monologue is the predominant type of discourse in artistic prose. True, there are novels or short stories where the dramatic technique or, to use Henry James' phrase, the "scenic method" reigns supreme. "The Killers" of Hemingway and *Jean Barois* by Roger Martin du Gard are cases in point. Yet a more typical work of fiction represents a complex interplay of dialogue and "monologue", with the latter taking over whenever the events are described, reported or commented on rather than actually rendered.

But, for our purposes at least, the Vinogradov-type definition is much too broad. Nor would the conventional, i.e. dramatic, interpretation of our key term be anymore apposite here. A "monologue" such as Dmitrij Karamazov's confession or Šatov's harangue in *The Possessed* occurs within, and is part of, a dialogue situation. What I henceforth propose to mean by "monologue" as used in narrative prose is neither "nondialogue" nor an extended utterance of a protagonist, but a mode of discourse or narration employed throughout a work of fiction or a large part of it in which the voice of an individual speaker or story-teller is distinctly heard and which is marked by the frequent use of the first-person pronoun.

But then, one could interpose at this point, why not speak about "Ich-Erzählung", as distinguished from "Er-Erzählung"? There is no question but that the concept is very germane to our discussion. If nonetheless I will persist in using the word "monologue", that is mainly because it reflects more closely the discursive, non-dramatic quality of some of our salient test-cases.

4. A further discrimination seems to be in order. For certain purposes at least, it might be useful to distinguish between *written and oral* monologue. Various types of the former have been employed in European prose fiction, ever since the eighteenth century when the sentimentalist quest for "authenticity" and intimacy encouraged the use of such nonfictional genres as a memoir, a diary or a letter. At the same time, there have been many instances where "Ich-Erzählung" was oriented towards actual, live speech. This narrative manner, known in Russian literary scholarship as the *skaz*, from the root "to say, speak, relate",[3] has been recently defined by Hugh McLean as "a stylistically

2. In Viktor Vinogradov, *O xudožestvennoj proze* (Moscow-Leningrad, 1938).
3. See especially Boris Èixenbaum, "Kak sdelana 'Šinel' Gogolja", Poètika, 1919; "Illjuzija skaza",

Skvoz' literaturu (Leningrad, 1924). Viktor Vinogradov, "Problema skaza v stilisktiké", Poètika, I (Leningrad, 1956).

individualized inner narrative placed in the mouth of a fictional character and designed to produce the illusion of oral speech."[4]

The only drawback of this succinct formula lies in its "inner-narrative" clause. The requirement of a frame story fits well enough McLean's test-case, Leskov's *Polunoščniki*, and a number of other relevant instances, e.g. that masterpiece of *skaz*, "The Tale about Captain Kopejkin", yet it disqualifies unnecessarily works which otherwise exemplify very neatly the *skaz* manner, be it Gogol's "The Overcoat" or Ring Lardner's "The Haircut." As McLean himself suggests further, the sole indispensable ingredients of this narrative mode are "orality" and "individualization."

During the last two centuries the skaz technique has been used by a number of prose writers, endowed with an uncannily keen ear for the vernacular. In Russia Gogol', Leskov, Zoščenko, and many others, in modern American prose such writers as R. Lardner or J. D. Salinger, in Yiddish literature that master of the folksy oral narrative, Šolem Aleixem, have sought to emulate the phonetic, grammatical and lexical patterns of ordinary discourse.

5. The *stylistic* ingredients of such a technique are obvious enough. Not unlike a "realistic" dialogue, a *skaz*-type monologue allows ample scope of sub-literary verbal materials—the relative formal incoherence and "sloppiness" typical of spoken language, the "slangy," substandard expressions, the dialectal peculiarities, inane misuses of language characteristic of the uneducated or semi-educated speakers. At the same time, as the last item may imply, *skaz* tends to function as *mode of characterization*. The class-determined deviations from the linguistic norm betray the speaker's or narrator's social and educational status,[5] even while his idiosyncratic verbal mannerisms often reveal his personality traits.

In a recent article Vinogradov called attention to Leskov's "Levša" as an instance of using the "expressive devices of *skaz* monologue in order to project a folksy, "non-literary" narrator. "These phraseological and syntactical forms of the *skaz* . . . embody the image of an epic story teller with clear-cut social characteristics."[6]

7. It could be interposed here that this character-forming and/or articulating function is no monopoly of monologue. Any strongly differentiated dialogue yields not only through the tenor, but also through the distinctive style of the alternating utterances, some clues as to the personalities involved. Yet the "monologist" is not merely one of the

4. Cf. *Harvard Slavic Studies*, II (1954), p. 299.
5. It goes without saying that this can be true of written monologue as well. Thus, an epistolary novel, such as Dostoevskij's *Poor Folk*, can emulate faithfully the stiff, pseudo-literary style of a semi-educated "little man", Makar Devuškin. The difference here is not of kind, but rather of degree. Since actual speech is less formalized (or more casual) than written language, the deviations from the norm assert themselves more exuberantly in "oral" monologue.
6. Cf. "Obščie problemy i zadači izučenija jazyka russkoj xudožestvennoj literatury," *Izvestija Akademii Nauk SSSR, otdel literatury i jazyka*, XVI, No. 5 (Moscow, 1957), pp. 407–429.

protagonists; his is a strategic position, since it is through him that the story—or a large part of it—is mediated. The narrator's moral and intellectual range defines the narrative focus, the vantage point from which the events are presented.

Whenever—as is so often the case with the *skaz*—the story-teller's personality is defined chiefly by limitations of sensibility and intelligence, betrayed by his use of language, we are confronted with what I would like to call "a worm's eye-view of reality." (Needless to say, this technique is quite compatible with the written brand of "Ich-Erzählung.") In R. Lardner's "The Haircut" the revolting exploits of a local bully are related admiringly by a barber whose moral coarseness prevents him from registering a proper response to the situation. In Gogol's "How Ivan Ivanovič Quarrelled with Ivan Nikiforovič" most of the story is told by a "local yokel" who is in no position to appreciate the utter stupidity and triviality of the squabble between the two Ivans. The same device is used, in a somewhat more subtle way, by Dostoevskij. In some of his novels, e.g. *The Possessed*, Dostoevskij interposes between himself and the reader a provincial chronicler, who is neither as vulgar as Lardner's narrator nor as inane as Gogol's, but who is clearly too naive and parochial to comprehend fully the moral implications of the events he painstakingly records. In Zoščenko's stories the constant misuses of the official Soviet lingo help dramatize the narrator's perpetual bewilderment in the face of new social realities. The narrative manner becomes thus a technique of indirection—a kind of compositional synecdoche. A tension is effected between two views of reality—the "overt"—and clearly inadequate view, offered by the speaker or chronicler, and the implicit one, presumably that of the author and of the "ideal" reader.

8. The problem of fictional monologue as a narrative focus is closely bound up with the narrator's position vis-a-vis the world he "transforms into language." To be sure, the relationship between the speaker and the other protagonists is in each individual case reflected in the general drift of the given monologue. But not infrequently the very fact of an extended utterance tends to underscore the precarious, not to say, *pre-posterous* social situation in which the speaker finds himself.

This is especially true of "oral" monologues, or, and more, of the skaz-like variety which makes a special point of its "orality". (Technically, many a retrospective tale by Turgenev is an "inner narrative" placed in the mouth of a wistful country squire who reminisces in front of a fireplace. Yet the frame is perceived here as mere contrivances. The point of departure is soon forgotten, since the style of this presumably oral narrative is scarely distinguishable from the author's polished prose). The monologue becomes something of an anomaly in a situation which seems to call for a "normal" verbal interaction. (As L. Ščerba has pointed out,[7] more often than not it is the dialogue which is the "natural" form,

7. Cf. *Russkaja reč'*, 1923, I.

while monologue—an "artificial" one). In "real life" a lengthy uninterrupted utterance requires a special setting, be it that of a church, a
conference hall, or a classroom. Where such a positive justification is
lacking, we sometimes drift into a monologue-situation by default, either
because the addressee is unable or unwilling to respond, or because the
speaker can not control his verbal urge.

The preposterousness of an interminable monologue in what pur-
ported to be a dialogue situation is at the core of some of Šolem Aleixem's
telling comic effects in such stories as "The Pot" *(Dos tepl)* and "An
Advice" *(An ejce)*. In both instances the monologue was to serve as a
starting point for a conversation; it was supposed to elicit an advice from
an "authority" (a rabbi—in "Dos tepl," a wise and experienced writer
in "An ejce"). In both stories the counselor is nearly or actually brought
to the state of mental collapse by the speaker's pathological loqua-
ciousness.

In "Dos tepl" Jente, a voluble poultry peddler roams all over creation,
digresses interminably about her late husband, her beloved son's Tal-
mudic studies, the vicious temper of her neighbor, unable to come to
the point, indeed to formulate the question which she presumably came
to ask. For a number of pages the rabbi endures this verbal onslaught,
punctuating it time and again by a sympathetic grunt. In the finale, he
faints, literally overwhelmed by Jente's grotesquely long "question."

The structure of "An Advice" is a bit more intricate: the fidgety young
man who presumably comes to the author in order to seek his advice
as to whether he ought to divorce his spoiled and hysterical young heiress-
wife, is clearly incapable of stating his case and then listening to the
older man's counsel. All he can do is to act out *ad nauseam* his paralyzing
indecision—the pendulum-like swing from the bitter resentment at being
an outsider in the house of his well-heeled father-in-law to the equally
acute fear of losing the social position he now enjoys. This verbal orgy
of ambivalence reduces the "author" to a mere echo of the speaker's
alternating attitudes. At each pause in the visitor's monologue he
promptly agrees with the last conclusion, be it a negative or a positive
one. But this reaction, instead of achieving its obvious goal—that of
bringing the tiresome interview to an end, has invariably the effect of
activating the "other voice," of setting off a harangue in favor of the
opposite solution. This pattern culminates in farcical dialogue where
each piece of "advice" elicits automatically a polemical response and
suddenly collapses as the exasperation of the long suffering author ex-
plodes in a blood curdling yell: "Divorce her, you rascal! Divorce her,
divorce her, divorce her!"

This violent outburst can be viewed as the author's last desperate act
of self-defense against the fate which befalls the rabbi in "The Post,"
and, more broadly, as the listener's last-minute attempt at asserting
himself as an active force rather than a mere passive victim of the
speaker's obsessive soliloquizing.

9. Indeed, the natural tendency of the compulsive oral monologue is to reduce the "other" to the status of a mere shadow. True, in "The Pot" each paragraph takes as a point of departure a phrase just uttered by the rabbi. But even this word or expression is usually but a by-product of Jente's irrepressible emoting, a perfunctory summing up by the rabbi of her preceeding harangue. Moreover, even these feeble echoes are given *indirectly*, through the medium of the woman's never-ending query.

One is reminded of quite a different literary monologue— the recent novel by Albert Camus, *La Chute*. At each juncture, the rambling confession of Camus' déclassé lawyer is addressed to someone, but the listener has no independent existence here. His occasional responses have to be *inferred* from the turgid monologue of Jean-Baptiste Clamence. His is the only voice to be heard in the moral desert of the Amsterdam bar which provides the backdrop of *La Chute*.

More importantly, the speaker's desperate attempt to provoke a counter-confession fails dismally. The embarrassing candor of Camus' "penitent-judge" is an elaborate moral trap. The routine of laying one's soul bare is designed to induce a commensurate act of penance on the listener's part. Yet, in the end, the nearly silent beneficiary of the narrator's ambivalent self-debunking, refuses to reciprocate. Characteristically, he turns out to be a lawyer—another lawyer!—rather than a prospective "client," in dire need of assistance and sympathy. Instead of setting off a dialogue, the monologue serves here to underscore its ultimate impossibility. No wonder that Camus' hero mutters sadly as the narrative draws to its close: "Ne sommes-nous pas tous semblables, *parlant sans tréve et à personne* (Italics mine, V. E.), confrontés toujours aux mêmes questions bien que nous connaissions d'avance les résponses?"

10. "Parlant sans trêve et à personne"—here is a singularly apposite, and I may add, a characteristically modern phrase. As I tried to show elsewhere at greater length[8] in narrative fiction of the last hundred years or so monologue, whether of the written or of the oral variety, has often served as a verbal epitome of loneliness and isolation.

Back in the formative period of the European novel the written monologue-forms had pointed up the distinctiveness of the "self" rather than its alienation. The first-person narrative tended to dramatize the narrator's inner life, to encourage emphasis on the personal, the private, the idiosyncratic. Yet, however subjective or even narcissistic the tenor of some of the picaresque, sentimentalist or early Romantic confessions may have been, a letter in those works always presupposed an addressee, a fictional memoir or a diary was usually directed toward a present or

8. "Some Uses of Monologue in Prose Fiction: Narrative Manner and World View," to appear in the Proceedings of the 7th Congress of the International Federation of Modern Languages and Literatures, *Problems of Style and Form in Literature*.

future reader. In other words, monologue tended to imply here at least a theoretical possiblility of a dialogue.

Conversely, in a number of more fictional soliloquies the "I" is not merely the principal subject of the utterance, but also perforce its only recipient, the only possible or available audience. Monologue becomes thus a matter of talking about oneself to oneself.

In nineteenth-century Russian literature this situation is epitomized by Dostoevskij's *Notes from the Underground* and Turgenev's "Diary of a Superfluous Man." Turgenev's diarist, a lonely and sad man of thirty who, as the narrative opens, learns from his doctor he is incurably ill, decides to pass away the remaining hours by writing a memoir. And as he embarks upon this thankless task, he says bleakly: "what can I write about? . . . *I know! I will tell myself my own life*" (author's emphasis, V. E.)

Dostoevskij's "underground man" is still more explicit. Toward the end of the ramblingly discursive part I of *Notes*, he declares with a kind of inverted pride: "I write only for myself, and I wish to declare once and for all that if I write as though I were addressing readers, that is simply because it is easier for me to write in that form. It is a form, an empty form, *I shall never have readers*."

It is hardly necessary to insist that, if Dostoevskij's hero finds it easier to write "as though (he) were addressing readers," much more is involved than mere personal preference or "an empty form." Speech-activity is by its very nature a two-way street. Any extended utterance implies a recipient, an audience, or at least, the illusion of an audience. Moreover, in spite of his professed intransigence (or does not the very shrillness of these assertions "give the show away"?), the "underground man" is morbidly preoccupied with others. He is much too "self-conscious," in the everyday, colloquial sense of this word, to be self-reliant. His utter inability to establish rapport with his fellow-man is matched only by his nearly pathological concern with the impression he is making on the outside world.

In his perceptive book, *Problemy tvorčestva Dostoevkogo (1929)*, Baxtin describes the manner of *Notes from the Underground* as a "*perpetuum mobile*" of internal polemics with others and with oneself, an interminable dialogue where one rebuttal gives rise to another and so *ad infinitum*. The critic is is certainly justified in pointing up this "internal dialogization" of the underground man's harangues. Yet, he pushes his thesis a bit too far when he denies to the *Notes* the label of "monologue." The "*other-directedness*" of Dostoevskij's diarist does not annul the fact that all "objections" he refuses so furiously are imaginary, that his frenzied argument keeps recoiling upon itself, because no one is listening and apparently no one ever will. Paradoxically, it is not so much the prevalence of "I" as it is the repeated and avowedly futile use of "you" ("*You* do not understand even now, gentlemen," "*You* believe in a palace of crystal", etc.) that underscores the total vacuum into which the monologue of the "underground man" projects itself.

For Dostoevskij's hero as for Turgenev's, for Camus' uprooted lawyer as for Salinger's half-crazed adolescent, in *Catcher in the Rye*, the soliloquy is not merely non-dialogue, but anti-dialogue, testimony to the impossibility of communication. All these men, "parlant sans trêve at à personne," are *outsiders*, increasingly and irretrievably isolated from the "world they never made."

11. The capacity of a literary "monologue"—whether a written or an oral one—to underscore a distinctive predicament of an individual protagonist tends to be enhanced whenever this form is used within the framework of a third-person narrative. A good case in point is *Lalka* (The Doll) by Boleslaw Prus, more specifically, that section of the novel which bears the title "A Diary of an Old Salesclerk." The diarist, Ignacy Rzecki, one of the last Mohicans of the pre-1863 period, is increasingly out of touch and sympathy with the emerging social forces. The author makes it amply clear that Rzecki's diary-keeping is an act of withdrawl, and a symptom of alienation. "Cut off voluntarily as he was from nature and from people . . . he felt increasingly the need for an exchange of ideas. Yet, as he distrusted some, and others did not care to listen to him, . . . he talked to himself and in strictest secrecy kept a diary."

A somewhat different instance is provided by Jurij Oleša's "Envy" (*Zavist'*). This novel, one of the most sophisticated works of early Soviet fiction, consists of two parts: Part I is written in the form of a quasi-diary kept by the chief protagonist Kavalerov, a Soviet "underground man," an unreconstructed individualist who leads a marginal existence in the shadow of a successful Soviet bureaucrat and neo-Philistine, Andrej Babičev. In part II the first-person narrative is abandoned as Kavalerov is made to share the limelight with his newly discovered ally Ivan Babičev. This flamboyant relic of "bourgeois" romanticism confronts the ultra-efficient and smug new men with a quixotic challenge in behalf of the old-fashioned emotions which they seek to discard.

At the purely technical level, the hybrid narrative manner of *Envy* is clearly a matter of experimenting with the point of view. (There is no question but that Oleša was one of the most form-conscious Soviet prose writers). Yet one is tempted to speculate as to the possible connection between this shift in the narrative focus and the change in the situation of the main protagonist. If Kavalerov's soliloquy, with its unmistakeable echoes from Dostoevskij's novel, with its shuttling between day-dreaming and bitter debunking of the powers that be, is a fit vehicle for the hero's unrelieved loneliness, the more "objective" narrative mode of the second part may correspond to the fact that Kavalerov is no longer alone. He remains unadjusted to the new society, but now he can share his maladjustment and frustration with a fellow "deviant." Both Ivan Babičev and Kavalerov are outsiders, the last Mohicans of an "obsolete" set of values and a doomed way of life. But now that they have found each other they can walk the plank *together*. The solipstic world-picture fades away, be it for a while, and so does its most telling emblem, the self-involved and self-addressed monologue.

ROBERT LOUIS JACKSON

[Freedom in *Notes from Underground*]†

* * *

House of the Dead constitutes the great divide in Dostoevsky's works. It profoundly influenced every work that followed it, in particular his important writings in the first half of the 1860s—*Winter Notes, Notes from the Underground, Crime and Punishment, and The Gambler*. It is the prologue, or *Urtext*, for *Notes from the Underground*, a work whose core endeavor is to explore the implications of the dead house for contemporary man and his rationalistic utopias. *Notes from the Underground* is marked dramatically by the ideological climate and polemics in the early 1860s. Indeed, it was called into being by Dostoevsky's need to respond to the rationalist and ethical utilitarian doctrines of the Russian "enlightenment" of his time.[1] But in its basic psychological and philosophical insights into the problem of beleaguered man, it is deeply rooted in, and indebted to, a master text: *House of the Dead*.

What indissolubly unites *House of the Dead* and *Notes from the Underground*, despite their radical differences in conception and design, is a vision of catastrophe. The essence of the dead house is man's reduction to the status of the living dead. The convict, confronted by the institutionalized suppression of his personality and freedom, sees all his vital energies pass into a desperate, unending, tragic struggle to maintain his sense of life. It is not only his objective loss of freedom that defines his situation, however, but his fatalistic orientation toward the world. The concomitant of that fatalism in the moral realm emerges as the absence of personal moral responsibility. In the face of universal misfortune, there are no guilty ones. The concept of a dead house contains the

† Robert Louis Jackson, *The Art of Dostoevsky: Deliriums and Nocturnes*. Copyright © 1981 by Princeton University Press. Excerpt, pp. 159–170, reprinted with permission of Princeton University Press.

1. The Soviet Russian scholar A. Skaftymov was the first to examine *Notes from the Underground* carefully in the social context of the 1860s and in the context of Dostoevsky's polemical writings and concerns of that period. See his "Zapiski iz podpol'ia sredi publitsistiki Dostoevskogo," in *Slavia* VIII (1929–1930), 101–117; 312–339. For a more recent examination in English of *Notes from the Underground* along similar lines, see Joseph Frank, "Nihilism and *Notes from the Underground*," in *The Sewanee Review* 69 (winter 1961), 1–33. The approaches of Skaftymov and Frank, while providing an indispensable perspective for understanding *Notes from the Underground*, do not, however, undertake a full presentation of the philosophical complexity and ambiguities of that work.

notion of a universe that is indeed dominated by fate and in which man is helpless prey to the forces of accident.[2] Yet the convict's entire behavior represents an unconscious protest against the idea of a meaningless universe. It is a protest, however, in which he is not ennobled, but humiliated.

The Underground Man, too, is the convict of a metaphysical underground, or fate-bound universe. *Notes from the Underground* differs from *House of the Dead*, however, and represents a radical shift in Dostoevsky's attitude, in its metamorphosis of the mute, uneducated convict-hero into an embattled, educated, and highly articulate antihero. The ruling paradox of *Notes from the Underground* is that Dostoevsky assigns to his malevolent antihero the essentially heroic task of signaling to his rationalist and utilitarian interlocutors (and to the reader) the basic and irreconcilable conflicts between human nature and all social or philosophical constructs that deny free will. But in Dostoevsky's conception, the Underground Man is not a representative of an oppressed class like the Russian convict or "little man" of his earliest stories (despite his psychological identification with this type), but the representative of an educated class that has lost its religious faith and connections with the national folk element or people. He is a member of a generation (the 1840s) that has yielded to the Western rationalist and skeptical impulse and has been crippled by it. He argues brilliantly with the rationalists and exposes their theories of behavior governed by rational self-interest and utopian societies where free will would be obsolescent (part one). But he also emerges in his own example and history (parts one and two), in the tragedy of his rationalistic intellect and seemingly fate-bound existence, as an embodiment of the very rationalism he rejects. Herein lies the double force of Dostoevsky's polemic against the rationalists in *Notes from the Underground*.

In the "logical tangle" of his own thinking, the Underground Man can conceive only of a meaningless universe, one dominated by fate and the iron laws of nature. Through spite, irrational will, and caprice, he seeks freedom from these laws, laws that have been humiliating him "more than anything else." He seeks to escape from the inwardly experienced and outwardly perceived rule of determinism. He is without moral or spiritual foundation. His life is a treadmill motion—of rebellious will, on the one hand, which hopelessly declares war on reality, and of consciousness on the other, which, rationalizing will's defeat, sanctions humiliating capitulation to that same reality.

The Underground Man, then, is not only devastated by the rationalistic principle; he is conscious of that devastation and continually in conflict with himself. The rationalists and utilitarians who step forth as the ideologists of the laws of nature and the prophets of a new utopia

---

2. It is interesting to note that in the period when Dostoevsky was working on *House of the Dead* he drew up a list of writing projects that included "A Plan for a tragedy 'Fatum'."

only exacerbate his sense of outrage and lead him to formulate an irrational will philosophy based upon his own experience. To those who confront him with the seemingly unanswerable certainties of "twice two is four," the laws of nature, the deductions of reason and mathematics, and the "stone wall,"he replies:

> Good Lord, what have I got to do with the laws of nature and arithmetic when for some reason these laws and twice two don't please me? It goes without saying I shall not break through such a wall with my forehead, if I am really lacking in the strength to do it, but at the same time I am not going to reconcile myself with it just because it is a stone wall and I am lacking in strength. . . . Is it not much better to understand everything, to be conscious of everything, all impossibilities and stone walls; not to be reconciled to any of those impossibilities or stone walls if it disgusts you to be reconciled to them; and by way of the most inevitable logical combinations to reach the most repulsive conclusions on the eternal theme that even for the stone wall you are yourself somehow to blame, though again it is clear as day that you are by no means guilty, and therefore, silently and impotently grinding your teeth, with a voluptuous feeling to sink into inertia. (I, 3)

The Underground Man's objective compromise before the wall, yet his uncompromising subjective rebellion, which takes the form of a masochistic delight in suffering; his rationalization of his whole situation as one in which he is "guilty but without guilt before the laws of nature"—all this barely conceals, as in a medieval palimpsest, the subjective world of the tortured convict and his unending duel with the authorities. The convict, as we have seen, outwardly accepts what comes to him from the order about him as "ineluctable fact"; he takes into account "fate" and bends his back passively to the terrible beatings and blows of misfortune. But his compromise, like that of the Underground Man, is part of "an established, passive but stubborn struggle" with the enemy. The convict, however, is unconscious of the tragic dialectic of this struggle, unaware of how the revolt of suffering expresses his profound anger and hatred. It is the Underground Man who brings the whole psychology of the revolt of suffering to the level of conscious ideology and who identifies it as the last defensive weapon of absolutely abased personality.

The Underground Man recognizes that in "certain circumstances" man may insist on the "right to desire even the very stupid." He may, indeed, deliberately desire something that is harmful and stupid. And this caprice, the Undergound Man believes, may be "more advantageous than any advantage, even in a case where it clearly is harmful to us and contradicts the most healthy conclusions of our reason about advantages, because in any case it preserves for us what is most important and dear, that is, our personality and our individuality. Indeed, some people maintain that this is even more precious than anything else for man." Dostoevsky's encounter with tragic circumstances in which man may perversely desire what is harmful took place in the dead house, where "almost any independent manifestation of personality" was regarded as a crime. In the face of the complete negation of his personality the convict often behaved in capricious and irrational ways; he insisted, as it were, upon the right to desire even the harmful and stupid.

For the Underground Man "certain circumstances" are not merely rationalistic utopia or dystopia; they are the whole tragic human condition. The tragedy of the underground, the tragedy of man's humiliation before the laws of nature, is not only a personal tragedy for him but the universal tragedy of man's alienation in a blind, meaningless universe. This universe is his prison, his underground. It is for this reason that he is certain that man will "never renounce real suffering, that is to say, destruction and chaos." Suffering, he insists, is man's defining trait. But in the end the Underground Man declares that he really does not stand "either for suffering or well-being. I stand for my own caprice and for its being guaranteed to me whenever I want it."

The Underground Man cannot escape the endless *perpetuum mobile* of his thought. Starting out with the legitimate idea of defending personality and individuality in certain circumstances by irrational, self-assertive acts, he ends up defending caprice and irrational will "whenever I want it." Indeed, in the whole development of his argument in part one—that is, in the realm of intellectual argument—and in the tragic dynamic of his relations with his school friends and the prostitute Liza in part two, we find an illustration of that very intoxication that Dostoevsky observed in the wild outbursts of convicts and in certain types of murderers: once having transgressed the boundary that had been sacred to them, these men are carried away and nothing will stop them. "And thus it would be better in every way not to bring him to this point," Goryanchikov remarks apropos of the convict's intoxicated rampage. "It would be more tranquil for everybody. Yes. But how is this to be done?" These lines could easily serve as an epigraph for *Notes from the Underground*. Although Dosteovsky's Christian solution is apparent in that work, the question, "Yes. But how?" speaks more directly to the tragic human condition that is exposed there.

The Underground Man finds man where he finds himself: at the "last wall," without hope or goal, yet—figuratively speaking—beating his head against that wall in order to affirm his existence. He posits a meaningless, treadmill existence: "The worker when he finishes his work at least receives his wages and goes to a tavern, ending up in the clink . . . but where can man go?" He suggests that "perhaps the whole aim mankind is striving to achieve on earth merely lies in this incessant process of achievement, in other words, in life itself, and not really in the attainment of any goal, which, it goes without saying, can be nothing more than twice two is four." Man is "instinctively afraid of reaching the goal and finishing the building he is erecting."

Dostoevsky certainly stands behind the Underground Man in his stress upon man's love of process and rejection of the idea of a terminal point to human strivings in life. The Underground Man's rejection of the "crystal palace," with its idea of final achievement and truth, echoes Dostoevsky's own ironical response to the Crystal Palace at the London World's Fair in *Winter Notes*: "Must we then accept all this indeed as the final truth and be rendered silent forever?" Yet the view of man laboring incessantly without any goal or purpose is one that Dostoevsky clearly did not share. Goryanchikov in *House of the Dead* recoils before the idea of Sisyphean, purposeless labor:

> The thought once occurred to me that if one's desire were to crush and destroy a man completely, punish him with the most frightful of punishments, it would be enough to give him work of a totally and utterly useless and nonsensical character. . . . If one compelled a convict, for example, to pour water from one bucket into another, and then back again into the first, to grind sand or to transfer a pile of earth from one spot to another and back again, I think he would hang himself after a few days or would commit a thousand crimes in order at least to die and in that way escape from such degradation, shame and torment. Of course, such punishment would amount to torture, revenge, and would be senseless, because it would not achieve any rational goal. But since some element of this kind of torture, senselessness, degradation and shame inevitably is a part of all compulsory labor, penal labor is incomparably more painful than any free labor just by virtue of the fact that it is compulsory.

The convict, Goryanchikov notes, works efficiently and rapidly when he is given a task that he can bring to a conclusion. In this he is like the free peasant who works better and longer because "he works for himself with a rational goal." Just as a rational, or tangible, goal makes the labor of a free peasant, or even a convict, meaningful and bearable, so in Dostoevsky's view man's strivings on earth are made meaningful by a spiritual goal or ideal. The concrete rational goal that man needs in his day-to-day labor if the labor is not to be torture and humiliation finds a direct counterpart in the spiritual and religious goal and ideal that he needs to make life meaningful. Striving in a world unillumined by lofty spiritual or religious ideals could only take on the tragic character of senseless forced labor in a penal camp. Such is the Sisyphean labor that the Underground Man projects for man in a universe where he has "no place to go." The Underground Man himself emerges in *Notes from the Underground* as a tragic convict of an age that has lost its faith, a prisoner doomed to the torture and humiliation of endless treadmill movement in a fate-bound universe of his own making.

Thus, like the Underground Man, Dostoevsky rejects the idea of a finite goal in human history, but unlike the Underground Man he posits a transcendent ideal that makes man's striving on earth rational and meaningful. Man, Dostoevsky agrees, prefers movement to inertia. But, he insists, man seeks more than simply movement: he seeks spiritual meaning in his strivings. Dostoevsky thus affirms a kind of Christian existentialist outlook wherein striving for an ideal itself introduces a creative tension and meaning into human existence. In contrast, the Underground Man lays the groundwork in part one of his notes for an atheistic existential outlook. Unlike some existentialists in the twentieth century (philosophers such as Camus), however, the Underground Man is unable to imagine either himself or the orphaned, Sisyphean man as happy.[3]

Dostoevsky's Christian existentialist point of view and the stark, despairing, unidealized, near-atheistic point of view of the Underground Man constitute intimately related polarities in Dostoevsky's philosophical thought. They also reflect the constructive dialectic of his own spiritual struggle in the period of his imprisonment in Omsk. But *Notes from the Underground*, at least in the form that it exists today, does not clearly bring into the foreground this dialectic or play of polarities. The reason lies, in part at least, in the censoring it underwent. In a letter to his brother Mikhail in 1864 Dostoevsky complained of "frightful misprints" in the printed text as well as other damage by the censor:

> It really would have been better not to have printed the penultimate chapter (the main one where the very idea is expressed) [ch. x, part one] than to have printed it as it is, that is, with sentences thrown together and contradicting each other. But what is to be done! The swinish censors let pass those places where I ridiculed everything and blasphemed for show, but where I deduce from all this the need for faith and Christ—this is forbidden. Just who are these censors, are they in a conspiracy against the government or something?[4]

It seems quite likely that Dostoevsky gave oblique expression in the penultimate chapter of the uncensored part one of *Notes from the Underground* to the ideas he had privately set down in his notebook in 1864

3. "There is no fate that cannot be surmounted by scorn," Albert Camus writes in his "Myth of Sisyphus." Camus leaves his Sisyphus at the foot of the mountain where he finds his burden again. He concludes: "This universe henceforth without a master seems to him neither sterile nor futile. Each atom of that stone, each mineral flake of that night-filled mountain, in itself forms a world. The struggle itself toward the heights is enough to fill a man's heart. One must imagine Sisyphus happy." A. Camus. *The Myth of Sisyphus and other Essays*, trans. Justin O'Brien (New York, 1959), pp. 90–91.

4. *Pis'ma* I, 353.

on "transitional" man eternally striving on earth for the ideal embodied in Christ. Here, undoubtedly, Dostoevsky in some way disclosed the inner Christian character of the Underground Man's "crown of desires," his hidden "ideals," his yearning for a "crystal palace" at which one would not want to stick out one's tongue. "I myself know, as twice two is four." he remarks at the end of part one, "that it is not at all the underground which is better, but something else, something quite different, for which I thirst but which I can in no way find! To the devil with the underground!⁵ The uncensored chapter, finally, was the counterpart to chapter nine, part two, where the theme of love and self-sacrifice finds symbolic embodiment in Liza and in that epiphanic moment when she and the Underground Man embrace in tears. But Dostoevsky did not restore the original, uncensored pages in subsequent editions of *Notes from the Underground*, and the manuscript of that work is not extant.

In the very first lines of *House of the Dead* Goryanchikov observes that the prison was situated on the "very edge of the fortress next to the fortress wall." Peering through the cracks in the stockade at "God's world," one could see besides the wall "a tiny strip of sky, not the sky above the prison, but another, distant, free sky." Beyond the locked gates of the fortress was

> a bright, free world where people lived like everybody else. But from this side of the stockade that world appeared to one as a kind of impossible fairy tale. Here is a special world unlike anything else; here are special laws, clothes, customs and ways, and a living dead house—life as nowhere else, and a people apart. Now it is this special corner that I have undertaken to describe. (I, i)

Starting out with God's world and the distant, free sky, Dostoevsky steadily narrows his focus until it concentrates on that special corner,

---

5. The Underground Man, of course, remains a skeptic and prisoner of the "underground." But insofar as his skepticism is directed against a rationalism that is devoid of spirituality or life, it serves the higher truth in which he is unable to believe. In all of this he bears a certain resemblance to Turgenev's Hamlet-type. In his important speech on "Hamlet and Don Quixote" in 1861, Turgenev observed: "The skepticism of Hamlet does not represent indifference . . . [Hamlet] who does not believe in the possibility of realizing the truth at the present moment, indefatigably struggles with falsity and in this way becomes one of the main champions of the truth in which he is unable fully to believe. But in negation, as in fire, there is an annihilating force, and how is one to keep this force within limits, how is one to indicate to it where, precisely, it must stop, when that which it must destroy and that which it ought to spare is often joined and indissolubly linked? Here is where one finds that tragic side of human life that has so often been noted: will is necessary for deeds, thought is necessary for deeds; but thought and will are disunited, and grow more and more disunited every day. (See "Hamlet i Don-kikhot," in Turgenev, *Polnoe sobranie sochinenii*, 15 vols. [Moscow-Leningrad, 1960–1968], VIII [1964], 183.) The Underground Man, as we have noted, is unconscious of the higher truth for which he yearns. Skepticism in him, moreover, takes on pathological forms. But in his irony, in the nature of his contradictions and in his uncontrolled instinct for negation, he is linked genetically with Turgenev's Hamlet-type.

the prison, a world he will shortly refer to as "hell—pitch darkness." The contrast between the outside and inside worlds serves at the very outset not only to accent the central theme of freedom but to establish in the reader's mind a cosmic frame for the prison recollections. In the course of his journey with the narrator, the reader will never lose a sense of the existence of God's world, the macrocosm. The house of the living dead is a special corner, but it will be presented and evaluated in terms of the ethical and spiritual values that are associated with God's world. What is important is not whether historical Russia beyond the prison walls lives by these values; it does not, and the prison, with its representatives from all corners of Russia, is clearly a model for that Russia. What is important, rather, is that in these opening passages Dostoevsky clearly establishes that vantage point, those moral-spiritual heights, from which he will survey his prison, his Russia, his hell, and address the conscience of man. In this connection it is of signal importance that Dostoevsky has chosen a narrator who has overcome his bitterness and despair and *learned how to see*.

The situation is quite different in *Notes from the Underground*. In *House of the Dead* the objective narrator and resentful convict constitute two separate entities. Here in *Notes* it is as though the convict has stepped out of his frame to become the narrator of his own story. His suffering ego (now the ego of the Underground Man) becomes the center and circumference of God's world. It eclipses God's world. He perceives the world through a "crack in the floor," and what he perceives is the same dark underground that surrounds him. The reader is without a Virgil in this hell, and his journey is a difficult one. It is up to him to discern the cosmic frame that encircles the seemingly boundless underground.

It is not easy to locate Dostoevsky in *Notes from the Underground*. Even in *House of the Dead* Dostoevsky places a fictional narrator (as well as an editor) between himself and his prison experiences. He does not want to speak directly about these experiences. Goryanchikov is a distancing device. The Underground man too is a distancing device, but one that operates in a different way, affording the author a certain cover or complicity with his narrator. The Underground Man carries on Dostoevsky's polemic: he discourses with a chilling frankness about human nature and history; he lashes out at the rationalists, the "stone wall," and the laws of nature. The Underground Man's tragedy, we come to recognize, is the central argument in Dostoevsky's polemic against the rationalists; but it is also part of the Underground Man's truth that Dostoevsky shares—up to a point. Again, however, it is for the reader to determine at what point the Underground Man's truth—the truth of a man buried alive—becomes unacceptable (as it indubitably does) to Dostoevsky. The reader, moreover, must decide whether truth in general, always shifting, even yields such a fixed point.

In allowing the Underground Man to dominate the stage, in investing him with the despair of his own darkest moments, and in turning that despair into a paradoxical weapon, Dostoevsky makes it difficult for the reader wholly to view the Underground Man in the didactic design of the work. At issue here is not Dostoevsky's intentional view—the organizing Christian perspective—but whether this view entirely succeeds in refuting those evidences of reality, that outlook on human nature and history that the Underground Man expresses and that, for him at least, validates a posture of despair. The underground paradoxicalist, in the final analysis, *lives*. He is more than a controlled satirical device by means of which Dostoevsky delivers a crushing blow to the rationalists of the 1860s and demonstrates the tragedy of a man divorced from the people and Christian faith. He is, also, quite clearly, a confession of the deep bitterness and despair that assailed Dostoevsky in the dead house. He is not simply a straw man whom Dostoevsky triumphantly exposes in a brilliant polemic. He also provides a certain viewpoint on human nature and history—a disorienting and pessimistic one—that is not easy to refute and that certainly must have been extremely difficult for Dostoevsky himself to transcend.

"You think I am one of those people who save souls, offer spiritual balm, put grief to flight?" Dostoevsky wrote to A. L. Ozhigina in 1878. "Sometimes people write this about me, but I know *for certain* that I am capable of instilling disillusionment and revulsion. I am not skilled in writing lullabies, though I have occasionally had a go at it. And, of course, many people demand nothing more than that they be lulled.[6] *Notes from the Underground* is not a lullaby; it is capable of instilling disillusionment, not because Dostoevsky stands with the Underground Man—he clearly does not—but because he could not stand at a sufficient distance from him.

In retrospect, the manner in which *Notes from the Underground* presented human reality did not wholly satisfy Dostoevsky. "It is really too gloomy," he remarked many years later. "*Es is schon ein überwundener Standpunkt.* Nowadays I *can* write in a more serene, conciliatory way."[7] At the time he was writing part two of *Notes from the Underground* he worried that "in its tone it is too strange, and the tone is harsh and wild."[8] Yet he nonetheless spoke of the work as "strong and frank; it will be the truth."[9] But did he feel in retrospect that its truth was more somber and divided than he had intended? Why did he not restore the

6. *Pis'ma* IV, 4.
7. V. V. Timofeeva (O. Pochinkovskaia), "God raboty s znamenitym pisatelem," in *F. M. Dostoevskii v vospominaniiakh sovremennikov* (Moscow, 1964), II, 176. Timofeeva recalls saying to Dostoevsky: " 'I read your *Notes from the Underground* all last night. And I can't get over my impressions. What a horror—the soul of man! But also what terrible truth!' Fyodor Mikhailovich responded with a broad and bright smile. 'Kraevsky told me at the time that [*Notes from*

the *Underground*] was my real *chef d'oeuvre* and that I should always write in that manner, but I don't agree with him. It is really too gloomy. *Es ist schon ein überwundener Standpunkt.* Nowadays I *can* write in a more serene, conciliatory way. At the moment I am writing a piece . . .'." (Ibid.) Dostoevsky was at work at the time on *The Raw Youth.*
8. *Pis'ma* II, 613.
9. *Pis'ma* I, 362.

pages that had been mangled by the censor? Did he feel, perhaps, that the Underground Man's blasphemy and ridicule had turned out to be more than something for show? Was he dissatisfied with the too tragic content of the work? Did the "external fatalism" of which he complained to his brother at the time he was writing lay too heavy a hand on *Notes from the Underground* itself? The prison recollections of Goryanchikov were broken in pieces by "some other narrative, some other kind of strange, terrible recollections jotted down in an uneven, convulsive sort of way"; they seemed to have been "written in madness." These recollections, we have suggested, might have dealt with Goryanchikov's domestic life. May we not, however, regard the Underground Man's reminiscences—in the figurative sense—as the other part of Goryanchikov's notebook? *Notes from the Underground*, in any case, lies deep in the shadow of the dead house.

*   *   *

GARY SAUL MORSON

[Anti-Utopianism in *Notes from Underground*]†

*   *   *

The most striking example of anti-utopian anti-closure is to be found in *Notes from Underground*. The narrator of that work, it will be recalled, promises, but fails, to end his potentially endless series of self-referential paradoxes; and so the "editor" arbitrarily ends the text, substituting an ellipsis for the "missing" section. "The 'notes' of this paradoxicalist do not end here, however," the editor explains. "He could not resist and continued them. But it also seems to me that we may stop here." The underground man's paradoxes of self-reference and infinite regress are closely related to one of his two key arguments against all-embracing explanatory systems: namely, that their starting points must be chosen arbitrarily and are consequently likely to appear, to someone not already committed to the system, as just what is most in need of justification. One system's axioms, he suggests, are another's theorems (and vice versa): there are no axioms *per se*. "Where are the primary causes on which I am to build?" he asks. "Where are my bases? Where am I to get them from? I exercise myself in the process of thinking, and consequently with me every primary cause at once draws after itself another still more primary, and so on to infinity." *Notes from Underground* itself is, indeed, the dramatization of this process, the logic of which is reflected not only

† Reprinted from Gary Saul Morson, *The Boundaries of Genre*, Copyright © 1981 by permission of the University of Texas Press and of the author.

in its non-ending, but also in its characteristic sequences of speech, speech about speech, and speech about speech about speech: "You will say that it is vulgar and base to drag all this into public after all the tears and raptures I have myself admitted. But why is it base? . . . And yet you are right—it really is vulgar and base. And what is most base of all is that I have now started to justify myself to you. And even more base than that is my making this remark now. But that's enough, or, after all, there will be no end to it; each step will be more base than the last."

The underground man's second argument against all-embracing explanatory systems is that they fail to account for the complex facts of history and human behavior—facts which are, he suggests, essentially unamenable to systematization. "Try it, and cast a look upon the history of mankind. . . . one may say anything about the history of the world— anything that might enter the most disordered imagination. The only thing one cannot say is that it is rational. The very word sticks in one's throat." Describing history as a succession of the contingent, irrational, and hence anomalous, he concludes that "all these fine systems—all these theories for explaining to mankind its real normal interests, so that inevitably striving to obtain these interests, it may at once become good and noble—are, in my opinion, so far, mere logical exercises! Yes, logical exercises. . . . But man is so fond of systems and abstract deductions that he is ready to distort the truth intentionally, he is ready to deny what he can see and hear just to justify his logic."

The first part of *Notes from Underground* could, indeed, be described as a series of encounters of system with anomaly. In chapter after chapter, the underground man (a) paraphrases a utopian explanatory system, (b) presents contrary cases from history or everyday behavior (e.g., the story of the educated man of the nineteenth century with a toothache), and (c) supplies the evidently inadequate answers that his opponents would probably give to explain away anomaly and so to "justify their logic." In chapter 7, in which the underground man's characterization of utopian explanatory systems as "logical exercises" occurs, this pattern is repeated a few times. "Oh tell me," he begins,

> who first declared, who first proclaimed, that man only does nasty things because he does not know his own real interests; and that if he were enlightened, if his eyes were opened to his real normal interests, man would at once become good and noble because being enlightened and understanding his real advantage, he would see his own advantage in the good and nothing else, and we all know that not a single man can knowingly act to his own disadvantage. . . . Oh, the babe! Oh, the pure, innocent child!

The one who "first proclaimed" this theory, or a version of it, was, of course, Socrates: and the underground man here seems to be answering both the *Republic* and a contemporary utopian target, *What Is to Be Done?*, which outlines a similar theory. Dostoevsky's "paradoxicalist" responds with his characteristic examples of quite different kinds of behavior; then supplies the "gentlemen's" likely defense of their system; and, returning to his starting point, both describes and engages in still more examples of the sort of paradoxical behavior which, he says, "breaks down all our classifications, and continually shatters all the systems evolved by lovers of mankind." The psychology of the underground thus refutes the Allegory of the Cave. In a number of chapters, the underground man concludes that "what is to be done"—he repeats the phrase a number of times—is not to escape from the "cellar" (as Chernyshevsky's heroine dreams) but to remain where the "sole vocation of every intelligent man is babble, that is, the intentional pouring of water through a sieve."

*   *   *

RICHARD H. WEISBERG

The Formalistic Model: *Notes from Underground*†

Against "Existentialism": Part 1 of the Tale

In Dostoevski's *Notes from Underground* (1864)[1] ressentiment achieves perhaps its most paradigmatic novelistic expression. This masterpiece of modern fiction is less representative of the independent "existential" philosophy for which it is known than of a personal history defined by frustrated vengefulness and distorted narrative formalism. The structure of the story, which still bears its original division into two distinct sections,[2] indicates that ressentiment is often motivated by external events working upon an overheated verbal imagination. The reverse chronology of the structure allows the reciprocity of this relationship to be clearly understood: the external events described in the second part have led to the romantic philosophizing of the first, just as the latter demonstrates the ressentiment perspective from which the protagonist's youthful experiences are viewed some fifteen years afterward.

The two parts of Dostoevski's well-known story have allowed critics sympathetic to the Underground Man's philosophy to limit their analysis to the first and virtually to ignore the incidents in the second that inspired that philosophy. Apologists for the protagonist, from the existentialist

† From Richard H. Weisberg, *The Failure of the Word* (New Haven: Yale U.P. 1984), pp. 28–41. Reprinted by permission of Yale University Press.
1. The title in Russian is *Zapiski iz podpol'ja*. I have followed the Constance Garnett translation in *Three Short Novels of Dostoyevsky*, ed. Avrahm Yarmolinsky (Garden City, N.Y.: Anchor, 1960), pp. 127–222, including at some points the original Russian in brackets.
2. *Notes from Underground* was first published in two separate numbers of the journal *Epokha*.

critic Lev Shestov to many recent analysts,[3] often choose to forget that the outpourings of the first half of the novel flow from the fictional pen of the same character whose pathetic attempts at human interaction are described thereafter. For in his "relationships" with the tavern officer, Zverkov, Liza, and even the servant Apollon, the diarist in part 2 passes through every stage of the phenomenon of ressentiment; these few failed human interactions have sent him into the underground to resense forever the humiliation they have produced. But even if an analysis ignores part 2, the internal evidence of part 1 establishes the pathetic enslavement of this protagonist to a narrative mode which utterly inhibits a free response to people and even to ideas.

The recognition that we are treating a story, not a treatise, refines our understanding of the tale's ultimate meaning. For if the underground protagonist has become a spokesman for twentieth-century existentialists, and if, as I will argue, his diatribe in part 1 subtly disguises a goading negativity, the story may finally be perceived as a brilliant critique of those who flaunt their freedom, but whose philosophy actually derives from (and leads to) passive resentment and repressed violence.

Part 1 establishes three fundamental aspects of the protagonist's character: his bellicosity, his obsessive self-awareness, and his verbosity. The very first paragraph centers on the adjective *zloi*, the closest Russian equivalent to the word *ressentient*, and one associated in all of Dostoevski with intellectual types. "I am a sick man, a spiteful [zloi] man," begins the underground "confession." We are immediately launched into a spiritual mode utterly at odds with that of the noble heroes of premodern literature. The Underground Man recognizes that he is no Achilles; the wordy Thersites has come home to roost as epic hero, and spitefulness has advanced from the fringes of Western literature to its very center.

The Underground Man quickly seeks an object for his characteristic rancor and chooses the reader of his diary. He gratuitously grafts onto us his own mocking insensitivity: "No. I refuse to consult a doctor from spite [zlost'i]. That you probably will not understand. Well, *I* understand it." And again, "Now, are not you fancying, gentlemen, that I am expressing remorse for something now, that I am asking your forgiveness for something? I am sure you are fancying that. . . . However, I assure you I do not care if you are." In a deliberate parody of the style of Rousseau's diarists, and presaging that of Camus' Clamence, Dostoevski's protagonist reveals his lack of genuine self-analysis. The mutual spite imposed on the relationship between speaker and listener by the Underground Man contrives to eliminate within all of part 1 of any forthright communication.

3. See especially Lev Shestov, *Na vesakh Iova* (Paris, 1929), pp. 27–94; and *Athens and Jerusalem* (1938), ed. Bernard Martin (Athens: Ohio University Press, 1966). For a recent apology, see Reed Merrill, "The Mistaken Endeavor: Dostoevski's Notes from Underground," *Modern Fiction Studies* 18 (1972–73), 505–16. See also my riposte to Mr. Merrill: Richard Weisberg, "An Example Not to Follow: *Ressentiment* and the Underground Man," *Modern Fiction Studies* 21 (1975–76), 553–63.

Using his exquisitely crafted tool of rationalization, the Underground Man generalizes from his own apparent negativity: *all* intelligent men suffer from the "illness of overconsciousness," he explains. Intelligence is thus depicted as a weakness imposed by hated "laws of nature" upon certain unfortunates. These people consequently lose the capacity for self-actualization, because "an intelligent man [*umni čelovek*] cannot become anything in the nineteenth century." Only in the act of writing can he become ("I have taken up my pen to explain this phenomenon," the protagonist says), for only writing can express his sole remaining emotion, "the enjoyment of one's own degradation." No meaningful approach to life is possible other than through narrative forms, and from these the protagonist significantly singles out the paradigm of insult and revenge:

> Finally, even if I had wanted to be anything but magnanimous, had desired on the contrary to revenge myself on the assailant, I could not have revenged myself on any one for anything because I should certainly never have made up my mind to do anything, even if I had been able to. Why should I not have made up my mind? About that in particular I want to say a few words.

Many readers have taken chapter 2 to heart, seeing in it the noble alienation and sensitivity of an existential hero. An alternate view identifies this chapter and the "few words" that follow as the expression of a hopelessly static or nonexistential consciousness. Causes are casually intertwined with effects in this masterpiece of rhetoric. Intelligence is gratuitously linked with nonactualization, and an idiosyncratic illness with a widespread social condition. Instead of proceeding from an awareness of some personal malady to a search for its cause (the usual path to cure), the narrator manages to work backward. He posits the cause first, the intangible "nineteenth century," and perversely concludes that a negative symptom (vindictiveness) must reflect a positive condition (intelligence). There is no way out of this logical fantasy, the first significant literary example of "mauvaise foi" since Hamlet observed, "The time is out of joint, O cursed spite, / That ever I was born to set it right!" Both characters grandiloquently blame their own most glaring inadequacies on an outside force, temporality.[4]

With immense sensitivity to the obsessive interests of such protagonists, Dostoevski now has the Underground Man advance his treatise with a dialectic on the subject that seems most to interest him: insult and revenge. When a nonintellectual senses himself to have been insulted, we learn, he rushes "straight toward his object like an infuriated

---

4. People occasionally express the ephemeral desire to have been born in earlier or later periods. But the narratively ressentient type exacerbates this "untimeliness" into a personal, enduring insult.

bull with his horns down, and nothing but a wall will stop him." On the other hand, the overconscious man, the self-defined "mouse," so complicates the issue of revenge that he does not even begin to charge. For decades, critics have quarreled over the meaning of the "wall," the force to which even the man of action "defers," and about which the "mouse" endlessly theorizes from the beginning of chapter 3.[5] The wall evidently stands between all men and a necessary act. When the "normal" man, in quest of such acts, confronts the wall, he concedes its unmistakable dominance over him and resumes other activities. He perceives the wall for what it is, a given:

> as though such a stone wall really were a consolation, and really did contain some word of conciliation, simply because it is as true as twice two makes four.

Existentialists such as Shestov embrace the protagonist's articulate refusal to accept unthinkingly even this basic external reality:

> But what do I care for the laws of nature and arithmetic, when, for some reason, I dislike those laws and the fact that twice two makes four? Of course I cannot break through the wall by battering my head against it if I really have not the strength to knock it down, but I am not going to be reconciled to it simply because it is a stone wall and I have not the strength.

Indeed, these passages superficially embody a fierce rejection of rationalism in the name of freedom. No wonder that Shestov, for example, compares the Underground Man to Nietzsche, Kierkegaard, and even Socrates.[6]

A careful look at the quality of the assumptions in the argument, even without an analysis of its source, reveals the protagonist's underlying deterministic stance. From the depths of his negative spirit, the narrator

---

5. See Shestov, *Athens and Jerusalem*, p. 371. For an excellent skeptical view of the Underground philosophy, see Viktor Shklovski, *Za i protiv; Zametki o Dostoevskom* (Moscow, 1957), 154–64: and A. Skaftimov, "Zapiski iz podpolja sredi publitsistiki Dostoevskogo," *Slavia* 8 (1929–30): 101–17, 312–39. For American views of the protagonist's philosophy closer to my own, see Joseph Frank, "Nihilism and *Notes From Underground*," *Sewanee Review* 69 (1961): 1–33; and Robert L. Jackson, "Aristotelian Movement and Design in Part Two of *Notes from the Underground*," in *Twentieth-Century Views on Dostoyevski*, ed. Robert L. Jackson (Englewood Cliffs, N.J.: Prentice Hall, 1984), pp. 66–81.

The Russian verb *pasovat'* in this passage is often mistranslated. Garnett, for example, translates as follows: "By the way: facing the wall, such gentle-

men—that is, the 'direct' persons and men of action—are genuinely *nonplussed*" (p. 134). David Magarshack, on the other hand, may render it too strongly: "Incidentally, before such a stone wall such people . . . as a rule *capitulate* at once"; *The Best Stories of Dostoevski*, ed. Ralph Matlaw (New York: Modern Library, 1955), p. 114. Active, ongoing consternation about the wall is absent in the original; since one usage of *pasovat'* is as a card-playing term meaning "to pass," it would seem that the "natural man" does no more than to *defer* to the wall.

6. See Shestov, *Na vesakh Iova*, p. 35. See also his *Dostojevski i Nitzsche: Philosophija tragedii* (St. Petersburg: 1903); and *Dostoevski, Tolstoi and Nietzsche*, trans. Bernard Martin (Athens: Ohio University Press, 1969).

first assumes that even the man of action will always defer to the stone wall. Such a man at least begins to act, however, whereas the protagonist has already identified himself as one who "could not have revenged myself on anyone for anything." The mouse would never dream of rushing toward the wall, much less of battering his head against it; instead, he creates so many doubts for himself about the wall that he does not even make a move toward resolving a deeply felt insult. Primary causes (the justice of the charge against the oppressor, no matter what the odds of success) are replaced by endless second-guessing (Should I act? Will there be a better time to act? Was my enemy really wrong? Don't I admire him deep down? Will I look ridiculous? etc.).

But the wall that occasionally hinders even the active man by definition does not allow for a great deal of inquiry. It is an axiom of human experience. Two plus two *does* equal four. There are things in the universe which are materially true, and which are insusceptible to human change. In Nietzsche's words (and the Underground Man is no Nietzschean!), "such truths do exist." The willingness at least to test his natural capacities to the fullest ennobles the not unintelligent "homme de la nature"; he will not allow imponderables to prevent him from confronting his destiny head-on. Thus, even if he is as mediocre as the Underground Man resentfully claims, the average nineteenth-century man is a step ahead of the narrator. The two are equally fascinated with the stone wall; neither has the heroic capacity to defy it. But whereas the normal man accepts its incontrovertible presence, the ressentient man makes it his personal enemy and determines his life in reaction to it. Thus the Underground Man, and not, as it may first appear, the natural man, converts a fundamental truth into a "satisfying determinism."[7]

Victor Shklovski, the gifted Russian formalist critic, recognizes the intrinsic fallacies of, and the autobiographical impetus for, the Underground Man's declaration of "freedom." As he puts it, "The narrator cannot even go to the wall to try his luck at bringing it down. Weakness thus becomes his amusement [B'essilie stanovitse ego razvlečeniem]." Unlike Shestov, Shklovski makes effective use of part 2, observing that "the stone wall is realized in the form of the officer who shoves everything

---

7. The term "satisfying determinism" is Reed Merrill's; see his "Mistaken Endeavor," p. 513n17. But rejecting certain absolutes as much as accepting them may lead to determinism!

Placing the case for a moment in an altered setting, assume that I decide one morning to paint the sky black. I make this decision because it occurred to me the night before (perhaps during a dream) that all "givens" of human experience are personally affronting to me. I call on my neighbor, Fred, to help out. Fred, less intelligent than I, loves action. While I watch from my sheltered vantage point, Fred rents a plane, buys some paint, and tries to effectuate my scheme. He quickly dis-

covers the impossibility of the task, and, deferring to forces beyond himself, lands the plane and heads off to work. Meanwhile, I sit at home, having attempted far less than Fred, but still doggedly unwilling to accept the material veracity of the sky's unalterably blue appearance. Who is the "freer" man, really—Fred, who goes on acting (however banally), or I, who sit at home railing against the laws of nature? More vital still, which of the two of us will be more likely to take steps against *actual* injustice—I, who do nothing but hypothesize such enemies as time, space, and matter, or Fred, who defers to external forces only after having tried his utmost to exert his free will?

aside as he walks. . . . The narrator cannot live because he is surrounded by *walls of this sort*. . . . The man, well-dressed, socially successful, is already a wall for the underground inhabitant.[8] Shklovski's approach is close to my own in that it affirms the unity of the story and the interaction of its parts. Indeed, the "stone wall" passage early in the tale merely restates and rationalizes the ressentient frustrations, weaknesses, and inaction of all of part 2. For there he recounts the galling truth that just such "normal" types as Zverkov and the tavern officer have "insulted" him by their self-confidence and popularity.

In the midst of the deceptive narrative in part 1, chapter 5 stands as a small oasis of veracity. It could be called the "soliloquy chapter," for in its single paragraph, the Underground Man expresses himself in a manner that echoes Hamlet at his most lucid. He tells us that he has "made up a life, so as at least to live in some way." Rejecting reality out of hand, he finds constant excuses for isolation and inaction; "the legitimate fruit of consciousness is inertia, that is, conscious sitting with the hands folded." And, although he continues to pretend to himself that only stupid men can act, he ends, like Hamlet, in an astounding confession:

> Oh, gentlemen, do you know, perhaps I consider myself an intelligent man only because all my life I have been able neither to begin nor to finish anything. Granted I am a babbler, a harmless vexatious blabber, like all of us. But what is to be done if the direct and sole vocation of every intelligent man is babble, that is, the intentional pouring of water through a sieve?

This comment, a strikingly and singularly honest one for the Underground Man, confirms that the internal logic of his diatribe against the "laws of nature" and the nineteenth century is organically false. The protagonist manages a brief confession; he admits that his sole virtue, intelligence, may itself be a figment of his mendacity. Having undermined this defining trait, the Underground Man is truly relegated to what Shklovski calls *ničtožnost'* (nothingness).

But while nothingness defines the protagonist, he paradoxically insists upon giving a narrative form to it. Could it be, he queries, that I only call myself intelligent to rationalize my inaction? For the Underground Man's diatribe in part 1 against observable reality is only partially justifiable as a critique of mediocre technological positivism. After all, the "homme de la nature" is far less a positivist than is the protagonist.

8. Viktor Shklovski, *Za i protiv*, pp. 154–56. In later pages of this perceptive analysis, Shklovski emphasizes the Underground Man's debilitating sense of being out of joint with his time (p. 159) and his constant reliance on "the muse of vengeance and sadness [*mesti i pečali*]." Shklovski associates these traits with Dostoevski himself (p. 159), seeing the work as a vengeful attack by the authors upon the writers Chernyshevski and Belinski.

The natural man spontaneously partakes of all the fullness of reality; the protagonist's only act, on the other hand, is to delimit that reality to the comforting material boundaries of his four underground walls and the pages of his diary.

From Insult to Mendacity: Part 2

Far from wanting to live, the protagonist has chosen a hermetic, moribund mode of mere existence. Yet he has adopted this stance not through rejection of alienating society, but by a cowardly acceptance of his own proclivity toward ressentiment.

The protagonist had been a middle-level bureaucrat before his "retirement." He despised his work but "did not openly abuse it" because he "got a salary for it." He considered himself intellectually superior to his fellow clerks ("they were all stupid"), but he envied their unselfconsciousness and feared their ridicule. "It somehow happened quite suddenly," he informs us, "that I alternated between despising them and thinking them superior to myself." He led a solitary existence; his only pastime was reading. By virtue of this reading he became what he calls a "romantic": an intelligent man who forms an ideal but "never stirs a finger for that ideal," and who "would rather go out of his mind—a thing though that very rarely happens—than take to open abuse." He was often "seething within because of external impressions," but smothered the flames in the "pleasure and pain" of reading and solitary acts of "filthy vice." "Even then I had my underground world in my soul."

With this background, only one or two specific events were needed to develop the seeds of envy and vindictiveness into a mature case of underground ressentiment. The narrator describes these few experiences in great detail, for petty as they are by normal standards, they are the only instances of human contact in his life. Dostoevski means us to test the compelling language of the Underground Man's philosophical freedom against the details of his biography.

The first of these "happenings" commences when the young clerk observes someone being thrown out of a tavern by an officer. Since, as he tells us, he "actually envied the gentleman thrown out the window," he naturally wishes to meet the perpetrator of the deed. By entering the tavern, he expresses the same mixture of fascination and fear which he has often felt toward his fellow clerks.[9] In addition, he hopes to place himself in a "literary" situation, but the defeat in violent battle which he romantically craves does not come to pass. Instead, he is bodily lifted and set down by the officer who "passed me by as though he had not

9. Several excellent psychoanalytic approaches to the Underground Man have been written in recent decades. See, for example, Dr. Herbert Walker, "Observations on Fyodor Dostoevski's *Notes from the Underground*," *American Imago* 19 (1962): 195–210; Barbara Smalley, "The Compulsive Pat- terns of Dostoyevski's *Underground Man*," *Studies in Short Fiction* 10 (1973): 389–96; and Bernard J. Paris, A *Psychological Approach to Fiction* (Bloomington: Indiana University Press, 1974), pp. 100–214.

noticed me." This ignominious confrontation, which has none of the anticipated frills, deeply offends the Underground Man's sensitivities. But even though he senses that he should protest, he "changed his mind and preferred to retreat resentfully [*ozloblenno*]."[1]

In the face of a direct insult, the young man can neither strike back nor even verbalize his outrage. Instead, he adopts Hamlet's "wait until next time" philosophy,[2] that fatal hesitancy derived from the verbal individual's legalistic approach to confrontation. As Hamlet sheathes his sword during Claudius' "prayer," so the Underground Man suppresses all outward reaction to the sense of insult. And, like the prince, he consoles himself with the promise that vengeance will occur in the context of a more perfect "justice." He returns to the tavern the next evening, but as the consciousness of his original weakness has been heightened, so too his consequent resentment has become generalized; thus, the entire group assembled in the tavern, "every one present, from the insolent marker down to the lowest, stinking, pimply clerk in a greasy collar," now becomes the object of his vindictiveness.

The effects of his pervasive negativity persist and expand as the Underground Man takes his problem to the fashionable milieu of the Nevski Prospect. Even here, however, he cannot translate his hatred of the officer into meaningful physical or verbal form. Instead, he adopts the visual mode of Plutarch's envious man: "But I—I stared at him with spite and hatred and so it went on . . . for several years! My resentment [*zloba*] grew even deeper with years. . . . Sometimes I was positively choked with resentment.

Chapter 3 introduces Zverkov, the character who inspires the Underground Man with *Existenzialneid*, the penultimate stage in the process of negativity. The protagonist notes that his former schoolmate had been "a pretty, playful boy whom everybody liked. . . . He was vulgar in the extreme, but at the same time he was a good-natured fellow even in his swaggering." Furthermore, Zverkov was the object of reverence to many "simply because he had been favored by the gifts of nature." How wonderfully the polemic against "the laws of nature" may now be understood in its personalized context, and how brilliantly Dostoevski demolishes complex statements of social criticism!

> I had hated him . . . just because he was a pretty and playful boy. . . . I hated his handsome but stupid face (for which I would, however, have gladly exchanged my intelligent one), and . . . the way in which he used to talk of his future conquests of women.

---

1. The root *zlo*, not by coincidence, frequently appears in words describing all of Dostoevski's tortured intellectual philosophers and lawyers. Other examples of the use of this root (which always carries with it connotations of ressentient behavior) are noted in brackets, below.

2. "Now might I do it pat, now he is praying / And now I'll do't. And so he goes to heaven, / And so am I reveng'd. That would be scann'd. . . . Up, sword, and know thou a more horrid hent" (III.iii. 72–75, 87).

Our understanding of this protagonist largely determines our sensitivity to modern fiction, and he deserves our pity, not our admiration. The Underground Man represents a culture whose lack of coherent values makes it necessary to compare ourselves to others, to adopt rather than to create a personal world view. The *imitatio Christi*,[3] in other words, has degenerated into a relativistic pattern of *imitatio alterorum*. The merest Zverkov may potentially inspire ressentiment. In such a culture, admiration rather than envy is made possible only through what Nietzsche (here somewhat anticipating John Rawls) calls an act of "good will operating among men of roughly equal power."[4] Neither reactive Christian "love" nor, for that matter, any legal system provides the modern protagonist with this sense of equanimity. Still less is it to be found in wordy philosophical or critical analyses uninformed by sympathetic values.

Few readers soon forget the picture of the protagonist during the party scene, desperately craving the attention of the envied being. "No one paid any attention to me, and I sat crushed and humiliated. . . . Zverkov, without a word, examined me as though I were an insect. I dropped my eyes." Once again, the narrator's shining dreams are brought down to the level of cold reality, just as they had been in the tavern and on the Nevski Prospect. Again, too, the Underground Man casts himself in the absurd role of avenging hero, challenging an irrelevant outsider, Ferfitchkin, to a duel. When others at the party greet this unexpected and incongruous challenge with mockery, the scene is set for the novel's quintessential act of repression:

"Now is the time to throw a bottle at their heads," I thought to myself. I picked up the bottle—and filled my glass.

3. Girard calls the Underground Man's attraction to Zverkov the finest literary example of the "imitation of Christ [becoming] the imitation of one's neighbor" (p. 59).

4. *Genealogy* 2.8.203. Reading Nietzsche on justice together with Rawls' widely discussed *A Theory of Justice* (Cambridge: Harvard University Press, 1971) raises interesting problems better handled in a different forum. Suffice it here to observe that both thinkers grapple with the triad of justice, equality, and resentment. For Nietzsche justice cannot emerge from a resentful community but rather controls the inevitable forces of ressentiment through the positive actions of well-motivated individuals. Nietzsche's principal aim is to locate the cultural norms which tend to produce a nonresentful (and hence just) community. Since Nietzsche believes in the inevitability of struggle, yet also proposes a notion of absolute justice, he clearly believes that justice and inequality can coexist. Equality for Nietzsche means equality of strength. For Rawls, equality of *opportunity* must

be sought: justice arises when the potential for equality in a group is maximized. He assumes away from his original position emotions such as envy and even moral approaches such as ressentiment until quite late in his book, when (in sections 80 and 81) he tries to deal briefly (citing Nietzsche and Scheler) with the implication that equality of opportunity, unmatched by equality of strength, is likely to increase resentment and hence to decrease the potential for justice.

While I treat here the relationship between justice and ressentiment, I do not pretend to analyze that between justice and equality. But even in the present context it is possible to argue that justice will not arise until members of a group *feel* both equal to one another and also good about themselves and each other. I do not think we can effectively discuss justice (except theoretically) without grappling with the forces in our culture which tend to eliminate such feelings. See on this point Helmut Schoeck, *Envy: A Theory of Social Behavior* (London: Secker and Warburg, 1969).

The brevity of the phrase belies its significance, for it describes a nonact which is the consistent trademark of intellectual and legalistic heroes. The lowered bottle symbolizes, as does Hamlet's sheathed sword ("Now might I do it, pat"), the failed attempt of a frustrated character to resolve a profound sense of personal injury. It also literally depicts the process of internalization. Rather than consummate the externally directed action—hurling the bottle at the others—the Underground Man merely consumes its contents. Hamlet's returning his sword to its sheath may symbolize a denial of manliness in a Freudian sense—again, an act of internalization. However petty the more modern situation as compared to Hamlet's, its implications for the pervasive negativity of novelistic heroes are profound. Neither protagonist effectively "lowers his horns."

As the ensuing brothel scene begins, Liza, the protagonist's last chance for human intimacy before he creeps underground forever, becomes the passive object on which he projects all his frustrated inclinations for revenge. As when he challenged Ferfitchkin, instead of Zverkov, he plans to avenge himself on Liza instead of on his truer "enemies." We also know that the Underground Man has always rejected those seeking to understand him; for example, the total devotion of the "one friend" he made in school, "a simple and devoted soul," caused the protagonist to "hate him immediately" and to "reduce him to tears and hysterics." Predictably, the Underground Man begins to work the gentle and quiet Liza into his grandiose fantasies. She will be the slavishly oppressed heroine of his "book." He will save her. But as he acts out in his mind the literary role of hero, he destroys her real existence just as the tavern officer and Zverkov had crushed his own. Liza's rejection of her role in this scenario is the insult that permanently debilitates the protagonist. Like several among Dostoevski's women, Liza possesses an indigenous and nonintellectualized sympathy for others which allows her remarkable insight into complex personalities. For just this reason, she cannot append herself to the hero's romantic forms. Her simple statement, "Why, you speak somehow like a book," shatters his glorious plans and warns him that she is a force to contend with.

Liza's insight, however threatening, almost succeeds in curing the narrator's soul of its bitterness. With her, he experiences the only moments of direct emotional response he reports. His admission that his bookish harangue was meaningless, his grasping of her hand, his sincere invitation to his house, his warm acceptance of her "self-defense" (the student's love letter)—all this implies that Liza has unexpectedly moved the young man. But because he is unused to such emotions, because he cannot defend against them with verbal structures (he says virtually nothing in the concluding paragraphs of chapter 7), he must run out of the brothel and return home.

Unfortunately, the moment of elation which might have saved him lasts only long enough for him to sink into an exhausted sleep. Soon

enough, the "inversion of the table of values" recommences. Vindictiveness so determines him that he makes good into evil and perverseness
into an ideal. He retreats once again into formalism, almost forgetting
Liza and writing a conciliatory note to one of the party-goers who had
insulted him. His resentful proclivities vie with Liza's positive but too
brief influence upon him. A passage in Scheler captures this tension in
such types:

> Such phenomena as joy, splendor, power, happiness, fortune,
> and strength magically attract the man of *ressentiment*. He
> cannot pass by, he has to look at them, whether he "wants"
> to or not. But at the same time he wants to avert his eyes, for
> he is tormented by the craving to possess them and knows that
> his desire is vain. The first result of this inner process is a
> characteristic *falsification* of the *world view*. Regardless of what
> he observes, his world has a peculiar structure of emotional
> stress. The more the impulse to turn away from those positive
> values prevails, the more he turns without transition to their
> negative opposites, on which he concentrates increasingly. He
> has an urge to scold, to depreciate, to belittle whatever he can.
> Thus he involuntarily "slanders" life and the world in order
> to justify his inner pattern of value experience. (*Ressentiment*,
> pp. 74–75)

But this instinctive falsification of the world view is of only limited
effectiveness. Again and again the ressentient man encounters happiness
(the Nevski passers-by), power (Anton Antonitch Syetotchkin), beauty
(Zverkov), goodness (Liza), and other positive forms of life. They exist
and impose themselves, however much he shakes his fist against them
and tries to explain them away. He cannot escape the tormenting conflict
between desire and impotence. Averting his eyes is sometimes impossible
and in the long run ineffective. When a positive quality irresistibly forces
itself upon his attention, the very recognition produces hatred against
its bearer, even if he or she has never hated or insulted him.

It is of the utmost importance to recognize that a single unresolved
incident, when perceived by a complex sensitivity as a reproach to its
existence, may well lead to a generalized vindictiveness which sees everything and everyone as potential sources of insult. Hence, prior even to
any real attachment, another person may be perceived as threatening.
Moreover, as the Underground Man's reaction to Liza illustrates, ressentient personalities perversely confuse goodness with enmity. Since
everyone attacks me, says the ressentient man, surely those who most
embody what others call "positive" traits pose the greatest threat to me.
Against them especially I must be on guard.

This perversion of perception through ressentiment is exemplified in
the Underground Man's confrontation with his servant Apollon, a scene

whose significance is frequently overlooked. Apollon's role is similar to that of Smerdyakov vis-a-vis Ivan Karamazov; he is the constant reminder to the Underground Man of his degradation. Each of these two obsequious figures contrives to reverse the master-servant relationship which ostensibly obtains. As in the brilliant Harold Pinter film *The Servant*, a seeming dependent assumes the status of moral better to his supposed superior, to the ultimate detriment of the latter. The table of values, implicitly reversed in the tortured minds of the Underground Man and Ivan, is explicitly reversed in these two demonic Dostoevskian relationships. Flustered, the Underground Man only with great difficulty brings himself to dismiss Apollon. "I will kill him!" he shouts, and bursts into tears. But then, strangely enough, "a horrible spite [strašnaya zloba] against *her* surged up in my heart; I believe I could have killed *her*" (emphasis mine).

In the space of seconds, the Underground Man's overheated imagination has substituted Liza for Apollon. Whatever "revenge" the narrator could not wreak upon his (or upon the officer or Zverkov), he will wreak upon her. But still his vengeance takes the form of a Hamlet-like torrent of words directed against an irrelevant object. Few innocent victims of ressentient frustrations in all of literature since Ophelia endure so gracefully the verbal "daggers" hurled by the anguished protagonist. Finally, incredibly, he attempts to pay the girl for her time with him. The cruelty of the gesture amazes even Liza, and she flees her tormentor forever. Unable to accept love, and shorn of the heroic stature of his elaborate fantasies, the protagonist now has no recourse but to the underground.

As noted earlier, the vocabulary and style of part 1 match the mendacity of the narrator; the consistent use of irony, paradox, and diatribe forces the reader to adopt an unflinching hermeneutical approach to the "diary." Nothing is to be taken at face value. But the compulsive aspect of the rhetoric of part 1 may be best understood in the protagonist's own terms during his outpourings to Liza:

> I knew I was speaking stiffly, artificially, even bookishly [knižke], in fact I could not speak except "like a book."

In a sense, all of part 1 can be analyzed as though it were a recapitulation of the pompous verbiage of the Liza-incident, as though "from a book" and not from the spontaneous workings of an existential consciousness. Organic mendacity becomes perpetual in the underground. We, and no longer Liza, are its victims.

Dostoevski's brilliant depiction of ressentient negativity thus succeeds in associating a seemingly "free" philosophy with the most falsifying and obsessive tendencies of a certain type of formalistic existence. As we shall see, the writer implicates his own enterprise when he makes such an association: the urge to structure reality within the artificial confines of a "book" is, of course, the writer's own. More explicitly, the two parts of the tale reveal the need to examine the premises upon which lofty articulations are based. This insight will enrich our understanding of such characters as Ivan Karamazov, Captain Vere, and Jean-Baptiste Clamence, but it is Dostoevski's next work, *Crime and Punishment*, that expands the verbalizing tendency beyond the confines of the underground mentality and into the courts of law. In his careful progression toward *The Brothers Karamazov*, Dostoevski came to recognize the social, as opposed to the merely personal, consequences of narrative ressentiment.

JOSEPH FRANK

Notes from Underground†

> If philosophy among other vagaries were also to have the notion that it could occur to a man to act in accordance with its teaching, one might make out of this a queer comedy.
>
> Søren Kierkegaard, *Fear and Trembling*

Few works in modern literature are more widely read than Dostoevsky's *Notes from Underground* or so often cited as a key text revelatory of the hidden depths of the sensibility of our time. The term "underground man" has become part of the vocabulary of contemporary culture, and this character has now achieved—like Hamlet, Don Quixote, Don Juan, and Faust—the stature of one of the great archetypal literary creations. No book or essay dealing with the precarious situation of modern man would be complete without some allusion to Dostoevsky's explosive figure. Most important cultural developments of the present century—Nietzscheanism, Freudianism, Expressionism, Surrealism, Crisis Theology, Existentialism—have claimed the underground man as their own or have been linked with him by zealous interpreters; and when the underground man has not been hailed as a prophetic anticipation, he has been held up to exhibition as a luridly repulsive warning.

The underground man has thus entered into the very warp and woof of modern culture in a fashion testifying to the philosophical suggestiveness and hypnotic power of this first great creation of Dostoevsky's post-Siberian years. At the same time, however, this widespread notoriety has given rise to a good deal of misunderstanding. It has led critics and commentators to enlist the underground man in the service of one or another contemporary point of view, and then to proclaim their particular emphasis to be identical with Dostoevsky's own (though, even more recently, it has become fashionable to profess a total unconcern about the need to establish any such identification). Most readings, in any

† Joseph Frank, *Dostoevsky: The Stir of Liberation, 1860–1865.* Copyright © 1986 by Princeton University Press. Excerpt, pp. 310–347, reprinted with permission of Princeton University Press.

case, exhibit a tendency to overstress one or the other of the work's two main aspects: either the conceptual level is taken as dominant (the first part has even been printed separately in an anthology of philosophical texts), or the emphasis has been placed on the perverse psychology of the main character.[1] In fact, however, the text cannot be properly understood without grasping the interaction between these two levels, which interpenetrate to motivate both the underground man's ideas and his behavior.

   Notes from Underground attracted very little attention when first published (no critical notice was taken of it in any Russian journal), and only many years later was it brought into prominence. In 1883, N. K. Mikhailovsky wrote his all-too-influential article "A Cruel Talent," citing some of the more sadistic passages of *Notes from Underground* and arguing that the utterances and actions of the character illustrated Dostoevsky's own "tendencies to torture."[2] Eight years later, writing from an opposed ideological perspective, V. V. Rozanov interpreted the work as essentially inspired by Dostoevsky's awareness of the irrational depths of the human soul, with all its conflicting impulses for evil as well as for good. No world order based on reason and rationality could possibly contain this seething chaos of the human psyche; only religion (Eastern Orthodoxy) could aid man to overcome his capricious and destructive propensities. Rozanov, to be sure, comes much closer than Mikhailovsky to grasping certain essential features of the text; but no notice at all is taken of the artistic strategy that Dostoevsky employs—a strategy, as we shall see, that makes the attack on "reason" far more subtle than the sort of head-on confrontation Rozanov thinks it to be. All the same, Rozanov was the first to make the insightful comparison between *Notes from Underground* and Diderot's *Le Neveu de Rameau*, which at least points the way to a better understanding of Dostoevsky's aims.[3]

   Another highly influential view of *Notes from Underground* was the one proposed by Lev Shestov, who read it in the context of Russian Nietzscheanism. The underground man dominates and tyrannizes everyone with whom he comes into contact; and Shestov interprets this as Dostoevsky's personal repudiation of the sentimental and humanitarian ideals of his early work, which have now been replaced by a recognition of the terrible reality of human egoism. Egoism finally triumphs in *Notes from Underground*, thus expressing Dostoevsky's acceptance of a universe of cruelty, pain, and suffering that no ultimate moral perspective can rationalize or justify. For Shestov, the essence of

---

1. *Existentialism from Dostoevsky to Sartre*. ed. Walter Kaufman (New York, 1957), 53–82. For a flat reassertion that the underground man is a universal psychological type, with no social or local coloration, see Wolf Schmid. *Der Textaufbau in den Erzählungen Dostoevskijs* (Munich, 1973). 260.

2. N.K. Mikhailovsky, "Zhestokii talant," in *F. M. Dostoevsky v russkoi kritike*, ed. A. A. Belkin (Moscow, 1956), 306–384.
3. V. V. Rozanov, *Dostoevsky and the Legend of the Grand Inquisitor*, trans. Spencer E. Roberts (Ithaca and London, 1972), 35.

the work is contained in the underground man's declaration: "Let the world go smash as long as I get my tea every day"—a profession of sublime selfishness in which, according to Shestov, Dostoevsky proclaims his reluctant but courageous acceptance of a philosophy of amoralism "beyond good and evil." Shestov's analysis unquestionably points to an important aspect of the underground man's character; but he simply takes him to be Dostoevsky's mouthpiece, and fails to understand how the figure is used to realize a more complex artistic purpose.[4]

It was evident from the day of publication that Dostoevsky's *Notes from Underground* was an attack, particularly in Part I, on Chernyshevsky's philosophy of "rational egoism"; but interpreters at the turn of the century paid very little attention to this ancient quarrel, which was considered quite incidental and of no artistic importance. Up to the early 1920s, the usual view of *Notes from Underground* assumed that Dostoevsky had been stimulated by opposition to Chernyshevsky, but had used radical ideas only as a foil. Chernyshevsky had believed that man was innately good and amenable to reason, and that, once enlightened as to his true interests, he would be able, with the help of reason and science, to construct a perfect society. Dostoevsky may have also believed man to be capable of good, but he considered him equally full of evil, irrational, capricious, and destructive inclinations; and it was *this* disturbing truth that he brilliantly presented through the underground man as an answer to Chernyshevsky's naive optimism.

Although such a view may seem quite plausible at first reading, it can hardly be sustained after a little reflection. For it would require us to consider Dostoevsky as just about the worst polemicist in all of literary history. He was, after all, supposedly writing to dissuade readers from accepting Chernyshevsky's ideas. Could he really have imagined that anyone in his right mind would *prefer* the life of the underground man to the radiant happiness of Chernyshevsky's denizens of Utopia? Obviously not; and since Dostoevsky was anything but a fool, it may be assumed that the invention of the underground man was not inspired by any such self-defeating notion. In reality, as another line of interpretation soon began to make clear, his attack on Chernyshevsky and the radicals is far more intricate and cunning than had previously been suspected.

The first true glimpse into the artistic logic of *Notes from Underground* appears in an article by V. L. Komarovich, who in 1921 pointed out that Dostoevsky's novella was structurally dependent on *What Is To Be Done?*[5] Whole sections of the work in the second part—the attempt of

4. Lev Shestov, "Dostoevsky and Nietzsche: The Philosophy of Tragedy," in *Essays in Russian Literature, The Conservative View: Leontiev, Rozanov, Shestov,* ed. and trans. Spencer E. Roberts

(Athens, Ga., 1968), 3–183.
5. V.L. Komarovich, " 'Mirovaya garmoniya,' Dostoevskogo," in *O Dostoevskom,* ed. Donald Fanger (Providence, R.I., 1966), 119–149.

the underground man to bump into an officer on the Nevsky Prospect, for example, or the famous encounter with the prostitute Liza—are modeled on specific episodes in Chernyshevsky's book, and are obvious *parodies* that inverted the meaning of those episodes in their original context. The use of such a literary technique was by no means a novelty for Dostoevsky, who had conceived his first novel, *Poor Folk*, essentially as a reply—though not a mockingly satirical one—to Gogol's *The Overcoat*. His works of the late 1850s and early 1860s, such as *Uncle's Dream*, *The Village of Stepanchikovo*, and *The Insulted and Injured*, are also filled with parodistic echoes and allusions.

The uncovering of such parodies in *Notes from Underground* opened the way to a new approach, and suggested that the relation to Chernyshevsky was far from being merely ancillary to what was, in substance, the portrayal of an aberrant personality. But while Komarovich pointed to the use of parody in the second part of the text, he continued to regard the imprecations of the underground man against "reason" in the first part simply as a straightforward argument with Utilitarianism. The underground man, in other words, was still speaking directly for Dostoevsky and could be identified with the author's own position.

A further decisive advance was made a few years later by another Russian critic, A. Skaftymov, who focused on the problem of whether, and to what extent, the underground man could be considered Dostoevsky's spokesman in any straightforward fashion. Without raising the issue of parody, Skaftymov argued that the negative views of the underground man could in no way be taken to represent Dostoevsky's own position. As Shestov had also pointed out, such an identification would constitute a flagrant repudiation of all the moral ideals that Dostoevsky was continuing to uphold in his journalism. "The underground man in *Notes*," wrote Skaftymov, "is not only the accuser but also one of the accused," whose objurgations and insults are as much (if not more) directed against himself as against others, and whose eccentric and self-destructive existence by no means represents anything that Dostoevsky was approving without qualification. Skaftymov also perceptively remarked (but only in a footnote, and without developing the full import of his observation) that Dostoevsky's strategy is that of destroying his opponents "from within, carrying their logical presuppositions and possibilities to their consistent conclusion and arriving at a destructively helpless blind alley."[6]

These words provide an essential insight into one of the main features of Dostoevsky's technique as an ideological novelist; but Skaftymov does not properly use his own aperçu for the analysis of *Notes from Underground*. Although fully aware that the novella is "a polemical work," he mentions Chernyshevsky only in another footnote and fails to see

---

6. Originally published in a Czech periodical, the essay has been reprinted in A. Skaftymov, *Nravstvennie iskaniya russkikh pisatelei* (Moscow, 1972), 70, 96.

how this polemical intent enters into the very creation of the character of the underground man. Skaftymov's analysis of the text thus remains on the level of moral-psychological generalities, and while accurate enough as far as it goes, does not penetrate to the heart of Dostoevsky's conception. This can be reached, in my view, only by combining and extending Komarovich's remarks on the parodistic element in *Notes from Underground* with Skaftymov's perception of how the underground man dramatizes within himself the ultimate consequences of the position that Dostoevsky was opposing. In other words, the underground man is not only a moral-psychological type whose egoism Dostoevsky wishes to expose; he is also a social-ideological one, whose psychology must be seen as intimately interconnected with the ideas he accepts and by which he tries to live.

Dostoevsky, it seems to me, overtly pointed to this aspect of the character in the footnote appended to the title of the novella. "Both the author of the *Notes* and the *Notes* themselves," he writes, "are of course fictitious. Nonetheless, such persons as the author of such memoirs not only may, but *must*, exist in our society, if we take into consideration the circumstances that led to the formation of our society. It was my intention to bring before our reading public, more conspicuously than is usually done, one of the characters of our most recent past. He is one of the representatives of a generation that is still with us" (italics added). Dostoevsky here is obviously talking about the formation of Russian ("our") society, which, as he could expect all readers of *Epoch* to know— had he not explained this endlessly in his articles in *Time*, most recently and explicitly in *Winter Notes*?—had been formed by the successive waves of European influence that had washed over Russia since the time of Peter the Great. The underground man *must* exist as a type because he is the inevitable product of such a cultural formation; and his character does in fact embody and reflect two phases of this historical evolution. He is, in short, conceived as a parodistic persona, whose life exemplifies the tragic-comic impasses resulting from the effects of such influences on the Russian national psyche. His diatribes in the first part thus do not arise, as has commonly been thought, because of his rejection of reason; on the contrary, they result from his acceptance of *all* the implications of reason in its then-current Russian incarnation—and particularly, all those consequences that advocates of reason such as Chernyshevsky blithely chose to disregard. In the second part, Dostoevsky extends the same technique to those more sentimental-humanitarian elements of Chernyshevsky's ideology that had revived some of the atmosphere of the 1840s.

Dostoevsky's footnote thus attempted to alert his audience to the satirical and parodistic nature of his conception; but it was too oblique to serve its purpose. Like many other examples of first-person satirical parody, *Notes from Underground* has usually been misunderstood and taken straight. Indeed, the intrinsic danger of such a form, used for such a purpose, is that it tends to wipe out any critical distance between the narrator and reader, and makes it difficult to *see through* the character to the target of the satire. A famous example of such a misunderstanding in English literature is Defoe's *The Shortest Way with Dissenters*, in which the dissenter Defoe, ironically speaking through the persona of a fanatical Tory, called for the physical extermination of all dissenters. But the irony was not understood, and Defoe, taken at his word, was sentenced to a term in the pillory as punishment. This danger can be avoided only if, as in *Gulliver's Travels*, the reader is disoriented from the very start by the strangeness of the situation, or if in other ways—linguistic exaggerations or manifestly grotesque behavior—he is made aware that the I-narrator is only a convention and not a genuine character. Although Dostoevsky makes some attempt to supplement his footnote in this direction, these efforts were not sufficient to balance the overwhelming psychological presence of the underground man and the force of his imprecations and anathemas against some of the most cherished dogmas of modern civilization. As a result, the parodistic function of his character has always been obscured by the immense vitality of its artistic embodiment, and it has, paradoxically, been Dostoevsky's very genius for the creation of character that has most interfered with the proper understanding of *Notes from Underground*.

It is not really difficult to comprehend why, in this instance, the passion that Dostoevsky poured into his character should have overshadowed the nature of the work as a satirical parody. Time and again we can hear Dostoevsky speaking about himself through his fictional guise, and he unquestionably endowed the underground man with some of his deepest and most intimate feelings. As the underground man belabors his own self-disgust and guilt, was not Dostoevsky also expressing his self-condemnation as a conscience-stricken spectator of his wife's death-agonies, and repenting of the egoism to which he confessed in his notebook? The self-critical references to the underground man's school years in the second part certainly draw on Dostoevsky's own unhappy sojourn long ago in the Academy of Engineers; and the frenzy of the character's revolt against a world of imprisonment by "the laws of nature" imaginatively revived all the despair and torment of the prison years. Besides, what a release it must have been for Dostoevsky, after all his guarded temporizing and cautious qualifying, finally to fling his defiance into the teeth of the radicals and expose the disastrous implications of their "advanced" ideas! No wonder he could not resist the temptation to impart more depth and vitality to his central figure than the literary form he had chosen really required!

These personal taproots of his inspiration, however, all flow into the service of an articulate and coherent satirical conception. *Notes from Underground* has been read as the psychological self-revelation of a pathological personality, or as a theological cry of despair over the evils of "human nature," or as a declaration of Dostoevsky's supposed adherence to Nietzsche's philosophy of "amoralism" and the will to power, or as a defiant assertion of the revolt of the human personality against all attempts to limit its inexhaustible potentialities—and the list can easily be continued. All these readings, and many more, can plausibly be supported if certain features of the text are singled out and placed in the foreground while others are simply overlooked or forgotten. But if we are interested in understanding Dostoevsky's own point of view, so far as this can be reconstructed, then we must take it for what it was initially meant to be—a brilliantly Swiftian satire, remarkable for the finesse of its conception and the brio of its execution, which dramatizes the dilemmas of a representative Russian personality attempting to live by the two European codes whose unhappy effects Dostoevsky explores.[7] And though the sections have a loose narrative link, the novella is above all a diptych depicting two episodes of a symbolic history of the Russian intelligentsia.

Part 1

1. THE DIALECTIC OF DETERMINISM

The first segment of *Notes from Underground* extends from Chapter I through Chapter VI, and its famous opening tirade gives us an unforgettable picture of the underground man stewing in his Petersburg

---

7. In these days of methodological self-consciousness, and so as to avoid the charge of hermeneutical naiveté, it may be advisable to state my own conception of my interpretative task. What I am primarily concerned with is the "meaning" of *Notes from Underground*, using this word in the sense given it by E. D. Hirsch. "Meaning," he writes, "is that which is represented by a text; it is what the author meant by the use of a particular sign sequence: it is what the signs represent." Hirsch distinguishes meaning of this kind from what he calls "significance," which he defines as being "a relationship between that meaning and a person, or a conception, or a situation, or indeed anything imaginable. . . . Significance always implies a relationship, and one constant, unchanging pole of that relationship is what the text means." In my view, the vast majority of commentators of *Notes from Underground* have always been concerned with its significance, and, as a result, its meaning has rather gotten lost in the shuffle.

I am fully aware that Hirsch's ideas have met with massive opposition, and I would agree that in practice meaning and significance cannot be separated as neatly as his definitions would seem to imply. Indeed, in relation to any work of the past, significance unavoidably enters along with the time gap between past and present. Yet I would also argue that it is empirically possible for a critic to direct his energies either toward meaning or toward significance, and to emphasize one or the other in full awareness of making such a choice—which is precisely what I have chosen to do.

One of the major objections to Hirsch, made by the followers of H.-G. Gadamer, is that the establishment of meaning in Hirsch's sense is a chimerical ideal; it is a false application of the standard of scientific objectivity, which is impossible to attain because of the historicity of human understanding. But my own reading of Gadamer does not persuade me that he is in favor of historical error and illusion, or that he positively *discourages* attempting to obtain as accurate a knowledge of the past as possible. If so, the "fusion of horizons" that he recommends would be nothing more than a series of mythical inventions, and the most delirious reconstruction would have the same value as the work of the most justly reputed scholar.

It thus seems to me that the preliminary establishment of meaning is an indispensable part of the hermeneutic process; and this is enough to justify my own attempt. Dostoevsky's work has already been subject to so much "fusion" that a sober effort to establish meaning can serve a very useful function. See E. D. Hirsch, *Validity in Interpretation* (New Haven and London, 1967), 8; also, for a succinct account of the current debates over hermeneutics, M. H. Abrams, *A Glossary of Literary Terms* (New York, 1981), 84–87.

"corner" and mulling over the peculiarities of his character and his life: "I am a sick man. . . . I am a spiteful man. I am an unpleasant man. I think my liver is diseased." The least one can say, at first contact, is that the underground man is not self-complacent; and we are immediately aware of his acute intelligence. He is ill but refuses to see a doctor, though he respects medicine: "Besides, I am extremely superstitious, let's say sufficiently so to respect medicine." Medicine is of course supposed to be a science—and had indeed become *the* science after Bazarov, Lopukhov, and Kirsanov; but the underground man sarcastically labels excessive respect for medicine as itself just an irrational superstition. He knows he should visit a doctor, but somehow—really for no good reason, simply out of spite—he prefers to stay home, untreated. Why? "You probably will not understand that," he says. "Well, I understand it." Whatever the explanation, there is a clear conflict between a rational course of beahvior and some obscure feeling labeled "spite." The underground man's "reason," which would prompt him to seek a doctor out of self-interest is evidently thwarted by some other motive.

We then learn that the underground man is an ex-civil servant, now retired on a small income, who in the past had engaged in incessant battles to tyrannize the humble petitioners that came his way in the course of business. But while he had enjoyed this sop to his ego, he confesses that "I was not only not spiteful but not even an embittered man. . . . I might foam at the mouth, but bring me some kind of toy, give me a cup of tea with sugar, and I would be appeased." The underground man's nature is by no means vicious and evil; he is more than ordinarily responsive to any manifestation of friendliness; but such responses are carefully kept bottled up no matter how strongly he might feel them: "Every moment I was conscious in myself of many, many elements completely opposed to that [spite]. . . . I knew that they had been teeming in me all my life, begging to be let out, but I would not let them, would not let them, purposely would not let them."

Such a passage should have been sufficient to scotch the prevalent notion that the underground man was perverse and evil "by nature," and that his behavior springs from a character innately deformed and distorted. But alas! The narrator's plain words have been far from enough to prevent precisely such a reading from being widely accepted (and they will no doubt prove as insufficient in the future as in the past). In fact, the underground man is shown as being caught in a conflict between the egoistic aspects of his character and the sympathetic, outgoing ones that he also possesses; but these latter are continually suppressed in favor of the former. At first, we observed a conflict beween the underground man's reason and his feelings that might be considered purely psychological (is reason or spite the stronger force?). To this is now added a struggle of a more moral character between egoism and altruism, or at least friendliness. The first conflict dominates Part I, where the underground man essentially talks to himself or to an imaginary interlocutor; the second comes to the fore in Part II, where he is still living (or trying to live) in society and in relation to other people. In both cases, though, we see him torn apart by an inner dissonance that prevents him from behaving in what might be considered a "normal" fashion—that is, acting in terms of self-interest and "reason" in Part I, or giving unhindered expression to his altruistic (or at least amiably social) impulses in Part II. What prevents him from doing so is precisely what Dostoevsky wishes to illuminate and explore.

The nature of these impediments becomes clear only gradually in Part I as the underground man continues to expose all his defects to the scornful contemplation of his assumed reader. For it turns out that the contradictory impulses struggling within him have literally paralyzed his character. "Not only could I not become spiteful," he says, "I could not even become anything: neither spiteful nor kind, neither a rascal nor an honest man, neither a hero nor an insect." The underground man's only consolation is that "an intelligent man in the nineteenth-century must and morally ought to be pre-eminently a characterless creature: a man of character, an active man is pre-eminently a limited creature," and he boastfully attributes his characterlessness to the fact that he is "hyperconscious." As a result of this "hyperconsciousness," he was "most capable of recognizing every refinement of 'all the sublime and the beautiful,' as we used to say at one time" (the 1840s). But "the more conscious I was of goodness, and of all that 'sublime and beautiful,' the more deeply I sank into my mire and the more capable I became of sinking into it completely."

This strange state of moral impotence, which the underground man both defends and despises, is complicated by the further admission that he positively *enjoys* the experience of his own degradation. "I reached the point," he confesses, "of feeling a sort of secret, abnormal, despicable enjoyment in returning home to my corner on some disgusting Petersburg night, and being acutely conscious that that day I had again done something loathsome, that what was done could never be undone, and secretly, inwardly gnaw, gnaw at myself for it, nagging and consuming myself till at last the bitterness turned into a sort of shameful accursed sweetness, and finally into real positive enjoyment."

The underground man frankly admits to being an unashamed masochist, and all too many commentators are quite happy to accept this admission as a sufficient explanation of his behavior. To do so, however, simply disregards the relation of the underground man's psychology to his social-cultural formation. For he goes on to explain that his sense of enjoyment derived from "the hyperconsciousness of [his] own degradation," a hyperconsciousness that persuaded him of the impossibility of becoming anything else or of behaving in any other way even if he had wished to do so. "For the root of it all," he says, "was that it all proceeded according to the normal and fundamental laws of hyperconsciousness, and with the inertia that was the direct result of those laws, and that consequently one was not only unable to change but could do absolutely nothing."

What does the underground man mean by this rather baffling assertion? What *are* the "normal and fundamental laws of hyperconsciousness," and why should they lead to immobility and inertia? This passage has often been taken as a reference to the underground man's "Hamletism," which links him with such figures as the protagonists of Turgenev's "Hamlet of the Shchigrovsky District" and "Diary of a Superfluous Man," both of whom are destroyed by an excess of consciousness that unfits them for the possibilities offered by their lives. Such thematic resemblances need not be denied; but this pervasive motif in Russian literature of the 1850s and 1860s is given a special twist by Dostoevsky and shown as the unexpected consequence of the doctrines advanced by the very people who had attacked the "Hamlets" most violently—the radicals of the 1860s themselves. For the pseudo-scientific terms of the underground man's declaration about "hyperconsciousness" are a parody of Chernyshevsky, and the statement is a paraphrase of Chernyshevsky's assertion, in *The Anthropological Principle in Philosophy*, that no such thing as free will exists or can exist, since whatever actions man attributes to his own initiative are really a result of the "laws of nature." The underground man reveals the effects on his character of the "hyperconsciousness" derived from a knowledge of such "laws," and thus mockingly exemplifies what such a doctrine really means in practice.

Such "hyperconsciousness," based on the conviction that free will is an illusion, leads to a bewildered demoralization dramatized by Dostoevsky with consummate dialectical ingenuity. The underground man, for instance, imagines that he wishes to forgive someone magnanimously for having slapped him in the face but the more he thinks about it, the more impossible such an intention becomes. "After all, I would probably never have been able to do anything with my magnanimity—neither to forgive, for my assailant may have slapped me because of the laws of nature, and one cannot forgive the laws of nature; nor to forget, for even if it were the laws of nature, *it is insulting all the same*" (italics added). Or suppose he wishes to act the other way round—not to forgive magnanimously, but to take revenge. How can one take revenge when no one is to blame for anything? "You look into it, the object flies off into air, your reasons evaporate, the criminal is not to be found, the insult becomes fate rather than an insult, something like the toothache, for which no one is to blame." This is why, as the underground man asserts, "the direct, legitimate, immediate fruit of consciousness is inertia—that is, conscious sitting on one's hands." Or, if one does not sit on one's hands but acts—say on the matter of revenge—then 'it would only be out of spite." Spite is not a *valid* cause for any kind of action, and hence it is the only one left when the laws of nature make any justified response impossible.

In such passages, the moral vacuum created by the thoroughgoing acceptance of determinism is depicted with masterly psychological insight. As a well-trained member of the intelligentsia, the underground man intellectually accepts such determinism; but it is impossible for him really to live with its conclusions. "Thus it would follow, as the result of hyperconsciousness, that one is not to blame for being a scoundrel, as though that were any consolation to the scoundrel once he himself has come to realize that he actually is a scoundrel." Or, as regards the slap in the face, it is impossible to forget because "even if it were the laws of nature, it is insulting all the same." Dostoevsky thus juxtaposes a *total* human reaction—a sense of self-revulsion at being a scoundrel, an upsurge of anger at the insult of being slapped—against a scientific rationale that dissolves all such moral-emotive feelings and hence the very possibility of a human response. Reason tells the underground man that guilt or indignation is totally irrational and meaningless; but conscience and a sense of dignity continue to exist all the same as ineradicable components of the human psyche.

Here, then, is the explanation for the so-called masochism of the underground man. Why does he refuse to see a doctor about his liver or insist that one may enjoy moaning needlessly and pointlessly about a toothache? It is because, in both instances, some mysterious, impersonal power—the laws of nature—has reduced the individual to complete helplessness; and his only method of expressing a *human* reaction to this power is to refuse to submit silently to its despotism, to protest against its pressure no matter in how ridiculous a fashion. The refusal to be treated is such a protest, self-defeating though it may be; and the moans over a toothache, says the underground man, express "all the aimlessness of your pain, which is so humiliating to your consciousness; all the system of the laws of nature on which you spit disdainfully, of course, but from which you suffer all the same while it does not."

Both these situations are analogous to the shameful "pleasure" that the underground man confesses at keeping alive the sense of his own degradation after his debauches. He refuses to be consoled by the alibi that the laws of nature are to blame; and his dubious enjoyment translates the moral-emotive response of his *human nature* to the blank nullity of the *laws of nature*. Far from being a sign of psychic abnormality, this sensation is in reality—given the topsy-turvy world in which he lives— a proof of the underground man's paradoxical spiritual health. For it indicates that, despite the convictions of his reason, he refuses to surrender his right to possess a conscience or an ability to feel outraged and insulted.

2. THE MAN OF ACTION

It is only by recognizing this ironic displacement of the normal moral-psychic horizon that we can accurately grasp the underground man's relation to the imaginary interlocutor with whom he argues all through the first part of *Notes from Underground*. This interlocutor is obviously a follower of Chernyshevsky, a man of action, who believes himself to be nothing less than *l'homme de la nature et de la vérité*. The underground man *agrees* with this gentleman's theory that all human conduct is nothing but a mechanical product of the laws of nature; but he also knows what the man of action does not—that this theory makes all human behavior impossible, or at least meaningless. "I envy such a man till my bile overflows," says the underground man. "He is stupid, I am not disputing that, but perhaps the normal man should be stupid—how do you know?" The normal man, the man of action, happily lacks the hyperconsciousness of the underground man; and when impelled by a desire to obtain revenge, for example, he "simply rushes straight toward his goal like an infuriated bull with its horns down, and nothing but a wall will stop him." He is totally unaware that whatever he may consider to be the basis for his headlong charge—for example, the need for justice—is a ludicrously old-fashioned and unscientific prejudice that has been replaced by the laws of nature. Only his stupidity allows him to maintain his complacent normality, and to remain so completely free from the paralyzing dilemmas of the underground man.

The men of action sometimes also run up against the stone wall of the laws of nature; but since they do not understand all its implications, the shock of impact has no effect on their convictions or their conduct. "For them a wall is not an excuse, as for example for us, people who think, and consequently who do nothing. . . . The stone wall has for them something tranquilizing, morally determining and final—even something, if you please, mystical. . . ." Confronted by the so-called tenets of natural science—such as, for example, "that in reality one drop of your own fat must be dearer to you than a hundred thousand of your fellow creatures, and that this conclusion is the final solution of all so-called virtues and duties and all such ravings and prejudices"—they stop all their questionings and reasonings. They simply do not understand that the stone wall of science eliminates their feeling of outraged justice as surely as it eliminates all nonsense about duty. Hence the men of action accept the doctrines of natural science with a smug awareness of keeping up with European progress, while they continue to profess the same moral indignation as people in the "unscientific" past.

The hyperconscious underground man, who lacks this saving grace of stupidity, knows only too well that the stone wall of science and determinism cuts the ground away from *any* type of moral reaction. Hence, when *he* feels aggrieved, he can only nurse a despicable resentment which, as he realizes only too clearly, cannot justly be discharged against anybody. Yet he cannot help behaving *as if* some sort of free human response were still possible and meaningful; "consequently there is only the same outlet left again—that is, to beat the wall as hard as you can." And, this gesture of despair at least has the consolation of lucidity and lack of self-deception: "Is it not much better to understand it all, to be conscious of it all, all the impossibilities and stone walls; not to resign yourself to a single one of these impossibilities and stone walls if it disgusts you to be resigned; to reach, by way of the most inevitable logical combinations, the most revolting conclusions on the everlasting theme that you are yourself somehow to blame even for the stone wall, though again it is as clear as day you are not to blame in the least, and therefore, silently and impotently gnashing your teeth, to sink sensuously into inertia, brooding over the fact that there is no one even for you to feel vindictive against?"

Here, we might think, the paradoxes of the underground man reach a paroxysm of psychopathic self-accusation; but psychology by itself does not take us very far in comprehending Dostoevsky's artistic logic. For once we understand the complex inversions of his creation, it is quite clear that no one in the world can be guilty of anything except the underground man. He knows that the idea of guilt, along with all other moral ideas, has been wiped off the slate by the laws of nature; yet he irrationally persists in having moral responses. And since there is nowhere else for him to assign moral responsibility, by the most irrefutable process of deduction he and he alone is to blame for everything. But, at the same time, he knows very well that he is *not* to blame, and he wishes it were possible to forget about the laws of nature long enough to convince himself that he could freely choose to become *anything*— a loafer, a glutton, or a person who spends his life drinking toasts to the health of everything "sublime and beautiful."

This analysis should be enough to illuminate the dialectic of determinism that Dostoevsky dramatizes in these first six chapters of *Notes from Underground*. It would be possible to show how every self-contradictory response of the underground man in these chapters derives from this dialectic, which is driven by the contradiction between the underground man's intellectual acceptance of Chernyshevsky's determinism and his simultaneous rejection of it with the entire intuitive-emotional level of personality identified with moral conscience. As a result, the underground man's self-derision and self-abuse are not meant to be taken literally. The rhetoric of the underground man contains an inverted irony similar to that of *Winter Notes*, which turns back on itself as a means of ridiculing his scornful interlocutor, the man of action. For the life of the underground man is the *reductio ad absurdum* of that of the man of action; and the more repulsive and obnoxious he portrays himself as being, the more he reveals the true meaning of what his self-confident judge so blindly holds dear. It is only the impenetrable obtuseness of the radical men of action that prevents them from seeing the underground man as their mirror image, and from acknowledging the greeting he might have given them (in Baudelaire's words): "hypocrite lecteur, mon semblable, mon frère!"

3. THE MOST ADVANTAGEOUS ADVANTAGE

The first chapters of *Notes from Underground* present a powerful picture of the existential dilemma of the underground man, whose life illustrates in action the split between reason and the moral-emotive sensibility arising from a total acceptance of *all* the implications of Chernyshevsky's philosophy. After showing the inherent inability of the human psyche to accommodate itself to such a "rational" world, and the strange and seemingly senseless ways in which this refusal can become manifest, the underground man turns more directly to demolish the arguments that Chernyshevsky and the men of action use to defend their position. It may seem as if this refutation contradicts the assertion that he *accepts* the basic tenets of Chernyshevsky's philosophy. But such acceptance has always included a sardonic realization of the total incongruity of those precepts with the norms of human experience; and this incongruity is now formulated more explicitly in the arguments developed throughout Chapters VII-IX.

"Oh, tell me," the underground man asks incredulously, "who first declared, who first proclaimed, that man only does nasty things because he does not know his real interests; and that if he were enlightened, if his eyes were opened to his real, normal interests, he would at once cease to do nasty things . . . he would see his own advantage in the good and nothing else, and since we all know that not a single man can knowingly act to his own disadvantage, consequently, so to say, he would begin doing good through necessity." This was indeed the essence of Chernyshevsky's position—that "rational egoism," once accepted, would so enlighten man that the very possibility of his behaving irrationally, that is, contrary to his interests, would entirely disappear. But this argument, as the underground man points out caustically, has one little flaw: it entirely overlooks that man has, and always will have, a supreme interest, which he will never surrender, in being able to exercise his free will.

The underground man's discourse in these chapters is composed of several strands. One is the repeated presentation of the way in which "statisticians, sages, and lovers of humanity" frequently end up by acting contrary to all their oft-proclaimed and solemnly high-minded principles of rationality. Another is to look at human history and to ask whether man ever was, or wished to be, totally rational: "In short, one may say anything about the history of the world—anything that might enter the most disordered imagination. The only thing one cannot say is that it is rational. The very word sticks in one's throat." A third comes much closer to the present and, in passing, takes a sideswipe at the British historian Henry Thomas Buckle, then very popular with the Russian radicals, who believed that the laws of history could be worked out according to those of the natural sciences. The underground man simply cannot control his merriment over Buckle's assertion "that through civilization mankind becomes softer, and consequently less bloodthirsty, and less fitted for warfare," and he appeals to the reader: "Take the whole of the nineteenth century in which Buckle lived. Take Napoleon—both the Great and the present one. Take North America—the eternal union [then racked by the Civil War]."

These examples show to what extent rationalists and logicians are apt to shut their eyes to the most obvious facts for the sake of their systems; and all these systems, for some reason, always define "human advantages" exclusively "from the average of statistical figures and scientific-economic formulas. Now then, your advantages are prosperity, wealth, freedom, peace—etc., etc. So that a man who, for instance, would openly and knowingly oppose the whole list would be, according to you, *and of course to me as well*, an obscurantist or an absolute madman, no?" (italics added). But while the underground man has often been taken for this kind of "absolute madman," such a reading is a clear violation of Dostoevsky's words. The underground man does *not* reject prosperity, wealth, freedom, and peace *in themselves*; he rejects the view that the only way to attain them is by the sacrifice of man's freedom and personality.

"There it is, gentlemen," he says commiseratingly, "does it not seem that something really exists that is dearer to almost every man than his greatest advantage, or (not to violate logic) that there is one most advantageous advantage (the very one omitted, about which we spoke just now) for which, if necessary, a man is ready to go against all laws, that is, against reason, honor, peace, prosperity—in short, against all those wonderful and useful things if only he can attain that fundamental, most advantageous advantage dearer to him than everything else?" The answer to this question, whose parentheses parody some of the more laborious passages in *The Anthropological Principle*, has been given in the first six chapters. The one "most advantageous advantage" for man is the preservation of his free will, which may or may not be exercised in harmony with reason but which, in any case, always wishes to preserve the right to *choose*; and this primary "advantage" cannot be included in the systems of the lovers of humanity because it makes forever impossible their dream of transforming human nature to desire *only* the rational.

4. THE CRYSTAL PALACE

Chernyshevsky embodied this dream of transformation, as we know, in his vision of the Crystal Palace, and Dostoevsky picks up this symbol to present it from the underground man's point of view. In this future Utopia of plenitude, man will have been completely re-educated so that "he will then voluntarily refrain from erring, and, so to say, by necessity will not want to set his will against his normal interests. More than that: then, you say, science itself will have taught man (though this, I think, is a luxury) that he does not really have either will or caprice and that he never has had them, and that he himself is nothing more than some sort of piano key or organ stop; and that moreover, there are laws of nature in the world; so that everything he does is not at all done by his will but by itself, according to the laws of nature."

The musical imagery here derives directly from Fourier, who believed he had discovered a "law of social harmony," and whose disciples liked to depict the organization of the passions in the phalanstery by analogy with the organization of keys on a clavier. (This latter comparison is made in a widely read work of Victor Considérant, *La Destinée sociale*, whose title Chernyshevsky managed to smuggle into *What Is To Be Done?* as a play on words.) Also, when the underground man comments that in the Crystal Palace "all human actions will . . . be tabulated according to these laws [of nature], mathematically, like tables of logarithms up to 108,000 and entered in a table," he is by no means exaggerating. Fourier had actually made the effort to work out an exhaustive table of the passions that were in his view, the immutable laws of (human) nature, and whose needs would have to be satisfied in any model social order. Dostoevsky thus combines Fourier's table of passions with Chernyshevsky's material determinism in his attack on the ideal of the Crystal Palace as involving the total elimination of the personality. For the empirical manifestation of personality is the right to *choose* a course of action whatever it may be; and no choice is involved when one is good, reasonable, satisfied, and happy by conformity with laws of nature that exclude the very possibility of their negation.

Even if one were to imagine attaining this state of perfection, the underground man warns, it might still prove to be terribly tedious. Once man has nothing further to strive toward or hope for, he falls prey to *ennui*; and Dostoevsky at this point falls back on some familiar motifs. *Ennui* immediately recalls the world of Prince Valkovsky and Cleopatra, and it is no surprise to see Pushkin's Egyptian queen turning up to stick gold pins into the breasts of her slave girls for amusement. Luckily, though, the underground man assures us, the Crystal Palace is *not* possible because "man is so phenomenally ungrateful . . . shower upon him every earthly blessing, drown him in bliss so that nothing but bubbles would dance on the surface of bliss, as on water; give him such economic prosperity that he has nothing else to do but sleep, eat cakes, and busy himself with ensuring the continuation of world history—even then man, out of sheer ingratitude, sheer slander, will play you some dirty trick." This "dirty trick" is precisely that he will "even risk his cakes and deliberately desire the most fatal rubbish, the most uneconomical absurdity, simply in order to prove to himself (as if this were so necessary) that men are still men and not piano keys."

At this point, the underground man rises to a climactic vision of universal chaos, which parallels, in terms of the socio-historical ideal of the Crystal Palace, the chaos of the underground man's private life in the first six chapters. In both cases, the cause of this chaos is the same: the revolt of the personality against a world in which free will (and hence moral categories of any kind) has no further reason for being. For if the world of the Crystal Palace really existed, "even if man really were nothing but a piano key, even if this were proved to him by natural science and mathematics—he will devise destruction and chaos, will devise sufferings of all sorts, and will insist on getting his way!" And if all this suffering and chaos can also be calculated and tabulated in advance, "then man would purposely go mad in order to be rid of reason and to insist on getting his way!" These words have been endlessly quoted out of context, as if Dostoevsky conceived of ordinary human life as some sort of metaphysical imprisonment that required and justified such a recourse to madness and chaos; but this reading goes against the clear sense of the text. The self-destructive revolt of freedom is not a value in itself; it is envisaged *only* as a last-ditch defense against the hypothetical accomplishment of the Crystal Palace ideal. As the underground man writes in relief: "And after this how is one not to sin by rejoicing that this is not yet, and that for the time being desire still depends on the devil alone knows what!"

Such is the terrible prospect of the proposed completion of the Crystal Palace ideal, and the underground man continues to question the buoyant assurance of Chernyshevsky and his followers that such an ideal is man's true desire. "Man likes to create and build roads, that is incontestable," he concedes, meaning that man wishes to occupy himself with useful and socially productive labor. But he denies that humanity is longing to achieve the static, secular apocalypse of the Crystal Palace, which would signify the end of history and the cessation of all further striving, aspiration and hope. "May it not be that he so loves chaos and destruction (surely this is incontestable, he sometimes loves it very much, that's so), because he instinctively fears to attain his goal and to complete the edifice under construction? How do you know, perhaps he only likes that edifice from a distance, not from close up; perhaps he only likes to build it and not to live in it, leaving it *aux animaux domestiques* such as ants, sheep, etc., etc. Now the ants have an entirely different taste. They have an astonishing edifice of this kind eternally indestructible— the anthill."

This comparison of the Socialist ideal to an anthill was a commonplace in the Russian journalism of the period, but Dostoevsky may have used this image in connection with the end of history as an allusion to Herzen. "If humanity went straight to some goal," Herzen had written in *From the Other Shore*, "there would be no history, only logic; humanity would stop in some finished form, in a spontaneous *status quo* like the animals. . . . Besides, if the libretto existed, history would lose all interest, it would become futile, boring, ridiculous."[8] The obvious similarity of these texts shows how much Dostoevsky had absorbed from

---

8. A. I. Gertsen, *Polnoe sobranie sochinenii*, 30 vols. (Moscow, 1954–1966), 6: 36.

the work he admired so greatly; it also reveals how accurately he was thematizing a profound ideological contrast between his own generation and that of the 1860s. For the intellectual and ideological physiognomy of the generation of the 1840s, nourished on Romantic literature and German Idealist philosophy, formed a sharp contrast to that of the 1860s; and Herzen, like Dostoevsky, always staunchly refused to accept Chernyshevsky's material determinism and denial of free will. It is thus appropriate that the underground man later attributes his opposition to the ideal of the Crystal Palace at least partly to having come of age when he did.

All these arguments are then focused in a final rejection of the Crystal Palace for leaving no room for "suffering." Once again, however, in order to do justice to Dostoevsky, it is necessary to stress the qualified nature of this assertion and the nuance of meaning that he gives it. "After all," the underground man says, "I do not really insist on suffering or on prosperity either. I insist . . . on my caprice, and that it be guaranteed to me when it's necessary." Suffering is no more an end in itself than madness or chaos, and remains subordinate to the supreme value of the assertion of moral autonomy; but it serves as a prod to keep alive this sense of moral autonomy in a world deprived of human significance by determinism: "In the Crystal Palace it [suffering] is even unthinkable: suffering is doubt, negation, and what kind of a Crystal Palace would that be in which doubts can be harbored?" The ability to doubt means that man is not yet transformed into a rational-ethical machine that can behave *only* in conformity with reason. This is why the underground man declares that "suffering is the sole origin of consciousness"; suffering and consciousness are inseparable because the latter is not only a psychological but primarily a moral attribute of the human personality.

5. THE PALATIAL CHICKEN COOP

Chapter X of *Notes from Underground* poses a special problem because it was so badly mutilated by the censorship. In this chapter, as we know, Dostoevsky claimed to have expressed "the essential idea" of his work, which he defined as "the necessity of faith and Christ"; but the passages in which he did so were suppressed and never restored in later reprintings. Dostoevsky's failure to return the text to its original form has sometimes been taken to mean that the sense of his initial affirmation could hardly have had any real importance for him and can thus be disregarded; but such an inference fails to take the problem of censorship into account. At no period of his life would Dostoevsky have relished the dangerous and time-consuming prospect of attempting to persuade the censors to reverse an earlier ruling. To have tried to do so would only have imperiled and delayed the publication of the reprints and collected editions of his work on which he counted for badly needed income. Tzvetan Todorov has recently argued, much more interestingly, that Dostoevsky did not restore the cuts for aesthetic reasons: he realized later that the true climax was the end of Part II, and decided it had been a mistake to provide another climax earlier.[9] But even this structural suggestion does not, in my view, offer any conclusive internal reason for Dostoevsky's choice to leave well enough alone.

For the moment, let us examine this "garbled" chapter to see what can still be found that may help us to come closer to Dostoevsky's "essential idea." In the first place, Chapter X brings home quite explicitly how literally unbearable the situation of the underground man has become. Up to this point, he had used his misery mainly as an ironic weapon; but now we realize that the underground revolt of the personality—important and necessary though it may be—cannot ever be taken as an end in itself. Torn between the convictions of "reason" and the revolt of his conscience and feelings, the underground man cries: "Can I have been made simply in order to come to the conclusion that the whole way I am made is a swindle? Can this be the whole purpose? I don't believe it." True, he rejects the Crystal Palace because it is impossible to be irreverent about it and stick out one's tongue at it, but "I did not at all say [this] because I am so fond of putting out my tongue. . . . On the contrary, I would let my tongue be cut off out of sheer gratitude if things could be so arranged that I myself would lose all desire to put it out."

Dostoevsky thus indicates that the underground man, far from rejecting all moral ideals in favor of an illimitable egoism, is desperately searching for one that would truly satisfy his spirit. Such an ideal would be one which, rather than spurring the personality to revolt in rabid frenzy, would instead lead to a willing surrender in its favor. Such an alternative ideal would thus be required to recognize the autonomy of the will and the freedom of the personality, and appeal to the moral nature of man rather than to his reason and self-interest conceived as working in harmony with the laws of nature. For Dostoevsky, this alternative ideal could be found in the teachings of Christ; and from a confusion that still exists in the text, we can catch a glimpse of how he may have tried to integrate this alternative into the framework of his imagery.

This confusion arises in the course of a comparison between the Crystal Palace and a chicken coop. "You see," says the underground man, "if it were not a palace but a chicken coop, and it started to rain, I might creep into the chicken coop to avoid getting wet, but all the same I would not take the chicken coop for a palace out of gratitude that it sheltered me from the rain. You laugh, you even say that, in such circumstances, a chicken coop and a mansion—it's all the same. Yes, I answer, if one has to live simply to avoid getting wet." It is not

9. Tzvetan Todorov, "Notes d'un souterrain," in Les Genres du discours (Paris, 1978), 158.

the usefulness of the chicken coop that is impugned by the underground man, but the fact that it is taken for a palace—the fact that, in return for its practical advantages, it has been elevated into mankind's ideal. One recalls Dostoevsky's remark in *Winter Notes* that the desperate English working class prefers the anthill to cannibalism; but the underground man refuses to accept the chicken coop qua palace as *his* ideal. "But what is to be done if I have taken it into my head that this [not to get wet; utility] is not the only object in life, and that if one must live, it may as well be in a mansion? That is my choice, my desire. You will only eradicate it when you have changed my desire. *Well, do change it, tempt me with something else, give me another ideal*" (italics added).

The underground man thus clearly opens up the possibility of "another ideal"; and, as the text goes along, he seems to envisage a different sort of Crystal Palace—one that would be a genuine mansion rather than a chicken coop satisfying purely material needs. For he then continues: "And meanwhile, I will not take a chicken coop for a palace. Let the Crystal edifice even be an idle dream, say it is inconsistent with the laws of nature, and I have invented it only as a result of my own stupidity, as a result of *some old-fashioned, irrational habits of my generation*. But what do I care if it is inconsistent? Isn't it all the same if it exists in my desires, or better, exists as long as my desires exist?" (italics added). At this point, we observe a shift to a "Crystal edifice" based on the very *opposite* principles from those represented by the Crystal Palace throughout the rest of the text: this new "Crystal edifice" is *inconsistent* with the laws of nature (while the Crystal Palace is their embodiment), and it owes its existence to desire rather than to reason. The change is so abrupt, and so incompatible with what has gone before, that one can only assume some material leading from one type of Crystal building to the other has been excised from the manuscript.

Dostoevsky, we may speculate, must have attempted here to indicate the nature of a true Crystal Palace, or mansion, or edifice (his terminology is not consistent), and to contrast it with the false one that was really a chicken coop. From his letter, we know that he did so in a way to identify a true Crystal Palace with the "need for faith and Christ"; but such an attempt may well have confused and frightened the censors, still terrified out of their wits by the recent blunder over *What Is To Be Done?* and now accustomed to view the Crystal Palace as the abhorrent image of atheistic Socialism. Hence, they would have excised the sentences in which Dostoevsky tried to give his own Christian significance to this symbol, perhaps considering it to be both subversive and blasphemous. These suppositions would explain the strange history of Dostoevsky's text, and account for the flagrant contradiction, clearly evident on close reading, which provoked his indignant outcry that his entire meaning had been distorted.

Although this alternative ideal may have originally been indicated more clearly, Dostoevsky's conception still requires the underground man to remain trapped in the negative phase of his revolt. An alternative is suggested only as a remote and, for the underground man, unattainable possibility; and this is why Todorov's theory explaining the failure to restore the original text does not seem tenable. Each episode was meant to have its own type of climax, and there would have been a distinct gradation between the first and the second. What appears in the underground man's thoughts only as an impossible dream in the first part becomes a living reality in the second, strongly presented in terms of dramatic action. Even if the first climax had been retained in its original form, it would thus not have weakened the second, as Todorov assumes, but rather exemplified its metamorphosis from a hope into a vividly concrete illustration of such a resolution. For the underground man in this first part longs for another ideal; he knows it must exist; but he is so committed to a belief in material determinism and the laws of nature that he cannot imagine what it could be. "I know, anyway, that I will not be appeased with a compromise, with an endlessly recurring zero, simply because it exists according to the laws of nature and *actually* exists. I will not take as the crown of all my desires—a block of buildings with apartments for the poor on a lease for a thousand years, and, for any contingency, a dentist's sign hanging out."

In the final Chapter XI, the underground man continues to oscillate between defiance and despair, both affirming and denying his life and convictions in the space of a few lines: "Though I have said that I envy the normal man to the last drop of my bile, in the conditions in which I see him now I do not wish to be him (though all the same I will not stop from envying him. No, no, the underground is in any case more advantageous!). There, at any rate, one can . . . Bah!, and now here I am lying! I am lying because I know myself, like two times two, that the underground is not at all better, but something else, something I long for but cannot find. To the devil with the underground!" What that something else is, and why the underground man cannot find it, provides the substance for the second part of Dostoevsky's novella.

Part II

1. APROPOS OF THE WET SNOW

The underground man, as we have seen, clings to his ideal of a "true" Crystal Palace because of "some old-fashioned, irrational habits of my generation." Dostoevsky thus locates the psychic-emotive responses of his character in a social-cultural context very clearly delimited in time. The underground man is forty years old in 1864 when he begins to write his *Notes*; he is twenty-four when the events in Part II take place, which would locate them in 1848; and this is the very year that Dostoevsky first assiduously began to attend the meetings of the Petrashevsky circle. These calculations are not intended to suggest that the second part of

Notes from Underground is about Dostoevsky himself in any literal sense. The underground man is primarily a social-cultural type and must be understood as such; but in the second part, where he becomes a parody of the attitudes of the 1840s, he was certainly nourished by Dostoevsky's judgment of himself as a member of that generation. Evaluating his state of mind at that time, Dostoevsky had written to General E. I. Todleben in 1856: "I believed in theories and Utopias. . . . I was a hypochondriac. . . . I was excessively irritable with an unhealthy susceptibility. I deformed the simplest facts, endowing them with another aspect and other dimensions."[1] This description applies, word for word, to the portrait we are given of the underground man's psychology in his youth.

The period tonality of this second part is also indicated in many other ways besides the precise chronology of dates. The subtitle, "Apropos of the Wet Snow," seems to have no intrinsic relation to the text, and to have been used only to trigger the association recalling the memory of the prostitute Liza. In fact, however, it also helps to set the action firmly in a symbolic setting. P. V. Annenkov had noted in 1849 that the writers of the Natural School were all fond of employing "wet snow" as a typical feature of the dreary Petersburg landscape; and Dostoevsky thus uses his subtitle to bring back an image of Petersburg in the 1840s—an image of what, in the first part, Dostoevsky had called "the most abstract and premeditated city in the world," a city whose very existence (ever since Pushkin's *The Bronze Horseman*) had become emblematic in Russian literature for the violence and inhuman cost of the Russian adaptation to Western culture.

The atmosphere of the 1840s, with all its social-humanitarian exaltations, is also evoked explicitly by the quotation from a poem of N. A. Nekrasov appended as epigraph to the second part. This is the same poem, dating from 1846, that had already been mentioned ironically in *The Village of Stepanchikovo*, the first work in which Dostoevsky explicitly dissociated himself from what he now considered the naive illusions of the Natural School and of his own past. Written from the point of view of the (male) benefactor of a repentant prostitute, who has saved her from a life of sin by his ardent and unprejudiced love, the poem describes her torments of conscience:

> When from the murk of corruption
> I delivered your fallen soul
> With the ardent speech of conviction;
> And, full of profound torment,
> Wringing your hands, you cursed
> The vice that had ensnared you;
> When, with memories punishing
> Forgetful conscience

1. *Pisma*, 1: 178; March 24, 1856.

You told me the tale
Of all that happened before me,
And suddenly, covering your face,
Full of shame and horror,
You tearfully resolved,
Outraged, shocked . . .
Etc., etc., etc.

By cutting this passage short with three etceteras, Dostoevsky manifestly indicates that the philanthropic lucubrations of the speaker are just
so much banal and conventional rhetoric. The redemption of a prostitute
theme, taken over by the Russians in the 1840s from French Social
Romantics like Eugène Sue, George Sand, and Victor Hugo, and continued up through Tolstoy's *Resurrection* (1899), had indeed become a
commonplace by the 1860s. It figures as a minor episode in *What Is
To Be Done?*, where one of the heroes salvages a fallen woman from a
life of debauchery, lives with her for a time, and turns her into a model
member of Vera Pavlovna's cooperative until she dies of tuberculosis.
The climactic episode in the second part of *Notes from Underground*—
the encounter between the underground man and the prostitute Liza—
is an ironic parody and reversal of this Social Romantic cliché.

The second part of *Notes from Underground*, then, satirizes the sentimental Social Romanticism of the 1840s just as the first part satirized
the metaphysics and ethics of the 1860s; and Dostoevsky draws for this
purpose on the image of the 1840s he had already sketched in the pages
of *Time*. It was a period, as he saw it, when the Russian intelligentsia
had turned itself inside out so as to conform to the ideological prescriptions coming from abroad: "Everything then was done according to
principle, we lived according to principle, and were terribly afraid to do
anything not in conformity with the new ideas." Russia thus produced
a race of "giants" (as he mockingly calls them), burning with a desire
to aid "humanity" but regrettably unable to find any outlet for their vast
powers. The 1840s had thus fostered its own kind of egoism and vanity,
which allowed the "superfluous men" of the gentry-liberal intelligentsia
to live in a dream world of "universal beneficence" while neglecting the
simplest and most obvious moral obligations. It was incumbent on them,
he had made clear, to live up to their own pretensions, and to turn their
abstract love of humanity into a concrete act directed toward a flesh-
and-blood individual. This is precisely the theme of the second part of
Notes from Underground, which has been transposed into the bureau-
cratic world of Dostoevsky's early work and embodied in a character who
is the lowly, but supremely self-conscious, administrative equivalent of
the superfluous man.

This shift of theme is reflected in Part II by a very noticeable change
of tone. Ultimate issues were at stake in the first part, where the final
argument against the world of the "false" Crystal Palace could only be

the rage of madness and self-destruction; and Dostoevsky's irony is accordingly bitter and twisted, his tonality harsh and abrasive. No such ultimate issues are involved in the misadventures of the underground man's early manhood, which are all provoked by that standard comic source—overweening vanity. Hence the second part is written in a much lighter tone of burlesque and caricature, and whole sections are nothing but an extended mockery of the underground man's stilted and pedantic responses to the simplest human situations. It is a tribute to the power of received ideas (as well as to the lingering effect of the first part on the reader's sensibility) that Dostoevsky's sharply derisive comedy should so long have gone unnoticed.

2. THE DIALECTIC OF VANITY

The opening pages of the second part recall the beginning of the first, where the underground man had spoken of his struggle to tyrannize the humble petitioners who came his way as a low-grade government bureaucrat. We recall that he had also felt more friendly impulses toward other members of the human species, but that "I would not let them, would not let them, purposely would not let them out." This conflict between the impulse to dominate and the desire to enter into a more amicable relation with others was not developed at all earlier; but it now comes to the fore and provides a more intimate background to the relative abstractions of Part I.

Why, we may well ask, did the youthful underground man behave in a fashion so much at variance with the promptings of his own inclinations? The answer once again emerges only gradually, and we first become aware that the underground man, consumed by a boundless vanity, is so acutely self-conscious that he cannot enter into normal social relations with anyone: "All my fellow clerks I, of course, hated from first to last, and I despised them all, and yet at the same time I was, as it were, afraid of them. . . . Somehow it then turned out this way quite suddenly: one moment I despised them, the next I placed them much above me." The underground man's vanity convinces him of his own superiority and he despises everyone; but since he desires such superiority to be *recognized* by others, he hates the world for its indifference and falls into self-loathing at his own humiliating dependence. This is the psychological dialectic of a self-conscious egoism that seeks to conquer recognition from the world and only arouses dislike and hostility in return. Such a dialectic of vanity parallels the dialectic of determinism in the first part, and has the same effect of immuring the ego in a world alienated from any human contact. Just as determinism dissolves the possibility of human response in the first part, so vanity blocks all social fraternity in the second.

Besides portraying this dialectic of vanity in action, Dostoevsky also traces it back to an ideological source—not a specific philosophical doctrine as in Part I, but the general cultural atmosphere of the 1840s, which fostered a forced and artificial Romantic egoism and a sense of superiority to ordinary Russian life that the underground man drank in through every pore. Indeed, what distinguishes him from the very earliest years is his marked intellectual prowess. "Moreover, they [his school fellows] all began to grasp slowly," he writes, "that I was already reading books none of them could read, and understood things (not forming part of our school curriculum) of which they had not even heard." Describing his later life, he says: "In the first place, at home I spent most of my time reading. . . . I tried to stifle all that was continually seething within me by means of external sensations. And the only source of external sensation possible for me was reading. Reading, of course, was a great help—it excited, delighted, and tormented me." Books are thus responsible for keeping the *real* feelings of the underground man bottled up—the feelings, that is, opposed to his vanity and desire to dominate. Books interpose a network of acquired and artificial responses between himself and other people; and since we are in the world of the Russian intelligentsia of the 1840s, these books could only have been the works of the French Utopian Socialists and the Social Romantics and their Russian disciples on which Dostoevsky himself had battened at this period.

Over and over again Dostoevsky stresses the connections between the dialectic of vanity in which the underground man is caught and his intellectual culture. "A *cultivated* and decent man cannot be vain," he remarks, "without setting an inordinately high standard for himself, and without despising himself at certain moments to the point of hatred" (italics added). Comparing his features with those of other clerks in his office, he thinks: "Let my face even be ugly . . . but let it be noble, expressive, and, above all, *extremely* intelligent." Again, while seeking to provoke a quarrel so as to attract attention, he is troubled for a moment by the sordid triviality of the whole business: "Devil knows what I would then have given for a real regular quarrel—a more decent, a more *literary* one, so to speak." And after needlessly insulting a group of old school fellows, he says to them silently: "Oh, if you only knew what thoughts and feeling I am capable of, how cultured I am!" As a result of imbibing the European culture popular in Russia in the 1840s, the underground man, it becomes clear, has lost any capacity for simple and direct human feeling in relation to others. Instead, his vanity and sense of self-importance have become inflated to a degree out of all proportion to his actual social situation; and the conflicts engendered by this discrepancy provide a comic analogue to the fratricidal war of all against all arising in Western European society from the dominance of the principle of egoistic individualism.

Dostoevsky is a master at portraying the psychology of pride and humiliation, and when the humiliation springs from some genuine oppression or suffering, he knows how to make it intensely moving; but it would be a flagrant misreading to take the underground man as such a victim. For he lives in a purely imaginary world and distorts and exaggerates everything with which he comes into contact. "It is perfectly clear to me now," he says, "that, owing to my unbounded vanity and, probably, to the high standard I set for myself, I very often looked at myself with furious discontent, which verged on loathing, *and so I inwardly attributed the same view to everyone*" (italics added). Anticipating the scorn he might encounter from his old school fellows, on whom he had forced his company, he comments: "I knew, too, perfectly well even then that I was monstrously exaggerating the facts." And, as he confesses, "I always recognized that [exaggeration] was a weak point of mine, and was sometimes very much afraid of it. 'I exaggerate everything, that's where I go wrong,' I repeated to myself every hour."

Very little objective basis thus exists for the underground man's "humiliations," or better, they are all brought on by the excesses of his vanity; but even if his humiliations are entirely self-caused, their effect on him is no less distressing. His inability to enter into human contact with other people plunges him into a savage isolation, and it is only through "petty vice" that he can emerge at all from his everlasting self-preoccupation and self-absorption. At the same time, though, he is acutely aware that his behavior is debasing and degrading: "I indulged my vice in solitude at night, furtively, timidly, filthily, with a feeling of shame that never deserted me, even at the most loathsome moments, and which at such moments drove me to curses. Even then I already had the underground in my soul. In the first part, "the underground" had referred to the revolt of the underground man's personality against his ideas. Here his "feeling of shame" (his ineradicable conscience) once again rises up in revolt—not against a theory that denies the right of conscience to exist, but against an actual indulgence in vice that the underground man cannot help regarding as loathsome even while it offers his only escape from claustrophobic solitude. The reference to vice at this point foreshadows the all-important Liza episode, but in these earlier chapters, filled with comic grotesquerie, the emphasis falls on the underground man's efforts to break out of his solitude through purely social (rather than sexual) intercourse.

All these episodes display the torments and tortures of the underground man as he attempts to assert his existence as an ego who desires above all that someone—anyone—acknowledge his right to be recognized in a fashion compatible with his absurdly inflated self-image. It is for this reason that he becomes involved in the slapstick, mock-heroic farce of trying to summon up enough courage to bump into an officer on the Nevsky Prospect. His preoccupation with this ridiculous problem merely illustrates the picayune obsessiveness of his vanity; but the episode is also a parody of an incident in *What Is To Be Done?* One of the heroes of that book takes a solemn resolution not to yield the right of way in the street to "dignitaries"; and when an outraged gentleman begins to berate the poorly dressed student for bumping into *him*, the dignitary promptly ends up with his face in the mud.

Ironically reversing the scale of values manifested by this democratic protest against the public humiliations of inequality, Dostoevsky depicts the frantic desire of the underground man to assert his "equality" as ludicrous vanity rather than staunchly independent self-respect. The parody of Chernyshevsky is coupled with an allusion to Gogol's *The Overcoat*, which Dostoevsky slips in at the point where the underground man, feverishly preparing the proper costume for his epical encounter, decides to replace the hideous raccoon collar on his overcoat with a more dignified one of beaver. Not only does this detail thicken the period atmosphere (Gogol's story was published in 1842), but it also enriches the ideological implications of the incident, since Gogol's work provided the initial inspiration for the philanthropic thematics of the Natural School of young writers to which Dostoevsky had once belonged.

The theme of "masochism," so prominent in Part I, re-appears again in this first chapter of the second part. For as he walks along the Nevsky Prospect, the underground man experiences "a regular martyrdom, a continual, intolerable humiliation at the thought, which passed into an incessant and direct sensation, that I was a fly in the eyes of this whole world, a nasty, disgusting fly—more intelligent, more cultured, more noble than any of them, of course, but a fly that was continually making way for everyone, insulted and humiliated by everyone. . . . Already then I began to experience a rush of the enjoyment of which I spoke in the first chapter [of the first part]. Once again, however, we must be careful not to take this psychological characterization as self-explanatory. The underground man's masochism is a part of the dialectic of vanity, and it has a more complex function than merely to illustrate a taste for self-abasement. In fact, as we see, the voluntary exposure to humiliation *strengthens* the underground man's sense of inner superiority to all those who look on him with such contempt. At the same time that it makes him painfully aware of his own preposterousness and ignominy, it also sustains him by reinforcing the conviction of his cultural pre-eminence.

Masochism is thus assigned much the same function in both parts of the work—just as it had led to suffering in Part I, and kept alive the faculty of conscience, so in Part II it also acquires a positive significance. The seemingly pathological cultivation of masochistic "enjoyment" by the underground man ultimately buttresses his ego, which refuses to submit docilely to the judgment of the world. The ego thus asserts its independence and autonomy, whatever the price it must pay in indignity and despite all the external pressure to bend to alien authority. Such self-assertion is precisely what enables the underground man, twenty years later, to resist the temptations of a Crystal Palace in which the laws of nature have simply abolished the human personality altogether. Hence, in both parts of the work, Dostoevsky assigns a *relative* value— the value of protecting the autonomy of the personality—to the ideology of the 1840s, regardless of its weaknesses and shortcomings in other respects.

3. MANFRED AT A PARTY

Chapter II of the second part finally brings into relief the true target of Dostoevsky's satire. At last we discover—of course, in the form of a carefully distorted caricature—what the underground man has been reading in the books he finds so important. For here he takes on the features of the Romantic "dreamer" whom Dostoevsky had depicted in his early works, and whose literary fantasies had been contrasted with the moral-social claims of "real life" from which he had taken refuge. Dostoevsky's pre-Siberian attitude toward the dreamer had been, on the whole, relatively sympathetic; but he had begun to debunk him more severely in *Uncle's Dream*, and now, in the second part of *Notes from Underground*, the dreamer is manhandled very harshly indeed. Nor is he any longer a purely literary Romantic lost in exotic fantasies of erotic gratification and artistic glory; he has become a Social Romantic filled with grandiose plans for transforming the world. But his new social mission has not really succeeded in altering the dreamer's endemic self-preoccupation, and his failure to meet the moral demands of real life becomes all the more unforgivable in view of the social conscience by which he believes himself to be inspired.

In this chapter, we observe what occurs when, exhausted by the seesaws of the dialectic of vanity, the underground man has recourse "to a means of escape that reconciled everything," that is, when he finds "a refuge in 'the sublime and the beautiful,' in dreams."

> I, for instance, was triumphant over everyone; everyone, of course, lay in the dust and was forced to recognize my superiority voluntarily, and I forgave them all. I, a famous poet and court official, fell in love; I inherited countless millions and immediately sacrificed them for humanity; and at the same time I confessed before all the people my shameful deeds, which, of course, were not completely shameful but also contained an enormous amount of "the sublime and the beautiful," something in the Manfred style. Everyone would weep and kiss me (what idiots they would be if they didn't), while I would go barefoot and hungry preaching new ideas and routing the reactionaries at Austerlitz.

During such delightful interludes, the underground man felt "that suddenly a vista of suitable activity—beneficial, good, and above all *ready-made* (what sort of activity I had no idea, but the great thing was that it should be all ready for me)—would rise up before me, and I should come into the light of day, almost riding a white horse and crowned with laurel." These dreams, of course, replace any actual moral effort on his part; even more, they stifle any awareness that such effort could exist otherwise than in hackneyed, "ready-made" forms. At such moments the underground man felt an overwhelming love for humanity, and, "though it was never applied to anything human in reality, yet there was so much of this love that afterward one did not even feel the impulse to apply it in reality; that would have been a superfluous luxury." Also, these lofty visions of magnanimity happily served as a sop to the stirrings of conscience, because to "an ordinary man, say, it is shameful to defile himself . . . [while] a hero is too noble to be utterly defiled, and so he is permitted to defile himself." The underground man, as he himself remarks, "had a noble loophole for everything."

Yet he cannot long remain content with these delectations of his solitude; inevitably he feels the need to exhibit them (and himself) to the admiring eyes of humanity. After three months of dreaming, his dreams invariably "reached such a state of bliss that it became essential to embrace my fellows and all mankind immediately. And for that purpose I needed one human being at hand who actually existed." These words prelude the lengthy and grotesquely amusing episode (Chapters III and IV) relating the encounter of the underground man with his old schoolfellows. The moment he catches sight of real people, of course, the underground man's exorbitant demands for esteem invariably lead to a rebuff. Only too ready to embrace mankind, he discovers that mankind would rather shake hands and keep a polite distance, and this rejection brings on the dialectic of vanity, with its accompanying duel for domination.

So it has been, it would seem, with the underground man from his earliest years. "Once, indeed, I did have a friend (at school)," he reminisces. "But I was already a tyrant at heart; I wanted to exercise unlimited power over him. I tried to instill into him a contempt for his surroundings . . . but when he submitted to me completely I began to hate him immediately and rejected him—as though all I needed him for was to win a victory over him, to subjugate him and nothing else. But I could not subjugate them all." The surrealistic comedy of the underground man's meeting with his erstwhile comrades, which rises to dizzy heights of hysterical farce, derives from this hopeless yet irresistible impulse to "subjugate them all." After forcing himself on their friendly little party, he insults the guest of honor simply out of resentment and envy, and then parades up and down the room for three solid hours while the others disregard him entirely and continue their festivies.

The intricacies of Dostoevsky's irony are best displayed in the comic pathos of the underground man's bewilderment at the spectacle of stupid, unself-conscious, and tipsy amiability, with its total (even if alcohol-induced) momentary oblivion of self. "It was clear that they were fond of him [the guest of honor]. 'But why? Why?' I wondered. From time to time they were moved to drunken enthusiasm and kissed each other. They talked of the Caucasus, of the nature of true passion, of cards, of cushy jobs in the service; of the income of a hussar named Podkharzevsky, whom none of them knew personally, and rejoiced that he had a large income; of the extraordinary grace and beauty of a Princess D., whom none of them had ever seen either; and finally they reached the point of declaring Shakespeare immortal." The underground man's old friends, as Dostoevsky indicates by such a passage, are just as dull-witted and pedestrian a lot as he thinks them to be; but they nonetheless represent a norm of sociability impossible for him to attain or even to comprehend.

The whole group eventually departs for a brothel to finish off the evening, leaving the underground man in solitary possession of the débris of the feast. But, by this time, he has gotten it into his head that only a duel will satisfy his injured honor—and besides, a duel can be the occasion for all sorts of noble reconciliations! "Either they'll all fall down on their knees to beg for my friendship—or I will give Zverkov a slap in the face!" The mention of a duel at once unleashes a flood of literary references (Russian literature is filled with famous duels), and the underground man pursues his companions in a mood that parodies Pushkin's story *The Shot*.

Imagining what might happen if he carries out his plan to insult Zverkov, the guest of honor, the underground man muses:

> I will be arrested. I will be tried, I will be dismissed from the service, thrown in prison, sent to Siberia, deported. Never mind! In fifteen years when they let me out of prison I will trudge off to him, a beggar in rags, I shall find him in some provincial city. He will be married and happy. He will have a grown-up daughter. . . . I will say to him: "Look, monster, at my hollow cheeks and my rags! I've lost everything—my career, my happiness, art, science, the woman I loved, and all through you. Here are pistols. I have come to discharge my pistol and—and I . . . forgive you." Then I will fire into the air and he will never hear of me again.
>
> I was actually on the point of tears, though I knew perfectly well at that very moment that all this was out of Pushkin's *Silvio* [Silvio is the hero of *The Shot*] and Lermontov's *Masquerade*.

As might have been expected, these shopworn heroics remain purely imaginary, and everyone has vanished from sight by the time the underground man enters the salon of the "dressmaking establishment."

4. LIZA

It is at this point, when the underground man finally encounters another human being more vulnerable than himself, that the comedy changes into tragedy. Dostoevsky was well aware of this shift in tonality, and we have earlier quoted his allusion to it as similar to "a transition . . . in music. . . . In the first chapter, seemingly, there's only chatter; but suddenly this chatter, in the last two chapters, is resolved by a catastrophe.[2] By "the first chapter," Dostoevsky probably means the action leading up to the brothel scene; the brothel scene itself, and Liza's visit to the underground man's home, would then form the remaining two units. But the final text is broken up into smaller chapters, and the catastrophe beginning with Chapter V runs through Chapter X. No part of *Notes from Underground* has been more wrenched out of context to support one or another theory about Dostoevsky, even though the function of this section is surely to drive home the contrast between imaginary, self-indulgent, self-glorifying, sentimental Social Romanticism and a genuine act of love—a love springing from that total forgetfulness of self which had now become Dostoevsky's highest value. By his ironic reversal both of Nekrasov's poem and of the incident in *What Is To Be Done?*, Dostoevsky wished to expose all the petty vainglory lying concealed in the intelligentsia's "ideals," and to set this off against the triumph over egoism that he saw embodied in the spontaneous Christian instincts of a simple Russian soul.

When the underground man arrives in the brothel, the madam, treating him like the old patron that he is, summons a girl. As he goes out with her, he catches sight of himself in a mirror. "My harassed face struck me as extremely revolting, pale, spiteful, nasty, with disheveled hair. 'No matter, I am glad of it.' I thought; 'I am glad that I shall seem revolting to her; I like that.' " Not having been able to subdue his companions or to insult them sufficiently to be taken seriously, the underground man typically anticipates revenging himself on the helpless girl; the more repulsive he is to her, the more his egoism will be satisfied by forcing her to submit to his desires. It is not by physical submission alone, however, that the underground man attains a triumph over Liza. For when, after making love, he becomes aware of her hostility and silent resentment, "a grim idea came into my brain and passed all over my body, like some nasty sensation, such as one feels when going into a damp and moldy underground." This idea takes the form of playing on Liza's feelings, with the intention of triumphing over her not only physically but spiritually as well.

The underground man thus proceeds very skillfully to break down the armor of feigned indifference and cynicism by which Liza protects herself against the debasing circumstances of her life. "I began to feel myself

2. Ibid., 1: 353; March 26, 1864.

what I was saying," he explains, "and warmed to the subject. I longed to expound the cherished *little ideas* I had brooded over in my corner." Mingling horrible details of degradation with images of felicity, whose banality makes them all the more poignant (Balzac's *Le Père Goriot* is parodied in the process), the underground man succeeds in bringing to the surface Liza's true feelings of shame about herself and precipitating her complete emotional breakdown. None of his apparent concern, of course, had been meant seriously; the underground man simply had been carried away by the power of his eloquence and because "the sport in it attracted me most." But Liza is too young, naive, and helpless to see through his falsity, which in this case sounded like truth and was, in fact, even half-true: "I worked myself up to such pathos that I began to have a lump in my throat myself, and . . . suddenly I stopped, sat up in dismay, and bending over apprehensively, began to listen with a beating heart." For Liza had lost control of herself completely, and "her youthful body was shuddering all over as though in convulsions."

The underground man, carried away by his victory, cannot resist attempting to live up to the exalted role of hero and benefactor that he had so often played in his fantasies. When he leaves, he gives Liza his address with a lordly magnanimity, urging her to come and visit him and quit her life of shame. It is this gesture that undoes him and provides Dostoevsky with his dénouement. For the moment the underground man emerges from the self-adulatory haze of his charlatanism, he is stricken with terror. He cannot bear the thought that Liza might see him as he really is—wrapped in his shabby dressing gown, living in his squalid "underground," completely under the thumb of his manservant, the impassive, dignified, Bible-reading peasant Apollon. Never for a moment does it occur to him that he might really try to help her all the same; he is so worried about how *he* will look in *her* eyes that the reality of her situation entirely vanishes from view. Or not entirely: "Something was not dead within me, in the depths of my heart and conscience it refused to die, and it expressed itself as a burning anguish."

After a few days pass and Liza fails to appear, the underground man becomes more cheerful; as usual, "I even began sometimes to dream, and rather sweetly." These dreams all revolved around the process of Liza's re-education, her confession of love for him, and his own confession that "I did not dare to approach you first, because I had an influence over you and was afraid that you would force yourself, out of gratitude, to respond to my love, would try to rouse in your heart a feeling which was perhaps absent, and I did not wish that because it would be . . . tyranny. . . . It would be indelicate (in short, I launch off at this point into European, George-Sandian inexplicably lofty subtleties), but now, now you are mine, you are my creation, you are pure, you are beautiful, you are my beautiful wife." And here Dostoevsky throws in two more lines from Nekrasov's poem.

Interspersed with these intoxicating reveries is the low comedy of the underground man's efforts to bend the stubborn and intractable Apollon to his will. Dostoevsky interweaves these two situations adroitly by co-ordinating Liza's entry with a moment at which the underground man, enraged by the imperturbable Apollon, is giving vent to all his weakly hysterical fury. By this time, he has reached an uncontrollable pitch of frustration and nervous exasperation; at the sight of the bewildered Liza he loses control completely, sobbing and complaining that he is being "tortured" by Apollon. All this is so humiliating that he turns on her in spiteful rage when, by stammering that she wishes to leave the brothel, she reminds him of all that has gone before. His reply is a vicious tirade, in which he tells her the truth about their earlier relation: "I vented my spleen on you and laughed at you. I had been humiliated, so I wanted to humiliate; I had been treated like a rag, so I wanted to show my power." With the typical inversion of his egoist's logic, he shouts: "And I shall never forgive you for the tears I could not help shedding before you just now, like some silly woman put to shame! And for what I am confessing to you now, I shall never forgive *you*, either!"

But now an unprecedented event occurs—unprecedented, at least, in the underground man's experience; instead of flaring up herself and hitting back (the only response to which the underground man has been accustomed), Liza throws herself into his arms to console *him*. Both forget themselves entirely and break into tears; but the unconquerable vanity of the underground man, which incapacitates him from respond-ing selflessly and spontaneously to others, soon regains the upper hand: "In my over-wrought brain the thought also occurred that our parts were after all completely reversed now, that she was now the heroine, while I was just such a crushed and humiliated creature as she had been before me that night—four days before." And then, not out of love but hate, the underground man takes her on the spot to revenge himself on *her* for having dared to try to console him. To make his revenge more complete and crush her entirely, he slips a five-ruble note into her hand when their embraces are finished. "But I can say this for certain: though I did that cruel thing purposely," he admits, "it was not an impulse from the heart, but came from my evil brain. This cruelty was so affected, so purposely made up, so completely a product of the brain, of *books*, that I could not keep it up for a minute." Dostoevsky could not have stated more explicitly that the heart of the underground man, the emotive core of his nature, had by no means lost its moral sensitivity. It was his brain, nourished by the education he had so thoroughly absorbed—an education based on Western prototypes, and on the images of such prototypes assimilated into Russian literature—that had perverted his character and was responsible for his despicable act.

Liza, however, manages to leave the money on the table unobserved before leaving. Noticing the crumpled bill, the underground man is filled with remorse and runs after Liza into the silent, snow-filled street to kneel at her feet and beg forgiveness. But then, pulling himself up short, he realizes the futility of all this agitation: " 'But—what for?' I thought. 'Would I not begin to hate her, perhaps, even tomorrow, just because I kissed her feet today?' " And later at home, "stifling the living pang of [his] heart with fantastic dreams," he conceives the most diabolic rationalization of all for his villainy. "Will it not be better that she carry the outrage with her forever?" he thinks. "Outrage—why, after all, that is purification: it is the most stinging and painful consciousness! Tomorrow I would have defiled her soul and have exhausted her heart, while now the feeling of humiliation will never die in her, and however loathsome the filth awaiting her, that outrage will elevate and purify her—by hatred—h'm—perhaps by forgiveness also. But will all that make things easier for her, though? . . . And, indeed, I will at this point ask an idle question on my account: which is better—cheap happiness or exalted sufferings? Well, which is better?"

With this final, stabbing irony, Dostoevsky allows the underground man to use the very idea of purification through suffering as an excuse for his moral-spiritual sadism—exactly as Prince Valkovsky had done to excuse a more vulgar crime. In so doing, Dostoevsky returns to the main theme of the first part and places it in a new light. "Consciousness" and "suffering" had been affirmed as values when the underground man, struggling to preserve his human identity, wished to suffer *himself* rather than to surrender to the laws of nature. But so long as this struggle springs only from the negative revolt of egoism to affirm its existence, so long as it is not oriented by anything positive, it inevitably runs the risk of a diabolic reversal; there is always the danger that the egoist, concerned only with himself, will cause *others* to suffer with the excuse of helping to purify *their* souls. Such a possibility, broached here in passing at the end of *Notes from Underground*, will be brilliantly developed in *Crime and Punishment*, when Raskolnikov tries to convince Sonya that his sacrifice of *another* for a noble end is morally equivalent to *her* self-sacrifice for the same purpose.

5. CONCLUSION

As the second part of *Notes from Underground* comes to a close, the underground man again returns to the frustrations of his solitude. For one moment he had caught a glimpse of how to escape from the dialectic of vanity: Liza's complete disregard of her own humiliation, her whole-souled identification with *his* torments—in short, her capacity for selfless love—is the only way to break the sorcerer's spell of egocentrism. When she rushes into his arms, thinking not of herself but of him, she illustrates that "something else" which his egoism will never allow him to attain— the ideal of the voluntary self-sacrifice of the personality out of love. In his encounter with Liza, the underground man had met this ideal in the flesh, and his inability to respond to its appeal dooms him irrevocably for the future. Nonetheless, as we look at *Notes from Underground* as a whole, we see that the egoistic Social Romanticism of the 1840s, with its cultivation of a sense of spiritual noblesse and its emphasis on *individual* moral responsibility, does not have a totally negative value. Egocentric though it may be, such sentimental Social Romanticism still stressed the importance of free will and preserved a sense of the inner autonomy of the personality; and without such a sense no truly human life is possible at all. Dostoevsky will continue to portray the relation between the generations in much the same fashion—most explicitly in *The Devils*, where the old Social Romantic Stepan Trofimovich Verkhovensky is morally outraged by the Utilitarian ruthlessness of his Nihilist offspring Peter while ruefully acknowledging the responsibility of his own generation in bringing such a monstrosity to birth.

As a coda to the entire work, Dostoevsky adds some remarks still nominally set down by his narrator, but in which his own voice is heard almost as distinctly as in the prefatory footnote. Indeed, in these final sentences Dostoevsky again endeavors to alert the reader to the nature of his literary technique. "A novel needs a hero," remarks the underground man, "and all the traits for an anti-hero are *expressly* gathered together here, and, what matters most, it all produces an unpleasant impression, for we are all divorced from life, we are all cripples, every one of us, more or less." When the imaginary reader protests angrily at this, begins "shouting and stamping," and tells the underground man to speak only for himself and not for others, the rejoinder lays bare Dostoevsky's use of inverted irony. "As for what concerns me in particular," he retorts, "I have only in my life carried to an extreme what you have not dared to carry halfway, and what's more, you have taken your cowardice for good sense, and have found comfort in deceiving yourselves." The full significance of this assertion should by now be clear: Dostoevsky is alluding to his consummate use of satirical exaggeration and parodistic caricature, and his technique of dramatization by what we have called ideological eschatology, that is, by carrying "the logical presuppositions and possibilities of ideas to their consistent conclusion. . . ."

The underground man, hyperconscious as always, knows exactly where the source of the trouble is located: "Leave us alone without books and we shall at once get lost and be confused—we will not know what to join, what to cling to and what to hate, what to respect and what to despise. We are even oppressed by being men—men with *real, our own* flesh and blood, we are ashamed of it, we think it a disgrace and try to be some sort of impossible generalized man." It may be inferred, then, that the only hope is to reject all these bookish, foreign, artificial Western ideologies, and to return to the Russian "soil" with its spontaneous incorporation of the Christian ideal of unselfish love.

So ends this remarkable little work, certainly the most powerful and concentrated expression that Dostoevsky ever gave to his genius as a satirist. *Notes from Underground*, it has often been said (and quite rightly), is the prelude to the great period in which Dostoevsky's talent finally came to maturity; and there is no question that with it he attains a new artistic level. For the first time, he motivates an action *entirely* in terms of a psychology shaped by radical ideology; every feature of the text serves to bring out the consequences in personal behavior of certain ideas; and the world that Dostoevsky creates is entirely conceived as a *function* of this purpose. Psychology has now become strictly subordinate to ideology; there is no longer a disturbing tug-of-war, as in *The Insulted and Injured*, between the moral-psychological and the ideological elements of the structure.

Dostoevsky has also at last found the great theme of his later novels, which will all be inspired by the same ambition to counter the moral-spiritual authority of the ideology of the radical Russian intelligentsia (depending on whatever nuance of that idealogy was prominent at the time of writing). In this respect, the nucleus of Dostoevsky's novels may be compared to that of an eighteenth-century *conte philosophique*, whose characters were also largely embodiments of ideas; but instead of remaining bloodless abstractions like Candide or Zadig, they will be fleshed out with all the verisimilitude and psychological density of the nineteenth-century novel of social realism and all the dramatic tension of the urban-Gothic *roman-feuilleton*. It is Dostoevsky's genius for blending these seemingly antithetical narrative styles that constitutes the originality of his art as a novelist.

Dostoevsky, though, never again attempted anything as hermetic and allusive as *Notes from Underground*. It is very likely that he considered the work a failure—as indeed it was, if we use as a measure its total lack of effectiveness as a polemic. No one really understood what Dostoevsky had been trying to do (with the exception, as we shall see, of Saltykov-Shchedrin); and even though Apollon Grigoryev, with his artistic flair, praised the novella and told his friend to continue writing in this vein, the silence of the remainder of the literary world was positively deafening. We have already quoted Suslova's letter, whose references to Dostoevsky's "scandalous novella" and the "cynical things" he was producing, well convey the general reaction. Since she had not yet read the text, her words manifestly report what she had heard in the literary salon of the novelist Evgenia Tur (which she was then frequenting in Paris), and whose habitués were only repeating the latest literary gossip from Petersburg. Such reactions probably persuaded Dostoevsky that he had perhaps counted too much on the perspicacity of his readers to discern his meaning. He would, in any case, never again place them before so difficult a challenge to their literary and ideological acumen.

A Chronology of Dostoevsky's Life and Work

1821   Fyodor Mikhailovich Dostoevsky born at St. Mary's Hospital for the Poor in Moscow, where his father was a staff doctor (October 30).

1837   Mother dies.

1838   Enters Military Engineering School in St. Petersburg.

1839   Father murdered by peasants on his small estate south of Moscow.

1842   Commissioned as a second lieutenant.

1843   Translates Balzac's *Eugenie Grandet*.

1844   Leaves the military service; starts writing *Poor Folk*.

1845   Finishes *Poor Folk*; befriended by the critic Vissarion Belinsky; enjoys popularity among literary circles.

1846   *Poor Folk* and *The Double*.

1847   Attends meetings of Petrashevsky's radical circle (and other groups).

1849   Arrested, condemned to death, led out for execution, but granted a reprieve at the last moment; sentence commuted to penal servitude followed by exile.

1850–54 Serves as a convict doing hard labor at Omsk Prison in western Siberia.

1854–59 Posted as a private in the army to a military battalion in Semipalatinsk in western Siberia.

1857   Marries Marya Dmitrievna Isaeva, a widow who suffers from hysteria and tuberculosis.

1859   Permitted to return to European Russia; moves first to Tver and then settles in St. Petersburg; resumes writing.

1860   Publishes first chapters of *Memoirs from the House of the Dead*, based on his Siberian experience.

1861   Embarks on publication of new literary journal *Vremya (Time)* with his brother Mikhail; *The Insulted and the Injured*.

1862   First visit to Western Europe; affair with Apollinaria Suslova.

1863   *Winter Notes on Summer Impressions*, based on European travel experience; *Vremya* is banned for political reasons.

1864   Launches second journal *Epokha (Epoch)* with his brother Mikhail; first wife, Marya Dmitrievna, dies (April); brother Mikhail dies (July); *Notes from Underground*.

1865   *Epokha* collapses for financial reasons.

1866   *Crime and Punishment*.

1867–71 *The Gambler*; marries Anna Grigoryevna Snitkina, his stenographer, and takes up residence abroad.

1868   *The Idiot*.

1871   Returns to St. Petersburg; *The Possessed* (or *The Devils*).

1873   Edits a weekly journal *Grazhdanin (Citizen)*, and starts contributing sections of *Diary of a Writer*.

1875   *A Raw Youth* (or *The Adolescent*).

1878   Three-year-old son, Alexei, dies from epilepsy; visits Optina Monastery with philosopher Vladimir Solovyov.

1879   *The Brothers Karamazov*.

1880   Delivers Pushkin speech to enthusiastic public at dedication of statue in Moscow.

1881   Dies in St. Petersburg after lung hemorrhages (January 28); buried in cemetery at Alexander Nevsky Monastery (February 1).

Selected Bibliography

PRINCIPAL TRANSLATIONS OF *NOTES FROM UNDERGROUND*

Coulson, Jessie.   *Notes from Underground* and *The Double*. Baltimore: Penguin, 1972.

Garnett, Constance.   *Notes from Underground, Poor People, The Friend of the Family*. New York: Dell, 1960.

Ginsburg, Mirra.   *Notes from Underground*. New York: Bantam, 1974.

Hogarth, C. J.   *Letters from the Underworld*. New York: Dutton, 1913.

MacAndrew, Andrew.   *Notes from Underground*. New York: New American Library, 1961.

Magarshack, David.   *Notes from the Underground* in *Great Short Works of Fyodor Dostoevsky*. New York: Harper and Row, 1968.

Matlaw, Ralph E.   *Notes from the Underground* and *The Grand Inquisitor*. New York: Dutton, 1960.

Shishkov, Serge.   *Notes from Underground*. New York: Crowell, 1969.

BOOKS ABOUT DOSTOEVSKY

Anderson, Roger B.   *Dostoevsky: Myths of Duality*. Gainesville: University of Florida, 1986.

de Jonge, Alex.   *Dostoevsky and the Age of Intensity*. London: Secker and Warburg, 1975.

Fanger, Donald.   *Dostoevsky and Romantic Realism*. Chicago: University of Chicago Press, 1967.

Frank, Joseph and Goldstein, David, eds.   *Selected Letters of Fyodor Dostoevsky*. New Brunswick: Rutgers University Press, 1987.

Holquist, Michael.   *Dostoevsky and the Novel*. Princeton: Princeton University Press, 1977.

Ivanov, Vyacheslav.   *A Study in Dostoevsky: Freedom and the Tragic Life*. New York: Noonday Press, Farrar, Straus and Giroux, 1968.

Jones, John.   *Dostoevsky*. Oxford: Oxford University Press, 1983.

Jones, Malcolm V.   *Dostoevsky: The Novel of Discord*. London: Elek, 1976.

Kabat, Geoffrey C.   *Ideology and Imagination: The Image of Society in Dostoevsky*. New York: Columbia University Press, 1978.

Leatherbarrow, William.   *Fedor Dostoevsky*. Boston: Twayne Publishers, 1981.

Mochulsky, Konstantin.   *Dostoevsky: His Life and Work*. Princeton: Princeton University Press, 1967.

Peace, Richard.   *Dostoevsky: An Examination of the Major Novels*. Cambridge: Cambridge University Press, 1971.

Rice, James L.   *Dostoevsky and the Healing Art: An Essay in Literary and Medical History*. Ann Arbor: Ardis Publishers, 1985.

Steiner, George.   *Tolstoy or Dostoevsky*. New York: Penguin Books, 1967.

Wasiolek, Edward.   *Dostoevsky: The Major Fiction*. Cambridge: The M.I.T. Press, 1973.

BOOKS AND ARTICLES ABOUT *NOTES FROM UNDERGROUND*

Beardsley, Monroe. "Dostoevsky's Metaphor of the Underground." *Journal of the History of Ideas* 3 (1942): 265–90.

Howard, Barbara F. "The Rhetoric of Confession: Dostoevskij's *Notes from Underground* and Rousseau's *Confessions*." *Slavic and East European Journal* 25. 4 (1981): 16–32.

Jackson, Robert Louis. *Dostoevsky's Underground Man in Russian Literature.* The Hague: Mouton, 1958.

Spilka, Mark. "Playing Crazy in the Underground." *Minnesota Review* 6.3 (1966): 233–43.

Sugarman, Richard Ira. *Rancor Against Time: The Phenomenology of 'Ressentiment.'* Hamburg: F. Meiner, 1980. 1–20.

ANDERSON Winesburg, Ohio edited by Charles E. Modlin and Ray Lewis White

AQUINAS St. Thomas Aquinas on Politics and Ethics translated and edited by
Paul E. Sigmund

AUSTEN Emma edited by Stephen M. Parrish Second Edition

AUSTEN Persuasion edited by Patricia Meyer Spacks

AUSTEN Pride and Prejudice edited by Donald Gray Second Edition

BEHN Oroonoko edited by Joanna Lipking

Beowulf (the Donaldson translation) edited by Joseph F. Tuso

BLAKE Blake's Poetry and Designs selected and edited by Mary Lynn Johnson and
John E. Grant

BOCCACCIO The Decameron selected, translated, and edited by Mark Musa and
Peter E. Bondanella

BRONTË CHARLOTTE Jane Eyre edited by Richard J. Dunn Second Edition

BRONTË EMILY Wuthering Heights edited by William M. Sale, Jr., and Richard Dunn
Third Edition

BROWNING Aurora Leigh edited by Margaret Reynolds

BROWNING, ROBERT Browning's Poetry selected and edited by James F. Loucks

BYRON Byron's Poetry selected and edited by Frank D. McConnell

CARROLL Alice in Wonderland edited by Donald J. Gray Second Edition

CERVANTES Don Quixote (the Ormsby translation, revised) edited by Joseph R. Jones and
Kenneth Douglas

CHAUCER The Canterbury Tales: Nine Tales and the General Prologue edited by
V. A. Kolve and Glending Olson

CHEKHOV Anton Chekhov's Plays translated and edited by Eugene K. Bristow

CHEKHOV Anton Chekhov's Short Stories selected and edited by Ralph E. Matlaw

CHOPIN The Awakening edited by Margo Culley Second Edition

CLEMENS Adventures of Huckleberry Finn edited by Sculley Bradley,
Richmond Croom Beatty, E. Hudson Long, and Thomas Cooley Second Edition

CLEMENS A Connecticut Yankee in King Arthur's Court edited by Allison R. Ensor

CLEMENS Pudd'nhead Wilson and Those Extraordinary Twins edited by Sidney E. Berger

CONRAD Heart of Darkness edited by Robert Kimbrough Third Edition

CONRAD Lord Jim edited by Thomas C. Moser Second Edition

CONRAD The Nigger of the "Narcissus" edited by Robert Kimbrough

CRANE Maggie: A Girl of the Streets edited by Thomas A. Gullason

CRANE The Red Badge of Courage edited by Donald Pizer Third Edition

DARWIN Darwin selected and edited by Philip Appleman Second Edition

DEFOE A Journal of the Plague Year edited by Paula R. Backscheider

DEFOE Moll Flanders edited by Edward Kelly

DEFOE Robinson Crusoe edited by Michael Shinagel Second Edition

DE PIZAN The Selected Writings of Christine de Pizan translated by Renate
Blumenfeld-Kosinski and Kevin Brownlee edited by Renate Blumenfeld-Kosinski

DICKENS Bleak House edited by George Ford and Sylvère Monod

DICKENS David Copperfield edited by Jerome H. Buckley

DICKENS Hard Times edited by George Ford and Sylvère Monod Second Edition

DICKENS Oliver Twist edited by Fred Kaplan

DONNE John Donne's Poetry selected and edited by Arthur L. Clements Second Edition

DOSTOEVSKY The Brothers Karamazov (the Garnett translation) edited by Ralph E. Matlaw

DOSTOEVSKY Crime and Punishment (the Coulson translation) edited by George Gibian
Third Edition

DOSTOEVSKY Notes from Underground translated and edited by Michael R. Katz

DOUGLASS Narrative of the Life of Frederick Douglass, an American Slave, Written by Himself
edited by William L. Andrews and William S. McFeely

DREISER Sister Carrie edited by Donald Pizer Second Edition

Eight Modern Plays edited by Anthony Caputi

ELIOT Middlemarch edited by Bert G. Hornback

ELIOT The Mill on the Floss edited by Carol T. Christ

ERASMUS The Praise of Folly and Other Writings translated and edited by Robert M. Adams

FAULKNER The Sound and the Fury edited by David Minter Second Edition

FIELDING Joseph Andrews with Shamela and Related Writings edited by Homer Goldberg

FIELDING Tom Jones edited by Sheridan Baker Second Edition

FLAUBERT Madame Bovary edited with a substantially new translation by Paul de Man

FORD The Good Soldier edited by Martin Stannard

FRANKLIN Benjamin Franklin's Autobiography edited by J. A. Leo Lemay and P. M. Zall

GOETHE Faust translated by Walter Arndt, edited by Cyrus Hamlin

GOGOL Dead Souls (the Reavey translation) edited by George Gibian

HARDY Far from the Madding Crowd edited by Robert C. Schweik

HARDY Jude the Obscure edited by Norman Page

HARDY The Mayor of Casterbridge edited by James K. Robinson

HARDY The Return of the Native edited by James Gindin

HARDY Tess of the d'Urbervilles edited by Scott Elledge Third Edition

HAWTHORNE The Blithedale Romance edited by Seymour Gross and Rosalie Murphy

HAWTHORNE The House of the Seven Gables edited by Seymour Gross

HAWTHORNE Nathaniel Hawthorne's Tales edited by James McIntosh

HAWTHORNE The Scarlet Letter edited by Seymour Gross, Sculley Bradley,
Richmond Croom Beatty, and E. Hudson Long Third Edition

HERBERT George Herbert and the Seventeenth-Century Religious Poets selected and edited by
Mario A. DiCesare

HERODOTUS The Histories translated and selected by Walter E. Blanco, edited by
Walter E. Blanco and Jennifer Roberts

HOBBES Leviathan edited by Richard E. Flathman and David Johnston

HOMER The Odyssey translated and edited by Albert Cook Second Edition

HOWELLS The Rise of Silas Lapham edited by Don L. Cook

IBSEN The Wild Duck translated and edited by Dounia B. Christiani

JAMES The Ambassadors edited by S. P. Rosenbaum Second Edition

JAMES The American edited by James W. Tuttleton

JAMES The Portrait of a Lady edited by Robert D. Bamberg Second Edition

JAMES Tales of Henry James edited by Christof Wegelin

JAMES The Turn of the Screw edited by Robert Kimbrough

JAMES The Wings of the Dove edited by J. Donald Crowley and Richard A. Hocks

JONSON Ben Jonson and the Cavalier Poets selected and edited by Hugh Maclean

JONSON Ben Jonson's Plays and Masques selected and edited by Robert M. Adams

KAFKA The Metamorphosis translated and edited by Stanley Corngold

LAFAYETTE The Princess of Clèves edited and with a revised translation by John D. Lyons

MACHIAVELLI The Prince translated and edited by Robert M. Adams Second Edition

MALTHUS An Essay on the Principle of Population edited by Philip Appleman

MANN Death in Venice translated and edited by Clayton Koelb

MARX The Communist Manifesto edited by Frederic L. Bender

MELVILLE The Confidence-Man edited by Hershel Parker

MELVILLE Moby-Dick edited by Harrison Hayford and Hershel Parker

MEREDITH The Egoist edited by Robert M. Adams

Middle English Lyrics selected and edited by Maxwell S. Luria and Richard L. Hoffman

Middle English Romances selected and edited by Stephen H. A. Shepherd

MILL Mill selected and edited by Alan Ryan

MILL On Liberty edited by David Spitz
MILTON Paradise Lost edited by Scott Elledge Second Edition
Modern Irish Drama edited by John P. Harrington
MORE Utopia translated and edited by Robert M. Adams Second Edition
NEWMAN Apologia Pro Vita Sua edited by David J. DeLaura
NEWTON Newton edited by I. Bernard Cohen and Richard S. Westfall
NORRIS McTeague edited by Donald Pizer Second Edition
Restoration and Eighteenth-Century Comedy edited by Scott McMillin Second Edition
RICH Adrienne Rich's Poetry and Prose edited by Barbara Charlesworth Gelpi and
Albert Gelpi
ROUSSEAU Rousseau's Political Writings edited by Alan Ritter and translated by
Julia Conaway Bondanella
ST. PAUL The Writings of St. Paul edited by Wayne A. Meeks
SHAKESPEARE Hamlet edited by Cyrus Hoy Second Edition
SHAKESPEARE Henry IV, Part I edited by James L. Sanderson Second Edition
SHAW Bernard Shaw's Plays edited by Warren Sylvester Smith
SHELLEY Frankenstein edited by Paul Hunter
SHELLEY Shelley's Poetry and Prose selected and edited by Donald H. Reiman and
Sharon B. Powers
SMOLLETT Humphry Clinker edited by James L. Thorson
SOPHOCLES Oedipus Tyrannus translated and edited by Luci Berkowitz and
Theodore F. Brunner
SPENSER Edmund Spenser's Poetry selected and edited by Hugh Maclean and
Anne Lake Prescott Third Edition
STENDHAL Red and Black translated and edited by Robert M. Adams
STERNE Tristram Shandy edited by Howard Anderson
STOKER Dracula edited by Nina Auerbach and David Skal
STOWE Uncle Tom's Cabin edited by Elizabeth Ammons
SWIFT Gulliver's Travels edited by Robert A. Greenberg Second Edition
SWIFT The Writings of Jonathan Swift edited by Robert A. Greenberg and William B. Piper
TENNYSON In Memoriam edited by Robert H. Ross
TENNYSON Tennyson's Poetry selected and edited by Robert W. Hill, Jr.
THACKERAY Vanity Fair edited by Peter Shillingsburg
THOREAU Walden and Resistance to Civil Government edited by William Rossi
Second Edition
TOLSTOY Anna Karenina edited and with a revised translation by George Gibian
Second Edition
TOLSTOY Tolstoy's Short Fiction edited and with revised translations by Michael R. Katz
TOLSTOY War and Peace (the Maude translation) edited by George Gibian Second Edition
TOOMER Cane edited by Darwin T. Turner
TURGENEV Fathers and Sons translated and edited by Michael R. Katz
VOLTAIRE Candide translated and edited by Robert M. Adams Second Edition
WASHINGTON Up from Slavery edited by William L. Andrews
WATSON The Double Helix: A Personal Account of the Discovery of the Structure of DNA
edited by Gunther S. Stent
WHARTON Ethan Frome edited by Kristin O. Lauer and Cynthia Griffin Wolff
WHARTON The House of Mirth edited by Elizabeth Ammons
WHITMAN Leaves of Grass edited by Sculley Bradley and Harold W. Blodgett
WILDE The Picture of Dorian Gray edited by Donald L. Lawler
WOLLSTONECRAFT A Vindication of the Rights of Woman edited by Carol H. Poston
Second Edition
WORDSWORTH The Prelude: 1799, 1805, 1850 edited by Jonathan Wordsworth,
M. H. Abrams, and Stephen Gill